XO, Xena

An Olympus Inc. Romance

Kate Healey

Contents

Content Note

XO, Xena is a contemporary romance mystery with a guaranteed happy ending. However, it deals with some dark material and violent situations, including murder, attempted murder, workplace fatalities and accidents, gun violence, unwanted sexual touch, abduction, non-consensual restraint, organized crime, and threatened harm to children.

For every girl who ever watched Xena and Gabrielle and thought *wait a minute...*

Chapter One

Polyxena Troiades was trying not to spend her sister's wedding reception feeling sorry for herself, and trying even harder not to show it.

She couldn't do much about her feelings, but she would hate herself forever if they cast a cloud over Laodice and Telfer's special day. So she was putting a lot of effort into maintaining the lie that everything was *perfect*.

Unfortunately, she'd never been a good liar.

The wedding celebration itself was spectacular. Of course it was. Laodice had not only been planning this event since she was a little girl marrying Mister Bones, their weird anatomical skeleton, she was the editor-in-chief of the Bridal department at Olympus Inc. Vendors had fallen over themselves to offer great deals and incredible work by their best people in the hope of impressing the woman who'd be choosing who to feature in upcoming issues.

Xena had half-expected Laodice to be a nightmare bride, dedicated to perfection and frustrated whenever it failed to show up. Instead, she'd seemed to float from the engagement announcement through the bridal shower to the ceremony and now to the reception on a cloud of serene joy, utterly impervious to the winds of fate.

There were two reasons for that. One was the stellar work of the vendors.

The other was the groom, who had spent the last six months making sure that absolutely *nothing* could go wrong for Laodice's big day.

"The orchid centerpiece on that westernmost table is missing the gold ribbon," Telfer said, stiffening like a bloodhound from his place at the high table.

Cassie, Xena's eldest sister, patted his hand. "One of the guests probably took it as a souvenir."

"I know there are spares in storage," Telfer said. "The speeches are scheduled to start in seven minutes. I could go and get a replacement if I leave now."

"Laodice won't notice," Xena said. The woman in question was laughing with Telfer's Uncle Burak and some of his many, many friends, leaning over their table in her beautiful waterfall-style gown, her gorgeous hair adorned with orchids and pearls.

Telfer frowned. "She's very observant."

"She's having so much fun she wouldn't notice if someone set all the tablecloths on fire," Xena told him. "Look at her. I've known her since I was born and I've never seen her so happy."

"Do you really think so?" Telfer asked anxiously, and then Laodice looked up and smiled at him, her face lit with love and joy. He smiled back, totally besotted, and completely forgot that he and Xena had been mid-conversation.

"Yeah, she's hating this," Xena muttered.

Cassie shot her a significant look, and Xena gritted her teeth. She was really, truly trying her best. She loved her sister, and though Telfer was kind of a Groomzilla, he was also a big, sexy nerd who was completely gone on Laodice, to the point where it might actually impede his higher brain functions.

No, that was a mean thought. Xena was trying to avoid mean thoughts and sarcastic comments and absolutely all comparisons to what Laodice had—which she *deserved*, she was *wonderful*, she should have *everything*—and what Xena *could* have had. If, almost two years ago, she hadn't humiliated herself, ruined the best relationship she'd ever had, and destroyed her career.

Cassie was suddenly sitting beside her. Cassie was an archivist, and secretly an advice columnist. This meant she was detail-oriented, perceptive, given to analyzing people and relationships, and usually right.

It was annoying.

"Are you okay?" she asked now, low-voiced. "Do you need a minute?"

"I'm fine."

"Okay. Because you're about to tear that napkin in half."

Xena glanced at the napkin in her clenched hands. It was made of cream linen, and had previously been immaculately folded into the shape of a swan. Now it looked as if she'd tried to wring the swan's neck.

Xena dropped the sad piece of crumpled fabric onto her lap and attempted to smooth it. "I'm fine. It's a beautiful wedding. Laodice and Telfer are the perfect couple, the food is great, the music is awesome, and we even got to pick our own dresses." Within Telfer's exacting color scheme, of course.

"We can postpone the speeches, if you need some fresh air."

"Leave it, Cassie. I don't want advice, okay?" She smiled. It was an effort, but she made it. "Besides, if we don't do the speeches soon, Mom and Dad are going to start fully making out on the dance floor."

It wasn't officially time for dancing yet. This had not prevented Hecuba and Priam from picking a corner to embrace each other and slowly sway back and forth to the soothing instrumental music, lost in each other's eyes. Priam's hands were resting perilously low on Hecuba's back, very close to the ass zone.

Cassie looked at them. "You know I'm a sex-positive person," she said.

Xena nodded. "Me too."

"It's great that our parents are so into each other. I definitely hope that Manny and I are still hot for each other at their age."

"Mm-hmm."

"And yet? I'm still fully grossed out."

"Right there with you," Xena said.

Priam and Hecuba kissed. Lingeringly.

Laodice was making her way back towards the high table, her hands already outstretched for her new husband. They held hands *constantly*. It was cute. It was definitely adorable, and not at all annoying.

Cassie stood up and nodded at the musicians. Their cousin Paris, frontwoman of Paris and the Archers, did something with her pedals that led to the gentle jazz instrumental fading out, just as Cassie hit the stage and grabbed the mic.

Xena plastered an enormous smile on her face. Back in her past life, she'd been a performer. That life was over, but she could damn well make this performance count.

The problem was, she'd only ever been performing as herself.

She'd never been good at performing a lie.

***

4

Three hours later, the speeches were done, the cake had been cut, the first dance had been danced, the couple had finished all their social obligations, and had been loudly and cheerfully farewelled to their honeymoon. Xena had smiled through it all. When she'd hugged Laodice goodbye, she'd been able to congratulate herself on not expressing a single negative emotion where her sister could see it.

As a special reward for all her efforts, she planned to get really drunk.

Her plans didn't include her parents giving her a hard time for getting really drunk, assuming they could stop sucking each other's faces long enough to notice, so she swiped two bottles of champagne and a glass and wandered casually out of the marquee set up on the grounds of the Tantalus Vineyard. As casually as someone who was six foot four in low heels could wander, anyway.

The wedding location was another nice piece of synergy—Cassie's partner Manny owned and ran the vineyard, and its associated hospitality ventures, and it meant the wedding party was able to stay in the luxury accommodations. Then all of Laodice's Bridal department friends would feature the vineyard on their social media and maybe in their official work, and Manny's family would benefit from the publicity. Everyone was gaining. Everyone was getting benefits from years of dedicated effort and networking and building a well-deserved reputation for excellence.

Xena popped the cork off the first bottle and drank half of it straight from the neck.

"Whoa," someone said behind her, and Xena whirled to find Manny himself.

"What?" she said, lowering the bottle defensively.

"That was just the sound of me being impressed," Manny told her. "And also wishing I could do that." He glanced towards the marquee, where Paris was belting out a cover for the pop song of the summer.

"Oh, right," Xena said, feeling bad. "Weddings."

Manny was a burly blond teddy bear of a man who was calm and resilient and genuinely nice, so it was hard to remember that he had plenty of reason to resent Paris. Who'd eloped with Manny's ex-wife six hours after *their* wedding. In the middle of their reception, in fact.

Xena offered him the bottle. After a moment, he took it.

"I'm surprised Laodice booked the Archers," Xena said. "She doesn't even like Paris that much."

"I think your mom played the family card. Cassie checked with me, and I said okay." He took a swig. "And it is okay. I just have the occasional stray feeling."

So, not a permanent miasma of anger, resentment and despair. Well, there was hope. In fourteen years, maybe she'd also be down to occasional stray feelings.

"At least Helen didn't come," she said.

Manny didn't quite roll his eyes. "Paris wanted her to. She decided to stay at home with Hermione."

Kids. That was another thing Xena had planned on starting by now. She popped the cork on the second bottle. Champagne froth spilled over her hand. Great, now she was going to be irritable *and* sticky.

"How's school going?" Manny asked.

Xena lowered the bottle. "I quit."

"Oh."

"I haven't told anyone yet. I just... It's not for me." Xena had completed one year of college before her influencer career had really taken off. Everyone had kind of gently implied they thought she should go back, now that her career was over, and she hadn't had any better ideas. Her business classes were fine, but the whispering and not at all subtle attempts to record her on campus had been unbearable. She'd switched to online learning instead, but that had just made her feel isolated and weird, and she'd gradually stopped attending seminars or watching lecture recordings. Last semester, she'd drifted into academic probation, then failure, without bothering to respond to any of the polite inquiries from the Dean's office.

It didn't matter. She could afford it. She could probably afford to live on her investment income for the rest of her life, if she wasn't too extravagant. She could sit in the apartment she owned and watch all the movies she'd missed the first time and play a bunch of video games and run on her treadmill and get food delivered every night and eat it alone.

"Xena?"

"Mm?"

"I — please don't think I want to pry, but Cassie mentioned you'd had that bout of depression. Is everything all right?"

"No," Xena said, and took another swallow. "But the depression is officially over. Psych cleared and everything. How's your PTSD? Any luck finding that long-lost cousin your grandfather and uncle hid from you?"

Manny accepted the redirect with no more than a slight raise of his shaggy eyebrows. "No luck finding Gus yet, no. And my PTSD is better." He considered. "Though we don't use a shotgun to scare birds from the grapes anymore."

No wonder, when his murderous uncle had tried to shoot him with one.

Xena nodded. "And I don't propose to my boyfriend in a livestream that gets mocked around the world when he turns me down anymore, so... I guess we're both avoiding our triggers." She looked at him, then at the bottle in her hand. "Oh. Were you trying to figure out if you should cut me off?"

Manny winced.

"No, it's okay. You have a responsibility as the venue owner."

"I also have a responsibility as your friend," Manny said, with more bite than she'd expected. "I mean, maybe I'm assuming, but—"

"No, we're friends. Good looking out." Xena sighed. "Look, I just... For the last six months, this wedding has been the thing I had to get through. I psyched myself up and I held it together. And now it's over, and I need something else. And I keep running into the part where I don't know what that is."

"I think I can help with that."

Manny and Xena both turned to regard the new speaker. Sometime in the last few minutes, Xena belatedly realized, the music had stopped.

"I'm going to head in again," Manny said. "Nice chatting with you, Xena. Night, Paris."

"Manny," Paris said, acknowledging him with a nod, and then, as far as Xena could tell, immediately forgetting him as soon as he wasn't in her field of vision.

Paris Chen wasn't Xena's favorite cousin either, but Xena did have to admire her singular ability to focus. Her focus, right now, appeared to be on Xena. "So you're looking for a job," she said.

Xena shrugged. "I guess. I don't really need to work."

Paris shook her head, but in disapproval, not disbelief. "I can't believe you made so much money from sponsorships that you never have to work again," she said. "I mean, for what?"

"For working non-stop, putting out daily, high quality content and building an audience of millions."

"Millions of people watching fat lady dancing videos," Paris said, and Xena rolled her eyes. One popular series of videos *had* been called Fat Lady Dancing, because she'd been the fat lady dancing in them. They'd been great.

"Yes. And I did sports advocacy for people of all sizes, and a lot of media and political commentary and—" Xena shut her mouth on the rest of the sentence. She didn't need to defend what she did anymore. It was maybe the one good thing about no longer doing it. "What's your point?"

"I want you to do social media for the Archers."

Xena looked at her face. Paris appeared to be serious.

"Do you," she said.

"We're good," Paris said. "You *know* we're good. We've been working steadily for nearly twenty years now, and we keep touring and putting out music and building a following, and we're finally getting ready to break away from this events crap." She waved at the marquee.

"Paris, this is my *sister's wedding*."

"Sure, I mean, not that *this* is crap," Paris said, her tone unconvincing. "Happy to do a favor for family. Which brings me back to the job. We've been offered a festival gig. A new thing, but I think it's going to be huge, real rich-lister stuff. A luxury festival on a tropical island, like Fyre Festival was supposed to be."

"Fyre Fest was a massive scam."

"This isn't." Paris's face was intent. "The contracts are good, and we got a deposit in advance. There are a few big names, but most of the performers are indie, from a lot of different disciplines—musicians, comedians, drag, circus stuff. The appeal for the audience is that you could be there when the next big thing takes off. The Archers could *be* that next big thing."

Xena frowned. Much as she disliked stoking Paris's sense of entitlement, the Archers *were* good. They made solid music and they had a passionate fanbase, especially among queer women. They even had the bonus of a charismatic frontwoman, so long as no one talked to her one-on-one for very long. They truly could be on the verge of a breakout.

"So I want you to do the social media," Paris went on. "You know how to make content that goes viral. And on top of that you could, like, chronicle us. Getting ready, then traveling to the festival, the festival itself."

"Like a documentary?"

"Yeah, but live!" Paris frowned. "Or nearly live, we want to avoid mistakes like you made."

"Wow," Xena said. "You're really selling this job to me."

Paris drew herself up to her full height. Since that was more than a foot shorter than Xena, it probably wasn't as effective as she'd hoped, but this had never slowed Paris down. "What else have you got to do?" she asked.

Xena considered that. Paris wouldn't be able to pay her much—definitely nowhere near her previous rates—but she could feel a sort of excited tremor at the back of her brain that she hadn't felt for a long time. It was the instinct that had steered her through the shark-infested waters of social media, until she'd sunk her own ship. This could work. This had legs.

"What's the island?" she asked.

Paris grinned, which made her look a little like a well-dressed shark herself. "It's called Aea. It looks *amazing*. Blue seas, white sand, tropical forest, spectacular waterfalls. And it's not like Fyre Fest, because there are already facilities. There's a little town, but the festival itself is going to be on a massive private estate, owned by one of the investors.

Xena could live on her investments if she wasn't extravagant. Extravagancies included travel. And she *missed* travel. In her old life, she'd been gifted trips and had actually been paid to stay in a number of gorgeous locations, and she'd hadn't appreciated it enough. She'd worked so hard filming magical moments for her followers that she'd kind of skipped actually experiencing them.

"Come on," Paris said. "It'll be great exposure."

Xena didn't even have to think about that. "No," she said firmly. "No exposure for me."

"But you have all those fans!"

"I *had* fans. I'm not appearing on camera, Paris. Definitely no cross-promotion with my old channels." She'd kept them all, on her lawyer's advice, to limit impersonation, but she hadn't posted a thing since her final apology and farewell video.

"Oh," Paris said, and her face fell. She'd evidently been envisioning all of Xena's followers becoming *hers*. "Well, uh, how would it work, then?"

"The same way it works for anyone. Great content, good timing, a lot of luck." She looked at Paris. "I know much more than I did when I started. That will help."

Paris nodded. "Right, exactly. We've been concentrating on the music, not the marketing." The airy gesture she made with her hand seemed to dismiss the entire field of "telling people about your work" as beneath her and all true creatives. "So, I can tell the Archers you're in?"

Xena could feel herself actually considering it. She should ask for more time to think it over. Making a decision when she was emotionally compromised and more than a little drunk wasn't a good idea.

On the other hand, Paris was right. She literally had nothing else to do.

"Yeah, okay," she said.

Paris's eyes lit up with genuine pleasure, and Xena remembered why people liked Paris. When she was happy, she made you happy. When she was interested in you, you felt like the most interesting person in the world. Probably, this was why her wife Helen stayed with her, even though Helen was absurdly sweet and nice, and Paris thought being nice was an outrageous societal expectation imposed by phallocentric hegemony.

She wasn't completely wrong about that, but she was also very Paris about it.

"That's *awesome*," Paris said. "That's really, really great. Thank you so much, Xena."

"Looking forward to it," Xena said, and meant it.

"Of course, if you're not going to cross-promote on your channels we can't pay you as much," Paris added. "Hey! Where are you going? You said yes, that's a verbal contract!"

"We'll talk about the details tomorrow," Xena said, without bothering to look over her shoulder. There was a sizeable hill at the back of the vineyard, and climbing it would put her a good distance from concerned friends *and* self-centered opportunists. She hefted her bottle. "Tonight, I'm getting drunk."

"Why?" Paris said, and she managed to sound actually concerned. "Wait, is everything all right?"

"Sure," Xena said, increasing her pace.

"You're a terrible liar."

Xena turned on her. "Oh, really?" she said sarcastically. "Because from where I'm standing, my life is just perfect."

And she took off, running up the hill before anyone could challenge her on the lie.

Chapter Two

Cressida O'Brien liked her job.

Sometimes she had to repeat this to her reflection in the studio's mirrored walls before her students came in, but on the whole, it was true. Her burlesque classes at the Evenwood community center were popular, most of her students tried hard and enjoyed themselves, and a lot of them were discovering pleasure in their bodies in a way they maybe never had before.

After her first month at the center, she'd also put a flat moratorium on any negative body talk, banning all discussion of diets, weight loss regimes, or whether eating a cupcake was "being bad," partly because it endorsed unhelpful stereotypes, and partly because all of the agonizing over calories was so boring she was afraid she was going to yawn in a student's face. She'd lost a couple of students who hadn't believed she'd meant it, but the remaining burlesque hopefuls had told their friends, and now she could count on being booked out every week.

Cressida discreetly checked the clock over the door. Yes, they had time for one more run-through of the new routine. "Let's stick it this time!" she said cheerfully, and turned her back, so her students could watch her in the studio mirrors. She chanted through the routine in choreography shorthand, keeping her voice clear and peppy, and was pleased to see nearly everyone hitting their marks. For now, they were miming the strip portions. It would be harder when actual clothes had to come off, because hooks and zips and buttons had no respect for the beat.

"And wriggle wriggle wriggle," she said, miming pushing a skirt down her hips. "And step out, oops!" A shocked hand over her mouth. "And pop! And pop! And lift that chest! Eye contact…sparkle! And pose!" She grinned at her class, and led them in a round of applause for themselves and each other. "Amazing work, folks! Let's call it for today, and I'll see you all next week for a costume run-through."

She'd brought feather fans for the earlier routine. Now she stacked the fluffy monsters in their custom bag, listening with half an ear to the excited chatter of her students as they finished water bottles and swapped heels for walking shoes.

"—thought it would be acting like a hooker, but actually it's really fun!"

Cressida straightened. The speaker was a newcomer, a tall white woman brought along by a friend, who was embarrassedly trying to shush her.

Cressida wandered over. "Breanne, isn't it?" she said. "We try to avoid disparaging sex workers here. Burlesque owes a lot to them."

"But it was a compliment!" Breanne said. "I was saying that what you do is like, fun and sexy, not gross." She brayed a laugh. "Not like *stripping*. Or *prostitution*."

Hazel, standing beside her, winced. Cressida hesitated. Hazel was an excellent dancer, and Cressida planned to make her the final act at the end of year showcase. She'd be sorry to lose Hazel, if she sided with her friend. But she'd sworn never to compromise herself again.

"Stripping and prostitution are jobs," she said. "Again, in burlesque spaces especially, we try not to denigrate them."

"Yeah, but *you* wouldn't do them," Breanne said.

"I have," Cressida said. "Stripping, pole, lap dancing, full escort services."

Breanne's mouth opened wide, then shut, then opened again. She looked like a fish. Cressida waited, keeping her face perfectly calm. She knew what she looked like. Short and curvy, with blonde curls and a sweetheart smile, she was the image of a wholesome homemaker or adored kindergarten teacher. She wasn't the "type" to strut around a stage wearing heels and a smile, or exchange sex for money—which was partly why she'd been so successful at it.

"But—" Breanne said, and then got enough of a grip on herself to start manifesting outrage. "There are *kids* at this community center!"

"Not in my classes," Cressida said.

"That's— you're a whore! You sleep with other women's husbands!"

"We're leaving," Hazel said, slipping her hand into the strap of Breanne's bag and tugging. "Sorry, Cressida."

"Don't apologize to *her*! You brought me to this—"

"Stop," Hazel said, with more force than Cressida would have thought she could summon. She yanked the bag again, more firmly. "Let's go."

"Hazel!"

"*Now*, Breanne," Hazel said, and then pronounced the magic words that could move an outraged WASP mom: "You're making a scene."

Cressida took a moment to rub the spot between her eyes as the door swung shut behind them. The only other student left in the room, a guy called Rory who was doing burlesque to broaden his drag skills, gave her a sympathetic glance. "You okay, queen?"

"Yeah. Just... People get so weirdly aggressive when you challenge their sanitized world-views."

"Honey, you don't need to tell *me*. Are you generally out with the sex worker stuff, or do you want me to keep my mouth shut?"

"It's past tense, and I don't really advertise it," Cressida admitted, rolling her shoulders. "I just don't pretend, unless it's an unsafe situation. But I think I could have taken her."

"Oh yes, you could. That skinny ass wouldn't stand a chance."

Cressida laughed, feeling better. "Thanks, Rory."

"Any time, honey. See you next week."

Her class finished at 9:00 p.m., right when the center closed its doors, so Cressida closed the windows, turned off the lights, and checked the lock on the dance-cum-martial arts studio room before she turned to go.

There was a hulking shadow lurking in the hallway. Cressida shrieked and dropped the fan bag, her hand reaching instinctively for her Mace.

"Whoa, no!" the shadow exclaimed, raising her hands. "It's Debra."

"Debra!" Cressida clutched at her heart. It thumped against her palm. "You scared the hell out of me!"

"I'm so sorry!" The hall lights flickered on. "These damn motion sensors, they take forever. Cheap pieces of crap." Debra was in what she called her should-have-been-retirement years, a large and sturdy woman of indeterminate age with an impressive 80s-style perm. "Cressida, we have to talk."

Cressida's heart sank. "Did Breanne lay a complaint?"

"Oh, her? She did, but that's not the thing. The truth is, the center's not doing great. We missed out on two big community grants this year, and we were kind of relying on getting them. The board of trustees have decided that they won't be open to night classes." Debra shrugged awkwardly. "That way they can save on paying someone to supervise, cut down on running costs..."

"Oh."

"But I told them your Thursday classes are really popular, and they said, well, what if she takes on the costs?"

"What would that be?"

Debra gave her the number, looking hopeful. Cressida blinked. "I mean, I can't. That's more than I make from the classes."

"You could raise prices?"

"I can't *double* them," Cressida said. "That's what I'd have to do, to make slightly less money than I do now, which is already too little to cover all my expenses."

It was Debra's turn to blink. "I thought this was a hobby?"

"It's a hobby for my *students*. For me, it buys groceries." And fewer of those every week, it seemed.

"Well, maybe day classes, then? A lot of your students are moms, or semi-retired."

"I look after my son during the day."

"Oh. Daycare?" Debra saw her face and winced. "Sorry. Sorry, I keep trying to solve the problem. But of course you know your business best."

"I'll have to think about it," Cressida said, and escaped into the warm night air. After a moment, she turned towards the subway sign. Normally, she treated herself to a cab ride after class, but if she was going to lose that income too...

The elevator in her apartment building was broken again. Cressida walked the eight flights up, feeling her glutes and calves burn. It was a free workout, at least. She hadn't been able to afford a gym membership for years. She couldn't pay for daycare without income, she couldn't *make* income without daycare, and she was only able to teach the Thursday night classes because that was her best friend's night off, and Anna was happy to watch Lucian.

And let them live with her rent-free. And cover groceries and utilities when Cressida was short.

Cressida wasn't sure what she'd done in a past life to deserve Anna, but it had evidently been something good.

When she opened their apartment door, Anna was snoring on the couch, an open bag of potato chips lying on her stomach. Cressida tried to close the door quietly, but Anna sat up. "Good night?" she asked, her voice husky with sleep.

"Yes," Cressida said automatically, and then sighed. "Ugh, actually, no. The center is planning to cancel all of their night classes. I'm going to need to find another room for hire."

"That sucks."

"Yeah." She braced herself. "About this month's utilities. I don't know how much I can contribute to—"

Anna shook her head firmly. "I told you. You don't need to worry about that."

Cressida sat on the end of the couch. "I'm going to have to worry about it eventually, Anna. You've been amazing, but my savings are gone and Lucian's getting bigger. We can't share the same room forever. Once he starts school, we need more room."

Anna pursed her lips. "I have some clients who'd hire a couple," she suggested, and when Cressida shook her head, "Well, the club would take you back in a second. If finding someone to look after Lucian is the issue, you'd easily make enough to pay for a good babysitter."

Cressida made a face. "My lawyer has categorically advised against it."

"Stripping is legal," Anna said indignantly.

"Sure, but if Dammond decides he wants to apply for custody, a hooker mom—even a stripper mom—is an easy target. Especially because it's night shift work. He could make a good case for me being neglectful. All he'd need is a sympathetic judge." She rubbed her eyes. "I was *really* counting on the pre-K lottery." Lucian qualified for free pre-K, but the only slot she'd been offered from the city lottery was a forty-minute commute away, for half-days only. She couldn't get the hours to pay rent with that kind of schedule.

"But hey," she said, trying to sound upbeat. "In eight months, he turns five." And that place, at a good public school they could walk to, was already secured for him. "I can work retail or waitress then."

Anna looked unconvinced. "You hate retail and you love dancing."

"I know," Cressida said. "Believe me, Anna, I am *aware*. I just... I gotta look after my kid. That's the number one priority."

"I know," Anna said, and her body language softened, her eyes losing their challenge. "But babe, I hate to see you so worn out. Number one priority doesn't mean the only priority, right?"

"Right," Cressida said, but her voice lacked conviction, even to herself.

***

Cressida downed half a cup of gone-cold black coffee and exhaled, trying to shake the tension from her jaw and shoulders. Lucian was on the couch, entranced by an old episode of *Sesame Street*, and there would be no better time for her to make the phone call she was dreading.

She stepped into the bedroom she shared with Lucian, made a mental note to visit the laundromat later that afternoon, cracked the door so that she could keep an eye on him, and navigated to the name *Dammond Argive* in her contact list.

She didn't have to wait long. The phone rang twice, and then the familiar, boyishly eager voice was on the line.

"Chrissy?"

"Hi, Dammond."

"Hey!"

She steeled herself for the pleasantries. "How's it going?"

"Good! Good. Thanks for sending me that card at the holidays," Dammond said. He sounded sincere. He was good at sounding sincere. Sometimes, Cressida thought, it might even be genuine.

"You're welcome," she said.

"He's a really cute kid."

Cressida smiled. "Well, I think so."

"We made a cute little guy," Dammond went on, and she heard the slosh of liquid and the clink of ice against glass. It was two in the afternoon.

"Are you taking the day off?" she asked.

"Nah. I'm in the office." He sighed. "Still a lot of stuff to deal with after Granddad died."

"I bet," Cressida said, trying her best to keep her tone neutral. Adrestus Argive had been a terrifying old monster, and when his death notice had appeared two months ago, she'd felt as if a piece of rigid wire in her spine had loosened. But Dammond had loved his grandfather as much as he'd feared him. "I'm sorry for your loss," she added, and even meant it, at least a little bit.

"Yeah," Dammond said. "I appreciate you saying that. I know you two didn't get on so well."

Cressida supposed "you didn't get on so well" was certainly one way to put "he threatened to kill you after you gave birth."

"I'm glad you called. I've been thinking about you lately." The clink of ice again. "And Lucian."

"Well, that's why I'm calling," Cressida said. "I'm sure you've heard about the increased cost of living."

"Yeah, sure."

"I was hoping you'd be open to increasing your parental support payment."

A long pause. "In return for me getting joint custody?" Dammond asked, and he no longer sounded relaxed.

"I think he's old enough to start supervised visits," Cressida said cautiously.

"No. Custodial rights. I want my son to have a place in my home."

"Our parenting agreement doesn't give you those, Dammond. You signed it."

"Yeah, because you said that you'd never ask for more than the minimum."

They both knew that was a lie. Adrestus had wanted Dammond to have full custody, or nothing. Dammond's lawyers had probably advised him he wouldn't be able to *get* full custody. Cressida's lawyer had advised her against trying to get Dammond's parental rights removed. The uneasy compromise had been a pittance payment that Cressida had never contested, in return for Dammond never claiming custodial rights.

Lucian knew he *had* a father, but not who that father was. He'd never met Dammond. With Adrestus dead, Cressida was less worried about that meeting. But her hackles were rising at the thought of Lucian being with Dammond alone, being *without her.*

"Splitting him between homes would be a lot right now," she said. "He's starting school soon; it's going to be a big shift. Maybe when he's older, when he can make up his own mind."

"When you've brainwashed him. The way you did me."

"I didn't brainwash you, Dammond."

"You made me think you loved me."

Cressida closed her eyes. "I did love you. It was real."

"You wanted my money."

"Dammond, I need you to think about this logically. I left you without a penny. I've gotten by for years on the bare minimum. You *assumed* all along that you'd be supporting me financially, because you and your grandfather both assumed I'd stop working. You were fine with that. It was me wanting to make my *own* money that you had a problem with."

This, typically, would be the moment where Dammond would start talking about how no good mother could be a stripper, how it would have made him a laughingstock to his buddies and business partners, how his mother would never have been able to look her fellow ladies who lunch in the eye.

Never mind that he'd *met* her at the club. Never mind that he'd been one of the people paying for her time.

At first, Dammond's offer to cover her expenses while they planned the wedding had seemed generous and caring. Cressida had already put a temporary pause on her escort work when Dammond had proposed exclusivity, and she'd been planning to stop stripping when the baby bump appeared anyway. There *was* a market for pregnant dancers, but it wasn't one she especially wanted to cater to. And true, she worked at a good club, with good management and security, but there were always customers who thought nudity was permission. She'd accept the risk to herself, but not her passenger.

But she'd kept the burlesque appearances on her calendar. She and Dammond had fought about it a few times, but she'd held firm. Burlesque didn't pay nearly as well, but it was what she loved most—playful sexuality, performance, dance, spectacle, and an audience primed to appreciation. There'd been a lot to do, preparing for the wedding and Lucian's arrival, so she hadn't sought any *new* bookings.

And Dammond had apparently taken that as her *quitting*.

At the rehearsal dinner, she'd just been trying to make conversation. She'd spent the entire evening uncomfortable, alternately sweaty and chilled. Her back ached, her feet hurt, and the "cute maternity cocktail dress" Dammond's mother had gifted her for the evening was an expensive black sack. Dammond's best man hadn't let that stop him from hitting on her, for maybe the tenth time. She'd been witnessing Adrestus Argive's unpleasant posturing and Dammond's obsequiousness all evening *and* she'd had to go to the bathroom way too often.

So when one of the guests had said something condescending about having her hands full after the baby came, she'd talked about her desire to go to school and study events management, or maybe marketing. It was a half-baked dream, nothing she'd brought up to Dammond or even Anna before, but the more she talked the more she liked it. Performance could stay her priority, but it was smart to have a Plan B. And that had led her on to enthusing about burlesque and cabaret events, how fun they were, how much she was looking forward to getting back on stage...

And realized, with growing horror, that she was talking into a hostile silence, while Adrestus Argive swelled and reddened, a volcano of rage ready to abrupt.

"The mothers in *our* family have *never* worked," he pronounced. "Much less in—" he made a sharp gesture, too refined even to say the word.

"Oh," Cressida had said. "Well, the mother in *our* family will."

And then she'd looked to Dammond for support.

That had been her final mistake.

Because the truth was, while she'd never considered quitting work for good, Dammond had never considered she wouldn't. And neither of them had ever brought it up.

They should never have gotten together in the first place, and when she was honest with herself, she could admit that that part wasn't really Dammond's fault. He'd just done what customers were supposed to do, and fallen for a dancer.

It was Cressida who'd done the stupidest thing possible and fallen back. All the yeses that should have been no. Yes, I'll tell you my real name, yes, I'll do a private session at your house, yes, I'll go on a proper date with you, yes, yes, yes, I love you too.

They probably would have broken up six months into the relationship. Chemistry couldn't combat basic incompatibility forever. But her birth control had failed, and a whirlwind romance had turned into a whirlwind of wedding planning, and then all that chemistry had... Blown up.

With a start, Cressida realized that Dammond hadn't said anything for a while.

"Are you still there?" she said.

He sighed. "You're right."

"Excuse me?"

"I said, you're right. I know you're not a gold-digger, Chrissy. You've proven that by now."

"Huh," Cressida said. "I'm... Honestly, I'm shocked. I never thought you'd recognize that, much less say it."

"Things change. People grow."

"I'm so glad to hear it. So, an extension of the child support payment..."

"In exchange for joint custody."

Cressida gritted her teeth and kept her voice pleasant. "We could do this through the court system, if you prefer. The state will set your payment a lot higher than I'm asking for."

"Sure, we could do that," Dammond said. "I mean, my lawyers are sharks, and my income is technically one dollar a year, so good luck."

"The court would look at your *assets*, including your investments and capital, not just your tax-avoidant income."

"Sounds expensive," Dammond said, not sounding very worried. "How much would you owe *your* lawyer?"

"I can find someone."

"You don't want to take me to court, Chrissy. A judge will definitely give me some custody. They have no reason not to."

He was right, and she hated him for saying it. But he'd never done anything to her or Lucian. He hadn't breached their agreement by trying to see Lucian, and he'd always made the payments on time. Sure, he could drop more in the club on one night than he had to pay her in a year, but she knew that relative wealth didn't necessarily mean people paid their obligations on time.

And Adrestus was dead now. He'd been the one obsessed with his heir, desperate to secure the succession before he died, like an ancient, miserable king telling his son's concubine she *would* be queen.

"Okay," she said. "We can talk about it."

Dammond's exhale was audible, and Cressida realized that he hadn't been as confident as he sounded. Well, if nothing else, he'd learned to respect that when she said something, she meant it.

"Good," he said. "I'm glad. Uh...how about, as a sign of goodwill, I'll put an extra payment through right now. And—" his voice brightened. "Actually, yeah, this works. I'm hosting a festival."

"You're what?"

"I'm working with some of the Events guys at Argive, and we're running a music and arts festival called Lotophagi. It's going to be incredible, like Glastonbury or Coachella, only on Aea. And smaller, obviously. But very luxe, very upmarket."

"Aea? The island where your grandfather had that holiday house?"

"My holiday house, now," Dammond said. "There's going to be music, of course, and interactive installation art, and yoga on the beach, and a bunch of performance art. Multiple stages, multiple tents. We open in three months. You should come! We could work it all out then!"

Cressida blinked. "I'd be performing?"

"Uh. Well, I meant you could come as my guest."

Cressida stifled her disappointment. "We're not getting back together, Dammond."

"No, of course not," he said, too quickly. "But you can still be my guest, as just friends."

"That might confuse things."

There was a pause. "Would you *like* to perform? There's a cabaret tent, with burlesque and circus and stuff."

"I-" she shook her head, even though he couldn't see her. "I appreciate the offer, Dammond, but I don't know if it's a good idea. You made it pretty clear you don't like me performing. I don't want you treating that as a provocation when we're trying to work out a new arrangement."

"I've changed, Chrissy. I really have. Granddad's death brought up a lot of stuff for me."

"I--"

"Give me a chance to prove it. Come to Lotophagi, as one of the acts. Not as my guest. Not even as my friend. If you like, I'll pretend I don't know you at all. We can talk after."

Cressida wavered. She'd *loved* doing festivals. The people, the music, the simmering potential. If she could have lived exclusively on burlesque clubs and festivals, she would have. But even if Lucian would be okay without her for a few days—and that wasn't something she was sure of—she couldn't ask Anna for that much time.

"I can't," she said, regret a little too plain in her voice. "I don't have anyone to look after Lucian."

"Bring him," Dammond said instantly.

"To a *festival*?"

"There'll be a whole family friendly area," Dammond said triumphantly. "*And* we've got 24-hour childcare with trained nannies, for parents who want to enjoy themselves without worrying about the kids. No reason performers couldn't take advantage of it too." His voice wavered. "Maybe I could meet him?"

"24-hour childcare does sound upmarket," Cressida said, avoiding the question for now.

"You know it," Dammond said, and took the bait, launching into a practiced spiel. Cressida had actually heard something about the new festival through her various networks, but this was the first time she was learning about Dammond's involvement.

Argive Holdings usually focused on real estate and construction. The last time they'd gotten involved in something unusual, it was some kind of pre-wedding retreat business that had ended with multiple murders. That wasn't the kind of publicity that venerable institutions wanted. No wonder Dammond was keeping his name out of the Lotophagi marketing.

"Okay," she said, interrupting Dammond's spiel on the ablutions block he was getting installed so that performers would have access to showers. "I'll come. I'll bring Lucian, I'll perform, and afterwards, you can meet him. And he can meet you. And then we'll decide what we do next."

"Chrissy. That's—thank you."

If Dammond had grown up, if he'd changed... For a moment, Cressida allowed herself to hope. Romance was out of the question—she could never love him again. But co-parenting, perhaps, wasn't so out of reach.

Then practicality reasserted itself. "But I get paid," she added. "I'm not doing you a favor for exposure."

"You're doing me a big favor," Dammon said, sounding unusually heartfelt. "I won't forget it. I'll get one of the producers on it now."

"Okay, then. Bye." Cressida hung up as he farewelled her, and considered the conversation.

She was very much hoping she'd made the right decision.

Chapter Three

Xena had never been a roadie before. She wasn't sure what she'd expected from her first day of filming, but it hadn't been hauling Paris's luggage through a tiny mainland airport while they tried to get to their chartered flight to Aea.

To be fair, Paris was also hauling luggage. The Archers didn't pack light, and while most of their technical needs would be covered by the festival, their instruments and some of their specialist equipment had to fly with them. They also had to bring nearly everything they needed to camp for the next five days. Tents, beds, and food were supposed to be provided free for performers, but Xena had apparently not been the only one worried about the possibility of another Fyre Festival debacle, where attendees and performers alike had been stranded without enough food, water or shelter. Prax, the drummer, had a bunch of dehydrated camp meals shoved in her backpack, along with a tarp, an inflatable five gallon container, water sterilizing pills, a camp stove, and a foldable set of pots, pans, and utensils.

Prax had been really unhappy when airport security at their first stop had confiscated the butane canisters for the stove.

"Right," Paris said suddenly. She unceremoniously dropped her backpack off her shoulder, then placed her guitar case beside it, with much more care. "We need a cart. And maybe an earlier flight to Aea." She darted off into the crowd, wearing an expression of grim determination.

"I need coffee," Sapph said, setting down her own burdens. She had dark brown skin and luscious curves, which Xena had once explored in a mutually satisfying and sadly brief encounter, pre-fame and pre-Zac. She liked Sapph, who was witty, occasionally melodramatic, and perpetually sleep-deprived because, as she put it, "we only have one lifetime for reading and we can sleep when we're dead." "Does anyone see a cafe?"

Xena dumped Paris's other backpack, her own smaller rucksack, and the case that held most of her AV equipment and stretched, surveying the airport. Mostly, what she could see was people. Lots of people in their twenties, wearing shorts and T-shirts, energetically sharing their thoughts. Those would be the volunteers, coming early for setup. Fewer people in their thirties and forties, wearing black jeans, t-shirts and stoic expressions, who she tagged as the festival tech crew. Harassed airport staff in their uniforms, various ages, not many of them, and all of them trying to do eight things at once.

And performers, like the Archers. These were the lower-ranking acts, not the big names who'd be getting the VIP treatment, so she didn't expect to recognize anyone, but she could pick out the types. A group of lithe people in leggings and crop tops might have been circus performers or dancers, but she thought the muscles on two of them pointed to the former. There was someone with tattooed eyebrows and a far-off gaze who was definitely an installation artist and a pair of DJs enthusiastically discussing new mixers. A bare-chested man was doing warrior pose in the middle of the airport. He could, realistically, be any kind of performer, but he was definitely being annoying.

"I don't see any coffee," she said.

"My life is misery," Sapph said, and folded onto the institutional carpet in a posture of extreme dejection.

"I have instant in my pack," Prax said. "If you want to, like, eat it dry."

"I'm not quite that desperate yet," Sapph said. "But keep it handy."

The last two members of the band, Corinna and Phryne, were sitting on their own mountain of luggage, half-asleep in the muggy heat. Xena felt something in her brain click open and reached for her camera.

She panned over the crowd, and came down to a wide group shot. "How are you feeling, guys?" she asked.

"Hot," Corinna said.

"Sticky," Phryne said, right after, and then laughed, leaning into her girlfriend's side. "And not in the good way."

Prax looked uncertain. She was the youngest, and had joined the band after their original drummer had quit six months ago. "What do I say?"

"Whatever you like," Xena told her. "I'm just catching the vibe."

"Okay, well... Down with capitalism." Prax raised a fist.

"Nice," Xena said. It probably wasn't the time to point out they were heading to a private estate for a festival funded by capitalists. The complexities of making independent art in a system geared to reward extractivist billionaires was a conversation for another time. "Sapph?"

Sapph pulled her shirt away from her skin and flapped it for air. "A subtle fire races under my skin."

"Great." Xena panned over the crowd again. She'd need to get releases for showing anyone in an identifiable way, but they were all going to be in the same place for a week, and she figured she could find most of them again. She made a mental note to check if the volunteers and attendees had signed some kind of release already. Lotophagi had probably made them consent to being filmed for publicity purposes. If it was loosely worded, she might be covered.

The camera jumped, obedient to the sudden jolt of her hand, halting to frame a woman who'd paused in the exit from the bathroom. She wore a denim jumpsuit, unbuttoned to show a form-fitting red T-shirt. Her yellow-gold curls were contained by a blue kerchief bound around her head, and her red mouth smiled as she surveyed her surroundings. In that heated, chaotic crowd, she looked cool and calm.

Her eyes focused on Xena, filming her from across the room.

Xena lowered her camera.

The woman was still looking at her, her expression unreadable. Xena kept eye contact. Something had snatched her breath. She couldn't move with this woman looking at her, and it was impossible to look away.

Then a kid came out of the bathroom door, and the moment was broken. He said something to the woman and she bent over him, touching the hands he held out for inspection and praise. Four or five, maybe, and obviously very proud of himself for going to the big boy bathroom. A muscular man in cut-offs and a tank top came out after him and said something to the woman, smiling broadly.

Ah. A happy little family. Well, that was nice.

"Xena!" Paris said. She'd popped up out of nowhere, dragging a baggage cart behind her. The others were dutifully piling their heaviest gear onto it. "The guy at the desk said we could take an earlier plane. Come on, load up!"

"Sure," Xena said. She took one last look at the beautiful blonde, happily chatting with the beefcake, and turned away to help load up.

It wasn't important. For the first time in a long time, she had a job to do.

***

"—and then I was like, so who's your mommy, and he said, my mommy is Cressida O'Brien! Like, what were the odds?"

"Mm, weird," Cressida said. Lucian had tucked himself against her leg, little fingers tugging at the knee of her jumpsuit. He didn't have these bouts of shyness very often anymore, but a crowded, noisy airport, topped off by a bellowing circus boy, seemed to be doing the trick.

"Yeah! Anyway, I made sure he washed his hands."

"Good work," Cressida said, and ruffled Lucian's hair. She'd meant the praise for her son, but Troy Chevalier puffed up. He was basically a superhero comic come to life, all sleek muscle and smooth skin. His dark eyes sparkled in his tan face, and his mouth, under his ostentatious curling moustache, was equally ready to pout or smile.

He could do a lot with that mouth, as Cressida had reason to know.

"It's been a long time!" he said, and rocked back on his heels, beaming at her. He was flexing a little, more of a reflexive habit than conscious effort. His muscles jumped under his skin like eager puppies.

"Do you know who that tall woman is?" she asked. "She looks kind of familiar, but I don't recognize her from the circuit." She'd been out of the game for nearly five years, time for a whole new generation of bright young things to emerge, but the woman hadn't looked that young. Maybe closer to her own twenty-seven.

Troy immediately climbed up on a bench to peer across the crowd. Cressida resisted the urge to scold him for being obvious. She hadn't specified discretion. You had to specify things, for Troy.

"Oh yeah!" he said, and jumped back down. "That's Xena Troiades! XO Xena! She proposed to her boyfriend on livestream." He frowned. "I thought she was canceled."

So that was why that Amazonian figure and long dark hair had looked familiar. Cressida had really enjoyed Xena's content, especially the videos where she'd tried lots of different disciplines. She was naturally strong and athletic, and also cheerfully willing to fail at things where being naturally strong and athletic wasn't enough. Her attempts at pole had been hilarious. When she'd managed a straddle invert for the first time, Cressida had cheered along with her.

She'd missed Xena's disastrous proposal and the subsequent cancellation—Lucian had been in a real toddler phase at the time, waking up throughout the night, getting picky over foods he'd previously loved, and having multiple meltdowns a day. When the developmental storm had cleared, Xena had vanished from her phone. Weirdly, Cressida had missed her, like a friend she hadn't heard from in a while.

Bizarre, of course. Parasocial relationship building at its finest.

"Did you ever get to Mardi Gras?" Troy was asking.

"No. I've been pretty busy."

"Oh, yeah? With what?"

He seemed to be serious. Did he think the four-year-old tugging at her pants was an accessory?

"We can go now, Mommy," Lucian said. This was probably meant to be a question, but he'd taken to making declarative statements and waiting for her response. "We can go back home now."

Cressida knelt down to meet his eyes. "We're on an adventure, Lucian. We're going to an island."

Lucian brightened. "To the beach."

"Yes."

"We go swimming at the beach." That *was* a declarative statement. She'd packed his swimsuit, but she hadn't had a chance to check if the beaches were swim safe.

"Cute," Troy said, his tone approving.

Well, if he insisted on hanging around, he could make himself useful. Cressida straightened and smiled at him. "Could you help us with our bags?" she said sweetly.

"Sure!" The muscles did their happy puppy dance again, and then he looked at the cases. "Is uh...is all this yours?"

"Oh, you know what costumes are like." Troy did most of his performing in leggings and a thin layer of coconut oil, but he'd spent enough time on the scene to know that burly girl packing was a workout all on its own. "Thanks so much, Troy! You're a doll." She took Lucian's hand and headed for the check-in desk, where a beleaguered young woman was trying to organize people into groups based on the chartered plane they were supposed to be catching. The airport's electronic screens were down, which definitely wasn't helping with the chaos.

"Cressida and Lucian O'Brien," she told the young woman, who glanced at her list.

"Oh, you're down as 'first available,'" she said, looking surprised. "Sorry, somebody should have met you as you got off your connecting flight."

Cressida shrugged. "I don't mind. You guys have clearly got a lot going on."

"Mm-hmm! Paul! Take over here!" She turned back to Cressida. "Where's your gear?"

Cressida nodded towards Troy, who was pushing the trunk towards them, her other bags piled on top.

The woman scanned the pile with a practiced eye. "I can get you on a plane now, and send the luggage later, or get you on a plane that leaves in three hours."

In earlier days, Cressida would never have flown without her gear. Now she had Lucian, and three more hours in this airport were not to be contemplated. "Plane now, thank you. That is, Troy, if you don't mind—"

"You can owe me one," Troy said, and winked at her.

Cressida scooped her giant tote bag off the top of the pile, the one that held all of her and Lucian's absolute necessities. "If I can take this, then we're good to go."

"Alrighty." The young woman smiled at Lucian, white teeth flashing in her dark face. "Do you like planes, little man?"

"We came here in a big plane," Lucian informed her, his tone important. "It had cartoons in the back of the seat and they gave me chips."

Cressida had been expecting a puddle jumper with noisy propellers. The young woman, whose badge named her Olivia, took them out onto the tarmac, where a small, but genuine private jet was waiting. Two cargo loaders were enthusiastically stowing bags and boxes in the cargo hold.

Lucian clambered up the stairs, taking big strides with his little legs, and Cressida followed, alert to any wobbles. The cabin was a little cramped and old-fashioned, maybe, but those were still leather seats with plenty of legroom, arranged train-carriage style around small side tables. Most of the seats were occupied by black-clad women.

One of them was Xena Troiades.

The rest of the women were apparently in a band. In a flurry of small talk while Cressida got her bag stowed in the back, the small woman sitting beside Xena introduced herself as Paris Chen, quickly worked out that Cressida had never heard of the Archers, and just as quickly lost all interest in her.

Lucian had gone quiet and clingy again, but he was looking at the free seats, both backward-facing, and Cressida braced herself for the storm.

"Would he like to have my seat?" Xena asked.

Her voice was quieter than Cressida had expected, less enthusiastic than her on-screen performance. But it was a lovely voice, rich and warm, and Cressida felt a frisson tremor down her spine. She'd always been a sucker for a good voice. Dammond had a great voice, when he remembered not to whine or sulk.

"If you wouldn't mind," she said apologetically. "Lucian sometimes feels unwell when he travels backwards."

"I throw up," Lucian said.

Paris looked alarmed.

"My sister used to do that," Xena said, looking gravely at Lucian. "It's no fun, huh?"

"What's her name?"

"Laodice."

"Does that start with an ell?"

"It sure does."

"My name starts with an ell. Ell for Lucian."

"My name starts with an X," Xena said. "X for Xena."

"That sounds like a zee!"

"I know! A lot of words that start with X sound like they start with zee. Isn't that weird?" She stood up, hunching to avoid hitting her head on the ceiling, and stepped back, letting Lucian climb into her seat. Cressida helped him with the seatbelt, very conscious of Xena's presence.

And also very conscious that it had been months since she'd had sex, or kissed someone, or, whew, even had a bad first date. Now a tall, black-haired woman with a soft voice was watching her buckle her son's seatbelt, and she felt...tingly.

Lucian was currently telling Xena all the words he knew that started with X. Some of them didn't, and some of them were repeats, but she was nodding seriously at each one, sometimes making a contribution of her own.

"Xenophobia," Lucian repeated. "What does that mean?"

"It's being scared of outsiders."

"Outside where? Outside the plane?"

"More like outside the groups you belong to. Like outside your family, or outside your school..."

"I don't go to school! I'm four."

"I'm sorry," Xena said. "I thought you were older."

Lucian looked suspicious, then decided it was a compliment. "I don't go to school until I'm five. You don't go to school because you're too big."

Xena had definitely made a conquest. Cressida settled into her own seat, facing Lucian, and watched as Lucian chattered at the woman seated diagonally across from him.

Then he went silent, plastered to the window as they rose into the air and the ocean spread beneath them. Thank goodness he had no fear of flying.

It was a forty-minute flight, much better than the six-hour ferry ride would have been. Cressida had never been invited to the hallowed ground of Aea. Adrestus had made noises about bringing the whole family out once "the boy" was born. From Dammond's descriptions, she would have thought the entire island of Aea was privately-owned, but her spotty online research had revealed that the Argive estate was only the largest and most luxurious of the island's retreats. There were other private homes, some resorts and hotels, and a small permanent township that provided for visitors.

"What brings you here?" she asked Xena.

"Work," Xena said, and nodded at the small woman seated across from her. "Nepotism, really. Paris is my cousin."

"Hey," Paris said, not looking up from her phone. The pilot had warned them they didn't have Wi-Fi, but she appeared to be playing a game.

"You're performing?"

"No. Filming." Xena shrugged, self-deprecating. "Streaming and social media. Maybe some documentary stuff?"

"Will you be starting XO Xena again?" Cressida asked.

Perhaps she sounded too eager. Xena's face closed like a door slamming in her face.

"See?" Paris said, putting her phone down.

"I don't do that anymore," Xena said.

"Oh. Sorry. I thought that maybe—it doesn't matter."

"Thought she was done beating herself up?" Paris asked. "Apparently not."

Xena glared at her cousin.

It was a good glare. Her strong brows drew together, and the dark eyes that had been calm and welcoming while she talked to Lucian went hard and dangerous. Muscles bunched in her shoulders as she leaned forward.

Paris didn't seem to care, but it had a certain effect on Cressida. Not fear. A sensation of danger that wasn't entirely unwelcome.

"Sorry, I've obviously stepped in it," she said cheerfully. "And outed myself as a fan, I think. But I'll look forward to whatever you do next, whether that's on camera or behind it."

Xena's frown slipped. She looked more confused now, as if the compliment were somehow unusual.

"And what brings you to Aea?" Paris asked.

"Mommy's going to dance," Lucian said, without looking away from the window.

"I do burlesque and cabaret performance," Cressida translated.

"Really?" Paris said, eyes flicking up and down her diminutive blondeness.

"Wow, that's really cool," Xena said. "I took on a few burlesque challenges."

"I watched," Cressida admitted.

Xena laughed. "Watched me fall on my ass?" She glanced guiltily at Lucian. "I mean butt."

"You were great!" Cressida said. "Actually, I haven't performed at festivals for a while. I mostly teach now."

This wasn't something she'd intended to tell anyone. Something about Xena—the admiration, the open body language—made it easy to reveal things. Including, apparently, her inconvenient nervousness about getting back on the festival stage.

It wasn't that she hadn't been performing at *all*. She'd been MCing and performing at burlesque showcases for her students, though that was mostly for an audience of their friends and family. She'd also taken part in half a dozen cabarets over the last couple of years, when she could make it work around her schedule and Anna's availability. Those were real gigs, with a real audience.

But it had been four years since she'd done something like *this*. And she'd never tried to perform with a child in tow.

For a moment, she doubted herself. Then her sensible inner voice, which sounded remarkably like Anna, kicked in. *Being a mother doesn't erase who you are*, she thought firmly. *You don't have to sacrifice your whole self.*

"I'm a little nervous," she admitted, and gestured subtly towards Lucian. "It's the first time I've done this with a four-year-old plus one."

Xena's eyes warmed. "I bet there are challenges I can't even imagine," she said.

"My daughter's almost four," Paris said, breaking into the conversation. "She's staying at home with her mom. But I think it's great, bringing your kid to something like this. Showing him that you're, like, a whole person, not just a single mom."

"*Paris*," Xena said, while Cressida wondered how the same sentiment could sound supportive from her inner self, and infuriatingly patronizing from this woman.

"Sorry," Paris said, not sounding apologetic at all. "I mean, I'm assuming you're single?"

Lucian looked up, and Cressida made sure her smile was reassuring. "It's fine," she told him, and then looked at Paris. "I'm technically single, yes," she said. "But we live with my best friend, Anna. She's pretty much Lucian's other parent."

"I love Anna," Lucian said, and went back to the window. "Mommy! I see an island!"

"That's where we're going to stay, buddy," Cressida said, and spent the descent and landing engaging with an excited four-year-old, while Xena glared at her cousin. There wasn't much opportunity for them to speak again.

But when it was time to disembark, Xena handed Cressida's bag forward and said, "See you around," with a hint of a question in it.

And Cressida felt the smile spread across her face, wide and real, and said, "I hope so."

Chapter Four

"You should be thanking me," Paris said, while Xena got B-footage from the mini-van windows. Cressida and Lucian had disappeared into a car with a uniformed driver, but whatever magic Paris had worked to get the Archers onto a private jet hadn't extended to the rest of their transportation.

"Nope," Xena said. Aea was beautiful. Lush growth, turquoise blue sea. Even the light brown gravel roads were pretty, though she had to be careful of shooting through the dust. "No thanks for you."

"Come on, now you know she's single! And she's got a kid, and you want kids."

"Lucian isn't an accessory," Xena said.

"No, but he's a nice bonus," Paris said cheerfully, and nudged her. "You were making heart eyes at her from the second she got on board. Got a real thing for the wholesome ones, don't you?"

"What the hell is that supposed to mean?" Xena demanded, lowering her camera. The van was pulling to a stop in a haphazard parking lot, outside an impressive gate. There were other vans, other passengers, and several people wearing Lotophagi T-shirts and carrying clipboards.

"You tell me," Paris said, which was both mysterious and annoying, and hauled open the van door, jumping out before it had come to a complete stop.

Xena followed her to a woman with a clipboard, with an increasing sense of doom.

"We're Paris and the Archers," Paris said, and gave the clipboard wielder her brightest smile.

The woman, whose name tag said "Stacey: General Services" glanced up at her, looked down at the clipboard, and then reflexively looked back at Paris again. Xena sighed internally. She was aware she had a fair amount of charisma herself, especially in front of the camera, but Paris wielded hers like a blunt instrument.

"Right, Paris and the Archers," Stacey said, scanning down the list. "Okay, you're staying in Lot D, next to the main house. Three tents, six beds, which should be already set up. You can drop your gear off, then report to registration for your schedule and welcome packs." She paused, bracing herself, and added, "Please check the schedule carefully. Some alterations have been made to the previous timetable."

Phryne groaned. Sappho muttered something.

Paris only nodded, maintaining her smile. "We've got some expensive instruments with us," she said. "Any place we could store them? More secure than a tent?"

"Performers and attendees are liable for the safety and security of their personal possessions," Stacey said automatically, and then visibly weakened. "But there's a security booth at the entrance to Lot D. They might have some space."

"Thanks so much," Paris said, her teeth gleaming. "Who should I talk to there?"

"Um, older guy called Ernest."

"Great! I'll tell him Stacey sent us." Paris winked at her. When the flustered woman moved on to the next arrivals, she looked at Xena with her eyebrows raised. "What?"

"You've been happily married for over a decade."

"I'm not going to *do* anything," Paris said. "But a little flirting never hurt anyone. You could try it yourself. Just don't stand there scowling when I do, or we'll never get anything done. Prax! Come carry things!"

"Why me?" Prax asked.

"You're the rookie. And probably the strongest." Paris looked at Xena. "Maybe second strongest."

"Come on," Xena told the tall woman. "Do you want to bunk with me? We'll grab the best tent."

Xena had been to plenty of music festivals, though she'd never worked one. She'd gone to a few one-day events as a nobody, then, as her star started to rise, she'd been invited as a VIP, given a full ride in exchange for her enthusiastic support.

She'd never watched a festival come into being around her. T-shirted volunteers and organizers were everywhere, showing each other tablets and clipboards, driving golf carts, shouting questions and instructions at each other.

It looked like Paris hadn't exaggerated the scale of the billionaire's estate. They were walking up a lengthy paved driveway, surrounded on all sides by lawns of velvety grass, which were no doubt going to take a real beating from the foot traffic. Xena noted some areas that looked as if someone had done some hasty forestry, cutting down ornamental groves or hedges.

Clearly a ton of work had already happened before they arrived. There were cleared areas that looked like they were for the campers bringing their own tents, then a smaller section of round pavilions for glampers. She'd spotted two huge outdoor stages from their path. A less enormous, but still impressive wood and canvas structure, with high stained-glass windows, sat beside an ornamental gazebo

"What's that?" Prax asked.

"A Spiegeltent. For smaller acts and cabaret." The kind of shows that Cressida would be performing in. Maybe she'd have enough time to sneak in and watch. The ground had been steadily trending upwards under their feet, a shallow slope, but noticeably climbing as she shoved the wheeled trunk ahead. As they summited the hill, she saw what it had been concealing. "Oh, huh. That's got to be the main house."

"That's a mansion," Prax said, sounding awed, and then she squared her shoulders. "Not that there's any such thing as a good billionaire."

"Agreed," Xena said. The massive three-story building looked like a Gilded Age masterwork, constructed from the local yellow stone. It had probably been considered gaudy by the old money aristocrats of the day, but the symmetrical wings and elaborate facade had aged gracefully. "So that will be Lot D." She nodded towards the rows of identical white tents with pointed roofs, fenced off with construction site gating.

Ernest-the-security-guy was waiting to check them in and scan their bags for weapons. And glass bottles and vessels, so apparently this was a safety-conscious festival. According to the contract Xena had dutiful-ly read before signing, drugs were also contraband. In practice, Ernest didn't seem too interested in checking for anything that might be hidden in their clothes or on their persons. Sapph was visibly relieved about that.

"I'm surprised they let us all the way in here before security," Xena said. "Are these lenses okay?"

Ernest was looking through her camera cases, his hands sure and competent. "Yeah, we're not worried about glass that you won't throw at the performers. And security will be on all the gates when the guests start arriving tomorrow morning. This is just for setup, to get the staff and performers checked in." He lowered the lid on the last case and snapped the catches. "This is great gear."

"Thanks."

"Do I know you from somewhere?"

"I used to be on the internet," Xena said. It was her standard response for people who couldn't place her. Actually, Ernest looked kind of familiar to her, too. He was a tall, squarish man, probably in his late forties or early fifties, with thick blond hair, wide shoulders and a neatly trimmed, graying mustache. She didn't think she'd met him before. Then again, she'd met a lot of people. She had a pretty good memory for faces, but it wasn't photographic. "We're doing some social media and documentary filming here. Do you mind if I interview you about your duties?"

She was looking right at him, face-to-face, so she saw the flash of wariness that crossed his face, before it was replaced with a look of resigned good humor. "I'm busy right now," he said. "Maybe later?"

"Sure," Xena said. That was a no. Well, not everyone wanted to be online.

A motor gunned behind them, and a black SUV, standing out among the dinky golf carts like a crow among pigeons, roared past startled performers and staff to pull up in front of the main house. Four white dudes in identical black suits got out and headed for the door, and Xena felt Ernest's attention swivel towards them.

"Private security?" she asked.

"I guess," he said, and shrugged. "For the VIPs."

Sapph laid a hand on her heart. "We're not the VIPs, Ernest? I'm shocked!"

"Sure," he said, and smiled. "Have a good stay." He looked past her to Paris.

"Hi!" Paris said brightly. "Stacey said you were the man to see about securely storing our instruments!"

Xena rolled her eyes and left her to it as the rest of them found their tents in the still mostly-empty performers' quarters. It all looked clean and new, the air mattresses were strong and soft and there was more room than Xena had been expecting. There was a brief moment where Sapph realized she was stuck rooming with Paris and had a minor meltdown, but on the whole, it was a pleasant way to spend half an hour.

Xena felt... Good. She didn't really know what she was doing, but she was sure she could figure it out. She hadn't realized how much she'd missed this—the anticipation of a new adventure, the start of something different.

She'd been doing the same thing for far too long.

She and Prax were almost finished organizing their gear in the tent when Paris poked her head through the open tent flap. "Let's go get our welcome packs and see what shitdickery has happened with the schedule."

"Oh, yeah," Xena said, reminded. "What was that about?"

Paris shrugged. "Festivals just love to drop stuff on you at the last minute. Come on. You too, Xena. Might be some good footage."

Xena raised her eyebrows.

"Plus, Cressida might be there," Paris added, and though Xena rolled her eyes, her step was light as she joined the others.

She'd missed this, too.

***

Cressida surveyed the space she and Lucian were to occupy, and indulged herself in some well-founded suspicions. Dammond had sworn up and down that he wouldn't be telling people who she and Lucian were to him, but he must have slipped a hint to someone along the way.

She was a supporting act, not a headliner. Supporting acts didn't get private jets and line-jumping privileges. Supporting acts didn't get housed in a mansion—not just in a room, but in a second-floor guest suite, with two bedrooms, a full bathroom, and a small sitting room, all to themselves. The temporary daycare was also going to be in the main house, so you could argue that it was for ease of transfer, but somehow Cressida didn't think the people camping in the family-friendly zone on the back lawn would believe her.

Besides, she'd caught a glimpse of the woman whisking past her in the hall, surrounded by an entourage, the light bouncing off her dark, glossy hair. Supporting acts didn't get to stay on the same floor as Kithara, genuine headliner, and one of Cressida's favorite musicians. Back in the old days, if she'd saved up and maybe worked a few extra shifts, she might have been able to afford a ticket to Kithara's Katabasis tour.

Now, or at least for the next few days, she was her next-door neighbor.

"Mommy, I have my own room and big bed," Lucian said. He sounded as if he wasn't too sure about it, and Cressida sat on the ornate couch and held her arms out to him. Personally, she wanted nothing more than to fling herself into her bed—alone—and starfish her limbs out to every corner of it. Lucian had his own daybed in the room they shared at Anna's, and sometimes even went to sleep in it, but he ended up in hers, seven nights a week.

But she was throwing a lot of new things and changes at Lucian, and she was setting him up for more, what with all the father-meeting and possible joint custody in his future. So she kept her voice calm and neutral. "You can stay in that bed if you like," she said. "Or you can stay with me, like at home." She gauged the reaction and added, a little hopefully, "but staying in your own bed here might be a big adventure."

"I'll think about it," Lucian decided, a phrase he'd definitely picked up from her. A few minutes later, he was happily arranging his most essential items in his room, while Cressida looked through her updated schedule.

Whoever had arranged their accommodation was clearly not the same person as the one who'd been in charge of the production schedule, because there was no favoritism on display there. She had after-midnight slots on two of the three cabaret performance nights, but her tech checks were in the morning, so good luck getting a full night's sleep. She was supposed to be doing crowd warm-up at one of the big stages on Saturday and Sunday evenings before her late-night burlesque performances, which hadn't been mentioned in her contract, and there was an ominous note about cabaret performers being expected to assist at the VIP welcome evening in the Spiegeltent tomorrow.

Cressida frowned. She could fix this with one phone call. But she'd said she wanted to be treated as a performer, and all of the C-listers probably had schedules like this. Dammond had already pulled strings to get her here at all, but he'd characterized it as her doing a favor for *him*. If she asked him for a favor now, he'd expect something in return.

She could deal with a few late nights, knowing that Lucian would be looked after.

In fact, it might be fun. She hadn't had a late night in a long time. If she was lucky, Xena might even be free to hang out on one or two of those nights.

There was an abrupt spatter of water against the sitting room windows, and she looked up to see the sky had darkened, rain pouring down as if from a hose.

Lucian skittered into the sitting room. "It's raining!"

Some half-forgotten synapse from her former life flared. Right. They were in the tropics. "Buddy, it's probably going to rain at this time every day," she said. "And then it'll stop, really fast."

But it meant wet lawns, and with nearly ten thousand people on them, that meant mud. She wondered if Dammond's people had taken that into account.

Someone knocked on the door, and Cressida padded over in her bare feet to answer. It was a young woman with dark brown hair wisping around her light brown face. "Hello? I'm Elena? With the childcare facility?"

"You are?" Cressida said. She wished she hadn't—it sounded like a mimicry of the girl's hesitant uptalk.

"Yes?"

"Come in," Cressida said, falling back on courtesy. "Nice to meet you, Elena. I'm Cressida, and this is Lucian." She sat down before Lucian could try to hide behind her leg, so he clung to her side instead, peering around at Elena, who instantly scored points by crouching down to his level.

"Hello, Lucian," she said. "I'm Elena. I'm going to be looking after you for a few days, starting tomorrow, and I wanted to say hi."

"My mommy looks after me," Lucian said.

"I bet she does a great job," Elena said.

Lucian nodded, and Cressida ruffled his hair. "We talked about this, buddy, remember? Mommy's going to be busy for the next few days, the way she is on Thursday nights."

"Anna looks after me on Thursday nights."

"And just like Anna looks after you, Elena's going to look after you," Cressida said. "In the daytime, you'll play with her and other kids, and at night she'll stay here with you, just like Anna."

Lucian's lip was trembling, the precursor to a full-on screaming fit.

Was this her fault? Had she made Lucian too dependent on her by spending so much time with him? But she couldn't *afford* daycare, and she didn't have family to call on, and except for Anna, all of her old friends had kind of faded away. Lucian played with other kids in the park and the library, and she'd made acquaintances among the moms there. They knew plenty of other people, but she didn't leave Lucian alone with them.

And now she was going to leave him with strangers while she pranced around a stage.

Augh, why was this so *hard*? It was *good* for her to work. She desperately needed more money and more entries on her resume if she had any hope of performing again. But just like always, the waves of guilt and fear washed over her, and she had to grit her teeth against the urge to tell Elena to get out. Who was this girl anyway? Could Cressida really trust her with her son?

Elena caught her eye, and Cressida knew that what she felt must be painted all over her face.

"Do you want to see where we'll be playing tomorrow?" Elena asked Lucian. "There are lots of toys and books and fun things, and there's a little pool outside. With a lifeguard on duty," she added, to Cressida.

"What kind of toys?" Lucian said. "Are there Lego?"

"*Lots* of Legos," Elena said, and Lucian conceded that he might want to see the Lego, although he did insist on telling Elena about the correct plural on the way.

Five minutes later, he was in the living room that had been temporarily converted to a daycare center, sorting through bricks in a haze of building bliss. Elena presented Cressida with her credentials without being asked. A Master's degree in psychology, an early childhood education postgraduate diploma, four years of experience at Argos Academy... Elena was more qualified to care for Lucian than she was.

Cressida consciously willed herself to relax. "Thank you."

"No worries," Elena said, her eyes clear. "I promise, he's in good hands."

Chapter Five

Xena hadn't spotted Cressida again, on either their first night or their first morning in Lot D. She'd kept an eye out for her, and had volunteered to grab dinner and then breakfast from the staff mess tent, but Cressida was probably on a different schedule, or maybe camping in the family-friendly zone behind the mansion.

It was silly to feel so disappointed.

Paris downed the last of her coffee and brushed her hands together. "Okay, band meeting," she said. "We're playing at the VIP thing tonight in the Spiegeltent. Tech call at noon, standby at six, we're on at eight. They want mostly background music, so wear your black and whites."

"Are we getting paid any extra for that?" Phryne asked.

"What do you think?"

Phryne sighed.

"Just think of the exposure," Paris said, her voice ironic. "Anyway, it's a good opportunity to break out a few of the folk and jazz instrumentals from the back catalog. My guess is that by nine or ten everyone will have loosened up enough that we can slip some of our newer stuff in there with no problem. Tomorrow, we're on Stage One from one to two. In the afternoon, before you start getting excited."

There was a chorus of groans. "Why is that bad?" Xena asked.

"Too early," Phryne said. "We were supposed to be on later. Half of the festival crowd will still be arriving."

Paris shrugged. "We're not headliners, ladies. We are medium sized fish in a much bigger pond. The good news is, people will still be mostly sober."

"Speak for yourself," Sapph muttered, but she waved it away when Paris gave her a dirty look.

"But you'll like Saturday," Paris said triumphantly. "Stage Two, eight-thirty till nine, opening for Aoide Waters, who's opening for Kithara."

"Oh!" Prax said, and even Phryne looked impressed.

"I had to trade a lot of favors for that spot," Paris said, with a smug glint in her eye. "It's going to be our biggest crowd ever, and *we* are going to give them the performance of a lifetime. And Xena will be there to film it all. We're going viral, guaranteed."

"Uh, no, you can't guarantee that," Xena said. "I can get good footage and push it, but if anyone could guarantee virality, they'd be doing it every day."

"Sure, sure," Paris said, like she was soothing a fractious toddler. Xena considered pushing the point, but Paris had an ego like a titanium shield. No amount of patient explanation would make a dent.

"So what do we do until the tech call?" she asked.

"*We* are going to practice," Paris said, looking sternly at her Archers. "Acoustic only, mutes on, but I want everyone note-perfect. We're not going to be sloppy tonight, just because it's background."

Prax raised her hand.

"Note *and beat* perfect," Paris said, and beamed at Xena. "And you—"

"I know. I can film it."

It wasn't very demanding work, though the lighting was a problem, with all that bright daylight bouncing off the white tents and washing out the contrast. She made a mental note for the editing stage, but they weren't supposed to be doing high art here. Besides, Xena's problem wasn't going to be a lack of material; it was going to be choosing and editing the clips that would put the Archers in the best light. They were talented, but so were so many people who never broke out and made it big. Her own media career had been a fluke, a bizarre combination of being in the right place at the right time with the right content for an audience that had fiercely claimed her—and then disowned her just as quickly.

Get over yourself, she thought, and while the Archers gathered around Paris for some intense notes, she panned her camera over the tents. Other performers were also taking advantage of the sunshine and the space between the tents to rehearse. A shirtless man was walking around on his hands, flipping onto his feet and back again, while a limber woman beside him bent her body into impossible shapes. A comedian she thought she recognized was sitting in a deck chair outside his tent, squinting at notecards and muttering to himself. Memorizing new material? This was good behind-the-scenes stuff, but she should check out the non-performer spaces, too.

"I'm going to film setup," she told Paris, who was engaged in an intense breakdown of a song she'd written fourteen years ago and barely spared her a glance.

Lotophagi, now open to guests, was coming alive. An army of assistants and security guards in hi-vis were directing a constant stream of new arrivals through the grounds to their camping grounds. Unlike some of the bigger festivals she'd been to, no one was driving here—it was all flights or passenger ferries—so not having to wrangle cars was probably making it easier, but even so, from what she could see, the organizers were doing a great job. Not Fyre Festival. Not a scam. The real deal.

So what was making her uneasy?

Xena had once been prone to ignoring the risks and plunging straight in, and okay, that instinct hadn't entirely left her, but she'd learned to listen to the alarm bells in the back of her head. She'd heard them before she'd taken a whitewater rafting trip that had ended with her breaking her own foot to get free of the rocks trapping her underwater. She'd heard them before she'd got into an unlicensed cab and had to fend off an assault from the driver, leaping out at a red light.

She'd heard them before she'd proposed to Zac live, in front of thousands of people. Her biggest live audience by far, all there to witness her biggest fuck up.

That, finally, had been enough for her to learn her lesson. This time, she was going to pay attention to the alarms.

She panned over the happy crowds passing through the security checkpoint, and after a moment she had it. There were plenty of normal security guards like Ernest, who was patiently explaining to a woman that the no weapons clause definitely included her Japanese war fan, no matter how essential it was to her outfit. Those security guards wore various combinations of khakis and festival polos, with hi-vis vests reading SECURITY and badges hanging from lanyards around their necks.

But there were some *other* security guards, or people who occupied that security-shaped space in her brain. She could see four of them, standing by the pop-up ATMs where people were getting cash. Again, it looked like Lotophagi was trying hard to disassociate itself from Fyre

Festival, where people had been encouraged to use a Wi Fi bracelet pre-loaded with their spending money, much of which had disappeared in the festival's collapse.

The four men looked uncannily similar. All white, all men, or at least male-presenting, all with the same wide-shouldered build, all wearing black suits and white buttonups totally unsuited to the weather, although they hadn't gone as far as ties. If they had hair, it was buzzed high and tight. If they didn't, their scalps glistened. It was difficult to tell what they were thinking, because they were wearing expensive black sunglasses.

They weren't wearing vests or lanyards or anything that indicated they were security, but the way they stood, with their feet planted and their hands clasped in front, just screamed *bruiser*.

The Xena of two years ago might have blithely gone up to them and asked what their deal was. The Xena of now, a little older and a lot wiser, let her camera pan over them with the same pace she'd used for her other shots, and pretended not to notice one of them noticing her at the end of the shot. She didn't stop filming and run off, either; she approached a group of attendees in cute, tiny outfits largely made out of rainbow string and asked if they'd be happy to give her some voxpop.

"Are you *Xena*?" one of them asked, wide-eyed. "XO Xena?"

"That's me. I'm here with Paris and the Archers."

"The *band?*" a different girl asked, and in her peripheral vision, Xena saw the bruiser go back to staring blankly ahead of him, while she asked leading questions she'd edit out later. She wasn't even sure why she'd bothered to take the shot of the bruisers in the first place—they were probably just some extra security hired by the ATM company, there to protect the cash.

But she was done ignoring those alarm bells.

***

Cressida lifted her tray of wine glasses, checked that her boobs were still contained by her corset, and stepped out of the blocked-off portion of the Spiegeltent into the main space, where the great and good were gathered. Or, at least, those willing to spend upwards of ten grand on a VIP ticket.

Her day had been *blissful*. Lucian had gone to daycare after lunch, and she'd read almost half of one of the novels Anna kept telling her she had to read, entirely free of interruptions. She'd finished with a leisurely dinner and a long shower without any interruptions, then taken her time to get ready for the gig. Childcare was *amazing*. And if she and Dammond could work this new arrangement out, she could afford more of it.

But for now, she had to get her mind on the job.

She ran a practiced eye over the crowd of about three hundred before she plunged into it. About two-thirds men, mostly corporate-sponsorship types, with expensive haircuts and "casual" clothes that cost ten times the average suit. Well, that made sense—Dammond would have wanted to spread the festival funding around, and he had plenty of contacts to call on. Nobody was looking too messy, but the tray emptied quickly, and she headed back for more champagne. Troy was getting loaded up with canapes at the same time.

"I wish we didn't have to do this in costume," he said.

"I hear that," Cressida said. "If I hadn't got this bustier dry-cleaned before we left, it'd be stinking up the place." As it was, the layers of ingrained performance sweat would build up again all too quickly. And she was out of practice for walking in these heels, spiky red numbers which boosted her height and made her bared legs look amazing, but also concentrated most of her body weight into a two-inch triangle on the ball of each foot.

"Well, you look good," Troy said.

"Thanks. So do you."

Cressida was wearing the costume Anna had dubbed "Circo-Slut", which was a red bustier and red frilly panties, only partially concealed by the stiff, short layers of black ruffles that made up the skirt. Teamed with a red wig in pigtails and stark black and white doll makeup, the costume went with a chair routine about a puppet coming to life. She'd been on the fence about including it in her act, but the costume had good close-up impact for the cocktail evening.

"How are you doing, Troy?" she asked.

"A lady slapped my butt," Troy said, lowering his voice.

Cressida frowned. Troy's butt, particularly in his shiny black leggings, was a monument to great genes and constant exercise, but that didn't excuse someone getting handsy. "That's no good. Want me to spill wine on her?"

"Oh, no," Troy said. "But maybe you could take this tray over instead of me?"

"Sure." Cressida lifted the tray and headed in the direction he indicated. It was a tight knot of people, all of them talking animatedly, and behind them Cressida could see a roped-off area for the most important

VIPs. Dammond was holding court there. Kithara was standing next to him, looking beautiful, and possibly a bit bored.

"Hey, are those for us?" someone asked.

"You bet," Cressida said.

"Where's the cute one?" a tall blonde woman asked, and Cressida tried not to glare at her.

"This one's plenty cute," the man beside her said, leering. "What's your name, honey?"

"Chrissy Bee," Cressida said. "I'm performing here tomorrow night."

The man snorted. "No, what's your *real* name?"

Cressida gave him a baffled look, blinking her enormous false eyelashes. "See you tomorrow!" she said brightly, and kept moving, heading towards the VIP area. An equal-opportunity harassment couple, how cute. Well, let them try to follow her past the velvet rope.

There were two security guys hanging out by the rope; a huge bullet-headed guy in his mid-thirties, and an older guy with an impressive mustache. They were ignoring each other and most of the patrons, but they let her through with no problem. Sometimes, it was handy to be the one holding the tray.

Dammond had his usual coterie of hangers-on. Some of them knew who she was, and even her doll costume might not be enough to conceal her identity. Marcus, Dammond's best friend, was telling a long and probably boring story to a model she'd seen on lingerie runways. Marcus was a sleazeball, but he'd been Dammond's almost-best man, and he and Cressida had unfortunately spent some time at the same parties. Cressida hesitated, wondering if it was worth the risk of him looking past the corset to the face.

Fortunately, Dammond looked up, his eyes brightening with recognition. Cressida stayed where she was as he excused himself and came towards her.

"Hey," he said, keeping his voice down. "Everything okay? Lucian settling in all right?"

"It's great," Cressida said honestly. "This is all really impressive, Dammond."

He gave her a sharp look, but relaxed when he saw she was sincere. "Thanks," he said, almost bashfully. "I'm not really, you know, running it. Just helping out with some of the financing. Hey, would it be weird if I came to your gigs?"

"No, if it wouldn't be weird for you," Cressida said carefully. He really was trying—letting her keep her connection to him on the downlow, asking permission instead of just crashing through her boundaries.

"I'd love to see your new stuff," he said, relaxing further. He took a glass from her tray and winked at her. "You look good."

"So do you," Cressida said. It was unfortunately true. Dammond always looked good, with the clean-cut all-American look she liked best in guys. He took good care of his appearance, getting his hair cut, his nails manicured, and using a regular skincare routine. Cressida was used to spaces where women were expected to put a great deal of effort into their appearance, and men could just show up. She appreciated Dammond putting in the time.

True, his eyes could turn hard and mean, and his mouth was perhaps a little too sulky, but she'd kind of liked it when he pouted. It had been so much fun to kiss him into a better mood.

Even now, knowing that they weren't getting back together, that they should never have *been* together, she felt the attraction.

"You look *really* good," Dammond said, and Cressida decided that she'd better leave before he got more intense about it.

"Well, I just wanted to say hi," she said, and headed back through the rope. The bouncers watched her walk through with no expression, but she had the uneasy feeling they might have been observed.

Never mind. She couldn't do anything about it, and she had to get back to work. Mr. and Ms. Grabby had hopefully lost interest by now.

Her tray cleared quickly after that. Most of what was happening in the tent was designed to make the guests feel cool and glamorous, but as always, it came off just a little desperate. You couldn't just tell people to have fun—you had to build atmosphere and craft experience. The guests weren't sure whether they were supposed to be paying attention to the performers moving around them, or treating them like invisible servants, and that uncertainty was making them jittery. A few performances announced *as* performances would have helped, but the only people actually performing were the band on the low stage, and they were background noise at best.

Cressida did a double take as she recognized them. That was Paris in front, sitting on a stool and strumming an acoustic guitar as she sang a blues cover. Nothing original or challenging in that; definitely not anything to grab attention. She was *good*, but it was just pleasant sound.

But if *Paris* was here... Cressida scanned the room again, and caught sight of the tall black-haired woman standing quietly at the perimeter, her camera in hand.

How on earth could a woman with so much presence fade into the walls like that? Even the other servers were ignoring her, which meant she was probably thirsty. Cressida hit the backstage, reloaded her tray, and headed back out again.

The crowd was drinking for lack of anything better to do, and even moving in a straight line, Cressida had only two glasses left by the time she made it to Xena.

"Hey," she said, and Xena jumped, as if she'd been trying so hard to make herself invisible that she'd forgotten she could be seen at all.

"Hey!" she said, and lowered her camera. Her eyes widened. "You look *incredible*."

Cressida did a little curtesy. "Thank you! This is my job."

"I didn't recognize you! I saw you, of course, and I was like, 'wow, who's that uh, that woman?'"

Cressida put the tray down on the table Xena was half-concealed behind and grinned at her. "You paused. What was the word you were going to say?"

"Hot," Xena admitted. "Who's that hot woman?"

Cressida tried to look severe, but was pretty sure she was giving smug instead. "Ogling the talent. My, my." She handed Xena a glass.

"Uh, I'm working..."

"So am I. We're allowed a break." Cressida took a sip from her own glass to prove it and paused as the bubbles exploded on her palate, buttery and smooth. Dammond really wasn't stinting on the luxuries.

"How's Lucian?" Xena asked, cautiously taking a sip herself. Cressida watched the long, smooth column of her throat as she swallowed.

"He's great," she said. "Loves his sitter, made lots of friends today. I was worried, but now I'm more concerned how he's going to feel when I take him away from all his new buddies." She hesitated, but Xena had brought Lucian up first, and genuinely seemed interested. "I'm not just here to perform. Lucian's father is here, and they've never met. After the festival, we're sticking around for a couple days for some introductions."

"Neutral territory," Xena said, nodding. "That's really smart."

Cressida wrinkled her nose. Xena had, all unknowing, put her finger on the thing Cressida was most uneasy about. Aea *wasn't* neutral territory, not when Dammond owned half the island. But he'd made concessions to get her here, and she could make some for him. That was what compromise was all about. "Something like that," she said. "We didn't part well, but I'm hoping for a better co-parenting relationship." She ducked her head, suddenly shy. "Sorry, I don't mean to dump all this on you."

"I don't mind," Xena said, so straight-forward that Cressida had to believe it. "I hope it goes well."

"Thank you. Me too."

Xena drank again, apparently content to let the topic drop without further questions. It was reassuring, that she didn't pry, but Cressida regretted saying anything. Not least because they'd made a great start on some flirting, and she wasn't sure how to get back to that.

Several of the performers, bored, or trying to drum up more attention for their acts the next day, had started showing off. Klara Krause, a contortionist Cressida knew from the European cabaret circuit, was delivering drinks from a tray laid on her flat stomach, while she was bent backwards in bridge position. She moved with elegant ease, and when the last drink was removed by a laughing man, she took the tray in one hand, and, balancing on the other, kicked up into a perfect scissor handstand. Troy put down his own tray and said something to her, and a second later, Klara was standing on his shoulders. There was scattered applause as Troy turned slowly, his arms outstretched. Klara upended herself, balancing on her hands as easily as on her bare feet.

"Wow," Xena said. "The *flexibility*."

"I know, right? I'm pretty flexible myself, but I think Klara might be made out of different material."

"What do you do? You said burlesque, but that can cover a lot of ground."

"Heh. Well, dance and strip, but also pole and aerial work."

"Like, silks?"

"Yes, though I won't be doing that here." She gestured at Klara, who'd been joined by a person she didn't recognize, both of them doing backbends and twists around Troy's sturdy base. Nothing dangerous or complicated, but impressive all the same. "No point, when they do it so much better. I'm more of a classic burly girl. Burlesque girl, that is."

Xena grinned. "I got it."

The band had noticed the action too, and Paris was wandering around her players, communicating something as they played out the final notes of the number. When they started again, the tempo had picked up considerably. One of the women had switched out her violin for a saxophone, and the music gained a sweeping sensuality even before Paris started to sing.

Oh, she was actually *good*. A little breathy to start, matching the uncertainty in the lyrics, but growing in intensity and strength until the audience, without even really knowing it, were refocusing away from the contortionists and towards the band.

Xena picked up her camera. "I'd better get back to work," she said, sounding professional, but also just a little sad about it.

Cressida, with a start, realized that she absolutely wanted to sleep with this woman. For the past four years, sex had been a hurried, carefully scheduled thing with an occasional date. Even in the throes of passion, she'd think of how much time they had left, what time she'd need to leave this apartment or hotel room and go back to Lucian.

But tonight, Lucian was being well-cared for.

And that meant Cressida was free. She smiled at Xena, letting some heat in her eyes. "Maybe we can catch up later tonight?" she suggested, and laid her hand on Xena's arm.

Xena jumped. Oh, this was *adorable*, she was *nervous*. "I'd like that," she said.

"I could demonstrate my flexibility," Cressida said sweetly, and Xena's pupils blew huge and black, visible even in the dim lighting. Cressida let her smile go wicked, hinting at much while promising nothing, and drifted away, swinging her hips perhaps just a little more than strictly necessary, her mood much brighter.

More performers had put down their trays and started impromptu demonstrations. Cressida didn't have any of her props, and there was no choreography for this music, but she let herself settle into the puppet persona, moving in short jerks, and presenting shocked, wide eyes to the guests. She wasn't really much of a mime but she could totter around in her spiky heels, apparently catching herself at the last moment with her hands on the floor to present her ruffled rear, the next second over-correcting as she went upright so that she bent backwards, boobs pressing at the top of her bustier.

If she'd had a better sense of the crowd, she might have tried some closer interaction, plopping herself into laps or clambering up someone sturdy, but no one had laid down any ground rules, and she didn't want to deal with grabby patrons.

Nevertheless, she was gaining a crowd of her own, and Paris must have noticed, because the next song was another cover; "I Wanna Be

Loved By You," made famous by Betty Boop and Marilyn Monroe and every cutesy sexpot who'd tried to totter in their high-heeled footsteps. Cressida almost suspected Paris of having a sense of humor. She held back the smile that threatened to crack her doll facade and started to lip sync, eyes wide and hips wiggling on the boop-doop-de-doos.

Klara had apparently finished using Troy as a climbing stand; he was loitering on the edge of the circle forming around Cressida. She boop-de-booped up to him, ran a finger slowly down his abs, and let her mouth drop open with shock, playing to the laughing crowd.

Troy blushed.

Whoa, that was a tricky thing to do on command. Troy was either a better performer than she thought, or he was having interesting memories of the last time she'd been up and personal with his abs. She pinched his cheeks, turned her back, and did a shoulder-tossing wiggle against him. From almost any angle, it would look like she was writhing against his body, but she was carefully keeping a little distance between their hips. If the poor guy was having some inconvenient thoughts, there was no need to make it harder for him. In all senses of the word.

Xena was behind the crowd directly opposite, her height making it possible for her to film above the heads of the people in front of her. Cressida winked and blew her a kiss, then turned back to Troy, intending to pull him into the middle of the circle.

But Mr. Grabby Hands got there first. He stepped out of the crowd—she hadn't even *seen* him—and took her outstretched arm, pulling her into a tango-style embrace.

Cressida didn't try to control her expression, but apparently the doll makeup made her shock and anger look playful, because the crowd laughed again.

Mr. Grabby dipped her low, so that she had no choice but to balance her weight against him or be dumped on her ass, and then swung her up again, his hand tight on her waist. Before she could do anything with this new balance, he whirled her around, and right into the hands of *Ms.* Grabby, who rubbed against Cressida's back with great enthusiasm, her arms going around Cressida's waist.

Awesome. Now she was trapped between them, and everyone watching thought it was the height of entertainment.

Well, not everyone. She could see Xena putting down her camera and scowling, obviously ready to do something, even if she wasn't sure what.

Cressida would have to take care of this before she did—creating a fuss and breaking the illusion of her performance would be better than a scuffle.

"You're beautiful," Ms. Grabby whispered in her ear, her breath warm and wet.

Cressida stiffened and opened her mouth, ready to issue a flat command.

But Troy arrived before she had to pull the trigger. He reached into the tangle of bodies, did something that made Mr. Grabby loosen his grip, and pulled Cressida up and out, turning her over his shoulder. From her position upside down, Cressida could make out the faces, some amused and some confused, as if they were just catching on this might not be part of the act.

Cressida kicked her legs and waved her arms for show, giving them wide, shocked eyes as Troy walked through the hastily parting circle, carrying her all the way back to the backstage area, where he set her down on her feet.

He looked angry, an emotion she wasn't sure she'd ever seen on his face before.

"Was that okay?" he asked immediately. "I wasn't sure, but I thought—"

"You're my hero," Cressida said, and went up on her tiptoes to kiss his cheek. "Thank you. Really. Knight in shining armor stuff."

"Aw," Troy said, and blushed again. "I mean, I may as well make myself useful."

"You're very useful," Cressida assured him. Her hands were shaking with the aftershock, a reaction that was as inevitable as it was annoying.

"Should we report them?" Troy asked.

Cressida frowned. If she'd been in the club, that was definitely the kind of behavior that got patrons kicked out and banned, but festivals could be a lot looser. "Who do we even report to?"

"Jenny?"

Jenny was the Spiegeltent production manager who'd given them their orders for the evening. Since those orders hadn't included impromptu performance, Cressida wasn't sure she'd be sympathetic. But she was probably the best option. Maybe they could talk her into giving the Grabbies a warning, at least.

"Sure," she said reluctantly.

"I'll take care of it," a voice said abruptly behind them, and Cressida whirled to see Dammond. He'd stepped through the curtain, looking very out of place in the makeshift staging area in his luxury casual wear. But his face was serious, his frown real.

"Mr. Argive!" Troy exclaimed, and Dammond blinked, maybe surprised to be recognized. "Sorry, we were just figuring out the correct channels..."

"Lotophagi is a harassment-free zone for guests *and* performers," Dammond said. "I'll make sure those two are removed from the festival immediately."

Cressida blinked at him, even as Troy moved into effusive thanks. Dammond hadn't always been so intolerant of harassment. He'd never quite said outright that sometimes people were asking for it, but he'd certainly implied it. They'd had a lot of fights about that.

He really *had* changed.

"—we really appreciate that," Troy said, and put his hand on Cressida's shoulder, which was when she realized she hadn't said anything.

"Uh, yes," she managed. "Thank you very much."

"No problem," Dammond said, after a slight pause. His eyes lingered on Troy's hand for a moment, and then he stepped back through the curtain and was gone.

"He's one of the sponsors," Troy said, sounding awed. "Man, you never expect one of those guys to stand up for you, you know?"

"Oh yeah," Cressida said. "I know."

Chapter Six

The performers had mostly stopped their impromptu exhibitions once Cressida had made that abrupt exit. They knew something had gone wrong, even if most of the guests had no idea. Xena had to stamp down very firmly on her desire to go and start a fight with that nasty couple. She had black belts from several disciplines, but it was the controlled breathing she'd learned in the dojo that she used now.

A sleek blond man had left the VIP zone and gone after Cressida and the strongman who'd rescued her. After a moment he came back, and issued some terse instructions to Ernest, who nodded, and approached the couple, his shaven-headed colleague in tow. The couple's ejection from the party was so smooth and conflict-free that if she hadn't been watching closely through her camera lens, she would have missed it. After a moment, Ernest came back into the tent and resumed his position at the VIP velvet rope. The larger guy from the good-suit coterie didn't return, and Xena assumed he was responsible for making sure the couple didn't come back.

With the performers going back to serving drinks, the party was losing its sparkle. Paris and the Archers went back to playing instrumental jazz covers, and after another couple of numbers, took a break.

Paris beckoned Xena over.

"Where's your girlfriend?" she asked.

Cressida hadn't returned to the main area, though the strongman had come back with a tray of canapes.

"She's not my—" Xena said, and then rolled her eyes at Paris's smug expression. "Are you going to play more of your own stuff after the break? I've mostly been getting—"

"Excuse me," said an authoritative voice behind her, and Xena turned to see the same blond man who'd had the couple ejected. "Can I ask why you're filming my guests?"

"This is our videographer," Paris said, flicking on her charm like a light switch. "We cleared everything with Katrina before the festival, and with Jenny again tonight."

The blond man didn't look charmed. He was looking Xena up and down, a challenge in his eyes. "Did you get consents?"

"That's covered by the general festival consent to be filmed," Paris said.

"Not everyone here is covered by that," the man said. "I'm going to need you to delete the footage."

Paris lost her smile.

"Sorry, who are you?" Xena asked.

"Dammond Argive," he said, and if Xena hadn't already been working on keeping a neutral expression, she might have lost it then. This was the nasty little shitstain who'd tried to get her sister Cassie fired four years ago. She'd written a—thankfully anonymous—advice column in response to his fiancée, advising her to leave. When the poor girl had actually done it, Dammond had tried to sue Olympus Inc, and failing that, tried to talk Cassie's bosses into kicking her out. And he'd had something to do with that awful pre-wedding retreat Laodice had been on, though Laodice never wanted to talk about that.

"That's right," Dammond said, reading something from her face. "This is my estate. I own this land. And *I* don't give you permission to film here, whatever Katrina or Jenny said. Delete the footage from tonight, and don't do it again, got it?"

He *owned* this place?

"Xena, take a walk," Paris said crisply, and turned to Dammond, switching from "charming musician" to "let's make a deal business-woman." Xena stalked off, consciously relaxing her jaw and fists. At times like this, she really regretted giving up vaping. She ducked out of the main entrance and took two deep breaths of the night air, warm and soft.

Lotophagi was all lit up. Dozens of people were working in the per-formance zone, working late to get set-up finished for the next day, and from the camping zones she could hear a steady roar of indistinguishable voices and music, like an ocean just out of sight.

It was beautiful. But if Dammond Argive owned it... She pulled out her phone.

The slow connection made her grit her teeth again, but she eventually navigated her way to the Lotophagi website. There, buried in a spon-sorship subpage, was a single reference to the generosity of the Argive Family Trust.

Had Paris known? Wait, even if she had, she had no reason to care. Most people would have no clue that Dammond had been the villain in that Ask Cassandra column, and almost no one knew that Cassie Troiades *was* Ask Cassandra. Paris definitely didn't.

And now, Dammond was going to make it impossible for Xena to do *her* job, the only thing she'd found that was worth doing since—

"Xena?"

Xena looked up from her phone and dropped it in shock.

"Zac," she said, staring at the man who'd broken her heart. "I didn't know you were here."

***

"And if you can just sign this waiver stating your satisfaction with the proceedings," Jenny said, and flashed a tablet in front of Cressida's face.

Cressida wasn't used to festivals giving that much of a fuck about performers' safety, but she had finely honed instincts against signing anything she hadn't read. "I'll need a hardcopy," she said politely. "And time to consult my lawyer, if necessary."

"Sure," Jenny said. She was wearing the traditional production black, but her teeth were eerily perfect, shining too white in the dim lighting backstage. "Unfortunately, you won't be able to proceed with your performance until this matter is resolved, so..."

"So I'd better get it at tech check tomorrow," Cressida said. "That's nine a.m. here for me."

"Oh, *absolutely*. Actually, that reminds me we don't have your Health and Safety documentation signed-off either. You'll need extra time to read everything over. Let's make your call time seven-thirty a.m."

I don't like you, Cressida thought, but the trap was too neat. "Seven-thirty," she said, not letting her smile drop for a moment. She didn't want to give Jenny the satisfaction.

"Great! See you then!"

Jenny left, and Cressida considered her options. Technically, she was scheduled to be here until midnight, but Jenny had just said she wouldn't

76

be able to proceed with her performance until the waiver was signed. Jenny probably didn't consider carrying a tray to be performance, but Cressida was wearing a costume, wasn't she? It counted. So she'd sneak out now, and maybe get some real sleep in before that absurdly early tech check for her after-midnight performance.

Assuming Lucian had actually gone to sleep, he'd stay dead to the world till morning. Cressida liked many things about her son, but she considered this particular trait a glorious blessing from the fates to give a single mom.

Unfortunately, this meant she'd have no time to jump Xena's bones, but a girl had to be practical. Sleep first, sex later.

She changed her shoes and slipped out the backstage exit before Jenny could notice she was gone. As she dodged around the side of the structure, she could hear a familiar voice coming from near the main entrance.

"Zac," Xena was saying, her voice stricken. "I didn't know you were here."

Zac? Oh man, Xena's former boyfriend, the one she'd proposed to on livestream. Cressida snuck a little closer, sticking to the shadows, until she could get a good look.

"That makes two of us," Zac said. He was an impressive blond, with slim hips and a runner's physique, almost as tall as Xena. He'd started his social media journey through college athletics, Cressida recalled, until he'd given up the track for fame. He looked as if he might run now, skittish as a horse who'd spied a potential predator.

"I'm sorry," Xena said. "If I'd known, I would have said something." She looked miserable, collapsing in on herself, and Cressida didn't like it.

"Me too." Zac settled back on his heels, though he was still looking wary.

Honestly, did he think that Xena would spring another surprise proposal on him, when he'd been so dismissive of the first one?

Cressida was taken aback by the cattiness of her own thoughts. Zac had every right to refuse a proposal, and it hadn't been his fault it was so public, she reminded herself. His reaction had been honest, and honestly devastating. It was Xena who'd messed up, as she'd quietly admitted in her apology video, before she'd disappeared from the internet entirely.

Still, Cressida didn't like the guy.

"How are you doing?" Xena asked.

"Great. Great. The new T-shirt line is taking off and I'm in discussion with Golden Apple about a TV show. Madison thinks she can swing me an invitation to the Olympus Winter Ball."

"That sounds really good."

"Yeah," Zac said, and Cressida noted that he didn't ask Xena how *she* was doing before he swung into a list of further achievements and opportunities. He did hesitate at the end of the litany, and said, "Um, and I don't know if you've heard about me and Deidamia Skyron?"

Xena looked almost natural. "No, I hadn't. Are you two together? That's awesome."

"We're engaged," Zac said.

"Oh," Xena said, and that was *it*, Cressida couldn't stand it anymore, Xena was far too strong to look so *broken*.

"Hey, babe," she sang out, and as both of them jumped, she sauntered up to Xena with a little bounce in her step. "Thanks for waiting! Ready to go?"

Xena blinked, but Cressida winked at her, and she rallied. "Uh, sure."

Zac was looking at her, bodice and tiny skirt and, okay, she was wearing her dirty laundry day sneakers, but she was still fucking hot, and she put all of that into her voice as she turned to him. "Hi! I'm Cressida."

"Nice to meet you," he said, and when she looked at him expectantly for long enough, he added. "I'm Zac."

"Are you a performer? Or production?"

He waited a moment, probably assuming it was a joke, but she out-stared him, keeping that look of polite lack of recognition on her face. "I'm an influencer," he said.

"Oh, neat," Cressida said. "Well, sorry to deprive you, Zac, but I have plans for this girl! Good night!"

He stuttered something, but Cressida was already turning, using her presence to turn Xena with her and start moving, without touching her. "It'll be more convincing if we hold hands," she murmured, and after a moment, Xena's hand wrapped around hers.

It was icy cold, and trembling a little, and Cressida got mad at Zac all over again.

"Thanks," Xena muttered after a moment.

"I might not have thought this through," Cressida admitted. "Do you need to go back and work?"

Xena groaned. "Ugh, no. The jackass who owns this place told me I wasn't allowed to film anymore."

"Dammond?" Cressida said.

"Yeah. You know him?"

Cressida made a lightning-fast decision. "We've bumped into each other," she said casually. "He is kind of a jackass."

Xena snorted. "I'll say. We got everything cleared in advance, and then he stormed over in the middle of the party and told me to get lost." She paused. "Well, okay, my cousin told me to get lost, but that was probably to save me from blowing up in his face."

"That would have been something to see," Cressida said lightly. "You can be pretty intimidating when you want. I really liked those simulated defense videos you did."

Xena made a grumbling sound. "Those were my old manager's idea. Zac told her I could disarm someone with a gun, and she got excited about the drama."

"Those moves wouldn't work?"

"Oh, they work. If you've practiced them over and over, and you're lucky, and you're close enough, and you don't freeze, or misjudge your opponent, or fail to get out the way fast enough. But I've only ever done it in a dojo, with simulated weapons. I'm not sure I could do it in real life, not until it happened." She paused. "I don't think it was responsible, me doing those videos. But I was twenty-two, and stupid."

"Two words that often go together," Cressida agreed. When *she* was twenty-two, she'd agreed to date the fun new customer at the club. "But for real, what should I do, if someone pulls a gun on me?"

"First option, give them what they want," Xena said. "If they want your wallet or your phone, or something like that, it's not worth the risk. Hand it over. Second option, if you can't or won't do that, and you've got some distance, run away."

"Just run?"

"Zig zag, and get behind cover if you can," Xena told her. "Especially if it's a handgun. They can be pretty erratic, and even professionals miss a lot of moving targets in live fire situations. That's why gun people like semi-automatics."

"Urgh," Cressida said. "Well, what if they're too close for me to run?"

"Give them what they want."

"But you did those moves where you were knocking the gun away, or taking it away from them."

"That's why it was irresponsible," Xena said. "You can't just learn that from a video. You've got to practice, over and over."

"You did say that in the video."

"Sure, but people don't listen. Or they do it a couple of times in front of the mirror, and think they've practiced. I worry that I might have encouraged people to take risks, or have more confidence than they should in that situation. It's only if you've trained until it's automatic motion that you stand any chance of getting the gun away from them." She sighed. "But there are a lot of risk factors before you get there. Gun defense—reliable, repeatable moves—is pretty much a myth. It's last-chance stuff."

"Okay," Cressida said. "And when our theoretical martial artist has gotten the gun from her assailant, what does she do then?"

Xena grinned. "She backs up, and when she's got distance, she runs."

"Hm," Cressida said. "I'm sensing a theme." Xena's hand was warming up. Zac was probably out of sight by now, but Cressida decided not to point this out to her. She was enjoying the touch. It wasn't particularly erotic, just a pleasant tingle. Cressida didn't get to touch adults very much, these days, and she was realizing that she'd missed it.

Well, as long as it was *wanted* touch. Mr. and Ms. Grabby Hands need not apply.

"Are you all right?" Xena asked, as if she'd picked up on Cressida's thought. "That seemed intense, in there."

"It's taken care of," Cressida said lightly. They'd walked halfway through the grounds by then, nearly to the entrance of Lot D. Her good intentions to go back to her room and get some sleep were melting away under the warmth of that hand in hers. "Should I take care of *you*?"

Xena stumbled to a halt. "Um," she said. "Okay, it's been a while and I might be missing something. Are you hitting on me?"

Cressida laughed. "Yes. Is that okay?"

"Yes," Xena said, but hesitantly, as if she wasn't sure. "I just...we're only here for a few days."

"Yes?"

"I don't..." Xena said, and then she took a deep breath and gently released Cressida's hand. "I'm sorry, I don't think I can."

"Oh. Okay."

"It's not you," Xena said, and then, perhaps aware of what a cliche she sounded, added, "I mean, *look* at you."

The fervent desire in her voice made Cressida's skin prickle.

"I just... I can't. I don't trust myself not to make it weird."

"Weird, how?"

"Getting too clingy. Expecting too much. *Assuming* too much." She made an aborted gesture towards the direction they'd come from, but Cressida could feel the ghost of Zac and that disastrous public proposal hanging over them.

"Even with a guaranteed end-date?" Cressida asked, but Xena's face turned even more tortured. "No, okay, forget I asked. I won't pretend I'm not disappointed, but I'm a big girl. You know, emotionally." She made a motion that indicated their height disparity, and after a moment, Xena smiled uncertainly. "I guess I'll see you around. If I don't, have a great time at the festival."

"Um, thanks," Xena said, "You too." And now *she* looked disappointed. Well, what did she expect, for them to become *friends* on the basis of a couple of good conversations? Sex would have been a lot easier.

"Good night," Cressida said, and set off towards the big house. It was a calm and beautiful night, with barely a breeze. What a pity that her libido couldn't be as tranquil.

Chapter Seven

Xena was standing on the deck of a gigantic cruise ship, holding a rope.

"What's this for?" she asked.

Cassie looked up from her deck chair. "If you don't hold that, we sink," she said.

"Oh," Xena said, gripping harder. There was some kind of weight on the other end of the rope, and her hands were getting sore. "It's really heavy."

Laodice was floating on her back in the pool. "You can do it," she said. "You're the brave one."

"It's *really* heavy," Xena said, and the rope tugged, jolting her off her feet and out of the dream.

She woke with Paris leaning over her and frowning, which was only a mild improvement.

"Oh good, you're awake," Paris said.

"What the hell?" Xena struggled free of her sleeping bag. Her hands ached, as if she'd been clenching them in her sleep. The light inside the tent was dim, and the campground was relatively quiet. "What time is it?"

"Nearly seven," Paris said.

From the other camp bed, Prax mumbled something and thrust her head under the pillow.

"You were asleep when we got back," Paris continued, her voice accusatory.

"You're the one who told me to take a walk."

"I meant around the Speigeltent, not all the way back to your bed!"

"Shut *up*," Prax moaned.

Xena massaged her aching palms, getting a vivid flash of Cressida's small hand in hers on that walk. It had been so nice. Until she'd ruined it.

"Why does it matter?" she asked. "I'm not allowed to film anymore anyway."

Paris rolled her eyes. "Dammond Argive is a *businessman*," she said. "That was his opening gambit, not his final offer. I talked him around."

Despite herself, Xena's heart leapt. "I can film?" *I can* do *something?*

"There are some restrictions. You can film the Archers and the ordinary paying guests without further permissions. But you're not allowed to film VIPs, other performers, or production staff without their explicit consent, and you have to delete any unconsented footage. He wanted a blanket ban, but I told him about how great the documentary's going to be and how great Lotophagi's going to look in it until he caved."

Xena considered the airport full of performers and volunteers, the background shots she'd taken in Lot D, the filming she'd done of the security teams at work and the production crew putting together the show. And the cabaret tent, of course, crammed with every no-no category. "Well, that's good, but it means I need to delete most of the work I've done over the last two days."

Paris stared at her. "No! Are you crazy? Only if it's unconsented."

"I didn't get individual consents, Paris!"

"Right! So you have to get them *retroactively*." Paris grabbed Xena's jeans from her open suitcase and thrust them into her hands. "I talked the schedule out of Jenny. Tech call for the Spiegeltent starts at seven. Go talk to as many performers and staff as you can find and get them to agree, on camera, to using their likeness for the documentary."

"I haven't agreed to the documentary."

"But when you *do*, you'll be glad you have those consents," Paris said triumphantly. "Stage One tech call starts at nine, and Stage Two at nine-thirty, so you'll have to hustle between them. Where's your camera? Time's a-wasting."

"You're insane," Xena said, with conviction.

Paris snorted. "What else are you gonna do? Do you want that asshole Dammond to *win*?"

And there it was, a direct hit on her buttons. Not just Xena's natural competitiveness, but her loathing for Dammond, which Paris had either recognized or intuited.

"Damn the man," Prax mumbled.

"You're the worst boss I've ever had," Xena said, but she wriggled out of her sleeping bag and yanked her leggings on. Where the hell was her bra?

Paris snorted. "I'm the only boss you've ever had."

"Yeah, well, this is why it's much better to be self-employed." Oh, there was the bra. Xena pulled out a fresh T-shirt and rummaged through her toiletry bag. There was no time for a visit to the shower block, or even to make some use of baby wipes, but she could at least apply deodorant and brush her hair into a pony tail before grabbing her camera. At the last minute she remembered to throw her lanyard over her head.

She walked out into a spectacular dawn. The sun was just rising over the trees to the east, a giant orb of molten gold in a candy-pink horizon. To the west, a few bright stars were still evident, disappearing into the lightening sky. In an hour or so, this would all be deep, blazing blue, but right now the effect was of infinite shades of translucent blue and pink melting into each other at the center, deepening into an outrageous intensity of color at the edges.

It was so impressive that for a moment, all Xena could do was gape.

Then she yanked her mind back down to earth, and the mundane demands of her insane cousin-boss, and headed towards the Lot D exit.

It must have rained again in the night; the grass was damp, and there were puddles in places on the gravel path. Tucked away in her weird cruise ship dream, she hadn't heard it, which was a shame. The sound of rain hammering on the roof of a tent, at least a well-erected one that wouldn't sag or leak, was one of the things she'd missed when she gave up her past life.

She paused, mid-thought. Was there any reason she'd had to give that up? She'd loved camping, even before XO, Xena had gained its following. Unlike the more glamorous sponsored trips she'd been on, she wouldn't need to strain her budget to repeat the experience.

There was nothing to stop her from buying some good boots and a decent backpack, and checking out a few National Parks in the Pacific Northwest, where she'd get all the rain-on-tent she could hope for.

It had just never occurred to her to try.

Ernest was on guard at the exit, yawning over a huge cup of coffee.

"Don't you sleep?" she asked. He'd been at the cabaret night too, and he would have been one of the last people to leave.

"Here and there," he said. "Have a good day."

"I will!" Xena said, with more enthusiasm than she'd thought she could muster. Sure, she was up early and unwashed, and she'd turned down what she was pretty sure would have been some great sex with a fascinating woman, but the sky was beautiful and the tropical air was cool and a little misty. Almost instinctively, she started to jog.

Her lanyard got her admitted to the concert zone, and she jogged over to the Spiegeltent, picking up her pace. Xena had been a big fan of sports bras since her D cup days, way back in the mists of her early teenage years. Cassie liked lingerie in rich colours, and Laodice went for sexy frills and lace, but Xena was all about structured materials and impact engineering. This one was less suited to strenuous activity than some of her more serious bras, one of which had thirteen hooks at the front, and she was aware of the bounce factor. But it was good to *move*, good to feel her blood warm and rush around her body as her breath deepened.

The Spiegeltent looked gaudy and gorgeous in the early light, its mirrors and ribbons glittering. The main entrance was closed, but there was a cluster of people waiting at the side entrance the performers had used.

One of them was Cressida O'Brien.

Xena's pace faltered. Oh, man, this was embarrassing. Cressida was wearing green dungarees over a yellow T-shirt and her hair was up in curlers, wrapped in a scarf. She looked cute as a button, fresh-faced and dewy, nothing like the sexy gothic creature of the night before. And yet, when her eyes met Xena's, giving absolutely nothing away, Xena felt the same electric charge go down her spine, the thrill of a danger she wanted to run towards.

Well, she'd run away instead. She dropped the eye contact and glanced around the group instead.

"Hey, everyone," she said. "I'm attached to Paris and the Archers, the band from last night? I'm doing some video promo and maybe a documentary for them, and I need to get on-camera consent from you before I can use the footage."

A short brunette in athleisurewear, who Xena thought was probably the woman who'd been turning herself into a human pretzel last night, looked her up and down. "You cannot sell video of my performance," she said, in some kind of European accent. "That is copyright infringement." The huge blond guy next to her, the one she'd mistaken for Cressida's partner in the airport, looked worried.

"No, for sure, I get that. This is just so that I can use you as background."

"It's fine, Klara," Cressida said. "She's filming for the band, not trying to steal your act. What do we need to do?"

Xena smiled at her gratefully. "Just state your name and that you give permission for me to use your likeness as background material."

"Piece of cake," Cressida said, smiling back, and then a ripple went through the group as two people arrived in a golf cart laden with equipment—a woman Xena thought she remembered from the night before, and a man with a heavy-duty aluminum laptop case.

"Sorry we're late," said the woman, not sounding very sorry. "Darnell needs someone to help lift these cases."

"On it," the big guy said cheerfully, and Xena volunteered as well. She wanted to blend in, and making herself useful might endear her to the others.

"Those two big cases," Darnell said, pointing the back of the golf cart, as the woman let the others in. It seemed sort of odd, to have a "tent" with lockable wooden doors, but the Spiegeltent was a weird mix of a structure; temporary, but sturdy. "You'll need to take two trips, one person on each side."

"I can probably carry one," the big guy said, and Xena could believe it, but Darnell shook his head.

"One each side," he said, and headed in.

"Hey," the big guy said. "I'm Troy."

"Xena."

"I know, man! I've seen you. I mean, I used to watch your channel."

"Oh."

"I thought it was really cool," he said, his eyes bright and guileless. "Are you bringing it back? Is that part of what you're doing here?"

Xena shook her head. "No, that's over. This is... This is something new."

"Cool, cool. Well, you've got my consent!" He glanced at her camera, currently riding on her hip. She'd actually have to be filming for that to count, but she appreciated the effort.

"Shall we?" she said, gesturing at the cases. They were identical, the size and shape of large suitcases, but made out of some kind of hard black plastic, with aluminum reinforcement at the seams.

"Oh! Sure!"

The first case would definitely have been too much for Xena to carry alone. Fortunately, the manufacturer had included handles on each end, and Troy chivalrously took the position where he'd have to walk backwards, but she still had to engage her core as she lifted and consciously remind herself to breathe.

"What's in these?" she said.

Troy shrugged. "Panels? Lights? It doesn't pay to ask. You always want to stay on the tech guy's good side."

"So Darnell's the tech guy?"

"Yeah. And the lady, Jenny, she's the production manager, and I think stage manager for tonight. Someone else is doing the afternoon acts."

Cressida was waiting at the door, holding it open for them. She flashed Xena a smile, and then started a low-voiced conversation with Klara. A few safety lights around the perimeter flickered into life; someone must have flicked a switch. It was kind of a miracle, if you thought about it. A complete theater, with a stage and space for seating, with raised platforms at the sides for sitting around tables, stained glass windows and electricity, popping up in the middle of an island estate. The floor was wooden, parquet panels fitting tightly together, and there was a freaking chandelier suspended from the canvas ceiling.

"Where do these go?" Troy called.

Darnell was setting up his laptop on a light and sound table near the entrance. "Put them by the bar," he said, jerking his head over to the high counter off the other side of the entrance. It had been the extra-VIP area last night, Xena remembered. No velvet rope now. A cadre of volunteers had turned up and were setting up rows of foldout chairs under Jenny's direction, but fortunately they weren't in the way. Xena wasn't sure she could handle a detour right now.

The Spiegeltent was eerie and seemed much bigger without an audience. Their footsteps echoed on the floor. Troy didn't seem at all concerned about the weight, but Xena was beginning to struggle.

"What's your act?" she asked. It took more effort than she liked, but at least she wasn't audibly panting.

"I'm a strong man," Troy said. "Basically, I just lift things, or hit stuff, but like, to music. Lots of audience interaction, challenging people to hold my hammer and lifting them and that."

"Do you tear phone books in half?"

Troy shook his head sadly. "Can't get them anymore. I bend a steel bar, though, that's popular."

They were moving slowly, and Troy grunted. "Watch out, there's some water on the floor. Put this down a minute?"

Xena gratefully lowered her side of the case in unison with him and stretched her back. "Is there a leak?" she asked, looking up. The canvas roof looked sturdy enough.

"I hope not," Troy said. He was crouching, squinting at the shallow puddle in the dim light. "But even that would be better than water seeping up from the ground. I played an arts festival in Munich once where the crew erected a tent over a boggy area without realizing. First big rainstorm, no worries. Second one, and the boards started sagging. Third one, they worked out what was happening, but by then the rot had set in. Half the floor panels were ruined. Hey, do you know Cressida? I saw you talking to her last night."

Xena tried to keep up with the conversational veer. "Uh, sort of? We met on the way here."

"She's a really cool chick. She doesn't deserve any of that stuff that happened to her."

"What do you mean?" Xena asked. Was it something to do with what Cressida had alluded to last night, that things with Lucian's father hadn't ended well?

"Oh, nothing," Troy said, sounding guilty, and sprang upright with the ease of a well-oiled machine. "Let's finish moving this."

Lifting the case from the ground was even more of an effort than taking it from the golf cart had been. Xena, with a sudden suspicion, looked closely at the face across from hers. Troy didn't look much like Lucian, but that wasn't conclusive.

"Does that kind of thing happen often?" Xena asked. "Setting up leaking tents, I mean?"

"Oh, sure. No matter how smoothly a festival's going, there's always *something* wrong. This one's been pretty good but—" He cut off abruptly, eyes wide and jaw locked.

At first, Xena thought that he'd seen something awful behind her. She startled to glance over her shoulder, and then found herself tipping, the weight tearing from her hands as Troy dropped the case and fell backwards.

Caught off balance, Xena fell bodily into the case, the impact jolting her ribs and shoulder. She barely noticed—Troy's face had been too awful for her own pain to be worth any attention.

"Troy!" she said. "Are you okay?"

He was having some kind of fit, lying on his back while shudders rippled up his body. Xena scrambled to her feet and took a step forward, meaning to go to his side.

"Stop!" Darnell shouted, the command strong enough to freeze her in her tracks. "Don't touch him! Don't move! That's a live wire!"

There was another puddle. Troy had stepped into the edge of it, in his canvas sneakers, and on the other end, snaking away into the shadows, was a black, sinuous line.

An electric cable.

Darnell was scrambling along the side of the tent, swearing frantically. Jenny was calling for an ambulance over her walkie talkie, her voice sharp and clear.

Troy's eyes were open, his face fixed in that agonized expression. With horror, Xena realized she could smell something burning.

Darnell made it to the bar and yanked something free. The lights abruptly died.

"It's clear!" Darnell shouted, and Xena lunged forward, using touch more than sight to find Troy's body. He'd gone limp, and she listened for air, took his pulse with a shaking hand. She was probably imagining the slight buzz against her fingers as she touched his throat.

Darnell was running towards her, a slim maglight in his hand. Jenny was right behind him, ordering the others to stay away, stay back, give him air.

"No pulse," Xena reported, and then, as something fluttered beneath her fingers. "Wait, there!" A wait, another long beat, and then again. Too slow, she thought, but worse, there was no rise and fall of breath. She started rescue breathing, pinching Troy's nose shut as she forced air into his lungs. His mouth was minty and cool. He'd brushed his teeth this morning, and put on this old, worn T-shirt, and now he was lying still, his eyelids only half-closed over his eyes.

"Do we do CPR?" Darnell asked. He was on his knees on the other side of Troy's unmoving torso, his hands hovering uncertainly over his chest.

"I don't know! He *has* a pulse, just slow. Would we hurt him?"

"Do it," Cressida said from behind them, her voice small, but clear. "I did a class in pediatric resuscitation. When in doubt, compressions."

Darnell nodded, and locked his arms together, one hand over the other, pushing rhythmically down into Troy's chest, while Xena tried to breathe for him. After what seemed like an hour, but was probably only a few minutes, they swapped, and Xena took over the compressions. It was *hard*. Troy's chest was banded in muscle, and even in his unconscious state, she wasn't sure how much traction she was getting.

There was a babble at the front, the main doors were flung open, and three paramedics ran in, red bags swinging at their sides and the scene turned from barely controlled desperation to efficient care-in-action. One of the men put an oxygen mask over Troy's face, while the other talked to Darnell—"Yes, definitely electrical shock," he was saying, his voice wobbling—and the third EMT unzipped her bag, pulled out some scissors, and cut Troy's T-shirt right up the middle.

Ridiculously, Xena almost told her not to. The T-shirt was worn enough to be an old favorite, and Troy wouldn't want it damaged. *More than he wants to be alive?* she asked herself harshly, and moved back from the scene without even properly getting up, even as the woman stuck pads to his chest, ordered everyone clear, and turned the machine on.

Troy's chest jumped, horribly reminiscent of the original shock. There was a tense moment of silence, a held breath in the vast darkness of the tent.

The monitor beeped once, then, again. The woman looked at her colleague and shook her head—a tiny motion, but Xena heard a gasp, and when she looked up, Cressida was standing right behind her, her face drawn and pale.

Xena scrambled to her feet and put her body between her and the body. "Don't look," she said, the words feeling strange, coming from her numb lips. "Cressida, don't look."

                                    ***

"Don't look," Xena said, but Cressida couldn't look away.

Troy was limp, his vitality abruptly disappeared. For someone who'd lived through his body, it was obscene for him to be so still.

The paramedics were still working, depressing syringes into his thighs and trying to shock his heart back into motion with chest compressions, but Cressida saw the look they exchanged. The grim eyes, the unhappy set of their mouths. If the defibrillator hadn't worked...

"He's dead," she said, acknowledging it as she said it.

Xena jolted, as if she'd been shocked too.

"I think—" she said, her voice strained, and then she paused and breathed in, an enormous inhale, and out again.

Cressida's own lungs were tight. She belatedly breathed herself.

"What do you need?" Xena said. Her voice was calmer.

"Get me out of here," Cressida said. She could feel the weight of the eyes on her, all the performers and crew clustered around, keeping vigil. Klara was weeping, huge tears rolling silently down her round cheeks, and Cressida felt distantly terrible for her, but she could not stay.

Xena walked her through the crowd and out of the Spiegeltent. Passersby, probably alerted by the ambulance arriving, were clustering, craning their necks and asking each other questions they couldn't answer.

Cressida could feel stillness descending over her. It was the same kind of awful clarity which had driven her to leave her rehearsal dinner, huge with Lucian's tender body low in her belly, no idea of where to go or whom she could ask for help, only knowing that she had to go. Her feelings were shutting down, leaving her with the crystalline will to act.

But there was no action she could take here. There was only the stark reality of Troy's limp body lying in that tent, the sad remnant of that big, kind, lovely boy.

"It's like someone ran over a puppy," she said, and then realized that it was a horrible thing to say. Troy was a human being, not a pet. She meant something more complicated than that, something about all that exuberance and friendliness so abruptly snatched away by mechanical means. But no one had heard her except Xena, who put her hand up like she was thinking of squeezing Cressida's shoulder, then let it fall again.

Cressida was grateful. She felt the boundaries of her body as jagged edges. If someone touched her, she might cut them. She took a few steps past the entrance, where they wouldn't be in anyone's way, and stopped.

"Do you need to go?" Xena asked.

Yes, Cressida almost said. She needed to go back to the big house, to walk into the daycare, to pick Lucian up and bury her face in the side of his neck, breathing in the scent of him. But she might be needed for something here, and besides, right now she wasn't sure she could walk that far.

"I was talking to him," Xena said. "I was just talking to him, and then he stopped and fell down. He said you were really cool. I thought he was sweet on you." She shook her head hard, as if she were trying to shake a thought loose. "I mean. Those weren't his final words or anything. We were talking about the leak when he fell."

"We had sex once," Cressida said. "It was good. He was so kind."

"Was he—?" Xena blurted out, then closed her mouth.

Cressida looked at her, puzzled, until the unspoken question abruptly clicked into place. "Oh! No, he isn't Lucian's father."

Xena let out a shaky breath, but she didn't look very relieved. "So, we're both in shock, right?"

"Oh yeah. I've been here before."

"Me too. Got any candy?"

Cressida shoved one hand in the pocket of her dungarees, and discovered that she had a snackbag of Teddy Grahams. She scrupulously divided the packet in two, and they crunched in silence. The sugary blandness was comforting, melting away into a faint suggestion of sweetness.

The silence was comforting too. She didn't feel any need to fill it, no urge to perform a version of herself. Maybe Xena just didn't know what to say, but she wasn't fidgeting. She seemed just to be there, a companion while the first wave of shock and grief ebbed.

The EMTs brought out a gurney. The large form on top of it was completely shrouded, a sheet over the face.

Xena bowed her head, and Cressida felt an additional stab at the confirmation. "I wish I still smoked," she said. "If ever there was a time…" She sighed. "I'd better go back in and figure out what the deal is with tech call."

"They won't shut it down? Troy *died*."

"Shut down the *show*?" Cressida said, genuinely surprised. "No. I don't think so, not unless they can't figure out what happened."

"Live wire in water," Xena said.

"Pretty easy fix, then." Cressida was impressed by her own even tone. "They might cancel the kids show this afternoon, though. I was going to take Lucian." She looked at Xena. "Are you going to be busy?"

"The Archers are on Stage One at one. I need to film that, but afterwards I'm free." Xena made a face. "Paris probably wants me to spend that time getting consents, though."

"She can't expect you to talk to everyone in the festival in one day."

"She sure can. Paris isn't really good at setting reasonable limits. For herself, or anyone else."

"That sounds exhausting."

"It *is*," Xena said, sounding more amused than exhausted. "But ninety-nine times out of a hundred, she gets what she wants."

Cressida pictured it. What would it be like, to live life with that much confidence, without having to negotiate or compromise, to get what you wanted because you were persistent and bloody-minded enough to make it happen? A queasy thought arose. Was that how *Dammond* felt? He was white, wealthy, male, and straight—all advantages Paris Chen couldn't claim. He was probably used to encountering much less resistance; people would just hand him things Paris had to fight for.

"And the last time?" she asked.

"Hm?" Xena was watching the ambulance bump over the grass with hooded eyes.

"You said ninety-nine times out of a hundred. What happens on the hundredth time?"

"Oh. Everything blows up in her face. She meets someone who can stick to *their* limits, and she can't find a reason for them to say yes, so they say no. Depending on how pushy she's been, there's backlash. And then she holds a grudge against them forever, when you'd think it'd be the other way around."

Cressida's heart was beating too fast. Dammond had *dropped* his grudge, she reminded herself. He was even learning how to compromise:

not exposing their connection, letting her set the limits on how interaction with Lucian would go. His grandfather's death had been very good for him.

"I used to be one of the people who could say no," Xena said, sounding thoughtful. Oh, she was talking about Paris. "But she talked me into this job without taking a breath, and now I'm running all over the festival for her."

"What does she do? When people say no?"

"She holds a grudge, like I said."

"But she doesn't try to get revenge or anything?"

Xena smiled. "No. Revenge would take time she could spend on getting the *next* thing she wants." She looked at Cressida. "I mean, she's not a psychopath. Just really driven and kind of selfish. She's annoying sometimes, but she's not a bad person."

"Right," Cressida said weakly. "That's good." The ambulance was out of sight. She knew what she was doing. She was following an alarming train of thought, because her brain was beginning to shake off the first shock of Troy's death and wanted to throw all that cortisol at something she might be able to escape or control. So she was inventing a problem to deal with, a completely fictional problem, because Dammond *could* accept no. He *had*. He wasn't after revenge, and he wasn't holding a grudge.

She knew what Xena was doing, too. This light conversation about a minor annoyance was meant to be distracting, to get them both back on even keel. Xena had no way of knowing that this topic was troubled water.

"I *really* miss smoking," Cressida said, and remembered what she'd meant to say before. "Hey, no pressure, but if you decide you do have the time, you'd be welcome to hang out with Lucian and me this afternoon."

"I'd like that," Xena said, looking touched. "Let me get your number?"

"Oh, the cell coverage is awful. I tried to call my best friend last night, and we heard one word in ten. Just come up to the big house around two or three and ask for me. I'll let security know you're welcome."

"You're staying there? No wonder I couldn't find you in Lot D." Xena startled, apparently hearing the words coming out of her own mouth, and then blushed from the roots of her dark hair to the throat of her T-shirt.

It was very cute, and distressingly sexy that Xena had been *looking* for her, even if, at the crucial moment, she'd turned Cressida down. Cressida bit her lip. Why couldn't she hold onto the mild snit she'd been in last night, disdainful that Xena wanted to be her *friend*?

Troy died, she thought. *You need a friend right now.*

But in her heart of hearts, she wasn't sure that was it. She suspected she'd forgiven Xena for turning her down even before Troy died, the moment she'd bounced up to the Spiegeltent with her ponytail flipping, energetic and alive. There was some kind of shade hanging over Xena, a cloud that dimmed that light most of the time, but she'd glimpsed Xena's glow once or twice, and Cressida was weak enough to want more opportunities to see it.

"Hey," she said, and touched Xena's arm. "Thanks for waiting with me. I really appreciate it."

She went up on her tiptoes, meaning to brush her lips against Xena's cheek—just a friendly gesture, no inappropriate lusts here, no sir—but

Xena turned her head to look at her with dark, startled eyes, and Cressida drifted off course, drawn to those soft lips.

She hesitated before she made contact, not wanting to scare Xena or breach a boundary—and Xena *had* said no, last night, but things had changed, hadn't they, everything had changed when Troy fell down—and Xena wasn't pulling back, wasn't moving away. Instead, she'd turned her arm under Cressida's hand, cupping her elbow and pulling her closer.

The moment was as sweet and slow as honey dripping off a spoon, stretching with a golden, liquid grace as Cressida tilted her chin, her intentions unmistakable now, and then Xena moved that last quarter-inch and kissed *her*.

The kiss was almost chaste. Lips barely parted, the gentlest touch of tongue.

Cressida's entire body came alive. Her nipples tightened, two throbbing tight buds that shot heat straight into her lower belly, and her thighs clenched in reaction. Xena gasped quietly, and Cressida leaned into that grip on her elbow, wanting to get closer, wanting *more*—

"Oh, that's nice," Jenny said, her voice disgusted.

Cressida came back to earth with a literal and metaphorical thud as Xena's hand dropped away. "It's none of your fucking business," she snapped.

Jenny obviously bit back her first response and took a deep breath to stifle her second. For her part, Cressida made herself remember that Jenny had also had a nasty shock that morning, and tried to soften the aggression of her stance.

"We're meeting backstage," Jenny said. Her voice was struggling towards neutral, but she more or less made it. Her eyes tracked to Xena. "The Archers aren't on the list."

"I need to get moving anyway," Xena said. "See you later, Cressida?"

"I hope so," Cressida said, and turned back to Jenny with difficulty. "I'm sorry for snapping at you."

Jenny nodded. "I'm sorry too," she said. "Were you and Troy close? I need to—someone needs to tell his family."

"Not that close," Cressida said, falling into step with her. She remembered a body moving under hers, the ease with which he'd lifted and turned her, the enormous enthusiasm he'd brought to their one encounter. They had not traded family stories. "Klara might know more. I think they've worked a few festivals together."

"Thanks. I'll ask." Jenny looked tired, and Cressida felt suddenly bad for her. Accidents happened, but no one wanted them to happen on their watch. And even in the gonzo world of circus arts, accidents were rarely fatal these days. Broken limbs, concussions, burns from equipment or some overly-enthusiastic torch juggling—Cressida had witnessed all of those. Death, never, until today.

Jenny led them around the Spiegeltent, back to the performer entrance, so that they didn't need to pass through the seating area. Through the open doors, Cressida saw that Darnell and two other techs had roped off the scene of the accident with yellow hazard tape. They were holding various tools and meters and talking urgently to each other.

Backstage, the atmosphere was equally tense, with too many people crowded into the small, open dressing area. Cressida saw tear marks on several faces, and Klara's spine was rigid with control as she sat perfectly straight on a make-up stool, but no one was showing any signs of hysteria.

Jenny took her place in front of them, and Cressida slipped into place beside Klara.

"Before I discuss the new schedule, I want to make it clear that no one is obliged to perform tonight," Jenny said, pitching her voice effortlessly to the back of the space. Cressida was willing to bet she had performance experience. "If you want to pull your act from the lineup, we'll treat it like any other kind of unavoidable cancellation."

Since their contracts all stated that even "unavoidable cancellation" meant you didn't get paid for the gig, this wasn't quite as generous as it sounded. Still, Jenny was saying there'd be no additional financial penalty—and also no hidden blacklist, no production rumor going around that you were *unreliable.*

A current went through the crowd, but no one said anything until Klara spoke, her face as smooth and still as mirrored glass. "If we all take advantage of this offer, there will be no show, correct?"

"We can attempt to fill a few gaps," Jenny said. "But yes, if too many people pull out, we'll have to pull the plug." She flinched at her own phrasing, but continued. "For now, the afternoon show is definitely canceled."

Just as Cressida had predicted. A few people frowned or grunted, probably slated to perform for the kids show. Cressida should have felt sorry for them, but instead she felt a glimmer of pleasure beneath her grief. Time for her and Lucian. And Xena, if she didn't change her mind again.

"We can't use any electricity until this place is fully cleared and we know it's not going to—that there won't be any more accidents," Jenny said. "If we can't guarantee that, it'll be a cancellation. Otherwise, tech call is five p.m. for a two hour speed-run. Email me your tracklist and lighting cues and we'll do the best we can."

Oh, hell. Two hours might get through the lighting cues for about half of the acts scheduled for the night. Anyone on after midnight—like Cressida—was doomed to a dry-run. That unspoken buzz went through the listening performers again.

"What about the rest of us?" someone asked. Cressida craned, but she couldn't put a face to the voice. "Not all of the performers are here."

"I'll wait around for the nine a.m. tech call people and let them know the story," Jenny said, looking even more exhausted.

Cressida glanced at her phone and was startled to see they were coming up on that anyway. The incident had taken longer than she'd thought. Maybe she'd lost more than a few minutes in that silent, comforting silence with Xena.

"And will they get the same offer?" the unfamiliar voice demanded. "They can pull out with no penalties?"

"Yes," Jenny said. "This is a nomadic business, but we all know this is a community, and someone in the community has been—" She stopped, and took a careful breath. "I won't pretend to know who all could be affected. I only ask that you let me know as soon as possible if you plan to cancel your act. And I ask for your discretion. We don't want word getting out before Troy's next-of-kin can be contacted."

That might do something to curb the firehose of gossip that was about to shoot out of this tent, but frankly, Cressida doubted it would be enough. She hoped Jenny had those contact details close at hand.

Klara, who had listened to all of this without moving, abruptly un-folded herself and stood on the stool she'd been sitting on. She was short and muscular, the typical gymnast's build, and even on the stool she was barely a head above most of the people gathered. But still, she pulled everyone's attention without effort. "I will perform," she announced flatly. "I will dedicate my act to Troy."

She sat down again, paying no apparent attention to the wave of empathetic nods and whispers that ran through the space. Cressida, beside her, felt tears prickle in her eyes for the first time, struck by the absolute rightness of that.

"The show must go on" was a cliche, but she'd never met a performer who didn't, deep down, believe it with their whole heart. Troy would want them to go on. He'd want them to do their best work, to use the incandescent alchemy of the stage to turn this into a night they, and the audience, would never forget.

It would be for him, in his name. In a way, it would be his final work. She raised her hand and Jenny nodded at her.

"Me too," Cressida said, and she'd rarely meant anything more. "I want to perform too."

Chapter Eight

Xena jogged over to Stage One, body still buzzing from the touch of Cressida's lips on hers, head still whirling from the horror of Troy's death. There was an uneasy mixture of sadness and joy churning in her chest, coupled with some shame for having been caught making out with a hot woman thirty minutes after a man had died. She should have had more self-control.

It had just seemed... inevitable.

Word got around fast. She'd only just started introducing herself to the musicians waiting for their tech call at Stage One and getting permission to film them when a red-haired man with a Scandinavian accent and a bedazzled guitar blew in, obviously full of urgent news.

"Did you hear someone got murdered in the cabaret tent?" he said.

Xena's jaw dropped. Becky Washington, the woman she was filming, whipped her head around, no longer interested in potential publicity.

"What?" she said. "Who was it?"

"It wasn't a murder," Xena said firmly. She figured she could do the festival that much of a favor without joining the gossip.

The redhead gave her a huffy look. "All right, a mysterious death," he said. "It was one of the circus boys, I heard."

A couple of other musicians were looking over, and more were pretending not to look, but obviously listening in with everything they had. Musicians obviously liked gossip as much as influencers did.

Someone else's phone beeped, and they audibly gasped. "I just got a whole bunch of texts at once," they said. "Sven's right! Like, all the people carrying equipment just keeled over!"

"One person," Sven said, obviously annoyed the focal point had drifted. "Dead without a mark on him."

"It was an accident," Xena said. It came out louder than she'd meant. "An electric shock."

"How do you know?" Sven demanded. "Who even are you?"

"I was there." Xena didn't bother to give her name. She didn't add that she'd been looking into Troy's eyes as he fell.

Sven glared, but the atmosphere shifted as everyone realized they should at least be pretending some respect for the dead.

"That's so sad," Becky said. "Did you, like, know him?"

"Not well."

"Who was it?" She couldn't quite control the avid gleam behind the question.

"I don't think I should tell you that," Xena said, to a sea of disappointed faces.

She got a few more permissions, each of them from musicians who tried to pump her for information with more or less subtlety. The tech crew were running them through soundcheck and lighting cues as quickly as they could. They weren't trying to get the news from Xena, but she figured it was because they already had it. There was a lot of muttering and some quiet walkie-talkie conversations from the tech booths, and one of the techs was checking the thick bundles of cables in the wings, referring to a clipboard as she went.

Paris and the Archers came in, and Paris gave Xena an approving nod. Xena was annoyed at herself for being pleased. But who was she fooling? She'd been a little less ego-happy and impervious to drama than some of the other people in influencer space, maybe, but a part of her had always wanted the attention. Typical middle child syndrome—she'd been the youngest of three sisters, and then Iulus had come along when she was five to suck up all that last baby and only boy energy. Her parents loved her, of course, but they didn't understand her. The only sports-mad kid in a family of big brains, the only one with a weird job—Priam and Hecuba didn't know about Cassie's side gig—the only college drop-out, unless Iulus managed to fuck up his 4.0 GPA in the final year of his degree.

The only multi-millionaire, but that didn't seem to count for anything. It was only money, after all.

The only single girl.

Oh, hell, she'd boarded the self-loathing train without noticing, and she definitely didn't want to revisit that final destination. Repeating her therapist's mantras always made her feel stupid. Unfortunately they worked. "I am enough," she muttered to herself. "I am good. I am complete."

Her therapist would want her saying them with conviction, to a mirror, but backstage while someone did something earsplitting to an amp was the best she could manage. Her mood did lift, if only because this really was kind of dumb, and she had enough sense of humor left to laugh at it.

"Hey, so, have you heard about this murder?" Paris said behind her.

Xena turned on her with a speed that might have made anyone but Paris flinch. "It wasn't a murder," she said, through clenched teeth. "I was there, I saw it. This isn't some fun gossip story, okay?"

"Whoa," Paris said. "Okay. I just wanted to know if they were going to cancel anything."

"Probably the afternoon show," Xena told her. That was purely based on what Cressida had told her, but she was betting Cressida had a pretty good idea of what was likely to happen. "But it was just an accident. They'll probably go ahead with the evening shows if they can make sure it won't happen again." She could picture the crew now, taking up the floorboards, inspecting the ceiling, taking their time to go through every cable.

"That's terrible," Paris said, looking more thoughtful than appalled. "Do you think anyone might pull out? They might need someone to cover any gaps."

Xena closed her eyes. "Paris, you have all the sensitivity of a rabid hyena."

Paris didn't say anything, and when Xena opened her eyes, her cousin was looking concerned. And maybe even a little bit hurt.

"Get in touch with Jenny," she said, instead of any of the meaner follow-ups lining up in her mouth. "She's the one in charge over there. I have to head to Stage Two now." She took off before Paris could make any kind of response.

There was a dull headache starting behind her left eye, and it was way too early to feel this rough. But what did she expect? She'd missed breakfast, she hadn't visited the showers yet and she'd just realized she'd kissed Cressida with unbrushed teeth. It was probably a good thing Jenny had interrupted them before things got more passionate, or Cressida would have got a mouthful of morning breath and run a mile.

She made herself stop by a food truck that was serving coffee and muffins and pulled out her phone while she waited. The sister group chat took a long time to load, but she needed to get at least some of the unpleasant emotion of the last two days out. She scrolled through some pictures of Laodice's latest knitting project, and got to the most recent entries.

[Cassie] Manny's pretty down today. The PI he hired came back with another dead end on the hunt for Gus.

[Laodice] Are you going to get him declared dead? He's been missing for more than seven years, right?

[Cassie] No, not unless someone finds actual proof of death. Manny's pretty clear that by rights, Gus owns a third of the vineyard. He's hoping that if he's still alive, he'll take that bait at least.

[Laodice] Wait, how does that work? I thought Manny and Augie owned half of Tantalus each?

[Cassie] No, because Manny's grandfather left the vineyard business to his sons, Arthur and Theo, *and* Chris, his third secret son. But Theo murdered Chris to keep the secret and that's how he and Arthur got half the vineyard each. Arthur left the vineyard to his sons, Manny and Augie, so they had a quarter each.

[Cassie] When Theo died last year, he also split his half between Augie and Manny. BUT it gets complicated, because murderers aren't entitled to the proceeds of their murders, and killing Chris meant Theo's inheritance was one-third blood money.

[Laodice] There are too many fractions here.

[Cassie] Short version, Chris should have got his third, and Gus, as his presumptive heir, should have it now.

[Cassie] Oh, and Theo also split his savings between the boys, and it was a *lot* of money.

[Cassie] Anyway, Manny told Augie they should split the business and that money three ways and advertise widely. Augie hit the roof, because blah blah, this is my inheritance, I need to leave it to my kids, Dad didn't know Theo was a murderer, he left us his half fair and square, I'll fight this through the courts every step of the way, *you* go ahead and give him the ownership out of *your* half etc etc.

[Cassie] Which Manny was fully prepared to do, btw. Which would have left Gus with one third, Augie with one half, and Manny with one-sixth of the business he is currently *running*.

[Cassie] But THEN! Aerope got involved.

[Laodice] Manny's mom is terrifying.

[Cassie] Yes, she is. And she terrified Augie into backing all the way back into his third with his tail between his legs.

[Laodice] Lolllll I love her

[Laodice] How widely is "advertise widely"? You're going to get a lot of con-artists with that kind of money on the line.

[Cassie] I did point that out. Aerope volunteered me to do the background checks.

[Laodice] Hah! Where did Theo get that extra cash from, anyway?

[Cassie] No one can work that out. It's got to be dirty, somehow. I thought embezzlement, but Manny thinks the vineyard wasn't even making that much money, let alone enough that Theo could hide stealing those kind of amounts. Hey, would Telfer mind having a look at the books? He's the finance guy.

[Laodice] Maybe? I don't know.

[Laodice] He's pretty busy

[Laodice] Lots going on at work.

[Cassie] *rolled eyes emoji* You can just say no.

[Xena has entered the chat]

[Laodice] Hey!

[Cassie] Hi! How's the festival?

[Xena] good, but you won't guess who's here

[Message did not send. Click to resend.]

Xena rolled her eyes and clicked. The whirling symbol on her screen seemed dubious about it, but eventually it got through.

[Laodice] WHo?

[Cassie] You're right, I won't guess. Just tell me.

[Xena] *rolled eyes emoji*

[Xena] Zac

[Laodice] oh no

[Cassie] Are you okay?

[Xena] he's engaged

She hesitated, but clicked send anyway. It wasn't like it was going to be a secret. She kept as far from Zac's socials as she could, but if he was doing as well as he claimed, she had no doubt this was already out.

[Xena] I just wish I knew before he told me

[Xena] I looked like an idiot

[Xena] hes doing great and I'm a mess

She deleted the last message before sending—way too self-pitying—and tried again.

[Xena] he's doing great and I'm filming my cousin's band

[Cassie] And I bet you're doing it well.

[Laodice] Zac was never good enough for you

"Pineapple-cranberry muffin and quad shot Americano for Sheena?" the food truck guy called.

Close enough. Xena stepped up and took the order from him. Time to change the subject.

[Xena] I'm okay

[Xena] mostly

[Xena] there was a pretty bad accident this morning

[Message did not send. Click to resend.]

Xena clicked.

[Message did not send. Click to resend.]

Ugh. She wasn't going to discuss Troy's death over patchy wi-fi. What else could she bring up? The presence of Dammond fucking Argive didn't seem as important now. Cressida stepping in to get her away from Zac, Cressida hitting on her in the warm evening air, kissing Cressida… No, she'd keep all of that to herself, for the moment. It could all turn out to be nothing. She couldn't rely on her instincts when it came to romance.

[Xena] Tell me something good?

That went through. Cassie's response was three dots in a bubble, shortly joined by Laodice. Xena slid her phone back into the side pocket of her leggings, took an enormous bite of her muffin, and a scalding sip of coffee. She'd check later, and hope the connection had cleared up. She really wanted to hear about something good.

She thought, again, of Cressida's mouth on hers.

The rumor about the murdered man in the cabaret tent had spread to Stage Two by the time she got there. She didn't bother to correct anyone anymore, just kept her head down and gave waiting artists the same spiel.

At least, the ones she was allowed to approach. A member of Kithara's entourage made it clear that Kithara would not be appearing in some two-bit band documentary without a hefty licensing fee. Aoide Waters didn't have quite as many people in her entourage, but her manager took a cue off Kithara's people, and was working himself into a big snit when Aoide herself said, "Sorry, did you say Paris and the Archers?"

"Yes," Xena said.

"Oh my gosh, I'm a huge fan! I'm so happy they're opening for me tomorrow."

"I'm Paris's cousin," Xena told her, because she recognized an opening when she saw one, and Aoide looked like she might faint with the thrill of it. So too bad about Kithara, but that was another permission gained, and a good one. Xena stuck around long enough to ask Aoide if they could set up a real interview later, and then went back out into the festival grounds.

Which were suddenly and overwhelmingly crowded. At some point while she'd been backstage at Stage Two, the gates had opened, and the paying guests had started flooding through them. She hesitated, behind the security fence that kept her separated from the mass of humanity.

Someone else was coming in the gate, someone with a runner's build and the eyes that had caught her attention immediately and the hands that had touched her with such love "Xena?"

"Hi, Zac," Xena said. Of course he was there. Of course he was. She had no idea why he sounded so surprised, now that they both knew the other was around. "Are you doing a gig today?" Zac's attempts to break into music had never been very successful, but maybe he was finally getting some traction.

"No, I'm MC for this afternoon."

"Oh, okay. Well, have fun." She shifted her weight, preparing to go.

"Wait," Zac said. "Xena, I'm glad I caught you. I was going to text, but the network..."

"I changed my phone," Xena said. It had been the only way she'd been able to get herself away from her old contacts list and the people that had once been so important; she'd refused to transfer it to the new phone, and steadfastly kept herself from downloading any of her old apps.

"Oh," Zac said. "Well, I'm glad I caught you, actually. I was talking to Madison about you being here, and she was like, actually, that's great, you should do a reconciliation video."

"What?"

"Yeah, like it could be a really good idea to do like a forgiveness video. You know, like a video where you explain yourself, and then I say, I forgive you and we, like, formally reconcile."

Had Zac always said like so often? It felt like something he'd picked up from Madison, his agent and manager.

"It would do amazing numbers," Zac added, and that sounded more like the man she remembered. He'd always had a good eye for trends.

"I'm sure it would," she said, "but I don't do that anymore."

"I thought you were getting back into it, though." He nodded at her camera. "Or are you still just thinking about it? Either way, it'd be an incredible relaunch opportunity for you."

"I'm behind the scenes," Xena said. "Shooting for someone else."

"Oh," Zac said, and she could see him thinking it through. That was Zac's charm. Everything he was thinking always appeared on his face. He sometimes said stupid or hurtful things, but he was never fake, and viewers responded to that.

She'd seen him think, "Fuck, no," as she went down on one knee, and felt the world crack around her. It was a wonder she'd ever been able to get up again.

"Well, if you ever did decide to go back to making content, this would clear a lot of ground for you," he said, and he was right about that too.

"This project is probably just a one-off," Xena said. "I don't know if I'll ever do anything like it again."

"Okay. Well, it would be great if you could do the duo video with me anyway."

"Why?" Xena said. "I feel like we've both said everything we need to say. I've apologized to you, several times, and I apologized to the fans before I shut everything down. I'm glad you feel able to say that you forgive me..." She left it hanging, because he'd never actually said that before. He'd said, "Thank you for apologizing," and she'd known he meant it. And, "I really thought I loved you," and meant that too. And then he'd cut her out of his life, as forgettable as a bad take.

"Oh, yeah," Zac said now, clear-eyed. "I do forgive you. I forgave you ages ago."

Something smoothed and settled in Xena, some spiky thing that liked to tear at her innards.

"I appreciate you saying that," she said quietly. "Very much."

"But you don't want to do the video."

"I mean, this is the part that counts," Xena said, gesturing between them. "It counts whether it's on camera or not."

"I know it counts," Zac said, looking frustrated. "It just doesn't have any breakthrough. Look, the truth is, a few of my metrics aren't looking so hot lately. The market is so fucking crowded now. And, you know, we always did better numbers together."

"Actually, my numbers were better on my own," Xena said, before she could help herself. It was true, though—Zac's solo channel had good numbers, and Zac and Xena pulled more audience for both of them, that was the whole point of crossover content—but when the spikes settled, Xena's solo channel had always pulled in more viewers and stronger demographics.

"It would really help me out," Zac said, and then leaned closer, his handsome face intent on hers. He was just an inch taller than her, but he'd always made it work for him. "Honestly? It would kind of make up for what you did."

Xena took a quick, stunned breath. "Okay," she said, fighting to keep her voice level. "Once again, I am sorry that I asked you to marry me on a livestream. It was wrong. I am sorry that I assumed so much about our relationship and the steps you wanted to take next and put you in a terrible position in front of thousands of people. None of that was good or fair. But I've acknowledged that, and I've apologized, and I think that's the best I can do without breaking my own boundaries."

"You could do this too," Zac said. "It would be amends on top of an apology. Put everything to bed, once and for all."

"I'll think about it," Xena said, Did she owe him? Would it help? She probably did owe him something, but this? She'd be exposing herself to the world again, bringing up all of those old videos, inviting the Internet to judge whether she'd been appropriately contrite, while Zac got credit for being merciful and gracious. All so that he could boost his numbers and maybe secure a few extra deals.

It left a sour taste in her mouth, but amends was one thing she'd never been able to offer him before. "I will think about it," she said.

"You do that." Zac tipped her the smile that had put him Number Four on the *Agora* list ranking the 30 hottest influencers under 30 and set off towards the stage. Xena glanced at her phone for the time. She could upload some short clips to the Archers social accounts and grab an early lunch before she had to go film their set.

There were so many *people* at Lotophagi and they were so *happy.* She'd used to do this sort of thing all the time, going to conventions and concerts and festivals without thinking about it, and she was beginning to realize just how isolated she'd become over the last two years. If the rumors of Troy's death had made it to the attendees, they weren't letting it affect the mood. People were buzzed and hyper, chattering to their friends, admiring outfits and hugging each other.

Unfortunately, with nearly ten thousand excited guests on the grounds, the network was spottier than ever. Xena was able to edit together some good clips, but uploading would have to wait for later that evening, when hopefully people would be less interested in their phones. Maybe not, though; too many people thought you weren't really at a concert unless you were filming it. She spent some of the cash she'd brought with her for a couple of fish tacos and half a plastic cup of terrible beer, and then headed to Stage One.

At first, she'd thought Paris and the Archers were overly pessimistic about their 1:00 p.m. slot. The gates had been open since 11:00 a.m. and there was a large-ish crowd gathered around the stage, listening to a pretty good set by a musical comedy duo. But as she set up in the wings, looking at the crowd through her lens instead of with her eyes, she could see what Paris had been talking about. There were people *there*, but they weren't paying much attention, apart from a die-hard group at the front who laughed at every cue the duo fed them. Mostly, people seemed to be drifting in, listening or half-listening for a song or two, and then drifting out again.

When the Archers went on stage, right on the dot at 1:00 p.m., there was a smattering of applause and some cheers. Half of the people up front left, but more pressed forward, some of them wearing Archers T-shirts. There were probably fifty Archers fans who had come to the festival *for* the Archers, and then another hundred or so who had heard of them, and made enough effort to get there on time for their first set. 150 was a decent audience for a barroom gig, but nothing compared to the total festival crowd.

But there were *many* more people just hanging around, happy to soak up the vibes, or maybe plotting to grab good spots for later acts, and that was who the Archers were aiming at.

Paris's attention to detail and practice had paid off. Even Prax, the newest member of the band, looked as if she'd been playing with them for decades, and Sapph, Corrina, and Phryne seemed to be communicating through telepathy as they swept through a mix of their older, folksier songs and some of their newer, more punk material. Paris worked the crowd in between songs, flirting and taunting, until some of the bystanders had been drawn in to join the audience near the front.

Xena tried for some decent audience shots, zooming in and framing them so that the rest of the concert grounds looked a little less empty. When Prax rolled out the staccato drums that opened the Archers' one genuine hit, a frisson went through the crowd. She caught that, and the surge forward from even more of the bystanders who collectively realized that hey, they knew that song.

Xena zoomed in on Paris at the bridge, electric with passion as she sang about the girl who'd almost got away: "But I meet you in that alley/with your white dress on/and I say I love you still/and you say it isn't gone/and all we can do is run," she sang, and some of the audience sang it with her.

Without a pause, the Archers rolled into their the second most-streamed song, one that Sapph and Paris had composed together. It was another energetic number, from the point of view of a woman who was setting fire to everything around her—first figuratively, then literally—to revenge herself on her cheating ex.

The last song of the set was new, and very quiet in comparison, a delicate, wistful number called "Good Enough" about someone finally going out with the girl of her dreams, deeply aware that the ghost of the woman's ex was haunting the relationship. Xena zoomed in on one listener to catch the girl's spellbound face, tears rolling down her cheeks as she listened, her hands clasped under her chin. "I just hope that I'm good enough, good enough," Paris sang into the echoes left by Corrina's last chord, and the applause was generous and sustained.

"Thank you!" Paris said. "We're Paris and the Archers, and we're opening for Aoide Waters on Stage Two tomorrow!" She waved to the crowd, picked up her guitar, and strutted off stage. Someone tried to start a chant for an encore, but it sputtered out after a minute, and the stagehands were already moving things around for the next act.

Paris's energetic, confident walk had sagged as soon as she hit stage left.

"That was a great set," Xena said. "And I got some good footage, too."

"Thanks," Paris said, looking tired, as the others joined them in the wings.

"That felt good!" Prax said, but there was an uncertain note in her voice.

"It was a great set," Sapph said, and shot a look at Paris, who for once picked up on a non-verbal cue.

"Yes," she said. "Excellent work, everyone. Remember, though, this is the warm-up. We've got to bring our A-game tomorrow."

"That's going to be tricky," Phryne said, her voice thrumming with barely contained anger. Xena looked at her squared shoulders and her out-thrust chin. Corrina was standing beside her, arms folded, and both of them were glaring at Paris. Something had happened, some rupture in the group.

"I said I'm sorry that I didn't ask," Paris said, but where she might normally sound impatient, unable to understand the problem, she just sounded tired again.

Sapph was standing behind Paris, ready to back her, and Prax was looking between the two camps, shifting from foot to foot.

"Paris signed us up for the evening show at the Spiegeltent tonight," Phryne informed Xena. "Without consultation. Five p.m. tech call, and we won't be on until at least ten, maybe after midnight. For a three song set between a contortionist and a fire-eater or whatever. And then, after springing that on us, we're supposed to bring our A-game tomorrow."

"I'll do a solo set," Paris said suddenly, and when Sapph looked like she might protest, she shook her head. "It'll be fine. Acoustic guitar and vocals. Phryne's right."

Phryne looked astonished for a second, then rallied. "Yes, I am," she said. "Can I get that in writing?"

"I'll text you," Paris said. "Oops, no reception."

Phryne gave her the finger, poking her tongue out to soften the sting. Corrina and Sapph relaxed, and the tension dissolved. But Paris's face was still sagging, her inexhaustible energy somehow exhausted.

It was the first time Xena could remember Paris backing away from a conflict.

"Oh," Xena said. "I forgot to tell you. Aoide Waters asked me to pass on that she loves you guys, and she's really excited you're opening for her tomorrow."

"Whoa, really?" Corrina said.

"Aoide Waters," Prax breathed, her eyes widening.

"Did she sound like she meant it?" Paris asked. "Do you think she'd be up for a guest spot, or interested in some kind of collaboration?"

"Can we get off the grind for two seconds?" Sapph said, nudging her, but Xena was satisfied. Paris's entire body had gone intent and sharp, like a cat narrowing in on the kill.

The Archers were piled into two volunteer-driven golf carts and driven away to Stage Two, and Xena waved them off without the slightest bit of envy. Soaking up the vibes would be fun, but she was betting a visit with Cressida and Lucian was going to be better.

Back at Lot D, she took a shower in the surprisingly nice ablutions block, brushed her teeth, and let down her hair.

As she headed for the mansion, for the first time in an hour or so she remembered that Troy had died. At first he'd been all she could think about, then he'd come to mind less and less frequently as the day wore on. She'd barely known the guy—a couple of sightings and one conversation was hardly a basis for real grief. But still, she'd liked him, and felt bad that he could slip out of focus so easily. Cressida had known him better, and Xena braced herself to be turned away at the security gate to the main house, in case Cressida had had second thoughts.

But one of the guards stationed there, one of the shaven-headed suit-wearers, checked her ID carefully and noted her name on a list. "Go up the main stairs, go to the right hallway, third door on the left," he said, in a heavy accent she couldn't place. Maybe South African?

"Thanks!" Xena said, taking her driver's license back. He glared at her, apparently unhappy about her enthusiasm, and she turned the bubbly up a notch, purely for the fun of poking the bear. "Wait, is that the third door on the left, like there are three doors on the left, or the third door in *total*, and that one's on the left?"

He looked both confused *and* annoyed. "Three doors. On the left."

"Um," Xena said, and toyed with the end of her ponytail. "Can I come back and ask you if I get lost?"

"Don't get lost," he said, narrow-eyed, and okay, that was too much threat for a doorman. Xena's glee died down a little, but her curiosity sharpened.

"Okay, thank you!" she said. "Say, that's an amazing accent. Where did you get it?"

He grunted something she didn't catch, and turned ostentatiously back to his computer screen. Xena mentally shrugged, and walked through the wide white arch at the back of the security area.

Something beeped twice, loud and sharp.

"What the—" Xena said.

"Don't move!" the guard barked, and two more suits appeared, their faces hard and, holy shit, *guns drawn*.

Xena stayed very still, her hands half-raised. It wasn't the first time she'd encountered threatening people with weaponry—some of the places she'd been in her former life weren't all that safe—but she'd always felt confident about her ability to talk or joke or intimidate her way out of trouble.

These guys didn't listen, they didn't laugh, and as for intimidation...that was going entirely the other way at the moment.

"Do you have weapon?" one of the new guys barked.

"No," Xena said. "Um, I have a camera?"

There was a rapid discussion in a language she didn't understand. "Put this camera down," she was ordered, and then someone produced a wand and waved it over her body. No beeps there. The camera got the same treatment, and got two beeps. The men nodded at each other, and the two newcomers vanished.

"You leave this here, pick up later," the original guard said, and Xena meekly placed the camera in a plastic tub on his desk.

Xena got the hazy impression that the house was beautiful, but she didn't stop to pay attention to the decor as she followed the guard's directions. Her mind was still turning over that peculiar interaction. That was *intense* security for a music festival, even when you accounted for the fact that the mansion probably housed some of the biggest VIPs. Her luggage had already been checked, after all. Those guards had been on a hair-trigger, ready for trouble. What were they protecting? What were they afraid of?

She slowed down as she turned down the right corridor. With an awful sense of doom, she recognized the man standing outside the third door on the left. Polished shoes. Popped collar shirt. Jeans that cost as much as the average family's rent for the year.

Dammond fucking Argive.

Chapter Nine

"What are you doing here?" Cressida asked, her voice pitched low. Lucian was happily playing in his room, but at any moment he might decide he was bored enough to find out who Mommy was talking to at the door. "Actually, never mind. Go away."

"I need to talk to you, Chrissy," Dammond said. His thumb was running restlessly over his fingers, but he kept his voice down. "Can I come in?"

"That's not the deal! We said *after* the festival. Come on, Dammond, I was just starting to think we could work this out. Don't ruin that."

Judging from the way Dammond's eyes widened, this was an effective argument, but he grimaced. "I know, I know. Can you come out for a minute or two, then?"

"Everything okay here?" a new voice asked, and even before she recognized it, Cressida felt a warm swelling of relief.

"Xena," she said, and Dammond gave her a startled look, then turned to stare at the tall figure coming down the corridor. "Yes, we're fine. I just need to talk to Mr. Argive for a second. Would you mind heading inside? Lucian's playing by himself, but just in case he needs something, or wonders where I've gone…"

"Of course," Xena said, though her eyes flashed from Dammond's face to Cressida's. Cressida couldn't blame her for being suspicious. This whole setup was suspicious.

Damn Dammond anyway.

She pushed the door open and stepped sideways to let Xena go past her. Her hair stirred with the movement of Xena's passage. A whisper of a clean, lemony scent; Xena's shampoo, maybe.

"Lucian, Xena is here," she called.

And then she was back in the hallway, facing Dammond again, closing the door firmly behind her. "All right," she said, keeping her voice down. "What's this about?"

"Not out here," Dammond said, and turned on his heel.

Cressida seriously considered turning around and going back inside. Lucian and Xena's company promised to be far more enjoyable than whatever this kind of posturing indicated.

But he'd looked genuinely worried, and he'd accepted her caveats. He really was trying.

She followed.

Dammond didn't go far. Just a few more doors down the corridor, past Kithara's suite, past a room whose occupant she hadn't spotted yet. There was the quick flash of a key as he unlocked a narrow door and gestured her inside.

Cressida felt another touch of unease. Dammond had the keys. Of course he did; this was his house. But that meant he had the keys to her room. If she'd shut the door in his face, might he have come in after her?

The room was narrow, but oddly wide for the janitor's closet it had been turned into, with a rack of cleaning supplies on one wall and a fire extinguisher on the other.

"I just heard about that guy dying," Dammond said, and looked at her intently. "Are you okay?"

His concern surprised her almost as much as the sudden wave of grief. Dammond wasn't much for empathy. He cared about the things and people he cared about, but mostly when they were right in front of him. She wasn't really a sensitive soul herself, but that had more to do with her completely justified trust issues.

She blinked back some inconvenient tears. "I'm fine. Thanks for asking."

"Did you know him?"

"Troy? Yes. Not very well, but I met him on my last European tour." And three weeks after that, she'd started at a new club so she could begin saving for her *next* tour. And she'd met Dammond instead.

"He helped you last night." A muscle was jumping in the corner of his jaw. "I couldn't help you. I wasn't supposed to even know you."

"You helped plenty," Cressida said, surprised. "You got that couple kicked out. I appreciate it."

Dammond nodded sharply. "They're gone," he said, with some satisfaction. "They won't bother you again. Anyway, I don't think you should perform tonight."

"Excuse me?" Cressida said. She wasn't trying to be sarcastic. For a second, she thought she must have misheard him.

But Dammond shrugged, his expression caught halfway between infuriatingly patient and duh-this-is-so-obvious, and said, "It's too dangerous."

"Are you canceling the show?"

"No?" Dammond said, and then saw her face. "I mean, it's not like, *dangerous* dangerous. It's just, what if it happens again? I don't want you to be there."

Cressida folded her arms. "If it's not too dangerous for everybody else, it's not too dangerous for me."

Dammond ran his hands through his hair, sticking it all up on end. He must really be worried; normally he didn't touch his hair once he'd arranged it to his satisfaction. She'd ruffled it herself, a time or two. Rumpled, he looked a lot more like the man she'd fallen in love with.

"Look, what if something happens to you?" he asked. "Think about Lucian. Don't you want to play it safe?"

Cressida's momentary fondness transitioned seamlessly into an urge to punch him in the face. "I think about Lucian more in one day than you have in his entire lifetime," she said.

"That's not fair! You don't know how much I've—"

"And don't talk to me about safety! You have a fire extinguisher hidden behind a locked door!"

Dammond looked at the fire extinguisher and visibly prevented himself from rolling his eyes. He picked it up, opened the door, placed it in the hallway with exaggerated care, and slammed the door with sudden force. The bottles on the cleaning rack rattled.

Cressida didn't jump, but only because she'd anticipated the move. In some ways, Dammond was very predictable.

"There are also fire alarms in every hallway," Dammond said. "Because I am actually concerned about people's safety, and especially yours."

Cressida hadn't noticed the alarms. She stuck her chin out. "Dammond, I'm going on tonight."

"I just don't think it's worth the risk," Dammond said.

"It's my risk, damn it. I appreciate the concern, but are you sure this isn't just about you not wanting me to take my clothes off in front of a crowd?"

Dammond made a face. "I mean, I'm not crazy about that, but I get it. That's your deal. I don't have to love your job to—anyway, I just want you to be all right."

Cressida very much didn't want him to finish the sentence he'd bitten off. "Okay."

"I've already talked to Jenny," Dammond added.

"You talked to Jenny?"

"Yeah, you know, just to make sure that there wouldn't be any problems if you pulled out now."

"There will be no problems," Cressida said, "because I will be performing. Everybody's performing. We're dedicating the night to Troy."

"Oh, sure," Dammond said. "Troy's the hero, but here I am trying to keep you safe, and I'm the bad guy."

"This conversation is over," Cressida said.

Dammond didn't move.

"Get out of my way, Dammond. If you think that this is making a good case for you to meet Lucian—"

"I knew you'd go there," Dammond said, a bitter twist to his lips. "Sure, threaten me with not meeting my son. But you'll ask some stranger to go in and sit with him, you trust her more than me, you *never* trusted me—"

"I loved you," Cressida said. She *had* asked Xena without hesitating, which wasn't her normal M.O. It had just seemed...right.

"But you never trusted me, Chrissy," Dammond said. "A lot of things could have been different if you had."

Cressida could have claimed that she *had* trusted him, and he'd betrayed her to stick by his terrible grandfather. But she didn't, because he was right. Part of her had never trusted Dammond. That was why she'd written that letter to Ask Cassandra, months before she'd left him. Even then, the doubt had been there.

"Dammond," she said, not sure whether she wanted to shout or soothe. "A lot of things could have been different, if we'd both done a lot of things differently. We didn't. Here we are. We can't take any of it back now. All we can do is try to figure out what happens next."

"I'm just worried for you," he said miserably.

For a moment, Cressida weakened. She *could* pull out of the show. Nobody would blame her for it. There wouldn't be any penalty. She could probably even talk Dammond into making sure she was paid.

But she had so few chances to perform. And she remembered again that moment of rightness when Klara had declared that tonight's show was for Troy.

"I'm sorry," she said, as gently as she could. "I understand that you're worried. But if the show is going ahead, I'm going to be in it."

Dammond didn't move for a moment. "Okay," he said finally. "What time? Maybe I'll show up to support you."

"I'm on after midnight," Cressida said. "More or less. Cabaret schedules can get a bit fuzzy."

"Okay," Dammond said, his head drooping. "I guess I'll see you then."

He stepped to the side, far enough that she could get past him to the door, not so far that she could do it without being close enough to touch. The air between them was charged with possibility. She could feel him looking at her, at her eyes, and her lips, and kept her gaze turned away. No invitation, no glimpse of an opening.

She was being kind, but she doubted he'd understand that. On the way out the door, she nearly tripped over the fire extinguisher. She propped it against the wall, and went back down the hall.

Lucian had come out of his room. He and Xena were sitting on the rug, playing with the Lego set Elena had let him take "home" from daycare. Elena had become Lucian's key conversational topic over the last two days. Elena had given everyone in daycare hot dogs for lunch. Elena was from New Zealand, which was in the Southern Hemisphere. New Zealand had lots of birds that couldn't fly. Tonight Elena was going to make him a special dessert called fairy bread.

"I've been to New Zealand," Xena said. "But I don't think I've ever had fairy bread."

"You should stay with me, and then you can have some too," Lucian said generously.

"Sorry, buddy. I have to go to work, like your mom." Xena looked up as Cressida closed the door behind her. Lucian hadn't heard it, over the noise of clattering blocks and his own happy chatter.

"Paris is doing a solo act tonight in the cabaret show," Xena said. There was something guarded in her face, a deliberate putting aside of questions. "Filling a gap."

"That sounds good. Tech call at five?"

Xena nodded, and Cressida folded herself down onto the rug. "What are we making, Lucy Goose?"

"A farm," Lucian said. "Elena lived on a farm when she was little. A farm with ten thousand cows."

"I don't know if we have ten thousand cows," Xena said seriously, looking through the box.

Lucian looked up at her. "It's pretend!"

"Oh! Thank you for explaining."

"Yes, because, cows are big."

"How big?" Xena asked. She held her hands a foot apart. "This big?"

"Bigger."

Xena expanded her arms. "This big?"

Lucian caught on. "Bigger!" he said, giggling, and devolved into screaming laughter as Xena fully extended her arms, then got off the floor to make the biggest shapes she could, mooing and tossing her hair—"That's horses! You're being horses!"—and threatening to charge at Lucian.

Once Lucian had lassoed the naughty cow and shooed it back to the ranch, he settled into building his farm, muttering happily to himself as he laid out the little figurines on what was probably a priceless antique rug. Cressida joined Xena on the couch, which had been designated the naughty cow's pen. Lucian had piled cushions around her—"this is your fence"—and Xena looked flushed and rosy and *delicious*.

"Do you have nieces and nephews?" Cressida asked.

"Not yet. My sister Cassie might get there." That guarded look again, for the first time since Cressida had first come in, as if mentioning Cassie had reminded her of something. "I definitely want kids, though. Can I get an expert opinion on how I'm doing?"

"Are you kidding?" Cressida said, and gestured at Lucian. "You're perfect. Can I keep you on call?" She heard what she'd said the second it left her mouth, and flinched at the thought it might be taken as pressure, but Xena just grinned at her.

"If you play your cards right," she said, her voice pitched to stay under Lucian's interest level.

Cressida coughed. "So, other than filming musicians and escorting shocked women out of terrible situations, what do you do with your time?"

"Less than I'd like," Xena said, but she swung easily enough into an explanation. Paid work didn't feature highly, but who was Cressida to judge? Exercise did.

"You do two workouts a day?" Cressida said. "No *wonder* your biceps are so impressive."

Xena laughed. "I really do like working out. I wasn't just doing it for the views." She looked thoughtful. "Actually, I probably work out *more* now. Fewer demands on my time."

"No, no, for sure," Cressida said. "If you want to try pole again, hit me up."

"Do you do private lessons?" Xena asked, and then blushed. "I mean, um, I don't usually like group classes."

"You used to do them," Cressida said. That had been another popular series on XO, Xena, Xena being introduced to a new sport or activity, and gamely attempting Zumba with the grannies, or soccer with a bunch of ponytailed eight-year-olds. For somebody who was such a competent athlete, she'd put herself in a lot of positions to be a beginner again.

Not her martial arts videos, though. There, she'd looked completely at home. The trolls got really frantic about those videos, because they didn't believe a fat person could be good at this, or they didn't like seeing a woman break boards and bricks, or they didn't like women existing in public, calm and deadly and absolutely uninterested in their opinions on the matter.

"I tried a few group classes, afterwards," Xena said, and she was talking to her hands, that cloud slipping over her again. "People stared."

Cressida's hand moved towards her, then stilled.

"I'm probably being stupid," Xena said. "My sister says there's this thing called the spotlight effect, where you're fifty percent more likely to think people are noticing or thinking about you than they actually are."

"Well, maybe that's true," Cressida said carefully. "But I don't think you're being stupid. You were pretty famous. I'm sure people did stare."

"Internet-famous," Xena said dryly. "I wasn't front-page news or anything." She straightened up, squared her shoulders. "Anyway, I need to find something else to do. I don't technically *need* to work, but living off my investments clearly isn't that good for me. I do some volunteering at an after-school sports program, but that's only twice a week."

Nice for some, Cressida almost said, thinking of the room she shared with Lucian and the frustrating, soul-tearing grind of trying to claw back some financial independence. If she couldn't work out a new deal with Dammond, she was going to have to go for waitressing, retail, or cleaning, and she hated all three.

"Tell me about you," Xena said. "You already know some stuff about my life. It was a curated version, but it was still real. What about you?"

Cressida shrugged. "I grew up in the system, mostly. I went back to my parents a few times, but I don't really remember them. After that, I was with foster families."

She watched Xena's face twitch. Nearly everybody did, when she talked about her childhood.

"No big traumas," she said. "The system gets a bad rap, and often it's deserved, but I lucked out. Nice families. I send them cards in the holidays. Some of my foster siblings could be a lot, but you get used to it. I got to stay in one school for junior high with one family, and then stayed with another family for the whole of high school. My last foster mom encouraged me to go to college, but I didn't know what I'd even study, and the debt..."

"So, burlesque?"

Cressida shook her head. "Not right away. I tried musical theatre first."

"Wow."

"I'd done dance squad, cheer, gymnastics, and every show I could at high school. No one wanted me to sing, but I could really dance. I figured I had a shot. So I waitressed, and took a bunch of classes, and auditioned and auditioned and auditioned. I was *this* close to getting a spot in a *Chicago* traveling tour." She held up her fingers, squeezed together. "But when they did the final line-up I was too short. And waitressing was only just paying the bills, not to mention I hated it. So I did some dancing at clubs."

Xena looked puzzled.

"Gentlemen's clubs," Cressida clarified, with a quick glance at Lucian. He was contentedly moving his cows around the rug. She wasn't ashamed of doing sex work, but the conversation about Mommy's employment history could definitely wait for another decade or so. "That's how I got into pole."

"Oh," Xena said. "Oh, yeah, I've met a few people in that line of work."

"Right, I remember," Cressida said. It was nice, knowing that the person you were talking to had gone on public record supporting sex workers. "I did some extras too, which is how I first met my best friend, Anna." She put the slightest emphasis on *extras* and watched. Even people who were publicly cool with prostitution could be weird about it, one-on-one.

Xena nodded. Message received, and not judged. That was another tick in the plus column for her. "So what led you into burlesque?"

"I landed regular shifts at a good club that became my home base. Some of the girls there were into burlesque, and they invited me to a show. I was hooked after that. There are no height restrictions in burlesque, and no weird weight stuff—well, some weird weight stuff, but less than I was used to, from my dance background. The props are a lot of fun. And it turned out I was really good at it, and I loved it enough to want to get even better. So much of burlesque is the story you're telling the audience, the game you're playing with them."

"I can't wait to see you," Xena said, her eyes soft.

Cressida thought of Dammond, jittery and angry in that cleaning closet, all but ordering her not to perform, and couldn't help making the inevitable comparison.

"Mommy, can we watch *Bluey*?" Lucian said, and climbed up onto the couch between them, all knees and elbows in various squishy places, the farm abandoned on the floor.

"What's *Bluey*?" Xena asked.

Cressida laughed. "You'll see. Hope you're not a crier."

***

Xena wasn't a crier, although she sniffed at a few poignant moments.

After, they traded more stories, with occasional comments from Lucian. Xena had stories about far off locations and interesting locales. Cressida had stories about traveling as part of a festival tour, some of which she censored, and she had the feeling that Xena was dropping certain details out of her stories too. More interesting was that Xena had actually lived in Cressida's old neighborhood for a while.

"Can't believe we never ran into each other at the deli."

Xena shrugged. "We—I wasn't home very much."

"Where do you live now?" Lucian demanded, and Xena told him. Cressida saw Lucian trying to fit this into his personal map of the city.

"Near the park with all the ducks," she told him.

Lucian nodded. "I know that park. You can come with us to feed the ducks."

Xena caught her breath and met Cressida's eyes.

"We'll have to see, Lucy Goose," Cressida said. "Xena might be busy." It was too easy, too fast. Lucian liked Xena, and that was fine, so did she, but you couldn't bring someone into a kid's life and then say they wouldn't be there anymore. And she definitely didn't know Xena well enough for that.

Lucian nodded again, satisfied with the equivocation, and she breathed more easily. Right now, Xena was just a friendly grown-up they'd met on Mommy's work trip. She'd have to think hard before repeating this kind of meeting in the city.

Just before four, it rained again. Lucian explained to Xena that this happened nearly every day on the island, and then they walked him back to the childcare center, where Elena made his entire week by announcing they could go play in the pool before dinner.

"And then I don't need a bath," he said, sliding his eyes towards Cressida.

She kissed the top of his head, and then sniffed it. "Depends how smelly you are, goose."

Lucian giggled, the kind of laugh that could go hysterical without warning. Cressida gave him a goodbye hug, distracted him by making him check he had his swimsuit in his backpack, and then shot out the door before he could get off-track again.

She met Xena in the hallway, giddy as a teenager cutting class.

"He's a great kid," Xena said, which was a perfect way to get herself into Cressida's good books, and therefore would have been suspicious, except that she clearly meant it.

"Light of my life," Cressida said. She made as if to pick up her giant duffel bag, carefully packed with her costume and props for the evening, but Xena hoisted it easily and slung it over one shoulder. Her biceps swelled with the motion. Cressida had to fight the urge to fan herself a little.

"Let's go," she said instead.

The rain hadn't slowed down the fun. The festival was going hard, music pounding from both big stages, and a lot of smaller acts and exhibits were getting audiences too, people spattered with body paint, glitter and mud as they roamed from site to site. Their bright clothes and brighter smiles lifted Cressida until she felt as if she were floating, skimming over the grass instead of walking on it, her heart pulsing to the beat of the crowd. Troy was dead, and she was sad about that, but there was joy there too.

And then Xena said, "So, Dammond Argive," and Cressida came back to earth with a thud.

"Yes, he's Lucian's father." It wasn't really worth denying—Lucian and Dammond weren't clones, and she could claim Lucian's blond curls came from her, because they might, but it was an easy conclusion to draw. She wouldn't insult Xena's perception by denying it. "Lucian doesn't know, of course."

"Right," Xena said. "I won't tell him. I won't tell anyone."

Cressida nodded. She hadn't been worried about that, and now she wondered why. *You trust her more than me, you* never *trusted me.*

"I'm wondering about something else," Xena said, very carefully. "Because of the timing, and Lucian's age. Have you heard about an advice column called *Ask Cassandra*?"

Cressida stopped moving. Xena stopped with her, and they stood for a moment, a still, silent spot in the middle of all that vibrant, noisy motion.

"You read *Ask Cassandra*," Cressida said after a moment. That email, the one she'd written in a moment of doubt, after yet another stupid argument about Adrestus's involvement in their lives. Cassandra had told her to leave. She'd ignored the response when it was published—dramatic stuff, she wasn't in the dire straits Cassandra seemed to be imagining, and anyway Cressida had probably been exaggerating in her original email. Pregnancy hormones messed with your head, everyone knew that.

But five months later, at that rehearsal dinner, she'd thought of Cassandra's blunt advice. *Leave him. Leave him as soon as possible.*

Well, she'd left *possible* to the very last minute.

But Cassandra's advice might have saved her life. Adrestus Argive had truly hated her. Cressida had gone back and forth over the events of that night a million times, but one thing she'd never doubted was that his threat had been real. Adrestus had genuinely thought of her as an inconvenient incubator for his grandson, and if she'd stuck with Dammond and refused to comply with Adrestus, he might have had her destroyed with as little thought as he spared on defective equipment.

But wait. Cressida frowned. The initial email and response had been public, but they'd also been anonymous, and no one had worked out the link between that letter and herself and Dammond until after the fact. There had to be way more than one pregnant girl worried that her Cinderella story wasn't a dream after all. Xena *couldn't* know about what had happened at rehearsal dinner or the terrible way everything had ended. It had probably been popular gossip among the Argives' well-heeled friends, but she didn't think Xena moved in those circles, and none of that story had ever made it into print.

"Can I ask why you bring that up?" she said carefully.

Xena let out a slow breath. "I'm close to the woman who writes it."

"Oh," Cressida said, and closed her eyes. So that was how she knew. "And Dammond tried to get her fired."

"How do you know that?"

"He threatened to sue me too. Breach of promise, if you can believe it. Later, my lawyer told me that he'd never have gotten anywhere, but I wasn't exactly rational at the time. I was sitting in Anna's apartment on a Sunday afternoon, big as a house and eating pickle and peanut butter sandwiches between crying jags, and then Hera Rheczack called me. Have you ever met her?"

"A couple of times," Xena admitted.

"She made an impression. She told me Dammond had threatened to sue Olympus and wanted Cassandra's head on a platter. She'd already spoken to several of the catering personnel, and didn't have a good impression of Dammond, but she wanted to hear my side of the story. Before she talked to me, I was wondering whether I had enough savings to leave the country, and getting really upset that none of the airlines would let me travel by plane because I was so close to full term. Afterwards…" Cressida picked at a loose fleck of skin beside her thumbnail. "I can't even remember exactly what she said. I just knew that she would do her best to make it right, and her best seemed really, really good."

"She's a good person to have on your side," Xena said. Her face was still guarded.

"Look," Cressida said. "I can see you want to say something about Dammond. I get it. He's not always a great guy, and he's pissed off a lot of people—including me. Can we just… Can we put it on hold? Until after tonight?" Hidden in that, she realized the implication that they'd see each other again after tonight. They'd been doing that all afternoon, references to restaurants the other had to try, parks they could visit…. If this was just friendship, then it was the fastest Cressida had ever made a friend.

But it had to be friendship. Cressida didn't believe in that U-Hauling lesbian stereotype, the cliche about the women who moved in together after the second date. Technically, she and Xena hadn't even gone on *one* date.

"We can put it on hold," Xena said. "Of course we can. I don't need to—you're a grown woman, you make your own decisions. I just wanted you to know what I knew."

"Got it," Cressida said, and reached for her hand, squeezing the long fingers.

Xena squeezed back, and something thumped hard into the pit of Cressida's stomach.

They walked the last five minutes to the Spiegeltent in silence, hand-in-hand, like any other happy couple in that bright throng.

Chapter Ten

Ernest was on duty at the main door of the Spiegeltent again.

"Seriously, man, don't you get a break?" Xena asked.

"Don't you?" he said, and tilted his head to one side. "I heard you were right there when it happened."

"Cressida, thank goodness," Jenny called. She was heading towards them at a fast clip, a thick sheaf of stapled paper in her hand. "What with everything this morning, I forgot to get your signature on the release. Can you take these backstage and read them over?"

Cressida took the papers. "I'd better," she said to Xena, and let go of her hand. "See you soon."

Not many of the performers had arrived yet, but Xena saw Paris sitting at the far end of a row of seats, her guitar case in her lap. She wasn't interacting with the others at all.

"Have a good night," she told Ernest, but he gestured for her to wait a moment.

"I just had a few security questions," he said quietly.

"Oh. Sure."

"There's a rumor going around that the wire was frayed," Ernest said.

Xena blinked at him. "I hadn't heard that."

"Did you see it? The wire?"

Xena thought back. She'd seen the cable in the shallow puddle, winding back into the shadows behind the bar. Once Darnell had declared the area safe, she hadn't paid it any mind. All her attention had been on Troy.

"I don't know if it was frayed. I didn't inspect it closely or anything."

"You couldn't say if it's been replaced now?" Ernest said, making a minute gesture with his chin towards the bar.

"I hope it has," Xena said, with more emotion than she'd intended. The thought of the same cable that had killed Troy powering his memorial show was obscene, somehow. "Probably, right? Better safe than sorry."

"Sure, that makes sense. You didn't see or hear anything suspicious before that?"

"Like what?" Xena said, staring at him.

Something flickered across Ernest's face, too fast for her to follow. "Like anything."

Xena looked at his burly frame and made an educated guess. "Were you maybe a cop before you went into security?" she asked.

"Ah, no," Ernest said ruefully. "Just a bouncer. Sometimes night watchman."

But he'd probably wanted to join the force. Watched a lot of cop shows, dreamed of himself being the heroic detective solving cases. Those guys somehow never dreamed of themselves being the asshole caught on video using excessive force at a traffic stop.

Xena tried to keep the judgment off her face, but Ernest must have seen it, because he sighed. "Sorry," he said. "I'm probably just jumping at shadows."

"You probably shouldn't go spreading rumors," she said carefully, not wanting to sound patronizing. From Ernest's wince, she didn't quite manage it.

"Yeah, I know," he said. His eyes tracked over her shoulder, and she turned to see one of the younger security guys in the dark suits striding in. He was still wearing his sunglasses in the tent. What a jackass.

"Uh, I'd take it as a kindness if you didn't share this conversation," Ernest said tentatively.

He probably didn't want the younger, more serious-looking guys to give him shit. "No problem," she said. "Have a good night."

Paris was still staring at the stage, where a comedian was running through his set in a quick monotone, pausing at various points to cue Darnell for the sound effects. She barely moved when Xena took a seat beside her.

"Hey," Xena said. "Just figured I'd ask if you wanted anything in particular for the filming tonight?"

"No," Paris said. After a moment, she blinked. "Uh, yeah, close-ups for the bridges, see if you can get my hands for some of the fingering at the start."

"A lot will depend on the lighting," Xena warned her.

Paris glanced at Darnell. "I'll ask for a spot." She made an obvious attempt to rouse herself further. "I look best in cool tones."

"That should work," Xena said. She should leave it there. Go and find something to eat, pick up an Archers T-shirt at the merch tent as a memento. "Is everything okay?" she asked instead.

Paris slumped. "I think the band's breaking up," she said bleakly. "Phryne and Corinna want to start a family, and Helen's not happy that I'm away so often." She shot Xena a defensive look. "Not that she's wrong. I know it's not fair. But tours are the only way to make money from music these days, and we're not making much."

"I thought you were doing okay with those corporate gigs?"

"I hate them," Paris said tonelessly. "We all hate them. I really hoped this would work. Opening for Aoide—I put a lot into that. It could be a real opportunity."

"So it might turn out okay?"

Paris straightened. "Yes. Maybe. We've still got a shot." She looked at the stage. "I should have asked them, before I offered to fill in for Jenny. But I just assumed they'd be with me. They're usually with me."

Xena thought back to that brief, uncomfortable moment backstage—Corinna and Phryne on one side, Paris and Sapph on the other, Prax caught between them like a kid trying to figure out which parent she should be supporting.

"I'll try and get some good footage for you," she said awkwardly. "Actually, let me see if the network's doing better. I might be able to upload some stuff now."

Paris tugged at her lip, looking thoughtful. "Cassie would have asked me if I wanted advice."

"I don't have any."

"And Laodice would have said something cheerful and positive."

"Yeah, also not me."

"What would your brother do, if he were here?"

"Iulus? I don't know," Xena said, impatient with this little game. "He'd probably say you should do what makes you happy. That's what he told me, when I quit."

"He thought you should keep XO, Xena going?" Paris said. "See, I told you—"

"No. Iulus thought I should do what made me *happy*, whether that was XO, Xena, or going back to school, or... Whatever." She thought. "Actually, he said I should find out what makes me happy, and then do it."

"Did you?"

"I'm doing okay." She stabbed at her phone. The network *was* doing better. She uploaded a few stills—Sapph in a pile of bags, Phryne still and poised with her violin, Prax grinning wildly, hand raised to catch the drumstick she'd just spun into the air.

"Are you wearing *cargo pants*?" Paris asked. Xena had been sitting beside her for an entire conversation, but of course she'd only noticed now.

"Yes," Xena said. "So I can carry my gear without a bag. This is an actual-use case for cargo pants." She glanced at Paris pointedly. "I'm surprised you can fit anything in those skinny jeans."

Paris took too long to come up with a come-back, so Xena checked the shortest video she'd been able to edit together from the cocktail meet-and-greet: Paris singing while Cressida tottered around in her sexy doll make-up. Troy wasn't in that one. Hang on, there was a split second shot of the VIP area in background. She'd need to fuzz the faces.

Editing on her phone *sucked* but she definitely had the experience. She pinch-zoomed in and scrubbed, then paused. Ernest and Dammond were in that frame, side-by-side as Dammond stood at the edge of the VIP space. Dammond was watching Cressida. Nearly everyone was.

Ernest was watching Dammond. There was no expression on his face. No smile for the big boss, no ingratiating body language. He was staring at Dammond as if he was sizing up a threat.

Or a target.

Xena hesitated. Then she cut the frame out altogether and sent it to herself as a still.

"All good?" she said, turning her phone to show Paris the completed video.

Paris watched. "There isn't enough of the Archers."

"We're trying to grab people's attention," Xena said. "New content, remember? Trust me."

"Okay, fine. Upload it."

"Yes, your highness," Xena said, rolling her eyes. She'd barely pressed the button when a shit-ton of notifications appeared. The sisters group chat had caught up on the action. She clicked without thinking and stared.

"What?" Paris said, already crowding her. "Oh, ew."

"Don't ew, some of us like boys too," Xena said, trying—and failing—to keep her giggles contained. She'd asked her sisters for 'something good' and they'd obviously conspired before sending photos of their men. Telfer, bent over a baseboard with a toothbrush, scrubbing it clean, his ass tight and round in his black slacks. Manny, lifting boxes onto the vineyard truck, his shoulders straining against his T-shirt. Telfer, scowling at a screen as if he could change the numbers on it with the power of his mind, the tip of his tongue toying with the top of his pen in an unconsciously suggestive way. Manny, on the dock at Lake Lydia in his red swimming shorts, obviously posing for a private joke, turning over his shoulder in coy pin-up girl pose, finger to his kissy-face lips.

Paris raised her eyebrows at that one. "Kind of hot, if he were a girl."

"That's a rude thing to say about the man whose wife you ran away with," Xena said severely.

"She was *barely* his wife," Paris said. "And she didn't want to marry him in the first place."

"Then she shouldn't have said she did," Xena said, but it lacked force. It was an old story now. Paris was never going to admit that she and Helen had done anything wrong, and Manny was way better off with Cassie anyway. She was really thinking about Cressida, who'd left just *before* her wedding, but was tied to Dammond Argive anyway through their son.

"What's that weird mark?" Paris said, pointing at the massive white splotch on Manny's shoulder blade.

"Oh, it's the family birthmark," she said, and then, with a sudden spirit of mischief, "Didn't Helen ever tell you about it?"

Paris scowled. "Ha ha. We don't talk about Manny."

Which would be a little tricky, because Helen's sister was married to Manny's brother Augie. But somehow, Xena wasn't surprised that Paris and Helen managed to live in a bubble where Manny never came up.

Still, it was fun to poke her. "Cassie says Manny's dad and grandfather had it too, and so does Orestes, Augie's son."

"Oh yeah, I remember it from Orestes's baby photos," Paris said, perking up. Apparently nephews were an allowed topic of conversation in the Chen-Laconia household.

"Cassie found some old love letters from the 1800s that mention it as well, so it must go back a ways."

"Those are some weird genes."

"I need silence off-stage," Darnell called, and they shut up while an acrobat-mime in a silver bodysuit unrolled a glittering ribbon and made gorgeous rippling patterns over a sound track of ocean noises and bird-calls. Xena wasn't sure how that would work for a rowdy cabaret crowd, but it was beautiful to watch. Darnell had to adjust several lighting cues.

The mime talked him through it in a broad Australian accent, which was weirdly disconcerting.

"So why did your sisters send you spank-bank material?" Paris asked, the second the mime left the stage.

"You're disgusting."

"Yeah, but also, why?"

"It's not spank-bank material. It's to cheer me up. Did you know Zac was here?"

Paris's eyes slid away, and Xena sat up from her slouch. "Paris. Did you know Zac was going to be here *before* we came?"

Paris inspected her short nails. "I might have seen something on his socials."

Xena stared at her. "You know, I would say this was unbelievable, but in fact I can totally believe you did this. Did you think I'd refuse to come, if I knew?"

Paris shrugged. "Would you have canceled?"

Xena gritted her teeth. "No. I made a commitment. But I would have appreciated a fucking heads-up!"

"Voices down off-stage!" Darnell called again, and this time it was with an annoyed glance directly at them. Xena made an apologetic gesture and stood up, heading towards the exit. She needed some dumplings, and maybe another half-cup of bad beer.

Ernest tipped her a conspiratorial smile as she went past. His shaven-headed buddy didn't bother to register her existence.

What Xena would have said to Paris, if she'd had the chance, was that the pictures weren't about the sexiness of the subjects, whether it was accidental or play-deliberate. It was about the happiness of the women who had taken them. "Look at this," her sisters were saying. "This is good. You can have this too."

She didn't want or love Zac anymore. But she'd loved him for so long, it had worn a groove into the pattern of her life.

Without letting herself think about it, she dropped a picture of Cressida into the chat. Cressida in her doll makeup, blowing a kiss at her across the room, VIPs in the background.

No response. Either they weren't in the chat, or the network was down again.

"Do what makes me happy," she muttered to herself, and grimaced. If only her little brother *could* tell her what that would be.

***

Cressida usually read her contracts very carefully. Tonight, she skimmed, flicking through pages while Klara made impossible shapes with her body, and two drag queens discussed their wig choices for the evening.

The top three sheets were a liability waiver for the assault from Mr. and Ms. Grabby Hands last night, acknowledging that the festival had removed them from the venue and promising not to sue Lotophagi, its owners, or investors. The waiver didn't say anything about not suing or pressing charges against the Grabby Handses, and Cressida entertained a nice little fantasy about them getting some well deserved comeuppance for a few moments, then sighed and let it go. It would never get anywhere. Juries and defense attorneys were notoriously unsympathetic even to women who were violently assaulted in their own homes while fully dressed. "Circo-Slut gets molested at a performance" wouldn't even make it to court.

The next pack was much thicker, a statement of liability for her act and a bunch of health and safety stuff where she had to state her performance had been certified safe by an independent inspector. Cressida rolled her eyes. Of course it hadn't. Everybody ignored those regulations. Most of what the circo kids did was completely insane, and what kept them safe was experience and common sense, not any kind of red tape strapped on by some bureaucrat who couldn't imagine anything riskier than climbing a stepladder. People looked after themselves and their equipment.

There were still accidents. Troy hadn't even been on stage.

There were risks to being a burly girl, too. If a heels dancer went on right after a martini glass bath had splashed soapy water all over the stage, you were just begging for trouble. And then there were the even more athletic acts. She'd seen a performance in Venezuela go completely haywire when a woman on rollerblades had accidentally broken her long strand of pearls, which had promptly acted like ball-bearings.

Cressida signed on the dotted line anyway. The festival was obviously just covering its ass.

The last form was some kind of insurance contract in impenetrable legalese, of a type she'd never seen before. Jenny was backstage with the props supervisor, and Cressida wandered over.

"Just had a few questions about this one," she said, and Jenny squinted at it.

"Oh, that's for if you get injured," she said. "We know a lot of performers aren't covered for injuries during their acts, especially if they need to go to a clinic out of network."

Klara snorted. "Americans," she said, not quietly.

Jenny ignored her. "And even if you are, it can be a hassle to deal with when you're on the road. So if you sign that, you're covered by the Lotophagi insurance policy. If anything happens, you file an incident report and the company claims on your behalf. Then they pay out to you."

"Whoa," Cressida said, impressed.

"Good, right?" Jenny said. "They're really trying to build a reputation here. The acts this year are kind of small potatoes—no offense—but Mr. Argive is keen on expansion, maybe branching out to several locations. He sees a lot of potential."

"This was Mr. Argive's idea?"

"Actually, it was mine," Jenny said, beaming. "I was part of the Events team at Argive Holdings, but he brought me with him when Lotophagi got off the drawing board. But he supported it right away, said it was a great measure." Jenny had clearly joined the Dammond fan club.

"So what's in it for him?" Cressida said.

Jenny looked mildly affronted for a minute, and then gave in. "Well, you also waive the right to lay suit in the event of an accident," she said. "But you wouldn't want to anyway, because the insurance payout would cover everything you need, you wouldn't have to pay for a lawyer, and you wouldn't run any risk of not getting a settlement. It's really best for everyone."

"Backed by Argive Holdings," Cressida said. When Dammond had first told her about Lotophagi, he'd given her the impression that it was something he'd joined for fun in the later stages. Investing, letting them hire his family's holiday estate as a venue; that made sense. But if he was involved from the beginning—from the *drawing board*—why hadn't he told her that?

Jenny was looking shifty. "Um, I'm not supposed to talk much about Argive involvement," she said, her voice lowered. "Can you keep that on the DL? Mr. Argive doesn't want the publicity. He's pretty modest."

Cressida nearly laughed in her face. *Modesty* and *Dammond Argive* didn't even belong in the same sentence. If he was trying for secrecy he had some sort of angle, but she'd be damned if she could be bothered figuring it out.

"Was Troy covered?" she asked instead. "Can his family be compensated?"

"Oh," Jenny said, her eyebrows drawing together. "Yes, I suppose they could be claimants."

"Life cover," Cressida said, flipping through the policy. "Yep, there it is. To named beneficiaries." She wrote Lucian's name in. It was an absurd amount of money to go to a four-year-old, but Anna was the executor of her will and would make sure it was handled appropriately.

Not that anything was going to happen to her. She rapped the props table with her knuckles.

"I'll let his parents know," Jenny said, looking cheered up. "It can't make up for what happened, of course but—"

"But it helps," Cressida said firmly. "Money makes a difference. Anyone who says it doesn't is trying to sell you something."

"Yes, I suppose."

"How are they? His parents, I mean?"

Jenny grimaced, and for the first time Cressida realized they were about the same age. Thirtyish, and just figuring out that the world could be unexpectedly awful.

Cressida had figured that out a lot earlier, but she was betting Jenny's life had been less tumultuous, up till now.

Klara had disappeared at some point during the conversation to go through her cues. She came back and pointed at Cressida. "You're up after the next one."

Jenny jumped and put her hand to her headset. "Darnell, put the runsheet through me," she said, sounding exasperated. She held her hand out for Cressida's papers.

"Whoa, okay," Cressida said. On the one hand, they were moving a lot faster than she'd expected, and a smooth tech was a good tech. On the other hand, she hadn't even unpacked her duffel yet. She signed the insurance POA and handed the whole pile to Jenny, who left at a trot. "I've got my music on this thumb drive, Klara, would you mind running it out?"

"I can do that."

The props manager was hovering. "Holy shit, is that an executioner's block?" they asked, as Cressida lined things up.

"Yep. Made out of yoga blocks, so it's not heavy. I need that placed front and center before I enter stage left, and then I need someone stage right ready to hand me this when I reach for it. On the very edge of stage right. I don't want to have to go off-stage to get them."

"An *ax*? What's your act?"

"The death of Mary, Queen of Scots. But sexy."

"Dark," the props manager said appreciatively. They were already beckoning a black-clad stage-hand over.

"It's a hit," Cressida assured them. She couldn't do the full costume until show time, but she kicked off her Converse and strapped on the costume shoes, then ran for stage left on her tip-toes, so that the heels didn't clack against the wooden floor. Her blood was fizzing. Finally, she could do what she did best.

***

Xena had vanished by the time Cressida had gone back to front of house, probably to grab dinner. She might not have even seen Cressida's tech run. Cressida, when she thought about it, was pleased by that. Let Xena see her in her full, bloody glory. Not a practice run, not an improvised cocktail entertainment, but the real deal.

She grabbed dinner herself, and skipped the first part of the evening show. Backstage space at the Spiegeltent was limited, but Lotophagi had set up a tent out back as a dressing room-slash-holding pen, with volunteers on walkie-talkies moving acts out in groups. The energy was good, people chatting while they borrowed makeup and wriggled into costumes. Some people came back after their acts to hang out. More would be vanishing into the night, enjoying the rest of the festival.

"Cressida can help," Klara said, and Cressida looked up from where she was squinting into a mirror.

Her German friend was coming towards her, a half-dressed drag queen in tow. "Cressida, this is Siri Alexa," she said. "She cannot open her jewelry box."

"I think I left the fucking key at home," Siri said, looking frantic. "My tiara's in there."

Cressida grabbed two bobby pins and opened them out. "A real tiara?"

"No, but I use the box for safe transport." Siri set the box down on the dressing table and watched anxiously as Cressida bent her attention to the task. It was a simple lock, but Cressida was out of practice, and it took a few tries before she could set the pins.

Siri still gasped with satisfying awe when the lid swung open, revealing a costume tiara constructed out of old phone parts. "You're amazing! How did you do that?"

"I dated a magician for a bit," Cressida said. "She taught me some stuff."

"Well, I love you forever," Siri promised, and hustled back to her dressing station to clamber into the rest of her costume.

Cressida's own costume took over an hour to assemble, which was hilarious, because it took less than five minutes to take most of it off. But the giant red wig needed careful handling, and her makeup was no joke. Three different shades went into her lipstick, the better to pout.

Then she had to sit and wait, sweating in the humidity, the excitement like champagne bubbles in her veins. Xena's cousin was sitting nearby, her hair slicked back into a pompadour, and her lean lines showed off to best effect in dark pants and a deep red button-up.

They were running faster than expected, which was much better for crowd energy than a dragging pace. It was well before midnight, when one of the volunteers said, "Copy that," into her walkie talkie, and then raised her voice. "The Amazing Klara, Samira, Chrissy Bee and Paris Chen, places please."

"Thank you, places," Cressida said, and stood as if a fuse had been lit in her spine. She walked with Klara silent beside her over to the Spiegeltent performers' entrance. Someone clever had made sure to lay down some temporary matting over the grass along the pathway, to protect the costumes. Even so, Cressida lifted her skirts and walked carefully. The music from the main stages was loud, though not deafening. It would be a distraction to the audience if they were allowed to notice it. She'd need to draw them into her world, make sure the focus was clear.

The second she stepped backstage she knew it was a good night. The drag act on stage finished her final belt and stepped off to laughter and rapturous applause. The MC bounced into the light in her ringmaster costume to banter with the audience and welcome the newcomers. People were drifting in and out between acts, which was always a little unnerving, but at least they weren't being allowed to enter *during* performances.

The drag queen was grinning wildly. "Break a leg, ladies," she whispered. "They are *on* tonight."

Cressida was only distantly aware of her, of the people murmuring and moving around them, of the props manager checking their table, of Jenny at her stool off to one side, muttering through a list, of Klara bouncing on her toes, going through one last absurd, arm-twisting stretch.

Two stagehands walked past with Klara's stepladder and set it in the middle of the stage, screwing into the rotating platform another stagehand wheeled in. There wasn't any way to be subtle about this, so they were opting for efficiency instead.

"And now, give it up for the Amazing Klara!" the MC concluded, and Klara hoisted her mop onto one shoulder and walked on whistling, to a generous round of applause.

Cressida had seen Klara practice portions of this routine before, but it was something else to see her friend in her bedazzled janitor's jumpsuit, planting her mop in a bucket (weighted, because Klara wasn't an idiot) and swinging around it. That got some laughs, and then Klara noticed the stepladder, squared herself up for the challenge, and marched towards it.

The audience gasped as she appeared to trip halfway up, then laughed as she turned it into an inversion, balancing on the top of the ladder on her head, arms outstretched in apparent panic.

"Go for platform rotation," Jenny murmured, and the ladder began to turn in place, prompting an excited murmur

The murmur got more tense as Klara's foot twitched, introducing the hint of a wobble. Samira, the comedian beside her, looked as if she was going to throw herself on stage and try to break Klara's fall.

"It's part of the act," Cressida whispered. "She's in perfect control."

"If you say so," Samira said, but went rigid again as Klara began to tumble.

The audience roared, high on the vibe, and probably a few other things, and roared again when Klara turned the tumble into smooth motion, swinging her body through the gap between the steps and rotating back to the top of the ladder, this time balancing on a single hand. She turned the pose into a handstand, and started jumping down the steps, still upside down on her hands, her legs dangling and her exaggerated makeup freezing her face in an expression of permanent surprise.

"Watch this," Cressida murmured. Klara's finale was a sinuous clamber up the steps, backwards in bridge position, in the best horror movie tradition, before she flung herself off in a double salto, to land with her arms outstretched. The flip wasn't that dangerous compared to most of her routine, but it looked impressive, and always got applause.

Samira winced as Klara started her backwards, upside down scuttle up the stairs.

Cressida frowned. Something was off. After a moment she had it. Klara wasn't moving in time to the music. She was slowing down, a beat or two behind, as if she wasn't as confident as her body proclaimed. Either the BPMs were off, or Klara was—and Klara was never off—or something was wrong.

Klara got to the top of the ladder, sat on it, crossed one leg over the other, and shrugged charmingly at the audience. After a second, someone at the lighting booth realized she'd finished the routine and dimmed the lights, and the audience clapped. Klara jumped off—not at all flashy—collected her mop and bucket, and stalked off.

Cressida put a hand out to catch her attention and whispered, "What's wrong?"

Klara's mouth was a thin line, her eyes glittering. "The ladder was not secure," she said, with barely repressed fury. Samira gave them both a panicked look, and sauntered on stage to start her set.

She had the audience roaring in thirty seconds, and Cressida took the chance to follow Klara to where her ladder had just been carried off. Klara was kneeling by it, checking the bolts on the rotating platform. "These are good," she said, almost to herself, and then methodically checked each step. Halfway up her hands slowed. "Here. A loose screw."

This close, Cressida could see the step rocking as Klara leaned her weight into it.

"Everything okay here?" someone asked, and Cressida looked up to see that burly middle-aged security guard, the one Xena liked. Ernest, that was it.

"An equipment malfunction," Klara said brusquely. She glanced at Cressida. "You must go."

Jenny was gesticulating wildly at her.

"Fuck, fuck, fuck," Cressida said, and hurried to her position, skirts swishing. She checked that her wig was firmly in place, and looked across the stage to where a nervous kid was hovering with her props. Oh hell, there'd better be nothing wrong with those.

"You've been an amazing audience, thank you so much, good night!" Samira said, and the MC passed her as she left.

"Wasn't she great? Another round of applause for Samira!" She lowered her voice conspiratorially. "Now, our next act is about to take us back in time, to a dark day in English and Scottish history. Folks, Lotophagi is proud to present Chrissy Bee, as Mary, Queen of Scots!"

Cressida tightened her core, dropped her shoulders, lengthened her neck, and stepped into the spotlight.

Chapter Eleven

There were no seats for hangers-on in the tent, even for those who had a job to do, so Xena was standing at the back when Cressida's act started.

The music started low and solemn, some kind of procession march, as the unexpectedly tall figure walked onto the stage, head erect and hands clasped at her waist. She was wearing some kind of huge Elizabethan-style costume, with full black skirts, a tight square bodice, and even a frilly ruff around her neck. The costume had to collapse down somehow, or she'd never have been able to pack it into that bag. The audience murmured in puzzled anticipation.

There was some sort of Latin chant over the music, now, as step by step Cressida moved slowly to the object at the front of the stage. Xena craned. Was that...ew, a chopping block? Was this the *execution* of this Queen Mary?

Sure enough, Cressida knelt behind it, put her hands up in prayer—and then flung them out from side to side, a sudden gesture demanding *stop*.

The music changed to a violent whirl of drums and violin, as Cressida got back to her feet in a single, sinuous motion, hands still outstretched, hips now swaying to the beat in a rustle of black, glittering fabric. She crossed her arms, reached down, *tugged,* and suddenly the whole skirt was coming away in her hands, revealing a short, scarlet underskirt in ruffled layers that swirled around the top of her thighs. And some matching strappy platform heels, very high, which accounted for the height.

The audience cheered as Cressida flicked the skirt around the stage, waving off imaginary guards with it before she flung it aside. Xena swallowed hard.

Cressida's square black bodice came off next, revealing a scarlet corset with big black bows down the front. She was up front with the block again, but now she was anything but reverent, sliding her body over it, straddling it and pretending to ride, her hands roaming over her body.

Xena could imagine her hands following Cressida's path, her hands on that sleek satin, tugging at those wide ribbons, exploring up under that scarlet skirt, ripping that ruff from her smooth throat with a single motion. She knew that was part of the show, that *everyone* could imagine their hands on Cressida right now. Still, when Cressida stretched and stood to survey the crowd, hip cocked, arm bent, and clearly so bored with all these people who had come to see a queen die, she couldn't help imagining those wicked eyes were looking for her.

Cressida turned on her spiked heel and strutted up stage, her red ruffled underskirt came off to show a black thong—curving over an *incredible* ass—and she reached into the darkness off stage.

A second later she was twirling a fucking *hand axe* like a baton. She waved it, flirted with it, tested the edge with her thumb and stuck the digit in her mouth coquettishly. Then she clutched one of the black bows that held her corset together, pulled it away from her body, and *cut it off.*

The audience lost their collective mind as she tossed the bow into the crowd, and without missing a beat, cut the second and third bows off, and shimmied forward out of the corset that collapsed behind her, axe still spinning in her hand. Xena was staring at a pair of perfect breasts, round and beautiful. Cressida's nipples were covered with two black pasties, each with a silver crucifix dangling off them and bouncing with every step.

It was profane, because violent death was profane, and Cressida/Mary was meeting it with courage and contempt, strutting around the stage, taunting the audience with teasing glances, slapping the ax against her ass and mocking them all.

Then the music shifted, a driving, undeniable bass, and the queen looked alarmed. She darted right, tried to leave to the left, and then, clutching her ax like a frightened child might hold a teddy bear, she approached the exeuctioner's block and knelt for a third time, this time with her neck outstretched over it.

The thunk of an ax coming down cut through a suddenly silent crowd and the lights went out. Then they came on again, but this time they were tinted red, and Cressida was rising to her feet with her arms raised in triumph. There was red smeared on her face and across her neck, red liquid pouring from her hands, down her arms, between her breasts and down her belly. The dead queen living again, the legend that could never die.

The crowd roared as one, stamping their feet as well as smacking their hands and the lights went out again.

Xena stood very still. Her breath was caught in her throat, her stomach tensed against the emotion that threatened to swallow her. Cressida was a star, a *real* star, brilliant and burning and liable to set her on fire if she got too close, but oh, it might be worth it, just to bask in her warmth.

She wanted nothing more than to run backstage and tell Cressida how magnificent she was, maybe kneel at her feet and do a little light worship, but she couldn't.

No one was leaving the tent after that act; they were all staying to see what happened next, and she could hear the murmuring of the front of house staff as they told people outside that they'd have to wait. Paris would be playing to a full house. Xena slipped down the aisle, knelt down so she wouldn't spoil anyone's view, and raised the camera to her eye.

"Holy shit!" the MC was yelling, hyping up the crowd as stagehands cleared away the block and hastily wiped up the fake blood. "Can you believe that? Chrissy Bee, everybody!" She wiped her forehead with an exaggerated gesture. "I'd hate to follow that, but you know, I have a feeling our next act is up to the challenge. Let's get a warm welcome for Paris Chen, of Paris and the Archers!"

The applause was slightly less rapturous—most of the audience would probably have preferred an encore from Cressida. But Paris strode on stage with her guitar, wearing black tuxedo pants and a red shirt, and now the audience was primed to appreciate that color scheme. She didn't waste time on banter. "Here's a song for all the lost girls out there," was all she said, her voice clear and resonant, and then she launched straight into her first number.

"Girls in the Woods" wasn't on the playlist she'd given Xena, and Xena realized Paris must have made a lightning-quick decision backstage, because one of the lyrics in the first verse was about Queen Mary "killed in crimson." The audience stirred at the line, their focus drawn wire-taut again.

The spotlight was good, a clear pool of white-blue light picking out Paris's sharp cheekbones and the blue highlights in her thick black hair. Xena zoomed in on her cousin's long fingers, picking through the intricate bridge, then panned back to her face, serene and severe. Oh, that was going to be an incredible clip.

The audience roared again. Paris took that as the tribute it was, her smile the slice of a blade as she took them into the next number, a slower ballad about losing your lover in winter. Xena had never quite worked out whether the narrator's "death of the heart" was literal or metaphorical, but Paris was working the expressions, her face angry, devastated and longing in turn.

Xena couldn't get great crowd shots from her position, not without standing up and spoiling someone's view, but during the brief instrumental she caught a couple of close-ups of women. One was staring, with her hands clenched tightly together over her stomach. Another who was leaning forward, lips parted. This really might go viral, if she uploaded it at the right time and could follow up with more material. There was a glittering expectation in the tent, invisible, but almost tangible.

Paris thumped the heel of her boot into the stage as she headed into the final chorus.

The pool of light swung sharply to one side of the stage and veered back again. It could have been a mistimed effect, but even above the music, Xena could hear a metallic pop from the rig above Paris's head.

Xena was standing before she knew it, her body lunging towards the stage before her conscious mind could draw any conclusions. Time slowed around her, every motion fluid and clear.

Paris saw her, and her hands and mouth didn't stop moving, but she took a step forward, guitar thrusting out as if to warn Xena away, to push her back, to stop her from ruining the performance.

Which was why the spotlight plummeting from the lighting rig hit her between the shoulder blades, and not right on the top of her head.

The suddenly-dim shape of Paris smashed into the stage.

The screaming started almost immediately.

Xena didn't pay any attention. She hurtled up onto the stage, as people hurried in from the wings—"Darnell, house lights!" she heard Jenny say—and Paris was suddenly revealed, crumpled on the wooden boards and moaning, her arms still wrapped protectively around her guitar.

"Don't move," Xena said. "Did you hit your head?"

"My face hurts," Paris complained, ignoring Xena and sitting up.

No wonder. There was blood all over her face, cuts around her nose and mouth, swelling around her eyes.

But she was conscious and talking and *breathing*, and Xena was so relieved about that that her legs went right out from under her. She turned the collapse into kneeling at the last second, and caught Paris's hand before she could bring it to her nose. "Don't touch it."

"It feels gross," Paris said, and then used her *other* hand to probe. "Ow!"

"It might be broken," Xena said.

Paris's eyes widened. "I can't sing with a broken nose!" she protested, and then coughed, and then flinched again. "Oww!"

"I want people checking that rig right now!" Jenny was saying, her voice nearly a snarl, and Xena inadvertently looked up, to the other lights above their heads, and then across to the heavy-looking black spotlight which had gouged the floorboards with its impact.

"Let's go," she said urgently, because Paris had been sitting up and moving her neck, so she probably wasn't going to do her spine any *more* damage by getting away, and Xena was suddenly not at all happy about the safety of their position under this rig. What the fuck, what the *actual fuck* was going on?

"I can *walk*," Paris said, but Xena ignored that. She got one arm around her cousin's back, and one under her knees and lifted, all of that weights training coming in very handy as she carried Paris off stage.

There had been people fluttering around them, volunteers freaking out, that comedian Samira with a tiny first aid kit, but none of them were properly real at that moment. Cressida was real, though, waiting for them in the wings. She'd thrown a big T-shirt on over her blood-smeared body, and was clearing a space on a long table, shoving various props aside.

Xena sat Paris on the table. "Stop touching your nose, or I'll tie your hands behind your back," she said.

"EMTs are on their way," Ernest said, and what the hell was he doing backstage? "Is she okay?"

Paris tried to glare at him, but seemed to forget what she was doing partway though. "What happened?" she said, sounding confused.

"Front of house cleared," Jenny said. "Shit. *Shit,* what a disaster."

"Not now," Cressida said sharply.

"Right, sorry." Jenny backed off. "I'm going to, I've got to…"

"What's going on?" an extremely unwelcome voice demanded, but Xena couldn't spare even a stinkeye for Dammond Argive, because Paris was slumping, eyes closed, and Xena caught her just in time.

***

When Dammond hustled Cressida away from the backstage crowd, the first thing he said was, "I told you not to perform tonight!"

"Not now, Dammond," Cressida said. "What are you even doing here?"

"I said I'd come, didn't I? You said you were performing *after midnight.*"

"The show was moving faster than that," Cressida said, trying to get a glimpse around his shoulders of Xena, who was hovering behind the paramedics and biting her own fist.

"Fucking Jenny, I *knew* she didn't have the experience for this."

"Dammond, do you mind? I don't have time for this right now."

"Chrissy," he said, and then took her hands, still smeared with red. "Oh fuck, is this blood?"

"It's just fake blood, from the act," Cressida said, startled enough to meet his eyes. Dammond looked awful. The corner of one eye was twitching, and the hands in hers were ice-cold and trembling a little.

"It could have been you," he whispered, his voice hoarse. "It could have hit you."

"Well, it didn't," Cressida said, trying to gentle her tone while she extricated her fingers. It must have been a shock for him, to arrive just as the flood of patrons were gently but firmly evacuated. One falling light was not necessarily a show-killing problem. One falling light that *hit someone*, when there'd already been a fatal electrocution—yeah, Jenny had been right to shut it down at that point. "I'm fine, Dammond, really, but it *did* hit my friend's cousin, and I need to check on her."

"Don't," Dammond said, and grabbed her shoulders this time. "Come back with me, back to the house where you're safe. I think you're being *targeted*, Chrissy."

Cressida jolted. "What? Dammond, that's crazy."

He nodded, looking serious. "That guy got electrocuted while you were in the tent. The light fell just after you were on stage!"

"Those were accidents," Cressida hissed. Behind his shoulders, the paramedics were strapping Paris onto a stretcher and carrying her out, Xena following behind. The tall woman paused before she left and glanced around, her eyes meeting Cressida's. Her eyebrows lifted.

Cressida shrugged at her, a gesture she hoped conveyed, "I'm okay, and I'll catch up with you as soon as I can, but I have to deal with my ex's weird delusions at the moment." It might have been a lot to ask of a shrug. Xena nodded as if she'd caught some of it anyway, and headed out.

"I'm not saying you should spread it around," Dammond said, keeping his own voice low. "But maybe someone who knows about the connection between you and me, maybe someone like that thought he could get at me by hurting you. Or maybe it's not a he, maybe a she." He glared after Xena. "How much do you really know about that woman? She comes out of nowhere, she gets close to our son. She could be dangerous!"

"She was a public personality for years," Cressida said, and then paused, because he might actually have a point there. She'd known *about* Xena, but she hadn't *known* her until very recently. And Xena had been right next to Troy when he died, and close enough to be the first person to get to Paris when the light fell. But Paris was Xena's *cousin*, and sure, she'd complained about her, but in a loving family way, not a psycho killer way.

And if Xena had wanted to hurt Cressida, she could have done it half a dozen times by now. She could have accepted Cressida's first offer, lured her to a quiet place, and done it right then. Cressida could be scrappy in a fight, but she wouldn't have expected it. She'd never have had a chance.

Obviously, though, that would never have happened in the first place. Xena hadn't faked her reaction to Troy's death, or her concern for Paris. Dammond was being paranoid, that was all, and while Cressida would give him some points for being concerned about her, she wasn't going to entertain his delusions.

"Dammond, I just want to go home and get some sleep," she said instead. Dammond's entourage were milling about, including the meathead who'd been his best man. Marcus waved cheerily at her, and then paused for a moment to leer at her legs. Cressida gave him the finger and turned back to Dammond. "I've got to be on Stage Two at four o'clock tomorrow, and I'd like to spend *some* time showing Lucian around beforehand."

"I'll give you a ride back."

"I'm *fine*," Cressida said, louder than she'd intended. Ugh, if she'd hoped to keep the connection between the two of them private for a little longer, all hope of that was lost. Dammond charging right up to her had made an impression, and no doubt their body language was telling its own story. Jenny was looking more than a little devastated. "Look, I've got to debrief with the others anyway," she added. "Let's get in touch on Monday, okay? We can discuss next steps then."

She gave him a meaningful look, and Dammond gained enough self-control to remember that he had a custody agreement to renegotiate, and also an opportunity to meet his son.

"Right," he said. "Monday." He leaned in close to her. "But if anything else happens, if anyone else around you gets hurt, or if you're scared about anything, come to me right away, okay? I'll keep you safe. Remember that."

"Sure," Cressida said. "I'll remember. Good night."

Chapter Twelve

Xena looked at Paris's wan face, almost as pale as the white hospital pillow, and felt a distinct urge to commit murder. For once, it wasn't aimed at her cousin.

They'd had to go to the little clinic that served as the island's hospital, which had a grand total of one doctor and one nurse on the overnight shift. The first aid tent wasn't equipped to deal with fractures and possible concussion. The EMTs had told her that most of what they'd been treating on-site was dehydration, overdoses, sunburn and heat exhaustion.

"It's not that hot," Xena had said, confused.

"It is if you dance for four hours without drinking any water," one of them replied cheerfully. "But head trauma via spotlight is a new one on me."

Paris had regained consciousness by the time they got there, but she was still confused, and Xena wasn't surprised when the doctor briskly diagnosed concussion and advised medical evacuation in the next day or so.

"We're leaving on Sunday night," Xena said. "Is that early enough?"

"Should be." She straighted up from where she'd been gently feeling along Paris's cheekbones. "From what I can tell, Paris, I don't think you have any maxillary fractures, but you'll need to be x-rayed on the mainland."

"What about my nose?" Paris asked. She was holding an icepack to it.

"Oh, that's definitely broken, but it's not a complex fracture. You can wait, or I can do a manual realignment now."

"Now," Paris said. "We might as well get all the gross things done at once. Is my guitar okay?"

"It's fine," Xena said. This might have been a lie. She hadn't bothered to look at Paris's guitar, which had been left behind in the Spiegeltent. But she said it as convincingly as possible, and Paris visibly relaxed, and let the doctor numb her nose before she did something that involved a lot of unpleasant crunching sounds.

"I'm going to pack this with gauze and then Paris can stay overnight for observation," the doctor said cheerfully. "What's up, Hilaire?"

The nurse who'd just entered shrugged. "Four women in the waiting room asking after Paris."

"The Archers!" Paris said, and made a move as if she'd get off the bed.

"Stay there," Xena said, frowning at her.

"I need to—"

"One of them can come in, maybe. There isn't room for four more people in here anyway."

"And we're well past visiting hours," the doctor said firmly.

"Ugh, fine," Paris said, and her exasperation was oddly comforting. If she was still being annoying, she'd probably be all right, Xena thought, and consciously relaxed her hands from the claws that had been digging into her thighs.

"Why are you so jittery?" Paris wanted to know.

"You could have died."

"Oh, please. Okay, tell the Archers they have to perform tomorrow."

"You cannot be serious," Xena said.

"Not with me," Paris said, scowling. "But *they* should. They've got to open for Aoide. Sapph can sing. And you've got to take some photos of me looking pitiful, and do an interview with them beforehand, the show must go on, that kind of thing. Did you get video of the light falling on me?" She sighed. "It was such a good set."

"You were amazing," Xena said, with complete honesty. "Um, are you sure you want photos right now?"

Paris snorted, and then winced, her hand going back to her nose. "Why, because I look like shit? People will eat that up."

She was right. Some of Xena's more popular videos had been her post-adventure injury round-ups, where she'd shown off every bruise and cut. She had some suspicions about the wider audience for that content, but numbers were numbers, and her core fans had also liked them. The time-lapse video of Zac decorating her cast the time she'd broken her arm had done really well.

"I'm not too proud to take pity views. Hey, we've got a lot of fans in Europe who'll be awake now. Maybe I should livestream?" Paris looked around the room. "Pity about the light."

"We don't normally host photoshoots," the doctor said dryly. "You need to get some rest."

"I'm fine," Paris said, in the face of all the evidence. She was squinting, holding up her hand to ward off the overhead light.

Xena held up her phone. She wasn't sure where her camera was—possibly still on the stage in the Spiegeltent where she'd dropped it. "I'll take the photos if you promise to go to sleep in ten minutes," she said. "Absolutely no livestream."

"Stop babying me."

"Do it, or I call Helen," Xena said ruthlessly.

Faced with the big guns, Paris agreed to no livestream, but insisted on Xena getting Sapph so that she could personally deliver her orders for the show tomorrow.

"Actually, today. It's after midnight," Xena said, snapping a few shots of Paris looking pitiful, and then some more of her smiling bravely. "What happened to 'I think the band is breaking up'?"

"Moment of weakness," Paris said, her face still screwed up against the light. "Darkness before the dawn, etcetera. This is our turnaround moment."

Xena went out to the waiting room, where the Archers were sitting or pacing, depending on temperament. "She wants to give you marching orders," she told Sapph, who stopped walking a circle in the tiles and headed in.

"How is she?" Corrina asked.

"Bitchy."

Phryne looked relieved. "So she's going to be okay."

"Yes," Xena said, and actually felt her shoulders drop. "She might have to rest for a while. Concussion sucks. But she'll be fine." She sat down in a worn chair and pulled out her phone. Away from the festival and its data-sucking thousands, she was actually able to upload the pictures of sad Paris. Responses started pinging in immediately.

The sisters group chat pinged too, with belated responses to the shot of Cressida she'd sent.

[Laodice] exCUSE me, who is this hot lady

[Laodice] and where can I get those undies??

[Cassie] Is this a recent thing or...

[Cassie] ?

Xena grinned.

[Xena] Cressida O'Brien, aka Chrissy Bee

[Xena] we're hanging out

[Laodice] looking her up now

[Cassie] Wait. THE Cressida O'Brien? The one who wrote to me?

[Xena] yup

[Laodice] Who what wrote to you when?

[Cassie] It was an Ask Cassandra thing. The letter Dammond Argive tried to sue and fire me for.

[Laodice] That asshole. She had a kid, right? What does "hanging out" mean?

[Xena] he's four, he's Lucian, he's great

[Xena] I dcunno, hanging out?

[Xena] just wanted to take part in the eye candy

[Xena] anyway, big news is Paris got injured at the show tonight but she's going to be okay

[Cassie] But you like her?

[Cassie] What? WHat happened to Paris?

[Xena] a fucking spotlight fell on her

[Laodice] Is it too mean to say IRONIC?

[Cassie] Probably.

[Xena] no

[Xena] she's going to be fine, concussion and broken nose

[Laodice] OKAY I take it back, that was too mean

A private message popped up from Laodice, and Xena blinked. They mostly talked in the group chat. The last time she and Laodice had been one-on-one was when they were trying to figure out what to get Cassie for her birthday.

[Laodice] Hey, about Cressida.

[Laodice] I'm sure she's awesome, or you wouldn't be into her

[Laodice] But if she's co-parenting with Dammond I have to say be careful

[Laodice] he's bad news

Xena rolled her eyes.

[Xena] I know

[Laodice] Not just the Cassie stuff

[Laodice] other things, really bad

[Xena] wdym?

There was a pause, and three dots appeared and reappeared, as if Laodice was typing—or typing and deleting—a lot of text.

Sapph came out looking subdued, but thoughtful.

"We good to go?" Prax said. She was running her thumbs across the fingers of her clenched hands, swallowing so hard her Adam's apple was bobbing in her throat.

"Yeah. You okay?"

"I hate hospitals," Prax said, but she'd come anyway, they'd all come to support Paris, and Xena felt a warm spark ignite in her chest. And then snuffed it, just as quickly. If she needed that kind of support, would it turn up? Her sisters would come, of course, but for someone who'd been really popular, Xena hadn't actually had many friends. It hadn't mattered. She'd been very content with her family, and Zac, and the dozens of friendly acquaintances who had all melted mysteriously away the second her career crashed and burned.

"Um, can I get a ride back with you guys?" she asked.

"Of course," Sapph said, looking faintly surprised that she'd even asked.

"Dibs on the front seat," Prax said immediately, and Corinna ended up sitting in Phryne's lap.

Xena checked her phone again in the car, a maneuver that involved a certain amount of nudging Sapph's generous curves as she pulled the phone from the thigh pocket.

[Laodice] I really can't say much about it.

[Laodice] Just be careful, please?

[Xena] lol mysterious

She waited, but Laodice either didn't want to say more or the network had let them down again. More pings from the bruised-Paris pictures and another short clip from the VIP evening meant it was probably the first.

"Is that good?" Sapph said, craning over her shoulder.

"It is, yeah," Xena said. Fast numbers, quickly climbing, a few new followers. Too soon to say if it had found a real new audience yet. She scheduled a few more photos to release later. At least the bad network would stop her compulsively reloading every few minutes to go through the responses. Zac had always been able to upload content and go on with his day, but she'd never been able to break the habit.

Oh, hell, she'd have to decide about that stupid reconciliation video for him, although if she was thinking of it as *stupid* her unconscious mind might have made the decision for her.

And she had to figure out where her camera was. If the Archers *were* going to go viral, she needed to have more content ready to go.

The taxi driver dropped them off outside the gates, and their performers' lanyards got them past the yawning security guard without any hassle. It was nearly 3:00 a.m. Stage One was still pumping out the oomph-oomph of some club act she'd never heard of, but Stage Two was dark and silent, and the camping grounds to the north and west looked quieter too.

"Bed," Sapph said, and yawned widely. "I'm getting too old for this."

Xena had been up since before seven. Had it really been just this morning that Troy had died? She'd tried to stop a man from dying, run from stage to stage, talked to dozens of people, and kissed Cressida O'Brien, which was more rejuvenating than exhausting, but had definitely spiked her heart-rate. She'd run into her ex, again. She'd played with an energetic four-year-old. She'd thrown herself on stage to pick up her downed cousin.

The adrenaline she'd been running on for most of the day was demanding payback, and Xena was suddenly so tired that her bones felt like cast iron. All she wanted to do was lie down in the mud-churned grass and sink into the earth.

"I've got to stop at the Spiegeltent to grab my gear," she said instead, and when the others kept going to Lot D, she peeled off, jogging the now familiar path. She was probably being an idiot, who didn't even know if there was someone to let her in, but it felt as if her day couldn't end until she went back to...

The scene of the crime, her brain supplied.

The scene of the accident, she thought firmly back at it, and slowed down as she approached the tent.

The main entrance was locked and dark, with a handwritten sign of black marker on the back of a poster announcing that due to "unforeseen events" the Spiegeltent would no longer be hosting performances, please check out the main stages for performances on Saturday and Sunday. It was probably for the best, but Xena thought of Cressida's act, so engaging and intimate. Could you even do something like that on an outdoor stage with an open-air audience?

She headed for the side door, more from hope than certainty. It was pretty clear no one was around. But something flashed out of the corner of her eye, above her head. She stopped and stared up at the stained glass panels high on the walls. The light flashed again, bouncing off some surface within.

Maybe it was just a ghost light, left there to ward off thieves and vandals. Or, more superstitiously, to appease theater ghosts, though she'd never put much stock in that particular show business superstition.

Then again, Troy had died in the Spiegeltent, and not well. Despite herself, Xena shivered. She wouldn't put it past someone to demand that a light stay on, keeping vigil for him. But why would it be moving?

The light flashed again, very quickly, and then again, in a pattern that—*oh*. It wasn't a ghost light. Or a ghost, which she definitely hadn't considered for even a second. It was just somebody with a flashlight, moving around the theater.

But the relief was almost immediately followed by suspicion.

The scene of the crime.

Xena hadn't wanted to think about the possibility of sabotage, or worse. Sure, two serious accidents in close proximity, one fatal, seemed like a lot, but that was probably just confirmation bias. A vintage, temporary theater, generator electronics, a lack of care on the lighting rig after a rushed tech rehearsal... it could all be coincidence.

Dammond Argive is bad news.

He'd been at the Spiegeltent last night, and Troy had died this morning. He'd come backstage after the light had nearly crushed Paris. He was an investor and sponsor for the festival, working on home ground, with almost unparalleled access. None of the security guards were going to tell him to go away or ask any awkward questions about what he was doing.

And Cressida, the mother of his son, had also been there, way too close to the danger on both occasions. What if the light had been meant to fall on *Cressida*? What happened to the custody renegotiation Cressida had referred to if she was killed or badly injured? Sure, she was staying in his house and it would presumably be easier to get to her there, but if he wanted it to look like an accident...

Xena's alarm bells were going off.

Without letting herself think about what she was doing, she reached for the handle of the side-door. It turned smoothly under her hand. She waited for a particularly loud burst of bass from Stage One, then slipped inside and closed the door behind her, listening hard. Nothing. She closed her eyes and counted to ten in her head, then opened them again. She'd always had good night vision, and she could see well enough to make out the outlines of the furniture backstage. She crept towards the stage left wing, her heart thumping, but her breathing calm and even.

She hadn't thought about what she'd do if she found someone, much less what she'd do if it was Dammond and he *was* doing something shady. She was acting on instinct, the old, bad habit of throwing herself into situations without thinking ahead, and oh, it felt good to just be *moving* without second-guessing herself.

There was a figure on stage, tall and broad-shouldered. The lighting rig had been lowered to sit on the stage, and he was leaning over it, playing his flashlight beam over the structure. Looking for something. Whatever it was, he found it; the beam paused, and there was a quick intake of breath, only audible because she was listening so hard. His hand darted out.

Removing evidence of his crimes?

"Stop," Xena said, and the man whirled to face her.

Not Dammond, she registered, and then, with a burst of fury, she recognized his face. "Ernest," she said.

Ernest, who had asked her about any rumors going around about a frayed wire. Ernest, who had been backstage when the light fell, and one of the last to leave the night before. A security guard could also get anywhere and do anything, even more unquestioned and unnoticed than Dammond.

It sounded crazy, it *was* crazy, but she saw his face. He didn't look like a man who'd been startled in the normal course of doing his job. His eyes had gone flat. His left hand clenched around whatever he'd taken, and his right hand was reflexively reaching into his shirt.

Weapon, Xena thought, with the part of her brain that wasn't calculating angles and trajectories. Her exhaustion was gone as if it had never weighed her down, her whole body light and fizzing with energy. Punches were more precise, but she wouldn't make the distance, so it was her foot that came up in a sidekick, planted in his solar plexus. Ernest grunted and went back a couple of steps, hands going out for balance.

Wide shoulders, good stance. He'd had training somewhere, but she had youth and surprise on her side, and she followed up her advantage, feinting a punch and then, when he came forward to block, grabbing him at shoulder and hip and going for the throw instead. If she could get him on the ground and get the gun away, she'd have the advantage.

The throw was easy. Too easy, she realized, her own momentum being turned against her, and she twisted just in time. There was a confused moment of tumbling bodies in the near-dark, and then they were both on their feet. She was holding a dark overshirt in her hands, torn off as they'd rolled. She dropped it. The flashlight was on the stage, teetering back and forth. Ernest's handgun harness was visible in the shifting light, dark leather straps over a white singlet top.

But the gun was still holstered. His hands were held up to her, palms out, placating.

"Wait a second, Xena," he said.

Xena's weight was on her toes, balanced evenly on both feet. If she ran now and zigzagged, he probably couldn't get a good shot at her in this light .

"What the fuck did you do to my cousin?" she demanded.

"Nothing," Ernest said.

She watched his shoulders, his eyes. "Don't lie. You were going to draw on me."

"I couldn't see who you were. Just a dark shape that said my name and kicked me in the gut." His hands were still, his shoulders relaxed. "Which hurt, by the way. Look, I'm not your enemy. I thought, two accidents in one day, that's weird. I was poking around a little, trying to find out if there was anything suspicious."

He sounded perfectly reasonable, even a little rueful, a middle-aged security guy with detective dreams. Xena wasn't sure why she was suddenly convinced that was a facade. Maybe it had been the speed of his response, the way he'd responded to her attack with fluid control. It was too professional for that persona.

"What did you take from the rig?" she asked.

Nothing moved in his face. "What?" he said, sounding perplexed.

"I saw you take something."

"Um, I didn't?" Ernest said. "I was kind of poking at it. I didn't take anything."

Had she mistaken the gesture in the dark? "If you think something's wrong, why haven't you called the cops?"

"I didn't want to look stupid if I'd made a mistake," he said. His shoulders were caving in. "And it looks like I did. I couldn't find anything. I thought maybe the rig screws had been loosened, or a fastening sawed halfway through, but there's nothing like that. Is your cousin okay?"

"She will be," Xena said. She shifted her own stance.

"I think it's this place," Ernest said. "It's kind of spooky, when it's empty."

Xena nodded. "I just came back for my camera."

"Your girlfriend took it."

Xena blinked.

"Oh, sorry, not your girlfriend? Your friend. The one who did the, uh, execution dance." Ernest walked forward and Xena tensed again, but he was only bending over to pick up his shirt. He turned his back to her as he put it on, and she thought he was probably trying to put her at ease—it would be hard to fire at her with his back turned.

Embarrassment was beginning to take the place of rage. She'd been so sure, when she saw his hand over the rig, that he was taking something away. She'd trusted her instincts and ignored her alarms, *again*, and it had backfired. She should—

Wait.

"Ernest," she said, and he turned his head over his shoulder. His silver, birthmarked shoulder. "What's your last name?"

"Jones," he said. It was a lie, delivered with instant and easy conviction, but she wasn't going to let that fool her this time.

"Really," she said. "Because you're walking around with the Pelopson family birthmark."

"The what?" Ernest said, with apparently real bafflement, but she'd been watching him very closely, close enough to catch the small tension when she said *Pelopson*, and the deliberate relaxation that came immediately afterwards.

"Mm-hmm," Xena said. "Pelopson. You know, like Manny and Augie Pelopson? I should have seen it before. You're a bit taller than Manny, but your face is the same shape, and your hair's the same color. Give him eleven years and two inches, shave off his beard and slap on a moustache, and he'll look just like you."

"I think you're confused," he said, looking genuinely concerned.

"No, I'm not. I was for a second. You're a really good liar. But I know who you are now. You're Gus, named after your grandmother Augusta. And I can't remember your real last name, but I know it's not Jones."

His eyes narrowed, and she had the bad feeling she'd just made a terrible mistake, and then he straightened, shoulders military straight, and shook his head. "It's Ippith-Simmonds," he said, and even his voice had changed, shifting to something more clipped and efficient, the slight drawl gone. "And I need you not to mention that to anyone else, Ms. Troiades."

"Why not?"

"I'm afraid I can't tell you—" he shook his head sharply, and sighed. "No, that won't work, will it? You know, I was warned that a Troiades sister in the middle of my investigation would be trouble. Shame on me for not taking that seriously."

"Who told you that?" Xena demanded. She wasn't ignoring *investigation*, that sounded *extremely* interesting, but if someone had been shit-talking her family...

"A colleague of mine. A friend of your sister Laodice, sort of. They were only briefly acquainted, but she made an impression."

What the fuck? This had to have something to do with the disastrous wedding retreat Laodice and Telfer had been on two years ago, the one where that hotel staffer had murdered two people, tried to murder two more, and had then died in a car crash right after her arrest. Xena had always thought there was a lot Laodice wasn't telling them about that week, but she'd assumed it was because of the fricking trauma, not *government investigation*. And it had to be the government. Laodice wouldn't roll over and shut up for anything unofficial or a private grudge.

Xena wasn't the smartest Troiades girl—that was Cassie—nor the most intuitive—Laodice—but it was hard to ignore all the pieces when they came tumbling out of the sky and arranged themselves into a pretty pattern at her feet. There was only one subject Laodice was cagey about.

"You're investigating Dammond Argive," she said.

He shook his head again, and she was about to argue, because weren't they *past* this part, but then he said, "It goes pretty far past Dammond, but yes. He's part of what I'm doing here."

"Which is?"

"Investigating," Gus said, face professionally blank again.

"Investigating what, for who?" She could hear Cassie's voice, saying *whom*.

Gus said nothing.

"You realize I'm just going to ask Laodice, right?"

He puffed out a breath. "She was asked to keep certain information quiet."

"Oh, she did. I'm totally going to yell at her about it later. But now I *know*. Do you—" She cut off abruptly. She'd been about to say, "Do you *have* any siblings?" But, of course, he didn't.

Cassie's research meant Xena knew far more about Gus than she should, including that he'd been the main suspect for murdering his own father. Theo Pelopson, the actual culprit, hadn't been exposed for more than two decades. Gus had been seventeen. The day of the murder, he'd argued with his father, stormed off, and seen a strange man waiting outside in his car. The police didn't believe the strange man had ever existed. They hadn't had enough evidence to charge Gus, but the suspicion had driven him and his widowed mother out of the neighborhood. She'd died a few years later. And Gus had disappeared. Manny had thought he might be unhoused and undocumented, that he might have left the country, that he could be quietly dead somewhere. Joining some kind of shadowy federal agency wasn't, as far as she knew, on the list.

"Trust me," she said instead. "Now that I know Laodice was keeping quiet, I *can* get her to talk."

Gus frowned. "You'll get her charged with obstruction," he said meaningfully.

"I can afford lawyers."

He was still hesitating.

"Come on," she said impatiently. "Who am I even going to tell?"

He shrugged. "If you put it that way, just how close *are* you to Cressida O'Brien?"

"We met on Wednesday," Xena said. And okay, she felt closer to Cressida than anyone she'd known that briefly in a very long time, but still. That was the truth.

"Two days ago? Really?"

Xena shrugged. "Sometimes you just click with someone." Even if you were then dumb enough to turn them down because you couldn't trust that feeling.

"Argive Holdings is the target of a long-term money laundering investigation," Gus said. "It's a damn delicate case, and the only reason I'm telling you anything is because I don't want you going off half-cocked. Do *not* tell Ms. O'Brien. I'm aware that she and Dammond aren't exactly buddies, but I don't want her dropping something in an argument with the ex, either."

Xena tilted her head. "Is that all?"

"Is *money laundering* all?"

"I mean. I figured all these billionaires were shady with their finances."

"This isn't tax evasion," Gus said, sounding exasperated. "Money laundering turns the proceeds of crime into clean money. We're talking drug lords, terrorists, slavers, human traffickers, brutal oligarchs and dictators. These people throw dirty money in and get clean money out to buy their mansions and jets and whatever the fuck else they want. They get away with all of it, they get to *enjoy* their crimes, because of people like Dammond."

"Oh."

"Yeah, *oh*." Gus's eyes were glittering with hate. This was clearly more than just a job to him. "If we take down Argive Holdings, we can hurt a lot of those guys. We can maybe even *get* some of those guys. So I don't need a civilian wandering around the middle of my investigation, and I definitely don't want you telling anyone anything that you know, think, guess, or dream up in your tent, okay?"

"What does that have to do with sabotage in the Spiegeltent? There *was* sabotage, right? I know I saw you take something off the rig."

"I don't think it has any connection to my case," Gus hedged, but when she glared at him, he sighed, apparently recognizing that she wasn't going to let it go. He grudgingly beckoned her over to the lighting rig, sitting awkwardly in the middle of the stage like a strange, spiky sea creature that had been tossed up on land. "Look, here, that gummy bit? It's an adhesive. I think it held a tiny shaped charge in place, maybe with a radio trigger. When the saboteur judged the time was right, they hit the trigger. They wouldn't even have to be in the building. The charge blew itself up and tore through one of the clips holding the spotlight to the rig. That's why the light started swinging around."

"And then it fell."

"And then it fell," Gus agreed. "It's not the most subtle crime in the world. Probably it would look like metal fatigue or a normal break to a civilian, but I knew the moment I got a good look at the light that it had been blown off intentionally. Whoever it was took no chances, though, because that light got cleaned off the stage, and then went missing. What's left is the adhesive. I took a sample for the guys in the lab, just in case it turned out to be relevant."

Xena clenched her fists. "Someone was trying to hurt Paris?"

"I don't know. Someone deliberately blew the light. That's the best I can do."

"And Troy?"

"Yeah. At first I thought that was an accident. I checked it out, because you check unexpected deaths in the vicinity, but I didn't expect to find anything."

"And?"

He spread his hands. "And nothing. Except that cable's gone missing too. Absence of evidence isn't evidence, but let's just say I'm keeping an open mind."

"Someone murdered Troy," Xena said. Her voice sounded all right. It was her knees that were wobbling.

"Maybe," Gus said. "But it doesn't have anything to do with my case. It wouldn't make any sense. Money laundering activities try to *avoid* attention."

"We should tell the police, right?"

"I am the police," Gus said patiently. "More or less. Besides, Dammond Argive literally owns half this island. If you don't think he's got the local law in his pocket, I've got a bridge to sell you."

Not just local law enforcement, Xena registered. The trigger-happy security guards with their expensive suits and unplaceable accents, they were on the payroll too. She hadn't seen any of those guys roaming the festival, or on duty at Stages One or Two. They'd been guarding the main house, the portable ATMs...and the Spiegeltent.

"Are they laundering the dirty money through the ATMs?" she asked. Was the whole of Lotophagi an international crime scene?

Gus's face didn't move.

"Oh, shit. I *have* to tell Cressida. She doesn't know about any of this. Her son is here!" Guarded by armed thugs who worked for terrorists, drug lords, and human traffickers. People like that wouldn't care about a brilliant woman and her enthusiastic little boy. They were collateral damage.

"Her son is safe," Gus said sharply. "That I can promise. As for her not knowing... Are you sure?"

"I—" Xena said, and stopped. She wanted to say yes. But she'd only known Cressida for three days.

"Ms. O'Brien's a smart cookie. Do you really think Dammond could keep this kind of operation from her?"

"They barely talk," Xena said, but she was thinking about Dammond visiting Cressida's room in his mansion. She could have sworn Cressida hadn't *wanted* to talk to him. But she'd done it anyway, gone away with him and come back looking mad and thoughtful.

"I'm not saying she's in on it," Gus said. "But she might have some ideas already, and if you confirm them, she's going to ask how you know. And if she figures out that her son's father is under criminal investigation, maybe she'll drop a hint or two to him."

Xena glared at him.

Gus shrugged. "I'm just saying. Very understandable. No one wants to take their kid to visit dad in prison. And if we get this right, he's going to be locked up for a long time." His eyes were glittering again, and Xena remembered that still frame she'd caught—Dammond staring at Cressida, and Gus staring at him.

This wasn't just a job for him; Gus really hated Dammond Argive. Maybe he wouldn't care so much about Cressida and Lucian either, if it came down to it.

"Okay," she said.

"You won't tell her?"

Xena wasn't a good liar. She leaned into what she was actually feeling, hoping he'd read resentment and frustration as an honest response, given against her will. "No," she said. "I won't tell."

She wasn't sure if he believed her. But he didn't have much choice, unless he wanted to take her in right now. "All right," he said finally. "Xena, this'll all be over soon. Try not to worry about it, okay?"

She sighed. "Okay."

"Good. Now go and get some sleep. You must be dead on your feet."

And she was. But as she left Gus to do his spy shit in the Spiegeltent, her feet didn't take her towards Lot D. She trudged through the grounds, exhausted but inexorable, towards the mansion.

Towards Cressida.

Chapter Thirteen

L ucian had gone to sleep in his own bed, in his own room, *at his usual bedtime.* Cressida wasn't sure what Elena was getting paid, but she was positive it wasn't enough, and she said so.

"He's a nice kid," Elena said, on a yawn. "Did you have a good night?"

"Um, yes and no," Cressida said, but when Elena looked an inquiry at her, she just shook her head. "You'll hear all about it tomorrow, I'm sure."

"Was there another death?" Elena asked sharply.

"No, just an accident." Right after she'd been on stage. Dammond *was* deluded about the danger to her, right? "But we can't use the Spiegeltent anymore." Which neatly eliminated her next real performance. She could do warm-up acts, but most of her work needed intimacy and attention. An open stage, to a crowd impatient for the next band...not so much.

"I'm sorry," Elena said, looking as if she meant it. "I, um, I looked up some of your old festival performances online. You're really good."

"Thank you," Cressida said, and saw her out with a feeling of benign good will that faded as soon as she was alone in the sitting room again.

"Fuck," she said quietly. So much for her big comeback. The Mary act had really hit, and she'd been sure she would bring in numbers for the Saturday cabaret show. But that wasn't going to happen now. Her dream of making it back to the festival circuit, hardly articulated even to herself, had fizzled into one last dance instead. She could still put it on her resume and shop herself around to more festivals, but the problem...

Her eyes strayed to Lucian's bedroom door, and she truly hated herself for a moment. Lucian wasn't a *problem*. He was the best person in her life, the greatest thing she'd ever done, a wonderful, funny, curious little boy, and she'd have died for him in an instant.

But she couldn't take him with her. Very few festivals were going to have these kinds of accommodations for a single mother. And her hope of co-parenting was also dissolving. Dammond was behaving too erratically. She didn't doubt that he was worried about her. She didn't doubt he genuinely wanted a relationship with Lucian. But could she leave Lucian with him for weeks while she traveled?

She headed to the bathroom and started a shower, idly wondering if Dammond was on something. He'd always been oddly puritanical about the coke and pills his business buddies were into, probably because Adrestus had despised them. The closest thing to a compliment Adrestus had ever paid her was, "At least she's not a junkie"—and, even that had been delivered to Dammond, not to Cressida herself, though she'd been standing right there.

But Dammond was acting not just suspicious, but paranoid. Maybe more than a few things had changed after his grandfather died.

The shower heated up as she peeled out of her clothes and used baby oil to remove the adhesive on her nipple pasties. Cold cream and baby wipes took care of most of her makeup, and the rest came off in the shower. She leaned against the wall and let water pound on her upper back, then washed her hair, sighing with bliss as her fingers worked against her scalp. No hasty wash in a gross dressing room or temporary camp shower this time. A girl could get used to the A-lister treatment.

Even if she wasn't going to get a chance to do it again.

Cressida soaped down, thinking about her performance. She was probably going to be known as the act before the accident, but she'd really nailed it tonight. Every move had felt effortless, every motion perfectly timed. She'd felt the audience's awe, their hunger, and it had tingled over her skin as she bared herself, every gesture an act of defiance.

Xena had been out there tonight, watching her dance. Xena had carried an injured woman off stage, her biceps swelling. What would it feel like, to be the focus of that kind of intensity, that kind of strength?

Cressida parted her labia carefully. She didn't go for her usual efficient orgasm, but a gentle tease, like an exploring lover finding out what worked for her. She was wet already, from the touching, from her overheated thoughts, and she crooked two fingers and slid them inside, bringing out more fluid to swirl around her opening. She brushed over her swelling clit, another tease, and thrust her fingers in again. Xena could hold her open like this, explore her like this. Xena's dark eyes could be looking up at her, her strong hands holding her thighs apart, her tongue darting in to lap at her clit.

She'd move softly first, tentative, and Cressida would have to tell her to do more, promise she could take it harder, until Xena was devouring her. Her fingers would be sinking into Cressida's shaking thighs, her lips and tongue would be working on her clit, stroking and sucking with the firm pressure Cressida needed until—

Cressida came, shaking, and leaned against the shower wall, breathlessly grateful for the sturdy construction and the plentiful hot water.

She could just stay in here, wait for the oversensitivity to pass, and then go for round two.

Ugh, but it was late, and she needed to get at least *some* sleep. With some reluctance, she finished washing, rinsed out her hair, and stepped out of the shower, wrapping herself in the enormous fluffy bath sheet. Hm. Lucian slept through a lot, but the hairdryer might be too much. Well, she'd be wearing a wig for her performance tomorrow. Air dry would do fine.

So she was sitting on the sitting room couch, squeezing excess water from her hair, when someone knocked quietly on the door of the suite.

Cressida paused, and put down the hand towel she'd been using for her hair. It was after 3:00 a.m. If this was Dammond, here to tell her more wild theories about how she was being *targeted*... She walked to the door in her shortie PJs, padding softly in her bare feet, and raised her voice just enough to get through the door. "Yes?"

"It's Xena," a voice said, equally quiet, and Cressida unlocked the door and pulled it open.

For a moment, it felt as if her dream lover version of Xena had been teleported to her door, all intense eyes and swollen lips.

But this Xena looked as if she'd gone three rounds with a steamroller. There were dark smudges under her eyes, her hair was tangled, and the lip swelling wasn't from lust.

"Who hit you?" Cressida demanded, her voice low and fierce.

"What?"

"Your mouth!"

Xena touched her mouth and frowned. "Oh, huh. I didn't notice." She thought, with obvious effort. "Might have been when we were rolling across the stage."

"When who—never mind. Come in."

"I'm sorry," Xena said, obeying. "I know it's late. I didn't want to wake you or Lucian, but..." she trailed off. "I have to tell you something."

"Tell me sitting *down*," Cressida said, and bullied her over to a small side table with two chairs. She felt, obscurely, that this would be a better place for a serious discussion than the sofa.

Also, if she put Xena on the sofa, she might do something dumb like launch herself at the woman. With her shower thoughts still lingering, the barrier of a table between them seemed like a really good idea.

"Listen," Xena said, and then sat there, her mouth parted, apparently unable to actually say anything.

"Animal, mineral, or vegetable?" Cressida asked, after a moment.

"Dammond's a criminal," Xena said.

"Animal, then," Cressida said, while her mind whirled. It wasn't totally unexpected. You didn't work in either theater or sex work without encountering illegal activity, and Dammond was definitely somebody who'd take shortcuts. But of course, he'd grown up with that as a baseline. She'd had to insist that the staff hired for their wedding be paid at least the minimum wage, instead of whatever Adrestus thought he could get away with giving them, and she was sure that a lot of Argive Holding's Finance department was devoted to exploiting tax law gaps and loopholes.

"Money laundering," Xena said, and Cressida froze. She'd watched enough crime dramas to know what that meant.

"How do you know?" she asked, and Xena told her. The story was confusing—something about her sister nearly being murdered, and another sister whose partner had been looking for his lost cousin—but the parts about Ernest the security guard being a federal investigator were very clear. And from what Xena was saying, not only was Dammond in bed with some incredibly unsavory people, but the feds were about to charge in and attempt a takedown.

"Oh shit," Cressida said, and sat there for a moment as her vision of a peaceful co-parenting existence dissolved and disappeared like mist in a strong wind. She couldn't let Dammond anywhere near Lucian. She was going to have to take active measures to keep him *away*, and that was going to be so hard, going up against a man who could buy almost any help he needed, legal or otherwise.

Unless he was in jail.

"What does Gus need to put Dammond away?" she asked.

"I don't know," Xena said, looking confused.

Cressida put aside the idea of talking some useful, tradeable information out of Dammond, at least for the moment. On further reflection, she probably didn't want to testify anyway. She couldn't imagine Dammond's criminal friends would approve.

"But there's another thing," Xena continued. "Cressida, I'm so sorry. It looks like what happened to Troy wasn't an accident. He might have been murdered."

There was a faint buzzing in Cressida's ears and her lips went numb. "By Dammond?"

"Gus doesn't think so. He says that would bring attention to the money laundering." Xena was obviously trying to be fair. "But Paris's accident definitely wasn't an accident. What happened to Troy could be something totally unconnected, but—"

"What are the odds of that?" Cressida finished, and sat still. She no longer had the urge to throw herself at Xena's mouth. She'd drawn into herself instead, huddling in her chair like a scared child. She forced herself to sit up straight and lift her chin. "Dammond told me he thought someone was targeting me to get at him. I thought he was being paranoid, but if he's doing all this criminal shit, then maybe he knows damn well that someone *is*."

She scrunched her eyes closed, not wanting to see anything resembling pity in Xena's eyes. Or worse, condemnation. She'd so wanted to believe that Dammond had changed. She'd always blamed Adrestus as the main villain in their broken love story. Because she'd *loved* Dammond, truly and tragically, and even her own frustration and fear hadn't been enough to completely kill the hope that he could be on her side. She should have known better. But she'd been lured in by the promise of change, and also, though she hated to admit it, the prospect of financial support. Not only for Lucian's sake. For her own, as well. She'd leapt at even the possibility that she might be able to truly pursue the life and career she wanted so badly.

So she'd trusted too much, and ignored too much, until it was almost too late.

Again.

"A rival gang or something?" Xena asked, and Cressida opened her eyes. There was no pity or blame in Xena's face. Just a steady, reassuring calm.

It crossed Cressida's mind again that she might be trusting *Xena* too much. The woman had burst in on her in the middle of the night with this wild story, and only the bruises on her mouth to corroborate that she'd clashed with Gus in the Spiegeltent at all. She didn't even have any evidence that "Gus" existed outside of Xena's invention. A long-lost cousin of Xena's sister's partner, who just happened to be investigating Argive Holdings? It was ludicrous.

But again, if Xena wanted to hurt her, she could have. And why would she lie?

Xena, apparently unaware of Cressida's confusion, was still looking at her.

"Oh," Cressida said, remembering the question. Rival gangs. "Uh, I guess so?"

Whoever was behind it—if anyone was behind it—Paris *had* been hurt. Troy *had* died. That was real.

Xena bit her lip. "You're not going to tell Dammond about the investigation, right?"

Cressida tensed. "Why not?" She had no intention of accusing Dammond to his face, but was Xena trying to stop Cressida from getting outside confirmation?

"I told Gus you wouldn't. He said I shouldn't tell you even if I believed that."

"Well, that's on you," Cressida said tartly, and Xena winced.

"Give me a second," Cressida said, and got up. Her hair was drying into wispy curls, bouncing around her face as she moved restlessly to the bathroom and back again. She did a lap of the sitting room and eased the door to Lucian's bedroom open, holding her breath. He didn't stir. He'd fallen asleep on his front, with his face squashed sideways into his pillow and his knees folded under him. She watched his back move gently up and down with his breathing, and felt love and fear battle within her.

She closed the door carefully. She'd been trying very hard not to panic, but something terrible was going on, and her son was right in the middle of it. The problem was she didn't have any evidence to rule out either Dammond *or* Xena.

So what did her gut say?

Her gut said Dammond was shifty, and Xena was steady. Her gut said Dammond had already hurt her badly, and Xena never had.

But her priority was Lucian. He had to be. If she trusted Xena and got it wrong...

"If you tell Dammond—" Xena started, with the *worst* timing, and Cressida turned on her.

"I know!" she said, and then, more quietly. "I know." She pressed her hands to her chest. "But consider things from my point of view. You're asking me to take a leap of faith here, and I'm not good at those!"

"Wait, what?" Xena said, but Cressida could see her already working it out. "You think *I'm* lying?"

"Would you blame me if I did?" Cressida demanded.

Xena blinked, and then swallowed hard. "Actually, no. This sounds crazy."

"So crazy," Cressida agreed, but her hackles were already settling. No matter how logical her head was, her heart, it seemed, had already decided to trust Xena.

At least, until further events proved her wrong.

"And you get points for not telling me to calm down," she added. Dammond would have. *You're being hysterical, Chrissy.*

Xena looked insulted. "I'd never tell anyone to calm down. It's rude, and it never works."

"Especially on toddlers," Cressida said, and nodded in response to Xena's wince. "Yep. Only tried that once."

"I don't know how I can prove I'm not making this up," Xena said hesitantly. "I can show you Laodice's messages? Though I could have faked those, I guess, and they're not very specific." She brightened. "Or I could tell Gus I told you, and have him confirm it."

"By what, arresting you?"

Xena shrugged. "Probably?" She frowned. "And maybe you too, which I don't like."

"I can't leave Lucian," Cressida said immediately. Her eyes went back to the room where her son was sleeping, and she sucked in a breath that was almost a sob. "I've got to get him out of here." The panic bubbled up in her again. How was she going to get him out of the house his father owned, past the guards he paid, out of the festival he was running, off the fucking *island*?

Xena nodded. "I'll help in any way I can." She hesitated, then added, "Even if it means staying away from you, if that'll set your mind at ease."

Cressida pursed her lips. "If I *did* let you help me, what about your job? Aren't the Archers performing tomorrow?"

"Fuck my job," Xena said, looking astonished. "Lucian first."

Oh, hell. What was the point in trying to erect barriers against this woman when gooey sentimentality kept threatening to undermine the foundations? Cressida was only human.

"I trust you," she said, and the raw emotion in her own voice astonished her. "I don't know why, exactly, but I do. And I'll be grateful for the help."

"I don't know either," Xena said, and reached across the table. Her hand was warm and strong as she laid it over Cressida's. "I don't know what this is, between us. But it's something, right?"

Cressida considered denial or deferral, but Xena's gaze was honest and direct, and she just couldn't do it. "It's something," she admitted. "I'm not sure what."

"Can I see you when we get back home?" Xena asked. "Wait, that's not a condition of me helping. Maybe I should take it back."

"Don't," Cressida said, and turned her palm upwards, so that she was returning the grip. Xena's fingers were long, and they swallowed her hand. Her thumb moved rhythmically over Cressida's wrist. "I'd like to see you too. But.. Lucian first." The beginnings of a plan was starting to sketch itself across her mind. She'd always been good at escape routes, even if her timing was sometimes off.

And the initial panic was dying down. The reassurance of having someone else who could shoulder some of the upcoming burdens was helping a lot.

"Do you want to stay here tonight?" she asked.

"Um," Xena said, and blood rushed to her face. "I'd love to. But I should say that I'm really tired, so I don't know if you—I might be assuming, but in case you did mean—"

"No funny business," Cressida said, before Xena had to hurt herself by completing the sentence. "Just sleep. Honestly, I'll feel better if you're here."

Xena relaxed the moment sex came off the table. That should have been a little insulting, if Cressida were totally honest, but instead it was just kind of adorable.

"Come to bed," she said, and extended a hand as she stood up. "We're going to have a busy day tomorrow."

***

Xena woke with her nose buried in the sweet-smelling, soft skin of somebody's neck.

Not Zac, she thought muzzily, and then she registered the compact, curvy body she was holding against her own and the soft curls drifting over her cheeks, moving with her breathing.

She wasn't quite nuzzling Cressida's boobs, but she was an inch from mouthing her collarbone. They'd gone to sleep chastely enough, curled back to back in the enormous bed. Sometime in the night, they'd turned towards each other.

Her own breasts were pressed against Cressida's stomach, her arms wrapped around the other woman's waist. Well, she assumed it was both arms. One of hers seemed to have gone to sleep.

At least she wasn't the only clingy one. One of Cressida's legs was crooked, the soft weight of her thigh pressed over Xena's waist. The other leg had somehow entwined itself *between* Xena's thighs and wrapped around the back. If Xena dared to move, she was pretty sure she'd feel a dainty foot flexing against the back of her knee.

"Hngrh," Cressida said, over her head.

It was still dark, but the room wasn't quiet. Xena could hear rain tapping at the windows, and a wail outside that suggested wind was rising. It was the sound of the storm that had woken her, not Cressida's embrace.

Lightning flashed through the curtains, and she instinctively tightened her grip.

"Whrr?" Cressida said, and Xena actually felt the consciousness flow back into her body, a kind of tense awareness coming back that hadn't been there in sleep. She tried to let go, but Cressida purred something and wriggled down the bed, until they were face to face. Her cheeks were pink, her mouth a sly curve.

"Hi," Xena said, breathless for more than one reason. "I think it's a storm."

"Mm," Cressida said, smiling with obvious intent. "How are you feeling? All rested up?"

It wasn't even dawn yet. They couldn't have had more than a nap, two or three hours sleep at the most. But Xena felt warm and loose, energy zinging around her body. From experience, it was the sort of precarious boost that would demand serious payback later. Right now, however...

"I feel great," she said, and proved it by pressing her mouth to Cressida's.

Cressida made an encouraging sound in her throat, clutching Xena closer with arms and legs, and Xena took that as permission to go deeper, licking through Cressida's parted lips. Their breath was mingling, wet gasps and little laughs spilling from their mouths. Cressida pushed at Xena's shoulder, and Xena took the hint, rolling onto her back.

Cressida sat up and straddled Xena's hips. Without ceremony, she grabbed the hem of the T-shirt she'd worn to bed and pulled it over her head.

"Touch me," she said, and Xena obeyed, reaching for the breasts that were swaying so enticingly close. She circled her thumbs around the nipples, and Cressida threw her head back.

"Sensitive?" Xena asked, exploring.

"Oh yes. It made breastfeeding awkward."

"Seriously?"

"Yep," Cressida said, panting slightly. "One of the many things they don't tell you about. I thought I was a total perv until I worked up enough courage to do some research. It's not super common, but more common than people—whoa. Oh, that's nice."

Xena was delicately tracing the areolae and branching out to follow each silvery stretchmark.

"They got bigger, too," Cressida said, more or less coherently. "My boobs, I mean. My corsets don't fit as well as they used to. Your hands are so big, I fucking love it."

"You talk a lot," Xena observed.

Cressida's eyes glinted. "Shut me up, then."

Xena obliged, sitting up to kiss her again. Lightning flashed through the curtains once more, lighting the entire room with a silvery blue burst. Surely she was dreaming? Surely she wasn't really here, kissing an enchanting woman who smelled like jasmine and tasted like mint?

Cressida made a growling noise in her throat and thrust her own hands up under the shirt she'd lent Xena, groping eagerly. "I've been wanting to touch these tits for days," she said, with obvious relish, and Xena found herself laughing with delight and helping Cressida peel the shirt off. Seconds later, she was flat on her back.

Cressida made a happy little growl in her throat and cupped both breasts together, then dove in, face-first. "Does this work for you?" she demanded, between licks and nibbles. Cressida was obviously big on communication during sex, another tick in the *she's so hot* column.

"It's not a huge turn-on," Xena said honestly. "I don't mind breast stuff, but it doesn't do much for me."

Cressida raised her head, looking thoughtful.

"But I get off on you liking it," Xena added, also truthfully, and Cressida grinned.

"Got it," she said, and wriggled her weight to the side until her thigh came down between Xena's, pressing firmly upward against the crotch of her panties.

"Oh shit," Xena said, as her clit, already pretty happy, woke all the way up.

"There," Cressida declared smugly. "You get off on that."

And with that blithe order, she headed straight back to Xena's breasts Xena's hips moved more or less involuntarily, rolling against the pressure Cressida was providing. She could feel the dancer's muscles flexing in her thigh, tight and strong. She lifted higher, chasing more sensation.

"Yeah, that's it, fuck yourself on me," Cressida whispered in her ear. She'd kissed her way up Xena's neck and was mouthing at the delicate skin beneath her jaw. "You'll come for me, won't you?"

"Yes," Xena gasped, and Cressida chuckled.

"Good girl," she said, her voice rich with approval. "I can feel you soaking through your panties." She shifted her thigh a little closer. Xena raised her knees, planting her feet firmly on the mattress as she thrust up. She could bring herself off with her hand with one movement right now, but this, this was perfect, the grinding roll of her hips, the pressure of Cressida's thigh bearing down on her, the slow wave rising until it was as powerful as it was undeniable.

The wave crested and dashed over her. Xena clapped a hand over her mouth just in time, muffling the cry that broke from her throat. Cressida laughed quietly and eased her thigh back a little, as Xena collapsed back into the mattress, panting heavily.

"Was that good?"

"Amazing," Xena said.

"Good, because I was getting a cramp at the end there. Nice to know it was worth it."

"Let me help you with that," Xena offered, and rolled Cressida onto her back. Their bedclothes had long ago been tossed aside. She slid down

Cressida's body, kissing nipples, ribs, belly-button on her way, raining licks and nibbles over everything she could reach. She was ravenous, but she slowed down when she reached the waistband of Cressida's panties, sliding her thumbs underneath and drawing them gently down her well-shaped legs.

The little triangle of blonde curls was damp. She smoothed exploratory hands up the thigh she'd been rubbing herself against, and felt a slickness there that wasn't just sweat.

"Oh no," she said, in mock dismay. "I got you all wet."

"Oops," Cressida said, and then she let out a measured breath as Xena wrapped both hands around her thigh and drew them down, thumbs digging firmly into the tight muscle. "Damn," she said breathlessly. "You're good at that."

"I took some massage classes," Xena told her. "I had a depressive episode and my therapist recommended that I return structured touch to my life."

"You do realize that talking about therapy in the middle of sex is the gayest shit ever, right?" Cressida asked, but thumped her head back into the pillow when Xena repeated the motion.

"Don't see you complaining," Xena said, and kept stroking, pausing on some of the tighter spots and pushing in until Cressida was groaning with mingled pain and pleasure. She kneaded her way down Cressida's calf, then lifted her foot to her mouth and kissed the soft inner arch.

"Oh no," Cressida said, her eyes flying open. "Am I suddenly into foot stuff?"

"We can check that out later," Xena offered, and switched legs. Cressida purred and did an excellent impression of melting into the mattress as Xena kept working on her. Xena might have thought she was falling asleep, except that every time Xena's hands moved around to the inner thigh, Cressida's hips twitched.

"So good," she said, sounding drugged. She let out a soft, satisfied sound as Xena let her fingers card through the tangled, damp curls, and finally part her folds.

Cressida's pussy was flushed and pink, inner lips poking out like they were curious to see what was going on. Xena used her index and pointer fingers to trace the slick protrusions up to the point where they met, and then walked her fingers higher still, to where Cressida's clit was quivering, swollen and glistening, even in the dim light of the fading storm.

"Can I taste you?" she asked huskily, and Cressida moaned assent.

Xena took her time, starting with the tip of her tongue and teasing around the clit.

"More," Cressida demanded.

"I'm getting there," Xena assured her, and gradually increased the pressure until her face was buried in Cressida's pussy, licking and suckling in turns as Cressida moaned and thrashed and finally pulled a pillow over her face to muffle the noise.

Cressida's legs wrapped around her shoulders and neck, pulling her closer, and Xena surged forward, tongue as flat and strong as she could make it against Cressida's clit.

Cressida made a noise that might have been a scream, and her muscles clenched totally rigid and tight, and then relaxed completely, all at once.

Xena allowed herself a smug, unseen grin, and flicked her tongue out again, testing.

"No, no," Cressida said, flinching away. She turned onto her side, hands cupping herself protectively.

"No good?" Xena asked, wiping her mouth and discreetly picking a pubic hair off her tongue with the same gesture. Sex was messy, especially when you did it right. She'd never minded, but some people got embarrassed by the reminders.

"I'm out for the next twenty minutes, at least," Cressida said, sounding dazed. "Holy shit. Who first taught you to eat pussy?"

"High school girlfriend, a year older than me."

"May blessings rain down upon her. She taught you *well*."

"Speaking of rain," Xena said, and padded to the window, twitching the heavy drapes aside. There was some light scattering off the cloud cover, enough that she could make out the waving of trees in the distance and the fluttering canvas of the family camping grounds, out the back of the mansion. This wasn't the light sprinkling that had dampened the soil and leaked in the Spiegeltent. "It's going to be a mud-bath out there tomorrow."

Cressida joined her at the window, and Xena tucked an arm around the smaller woman's shoulders. "That won't matter to us," she said grimly. "We won't be there."

"No," Xena said, and turned to look down at her. They hadn't talked about it while they made love—*had sex*—Xena internally amended. For those minutes, the danger and fear had been pushed away. Not forgotten, but set aside.

Now the threat was back, nearly palpably present in the quiet room.

"You can back out," Cressida said, her eyes intent. "This isn't your fight, you know. I appreciate everything you've done, but you don't have to put yourself on the line for me."

"I want to help," Xena said quietly. "I'm in."

"Okay," Cressida said, and walked across the room to pluck a robe from a hook. Xena watched the curves disappear into the fluffy toweling with some regret, but Cressida was right. It would be daylight soon. It was time to get serious.

Xena put her own shirt back on and found her cargo pants. She'd showered before sleeping, but she was beginning to regret not stopping at her tent for a change of clothes.

"How did you get in here?" Cressida asked, sitting cross-legged on the bed.

"I talked my way past the security guy," Xena said. "I was on the list from earlier today, and there were still people at Stage Two. He bought it."

Cressida looked disappointed. "I was kind of hoping you'd found a secret place to get through the fence or something," she admitted.

Xena grinned. "If you want me to stand underneath your balcony and throw pebbles at the window, I will."

"Maybe another day. Okay. If we can't sneak out, I think we'd better just leave, looking like we're heading out to enjoy the festival. Mix with the crowd, get out one of the gates that doesn't have any of Dammond's goons on it, and head to the ferry docks."

"Not the airport?"

"The planes are too small. More people will be on the ferries."

"Smart," Xena said, and meant it. She wasn't much of a planner, but Cressida definitely had this handled.

"Okay. Looking normal means we can't carry any obvious luggage. A small backpack is okay, but nothing bigger than you'd take to a festival." She looked mournfully at the two trunks stashed against the wall. "No costumes."

"I can carry a pack for you," Xena said. "I don't have anything with me."

Cressida looked taken aback. "You don't want to stop off at Lot D?"

"I think that's Gus's home base. I don't want to answer any awkward questions. I've got my phone, my wallet, my camera. That's enough." Not her laptop, or her small lighting setup, or her favorite pair of gold sneakers. Or her house key, come to think of it. She'd have to ask Laodice for her spare.

Which reminded her of the other things she needed to ask Laodice. She pulled out her phone, sighed at the lack of bars, and put it away again.

"I think the network's bad on purpose," Cressida said suddenly.

"Why?"

"Remember all the publicity before Lotophagi opened? They kept saying it's not like Fyre Festival, we're going to be upfront that the network won't be able to handle card payments, you're going to need cash and plenty of it."

"The ATMs worked fine."

Cressida snorted. "Well, they would. That's people's clean electronic money, traded for dirty cash. But a one-to-one deal doesn't work for launderers. All weekend, people have been paying in cash, buying food and drink, handing over money for merchandise... How many of those businesses are controlled by Argive Holdings, do you think? All they have to do is collect the legitimate takings, report them at double or triple the actual amount, and boom, there's the explanation for how all this money suddenly appeared."

"That's how it works?" Xena asked, feeling stupid. To be fair, normally she'd have looked it up on the internet. Now she had to contend with her own ignorance.

Cressida didn't seem to be concerned, though. "Yep. The mob used to do it through restaurants and laundromats—cash businesses, no easy way to say that isn't the profit you should be making. That's why it's called laundering."

"Oh," Xena said. "Well, that must be harder these days. Fewer and fewer places dealing in cash." Other than at Lotophagi and the occasional street food vendor, she couldn't remember the last time she'd bought something with paper money.

Cressida nodded. "Exactly. And there are nearly ten thousand people out there with a completely normal reason to be spending a lot of cash. Claim that they spent six or seven hundred each over what they actually did, and that's seven million that now looks totally legitimate."

"Seven million *dollars*?"

"Easy. Over just three days. And they're probably moving way more than that around the festival, because something this big has a lot of moving parts, and moving parts is where you hide dirty money. Vendor fees, perks for the VIPs, tax write-offs—oh damn, I bet Dammond is paying *himself* money to rent out his land for the festival. And then Dammond 'invests' in a company owned by the people who are paying for his services, or orders materials from a front business for any one of Argive's construction projects or redevelopments that never arrive, and that's it. Dammond's clients have their money back, clean and ready to spend. Minus Dammond's cut."

Cressida chewed her bottom lip. "And Dammond's thinking of doing this more often. He told me. He wants to take it international, run Lotophagi in multiple places a year." She grimaced. "This is just a prototype. He's *testing* it."

She looked physically ill, and Xena's alarm spiked.

"Are you all right?"

"No," Cressida said. "My ex is a dangerous criminal, and he's pulled me into this stupid fucking scheme. I came here at his invitation, *with our child*, and I'm living in his *house*, and no federal prosecutor is going to accept *sorry, I don't know anything, I just came for the show*. I'm going to have to testify, probably, and hope the government can keep Lucian and me safe, because otherwise..." She dragged her hands over her face. "He told me he thought I was being targeted," she said, her voice flat and level. "That someone was causing these *accidents* to try and hurt me, and get to him. He tried to make me think it was you. But of course he's worried that I'm a target, because somewhere at the back of his mind, he knows that's a possibility. That the people he's playing this game with don't fuck around."

Xena wasn't surprised. She was, however, suddenly furious.

"I really hate him," she said, without thinking, and Cressida winced.

"I'm sorry," Xena said awkwardly. "I know that you were close."

"We were in love," Cressida said, honest and unflinching. "I should probably hate his guts, and part of me does, but the rest of me remembers. What it was like, at the beginning." Her gaze strayed to the door, to the sitting room, and Lucian's room on the other side.

Xena wondered whether it was better or worse for Cressida that Lucian had been conceived in love. She hadn't really thought about the courage it must have taken for Cressida to walk away from that wedding. How brave and clearsighted Cressida had had to be, to recognize the threat levelled against her and her son and not brush it off or ignore it or hope everything would be okay. In retrospect, learning that your ex's family were huge crooks must have confirmed it was a smart choice, but at the time, she couldn't know. And yet, she'd walked out on the man she loved and a promised lifetime of stability and security, for her son and her freedom. And ever since, she'd paid for that decision, in precarity and labor and watching her career fade away.

In comparison, Xena's biggest disaster was a shitshow she'd put into motion all by herself. The consequences had included a lost relationship, which was maybe the only similar point. And then, what? Some people on the internet had been a little mean? She'd been a joke on a few late-night shows? She was financially independent at twenty-six, for goodness's sake. What was mild humiliation and the loss of her first career, compared to what Cressida had gone through?

And on top of that, instead of wasting her time by restarting a college degree she didn't want or increasing her lifting personal bests, Cressida had raised a bright, cheerful little boy, maintained her performance skills, and was even now doggedly trying to pursue re-entry to the theatrical world she loved so much.

With the steadfast help of the mysterious Anna, of course. Xena was suddenly very interested in meeting Anna. If she had any interest in maybe joining this family herself, she definitely needed to get the approval of Lucian's other mom.

And yes, okay, she had to admit that she *did* want to be part of this family, however wildly ridiculous it was to decide that on three days of acquaintance. Lucian was a great kid, and Cressida was beautiful, smart, strong-willed, and sexy as hell. Xena would stick around as long as she let her.

Cressida appeared oblivious to the dizzying cascade of epiphanies flooding through Xena's brain. She was twisting a curl around her finger and chewing at her lip again. There was definitely more light in the room, the grey pre-dawn filtering through the curtains. "All right," she said, and tugged her finger free of her hair. "Let's get moving."

Chapter Fourteen

Lucian was unhappy that they were leaving early. Cressida had thought about just not telling him until they were on the ferry, but she'd never lied to her son, and the thought of potentially breaking his trust right now made her stomach hurt.

So she tried to emphasize the good parts about their early departure. "The boat ride will be fun," she said. "We might see dolphins."

Lucian's small, stubborn face was frowning. "Elena is going to read me a book from New Zealand."

"I know she was going to, buddy, and I'm really sorry. But Mommy isn't going to dance any more, and the storm made the grass all muddy. Lots of people are leaving early, see?"

Lucian looked out the mullioned windows to the families busily packing up their tents, and sank a little lower into his high wooden chair. In one way, the storm had helped them out. It looked like nearly a quarter of the families were cutting their losses and going home, and that was a crowd they could blend into. But they needed to get to the ferry terminal before all the tickets were gone.

"Eat your breakfast," she said. "Look, your cereal has marshmallows."

"I want to say goodbye to Elena."

"That cereal looks good, Lucian," Xena said, on his other side. "Can I have a bite?"

"No," Lucian said, chin sticking out.

"Are you sure?" Xena asked, making an exaggerated move towards his spoon. Lucian picked it up, but in the end he only managed three or four spoonfuls, chewing with an agonizing pace and looking like a tortured angel. He was equally sluggish through the rest of the morning routine, with big mournful eyes and a pout that was more alarming than his rare tantrums.

He was even unhappier about the notion that they were leaving without his little wheeled suitcase. In the end, Cressida gave up and helped him pack it, stuffing the bare necessities into her own day pack and a tote she found for Xena. Lucian rolling a bright pink mini-suitcase around would look a lot less suspicious than a kid screaming for all the toys that they'd left behind. By the time she'd "helped" him fold his special blanket and zipped up the sides, he was even smiling again, and Cressida let herself dare to hope.

The plan was simple. They'd leave the mansion as if it was a normal festival day, then slip out one of the exits and head for the docks. Hopefully they could hire or talk someone into giving them a lift, but they could walk it if they had to. Then it was tickets at the ferry terminal, a four-hour boat ride, and then... Well, she was keeping things vague after that. Maybe they'd try and fly from the tiny mainland airport, or hire a car and drive to somewhere bigger. Maybe they'd road-trip across the country.

Xena had offered to pay for everything, with so little concern that Cressida hadn't let herself feel a moment's guilt. If they wanted to evade pursuit, from the law or from Dammond—or from Dammond's scary friends—a woman with deep pockets and a lot of experience with adventure was a handy person to have on your side.

Or on her back.

Cressida let herself have a brief cross-country fantasy, with steamy hotel bathtub sex after Lucian went to bed each night, and then let it go. Xena was being wonderful, but at any point she might decide that this was all too much trouble and expense, and Cressida wouldn't even be able to blame her. She trusted Xena, wanted to trust that she'd be there the whole way, but she'd trusted Dammond once too.

"Okay," she said, and scanned the suite again. If she'd forgotten anything vital, it refused to jump out and bring itself to her attention, so this was as good as it was going to get. She checked herself in the full-length mirror: denim shorts, a white short-sleeved blouse and gold sandals. A wide-brimmed red picture hat gave the carefree impression of a woman set on enjoying a beautiful day, without a care in the world or a thought in her head. Lucian was wearing his favorite dinosaur T-shirt and khaki shorts.

Xena was wearing her cargoes and a borrowed shirt that was loose on Cressida, but borderline scandalous on Xena's larger frame. She'd pulled her hair back and added earrings when Cressida had pressed them on her, for more of a holiday atmosphere, but her face was still serious.

Cressida smiled at her. "Showtime," she said under her breath, and stepped into the hallway.

Dammond was coming down the corridor, two men at his back.

Cressida felt her smile waver, and snapped it back in place just as he looked at her. He looked surprised, she registered. That didn't make sense. If he was coming for her, why would he look surprised to see her?

Then the door down the hall was flung open, and a furious megastar in a short black robe strode out.

"You!" Kithara said. Her voice was beautiful, melodious even when it was raised. She pointed at Dammond, her bejewelled finger sparkling. "You told me the screens would be ready! You told me these rains would do nothing but dampen the grass! Now I am to perform without visuals, without all my dancers, while my audience writhe in the *mud*?"

Dammond was here for *Kithara*. Relief came hard on the heels of understanding. Cressida let her features drop into a sympathetic grimace. *Stars, huh*? her face said.

Tell me about it, Dammond's quick glance said.

"Excuse me!" Kithara shouted. "Am I not here? Am I somehow vanished? Do you not see me?"

"Of course I see you," Dammond said, snapping smoothly into networking mode. "I'm so sorry, Kithara. Let me make some calls and see what I can do."

"Make them now, here, so I can hear what you say! Always I hear yes, Kithara, this will be done, Kithara, and then it is *not* done." She turned to look over her shoulder and said something in rapid French at one of the assistants clustered behind her, then took the tablet she'd been handed and thrust it in Dammond's direction. "Look! Look, this deposit has not been made, you see? The payment for last night!"

"I'm so sorry," Dammond said humbly. "The network—"

"The network, the network!" Kithara snapped her fingers. "This for the network, this for your excuses! I am your headliner! I deserve your respect!"

"Why don't we talk about it inside," Dammond said. He passed the open doorway where Cressida was hovering, his two goons behind him, clearly hoping to get Kithara to lower her voice.

But other doors were opening, lured by the noise, and Kithara was pitching her voice to carry, playing to her audience. "Oh, inside, hm? What are you afraid I will say?"

If it wasn't for how damn inconvenient this was, Cressida would have been lost in admiration. A true diva meltdown—when it wasn't directed at you—was a thing of appalling beauty.

And while she would have preferred to leave without witnesses, especially Dammond, she couldn't deny Kithara was providing one hell of a good distraction. She met Xena's eyes and reached for Lucian's hand, and they stepped into the hallway.

"—will have that wired directly to your account by—" Dammond was saying behind her, and then he stopped, cutting off in mid-sentence.

Cressida couldn't help herself. The crawling sensation between her shoulder blades was too much. She looked behind.

Dammond wasn't looking at her. He was gazing at his son, his face absolutely blank, with no hint as to what he was thinking or feeling.

And then Lucian responded to Cressida's halted movement and looked curiously over his shoulder at the yelling adults.

Cressida jerked, her grip tightening on Lucian's hand.

"Mommy, ow," Lucian said, his voice reproving, and Dammond raised his gaze to meet Cressida's. His eyes flickered to Xena as she pulled the door closed behind them, keeping her face turned away. She was scowling, and Cressida thought that she was probably trying to avoid giving Dammond any insight into what she thought of him.

What Dammond thought of Xena was clear. His eyes were narrowed with hate.

Cressida's brain abruptly exploded into flame. What right did Dammond have to hate Xena? Xena wasn't a criminal or a liar. Xena was doing her best to protect Dammond's son, while Dammond himself was endangering him.

"Hey," Xena said softly, and Cressida realized that she was glaring at Dammond herself. She turned it into a cool look, with a little flick of her head, hoping that he'd read it as *yeah, I slept with her. So?*

Kithara, unhappy about Dammond's diverted attention, burst into another list of Dammond's failings, rising impressively in both volume and pitch.

"Mommy," Lucian said uneasily, and tugged harder on her hand.

"Yes, Lucy Goose, I'm coming," Cressida said, and turned away. She could still feel Dammond's eyes on her back. She was abruptly, desperately relieved that she'd insisted on pretending this was a day trip as they left the mansion. She was certain that Dammond would never have let them leave if he'd seen them with the bags.

Lucian needed assurance about the yelling lady, and Cressida kept up a running patter as they headed out past the guard, who nodded familiarly at Xena, then yawned. The festival grounds were chaotic. Half the food vendors were closed—something to do with an unexpected power cut—and the chattering crowds were even more boisterous as they queued at the remaining vendors. Cressida saw bills changing hands and felt sick again. She hadn't been able to force down any breakfast herself.

The wheels of Lucian's little case did not cope well with the rough ground. After a few attempts to manage by himself, he allowed Xena to pick it up. He then requested that she carry him as well.

"Sure," Xena said, before Cressida could tell Lucian that he was too big for carrying. She bent down and hoisted him up with no apparent effort.

She looked calm and comfortable, her ponytail swinging with the motion, her forearm flexing slightly around Lucian's wriggling body as he nestled against her hip.

"If he's too heavy," Cressida began, and Xena shook her head.

"It's fine," she said. Her lips quirked, and Cressida realized that she was blatantly staring.

Well, who could blame her? "I'll take the case," Cressida said, and they kept going, weaving in and out of the flood. The smaller outdoor stages and visual art installations were getting a lot of attention, while people waited for the main stages to open for the bigger acts. Cressida caught a glimpse of Klara diving through a series of hoops and felt her throat catch with disappointment. Whatever happened, this was probably the end of her festival career. No one would hire a performer who'd just taken off on her second-chance contract.

"Xena!"

A short, round, dark-skinned woman had tumbled out of the flow, stepping into Xena's path. One of the Archers. Cressida took a moment to recall her name. Sapph, that was it. She noted the familiar way the woman stepped into Xena's personal space, and felt her eyebrows twitch.

Down girl. You can't be possessive after one night.

Xena herself was looking trapped, a fish stunned by a sudden blow.

Sapph's eyes tracked over Lucian and then to Cressida. Then she smiled, so warm and approving that Cressida felt herself smile in response.

"Oh, okay," she said. "Mystery solved."

"Mystery?" Xena asked.

"Well, Prax said you didn't come back to the tent last night. She was worried, but I thought you must have—" Sapph stopped, glanced at Lucian, and said, "been busy with something." She waggled her eyebrows, just in case none of them had heard the hidden subtext, and turned back to Xena. "Lucky for you, tech's been pushed back to ten a.m. You don't *have* to be there, if you had other plans? But it might be good B-roll."

"Um," Xena said, and Cressida was already wincing on her behalf. "I can't."

"Okay, no worries! Call time for us is four p.m. I've shifted the playlist a bit, so if I can go over the order with you beforehand—"

"I can't film you tonight."

Sapph's mouth parted. "You. What?"

"I'm leaving the island. Right now."

"Uh... Okay. Why?"

Xena hesitated again. "I'm sorry. I can't explain."

Sapph's eyes flickered to Cressida, to the child on Xena's hip, and her mouth turned down, as if she were suppressing a number of things she wanted to say that weren't appropriate for young ears.

"Okay," she said, the word carefully controlled. She waved away the explanation when Xena tried to say something more. "Never mind. I'm assuming it's important."

Xena nodded fervently. "It is."

"What did Paris say?"

"I—"

Sapph's control broke at that. "You haven't *told* her?"

"The phones don't work!" Xena said.

"So you're leaving it to me to tell her? In her hospital bed?" Sapph threw up her hands. "Xena! She's going to pitch a fit."

"I'm going to call her as soon as I can."

"You *better*." Sapph pressed her fingers to her temples. "Xena, this is not great for us!"

"I know. I'm so sorry," Xena said, sounding more than a little desperate. "I hope it goes really well. You'll be amazing, you and the Archers."

"I guess we'll find out," Sapph said crisply, and walked away without a farewell, the crowd parting around her.

"I don't like her," Lucian said.

"She's really nice," Xena assured him. "She's upset for good reasons."

"Remember how sometimes we need to feel our feelings?" Cressida added.

Lucian looked thoughtful. "Is she going to the time-out rug?"

"Something like that, buddy," Cressida said, trying not to giggle at the thought of Sapph sitting cross-legged on the striped rug Lucian went to when he needed some downtime. Xena didn't look as if she thought any part of the situation was funny.

Cressida clearly wasn't the only one leaving with regrets.

But Lucian came first.

By the time they got to the side gates, every muscle in Cressida's body felt tense, thrumming with anticipation. There were no problems with their leaving. The security guards were both the hi-vis lanyard-wearing variety she'd learned to identify as festival security, not Dammond's personal attendants. Everyone else probably assumed they were another family leaving early. Anyone observant enough to note their lack of bags would probably assume they were heading into the small town for a sit-down meal or a playground visit.

There were taxis—and lots of private cars—waiting at the gate. Word of the exodus had obviously spread.

Cressida made sure Lucian was settled in his inflatable booster seat, and relaxed incrementally as the car pulled away from the gates. They hadn't escaped yet, but the first stages were over.

Xena had pulled out her phone again—honestly, she was addicted to the thing, but that made sense, given her former profession. Cressida thought about teasing her, but then she caught the tension in her lips, the tightness around her eyes, and put a hand on her thigh instead.

"Everything okay?" she asked, and Xena handed her phone over without a word.

The battery icon at the top was blinking red, and it took Cressida a moment to figure out what she was reading. It was a group chat called "Boggle Bitches," for what were probably esoteric in-joke reasons, and it seemed to be exclusive to Xena and her sisters. Cressida was weirdly touched that Xena had so easily let her in to such a private space, but as she scrolled down, the pleasure was replaced with growing horror.

[Cassie] Laodice, do you have any ideas for Telfer's birthday this year? Manny and I were planning to be in the city around then, so maybe we could all meet up for dinner.

[Laodice] Okay. So I talked this over with Telfer and we agreed that I need to tell you both some things we kept back about the wedding retreat at Halcyon.

[Cassie] Okay? Xena's not online, do you want to wait for her?

[Laodice] I'll say it all now, and then she can read it when she can.

[Laodice] Danielle, the girl at the retreat, wasn't just murdering people randomly. She killed Jesse because he found out there were bugs at Halcyon when he tried to set up his own bugs.

[Laodice] Like, listening device bugs, not germs or insects.

[Cassie] Why was Jesse setting up bugs?

[Laodice] unimportant. Just let me tell it before I lose my nerve.

[Laodice] Danielle killed Sarah because she (Sarah) was running a different scheme that risked discovery, and she (Danielle) tried to kill Kyle and me for the same reason, and when she was arrested she didn't die in a car accident. The police car was stopped by two guys on motorcycles, and they shot her and left. Because she was working for scary people who were trying to run an extortion/espionage thing at Halcyon, recording everything that was happening in the building so they could listen to it later and pick out things they could use against the rich guests. and they didn't want her testifying. Those were the bugs Jesse found.

[Cassie] Holy shit

[Laodice] No, wait, this isn't even half of it. I'll tell you when I'm done.

[Laodice] Halcyon was an Argive Holdings venture. I don't know for sure, but I think Danielle was working either directly for Dammond Argive, or for whoever is behind him. And they killed her without blinking, for even the *possibility* that she might turn on them.

[Laodice] the reason I wasn't able to tell you any of this is because Argive Holdings is under federal investigation for money laundering, and has been for years. One of the other guests was an undercover agent trying to work her way into Dammond's inner circle but saving me blew her cover

[Laodice] she said we couldn't report on it, or even tell you guys, because it might risk the case

[Laodice] but fuck that, and fuck whatever NSA agent is reading this, my obligation to the government stops when my family is in danger.

[Laodice] Xena, I'm sure Cressida is really nice, but you've got to stay away from her. Dammond isn't just an asshole, he's a killer. Guys like that don't have rules.

[Laodice] And Cassie, I'm so sorry, but I'm like 90% sure that Theo was acting as a front, money laundering for Argive. That's where the extra money in his accounts came from, from his cut.

[Laodice] Are you there?

[Laodice] Oh, right, I'm done.

[Cassie] That's why the Tantalus accounts were a mess.

[Laodice] yes

[Cassie] That's why Theo killed Arthur too, and tried to kill me and Manny. Not just to cover up what he did to Chris, but so that no one could investigate him and find out about Argive.

[Laodice] I don't know for sure, but it makes sense

[Cassie] Well. He never talked. So I guess they got their money's worth.

[Cassie] oh okay that's why Theo's house was burned down the night he was arrested

[Cassie] A lot of things make more sense now

[Laodice] I'm really sorry I didn't tell you. I wanted to so bad.

[Cassie] Did he really die of a heart attack, in jail?

[Laodice] I don't know

[Cassie] I'm going to call you.

[Cassie] Xena, L's right. Get out of there. Contact us when you can.

[Xena has entered the chat]

[Xena] I'm leaving now.

Her sisters' grateful, relieved responses were still pinging into the chat.

Cressida closed her eyes. She'd been clinging to one final hope without even knowing it. Dammond had never once been violent towards her, or any of the other girls at the club. She'd never have considered dating him if he had been. And so part of her had always considered him non-violent. But even if he wasn't committing these murders personally, he knew of them. He might even be ordering them.

She'd read about those deaths at Halcyon. It had been an interesting story, something to shake her head at over her morning coffee.

Now, knowing that Xena's sister had nearly been one of his victims, that her other sister might have been collateral damage for Dammond's greed, the story couldn't be so easily forgotten.

She'd welcomed him into her body, she'd loved him with all her heart, she was holding their son in her arms, and he was capable of *this*?

"Mommy?"

"I'm fine, baby," she gasped. And that was it, her first lie to her son. She was going to have to do that a lot from now on, if she was going to shield him from any of this. "Mommy's just a bit carsick."

"I'm not a baby," Lucian said, but his eyes were still anxious.

"No, you're my big boy." She handed the phone back to Xena and hugged him. Xena was typing into her phone, her head down. She must think Cressida was an idiot.

Because she was. How could she never have *noticed*?

On the other hand, Xena hadn't told her sisters that she was leaving *with* Cressida.

"We've got three tickets on a ferry leaving in thirty minutes," Xena said.

"It would be nice if you can travel with us, but you don't have to," Cressida said brightly. She was trying to convey *your sisters are right, this is dangerous, maybe you should go.* It was difficult. Not just because Lucian was listening, but because, selfishly, the last thing she wanted was for Xena to desert them now.

"I want you to come!" Lucian said instantly, and over top of him Xena was saying, "We already talked about this."

Back at the mansion, she meant, when they'd both been touch-drunk and orgasm-hazy. "*I'm in,*" she'd said, her voice low and quiet, her eyes intense.

They weren't in bed now. But Xena had the same look in her eyes, a kind of steadfast burning. A fire Cressida could warm her hands at, a strength she could lean upon.

"Unless you want me to go?" Xena added, and Cressida adored her for that too. She didn't doubt for a moment that Xena meant it. If Cressida said go, she'd go.

"Stay," Cressida said.

The docks were busy, the little plaza where people waited for the boats absolutely heaving with bodies. It wasn't just the families leaving early. Cressida spotted people in twos and threes and larger groups, several of her fellow performers, and even a few people in volunteer T-shirts, looking muddy and tired. The queue outside the ticket booth was long, but while Lucian and Cressida waited to the side, Xena walked right up to the front of it and showed the woman behind the glass her phone screen.

The woman shook her head, and Cressida gritted her teeth, already wondering where they could hide until another boat was available. But Xena just kept talking, ignoring the complaining crowd behind her and the woman's scowl. At one point, Xena half-turned and pointed at

Lucian and Cressida. Cressida waved back. The woman's eyes snagged on Lucian, then rolled up and away.

She gave in all at once, pushing three slips of card across the counter, and Xena said something that prompted a reluctant laugh.

Xena turned away from the booth, fanning herself with the tickets, a faint trace of smugness to her smile.

"What did you say at the end?" Cressida asked.

"Said I hoped I was the most annoying person she had to deal with all day." Xena grimaced at her phone. "And that's the last of my battery. Probably karma."

Cressida laughed, and Xena bent down to Lucian's level, handing him a brochure. "Lucian, guess what? There's a gift store on board, and they have little ferry plushies."

While Lucian looked at the pictures, Cressida murmured, "I was thinking about the bugs at Halcyon."

"Me too," Xena said, equally low-voiced. "But your suite can't have been bugged, right? Or they'd have stopped us already."

"Your sister said they were recording everyone, planning to listen to it later."

Xena frowned, then her eyes went wide. "But I talked about... a lot of things." Gus's identity, she meant. The case against Dammond.

There wasn't anything they could do about it now, but Cressida's thoughts kept cringing away from the idea of some black-clad goon—or worse, Dammond—listen to Xena and herself laugh and whisper as they made love. She should probably be more concerned about the whole revelations-of-crimes thing, but somehow she wasn't.

"That's our boat," Xena said, pointing, with a twist to her mouth that said she'd had some similar thoughts and was trying to put them aside. "We'd better get boarded."

And that, with consummately terrible timing, was when three black SUVs pulled up outside the plaza.

Cressida was tensing even before she saw Dammond's trim form jump out of one of them, one giant man in a black suit coming around to join him at his shoulder. Other men boiled out of the other cars, all of them looking like smaller clones of the big man. They went straight into the crowd, holding up their phones and scanning faces.

Cressida could guess whose faces were on those screens.

She turned her back on them smoothly and snatched her red picture hat off her head—it felt like a flare—but that wasn't going to be enough. There were plenty of little blond boys in the crowd, and Xena's height made her stand out, but she wasn't wearing anything flashy. It was Cressida who was the problem.

Before she could think about it, Cressida plucked one of the tickets from Xena's hand and bent down to Lucian. "I have to go talk to somebody before I get on the boat," she said. "You go with Xena and be good." She kissed the top of his head, breathing in his sweet boy-smell.

"Cressida," Xena said, her eyes wide with understanding and horror. "You can't."

"We need to distract Dammond."

"Then I'll do it!"

"*No*," Cressida said. "He won't listen to you." And over Lucian's head, she glared a warning at Xena. Dammond was a killer, but some part of him seemed to still care about Cressida, and what she thought of him. With her, he might hesitate to give the order.

With Xena, who he already thought was a rival?

No.

Lucian was still catching up with the changes. "Mommy, don't go," he said. She could hear the tremor in his voice. He was on the verge of breaking into a full-voiced wail, the kind of noise that attracted eyes across a crowded store. Or the docks.

She wrapped her arms around his squirmy little body. His arms were like tentacles clinging to her neck, stronger than they had any right to be, but she gently untangled herself and looked into his watering eyes. He was her entire life. She had to protect him.

So she lied.

"I'm just going to be a minute," she promised. "You get on the boat with Xena, and she'll buy you a snack and a plushie, and I'll come find you on board. I love you, Lucy Goose. I'll be *right* back."

He believed her. Grumpy, but reassured, he took Xena's hand. "Can I have ice cream?" he asked.

"Let's see if they have that," Xena said, her voice calm. She shot one agonized look at Cressida, and then turned to take him on board.

Cressida waited long enough to see the long dark ponytail and the bobbing head of blond curls go across the docking bridge, and then turned back, shifting through the crowd while keeping an eye out. She shoved her ticket in her pocket. She'd use it if she could, but it looked as if Dammond's men were targeting the boats scheduled to leave first. It was a good strategy. She didn't like that they were dangerous *and* smart.

She spotted one of them heading towards the ferry Xena and Lucian had disappeared onto. Shit. If she was going to be a distraction, it had to be now.

"Dammond!" she called, pitching her voice across the space, and waving her red hat enthusiastically.

His eyes locked onto hers, and he charged forward, his enormous goon in tow. "What are you doing here?" he demanded. "Where's Lucian?"

"With Elena," Cressida said, with her best *you-idiot* tone. "I dropped him off with her and came down to say goodbye to Xena. She had to leave early. Her cousin, you know."

It was a bunch of vague nonsense that only sounded plausible because she was saying it with conviction. If Dammond *had* heard those theoretical recordings, even if he'd just checked with the daycare center before he left the house, she was fucked.

Dammond's eyes widened in what appeared to be honest surprise. Behind him, the goon was muttering instructions to someone to pull back from the airport. So they hadn't actually *known* Cressida and Xena were planning an escape, only acted on Dammond's instincts.

Which, for once, had been dead on.

"He's not with you?" Dammond said. "You're not taking him away?"

Cressida blinked at him. She had to be careful—theatrics that worked on stage would be too big for a conversation—but she thought she'd judged the pleasant disbelief just right. "*Taking* him? No! We're supposed to be staying till Wednesday, right?"

She judged the effect of that, and added, with a tinge of righteous disappointment. "Or have you changed your mind? Because I *told* Lucian we were staying to meet someone special, and if you've—"

"No!" Dammond said. "No, I mean, I haven't changed my mind. I want to meet him too."

"Well, good," Cressida said, still frowning. "Obviously the hallway this morning wasn't the right place, but I'd really like to get this new agreement figured out." She gave him a glance under her eyelashes that she hoped he'd read as shy, not seductive. "And then maybe we can all hang out a bit, as parents. It's... You're right. A lot of things changed when your grandfather died. It's taken me a while to work it all out. But it's been really nice, coming here, knowing that we're starting to trust each other again."

And that put Dammond on the spot, because if he admitted he'd sent his entourage down to the docks to search for her and Lucian, he was admitting he *didn't* trust her. Which he shouldn't, because he was a criminal shithead, and the *second* she could she was going to rat him out to the feds for whatever protection that might get her and Lucian. But right now, she'd use everything she had to make sure that ferry set sail.

Out of the corner of her eye, she saw one of the thugs go over the walkbridge, showing a picture on his phone to the ticket collector, who shrugged, but let the guy walk onboard.

She hoped that Xena had the sense to hide with Lucian in a bathroom or something, but she couldn't waste time worrying about that. She had to trust Xena to think of it, trust her to keep Lucian safe.

Oddly, it wasn't hard.

And that meant *her* next move was getting Dammond and his people away.

"Well, I was going to head back to the house," she said.

"Let me give you a ride," Dammond said instantly, and she happily agreed, pretending not to notice as he called the hounds off with some not-very-subtle mutterings at the big man hovering at his shoulder.

"It's a shame about the storm last night," she said, and chattered about how much *fun* it had been, how *sad* she was that the weather had marred the festival, even as she walked Dammond towards the exit, and the men in dark suits melted out of the crowd, converged together by the big bodyguard, and then followed his curt instructions, climbing back into their SUVs.

She couldn't be positive that the one who'd walked onto the ferry had returned. They all looked the same to her. But no one was hauling a weeping child, and no one seemed to be worried about a missing member.

"Wow," she said, climbing into the back of the SUV. "This is nice."

Dammond grinned at her. "Nothing wrong with a little luxury."

"Not at all," Cressida agreed, reclining back against the soft leather. She had to keep him focused on her until Xena and Lucian were well on their way. It was hard to keep tension out of her body, hard to keep her smile bright and sincere, but damn it, she was a professional.

She could sell Dammond the lie, to keep the people she cared for safe.

***

Chapter Fifteen

For maybe the first time in her adult life, Xena wished she wasn't so tall.

People on the internet had tried to make her feel shitty about it, but people on the internet had tried to make Xena feel shitty about a lot of things, and never succeeded until the end. She could grab things on high shelves, the extra reach was an asset in the dojo, and she'd been starter power forward on the varsity basketball team since she was a sophomore. Being tall was awesome.

Now, standing in this crowd where only a couple of men were taller than she was, it felt like she was a lightning rod in a thunderstorm.

"Mommy will be here soon," she told Lucian, who looked suspicious, but followed her easily enough to the gift shop. There, in a frenzy of guilt, she bought him all three sizes of ferry plushie as well as a larger suitcase so she could consolidate all the bags. Everything was vastly overpriced, but her main concern was that Dammond might be able to track them through her credit card.

She was probably being paranoid, but paranoia seemed to be a reasonable response.

And she couldn't stop thinking about Sapph and the disappointment and hurt in her eyes.

Did everyone think she was some kind of dilettante? Did Sapph really think that she'd leave a job she committed to just so she could get laid?

All right. It didn't matter what people thought of her. What mattered right now was that the overhead speakers were announcing boarding was complete, and Lucian was safe.

Xena was very much afraid that Cressida wasn't.

She sat with Lucian in the glass-walled lounge room, trying to distract him with a little book about the history of the ferry that she'd also grabbed from the gift store, while he ate Dippin' Dots and wriggled, periodically looking around for his mother. Xena had been hoping against hope that Cressida had made it on board, but now she was just hoping Lucian wouldn't realize she wasn't joining them until they were underway.

The boat's engines moved up a gear. Xena was looking at the windows to try and gauge if they'd left dock yet. The hilly sides of the bay started to drift past, and Xena blew out a relieved breath, at the very moment a black-clad man walked into the lounge.

Her reaction was pure instinct. He could, she thought later, have been a normal passenger in a black suit, but something about the habitual clothing of the private security guards had been tagged in her subconscious, the same way that black and yellow stripes said *wasp*.

She bent towards Lucian. "I need to go to the bathroom," she said, her voice cheery and upbeat. "Do you need to go the bathroom?"

"Yes," Lucian decided, so she took his hand and walked towards the corridor on the other side of the room with the familiar cutout outlines. Another family took their seats immediately.

Xena glanced over her shoulder. The man in black was scanning the room.

What could she do if he saw them, confronted them? Call for help, of course. But there was nothing to say that Lucian belonged with her. She wasn't his parent, and she didn't have anything from his mother that indicated she was allowed to be looking after him.

Lucian could tell people that his mother had said he should go with Xena, but he could also tell them that his mother had promised to be on the boat. And how many people were going to trust a four-year-old to have a firm grip on current events anyway?

"Where's Mommy?" Lucian said, with devastating loudness.

A young couple looked up at that, and standing behind them, leaning against a pole, was Zac.

They recognized each other in the same moment, and Xena hurried towards him, Lucian jumping from foot to foot.

"I'm so glad you're here!" Zac said, looking relieved. "I couldn't get hold of you, to tell you I was leaving early."

"Turning your back on adventure?" Xena asked.

Zac laughed. "No, onto the next thing. I got an offer for a gig last night, and I didn't have anything to do today but kind of hang around and soak up the vibe. But this is great! We can do that forgiveness video on the boat!"

Xena nodded towards Lucian. "I'm kind of in the middle of something right now." She was turning as they talked, trying to get a glimpse of the man in black out of the corner of her eye. He'd passed by them, but she couldn't tell whether he'd spotted them or not.

"Okay, but maybe later, we can—"

"I need to go to the bathroom," Lucian interrupted. He was stepping from foot to foot. Shit. Little kids had tiny bladders, Xena knew at least that much about childcare.

Zac bent down, grinning at him. "Is that so, little man?" he said heartily. "Do you want a guy to go with you?"

Lucian's grip tightened on Xena's hand. "No, Xena will take me. Or my mommy." He looked around the boat. "My mommy will be here soon," he told Zac, and did his little foot-shifting dance again. "Xena, I need to go to the bathroom *now*."

"Okay, buddy," Xena said. Where the hell was the man in black? She'd lost track of him during the conversation.

He was two rows of seats away, frowning at his phone. He looked up and caught her eye.

His face stayed totally blank. After a moment, his gaze moved on, unhurried. A shark lazily scanning the ocean for its next meal. He hadn't reacted to her in any particular way, and she wasn't sure why she was suddenly convinced he'd tagged her. But she was.

"Zac, I want to talk about this more. We'll be right back, okay?" She said it loudly, hoping the man in black would pick up the message—if you do anything terrible to me, someone will notice. Maybe she and Lucian could stick with Zac the whole journey. She squashed a moment of guilt that she might be endangering Zac. He was a big boy, and he could take care of himself.

The little boy who couldn't tugged at her hand again.

"Yes, buddy, we're going," she said, and hustled him into the corridor.

The bathrooms were empty, which wasn't ideal. Xena looked at the woman's bathroom, and then dismissed it as a possibility. A picture of a dress on the front wasn't going to stop a criminal. Instead, she hustled Lucian down the hall to a self-contained and surprisingly large family room, which held a toilet in a cubicle with its own door, a changing table and one of those weird UV hand dryers.

The floor was starting to rock and roll as they moved away from the shore.

Xena locked the door behind them, wishing for a sturdy deadbolt. This simple twist latch wouldn't stop anyone determined.

Lucian dropped her hand and went to the cubicle. "Do you need help?" Xena asked, hoping he didn't. The whole "look after my son" thing was becoming increasingly precarious.

"No, I can do it," Lucian said. He was frowning, but it looked more like concentration than concern. Xena turned away as he took his pants down. Apparently closing the cubicle door wasn't in his repertoire, but from the gentle splashing sound, he had aiming sorted.

Xena eyed the door instead, wondering if she could barricade it somehow.

There was a creak from the corridor, as if someone large were trying to move silently, but had put their foot wrong on unfamiliar floors. Xena wouldn't have heard it if she hadn't been listening for it, but now she was sure what she'd see if she opened the door. If Mr. Black Suit was waiting outside, he could be planning to ambush her and snatch Lucian when she emerged.

She stepped back to the cubicle, where Lucian was pulling up his pants, looking pleased with himself.

"Lucian," Xena whispered. "I'm going to close the door and I want you to lock it, okay? I want you to sit on the toilet and be like this." She scrunched down, closing her eyes and putting her hands over her ears.

Lucian opened his mouth, and Xena put her finger to his lips. She closed the toilet lid, picked him up bodily, and plunked him on it. "Scrunch up," she whispered.

"Like hide and seek?" Lucian whispered, looking uncertain.

"Yes, that's right, like hide and seek. You hide, and I'll come and find you. Lock the door behind me, then go back to here, okay?"

He nodded, and she went back to the main room, eying the door. The lever handle was turning, silently and slowly, and then the door pressed inwards, held only by the cheap latch.

"Occupied!" Xena trilled, in a high, cheery voice nothing like her own.

The latch burst off the door with a single hard shove from the outside. Xena kicked the door back at him.

She was rewarded with a slight grunt before the man in black came in swinging. She kept her arms up and muscles loose, and didn't try anything fancy. This wasn't a dojo fight, and this guy wasn't going to be impressed by the height on her ushiro geri. She blocked the first two blows towards her solar plexus and throat and threw one punch that he also blocked, eyes narrowing.

And then he just rushed her. She got another hit in and tried to slide sideways, but he stepped with her and shoved, his bulk bouncing her off the far wall.

Xena heard a yelp from the closed cubicle.

The man's head turned towards it and she threw a two-knuckle jab at his momentarily exposed throat. It landed, but he reared back, softening the impact, and caught her arm as she over-extended.

Fuck. It was an amateur mistake, and she paid for it, her weight too far forward as he tossed her.

The floor moved beneath her, rolling with the waves, and it gave her just enough momentum to roll out from under the blow that would have hit her jaw with stunning force. She tried to scramble up, using the wall for support, but the man jumped her, his weight bearing her down, and they grappled in silence.

She shouldn't *be* silent, Xena realized abruptly. She'd been too focused on the part where Lucian didn't belong to her, but no bystander or crew member was going to be happy about a man attacking a woman and child in a bathroom. She drew breath to yell, and took a jab in the ribs that knocked the air out.

It slowed her down just enough for him to catch her in a chokehold.

His form was perfect, his arm tight across her windpipe, his free hand on the back of her head. In a tournament, she'd tap out.

If she tapped out now, she'd die.

Through her darkening vision, Xena saw Lucian's terrified face peeking under the flimsy stall door. The fight had taken place in almost complete silence, with only the sounds of impact and their heavy breathing to give anything away. The man hadn't cursed her or threatened her or even muttered anything while he tried to choke her out.

Xena stared at Lucian, willing him to scream.

The parent room door banged open again.

"What the fuck?" exclaimed a familiar voice. Zac.

For a split-second, the man's grip loosened with surprise. Xena dug her chin into his arm, spent the last of her fading strength, and surged upwards.

She didn't have the leverage to throw him, but she made enough space to strike, hammering the inside of his knee with her fist. It buckled, and she reached up, straining to the limits of her flexibility to claw open-handed at his face.

Zac was moving in, ready to help, but she couldn't wait for him. She thrust back, slamming into the man with her full body weight.

There was a dull thud, and his body went limp against her back.

She stepped away and spun, weight balanced, fists raised, but he was falling boneless to the heaving floor. That last push had smashed the back of his skull against the hand dryer.

Xena bent over her knees, gulping in air.

"What the *fuck*," Zac said again.

There was a thin, high noise from the cubicle.

"Hey," Xena croaked, her voice rasping. "Hey, Lucian, it's okay. Zac, close that door."

Zac did, stepping into the room with them. Three adults in the room made a crowd, but Xena barely spared him a glance as he bent over her downed attacker.

"Lucian, you were super good," she said, crouching by the cubicle door. "Great hiding, buddy. Can you open the door for me now?"

There was a long pause, and Xena closed her eyes, rubbing at her aching throat. Then the latch clicked, and the door opened. Lucian was standing there, staring at her warily.

Xena tried not to flinch.

After a moment, he slunk forward and leaned against her, his skinny arms going around her neck. Xena hugged him back, feeling tears press against her eyelids. "Thank you, buddy," she mumbled. "I needed that."

"He's a scary man," Lucian whispered.

"Yes, but I won't let him hurt you. I won't let anyone hurt you."

Lucian didn't say anything in response, but his arms tightened around her neck.

Zac was bent over the guy, who was twitching a little and breathing heavily. Xena discovered that she was relieved about that. A living attacker posed a lot of problems, but not nearly as many as a dead man.

"Check the belt," she croaked, and Zac gingerly reached inside his jacket, feeling around the leather belt. He paused, eyebrows popping, then withdrew his hand and wrapped toilet paper around it. "Fingerprints," he explained importantly, and then went back to pull out the gun Xena had been positive was there.

Thank goodness Mr. Black Suit had tried to take her down instead of just threatening her—or Lucian—into doing whatever he wanted. He probably hadn't wanted the noise and notice of a gunshot, and had been confident in his ability to overpower one unarmed woman. Xena was lucky she hadn't had to put her training to the test.

"Um," Zac said, holding the gun as if it were a dead rat. "What do I do with this?"

Xena contemplated talking him through unloading, and then sighed. "Lucian, I need to take care of some things," she said, and gently put his warm little body away from her. "Do you want to stay in the toilet or the big room?"

"Big room," Lucian said, and scuttled around the wall, watching with huge eyes as she carefully took the gun from Zac.

Xena's experience with firearms was limited, but she'd filmed a few videos at a range, and the instructor had hammered safety into them. She kept the muzzle canted down and away from all of them, and kept her trigger finger on home position, far from the danger zone. Safety check? Okay, yeah, that was a bullet in the chamber. She released the magazine and shoved it in her pocket. What was next?

"Release, eject, slide," she muttered to herself, and gingerly pulled the slide back. The chambered bullet popped out the back, and she checked the chamber and barrel were empty. Something eased in her shoulders when she could confirm it was no longer loaded. Getting the slide off took a little more dexterity, but she finally worked out the combination of slide release lever and gentle yanking to get it free of the frame. There. Mostly disassembled. She stuffed the slide and frame into separate pockets. People really didn't appreciate cargo pants enough.

"Wallet," Zac reported, still rifling through the man's pockets. "$300 cash, no cards, no ID. Phone."

Xena reached out for the phone and snapped it in half. Lucian came back towards her. He was trembling, a response she found much scarier than a crying fit. She wrapped her arm around him, trying to provide any comfort she could.

"Okay," Zac said, and sat back on his heels, looking at her expectantly. "Now I get an explanation, I think. What's going on?"

"I can't tell you," Xena said, and grimaced. No, he deserved better than that. "I can't tell you everything," she amended. "Lucian's mom wants me to keep him safe."

"Right. So...who do we report this to? The captain? Is there security on board?"

"No," Xena said sharply. "We can't. No one can find this guy until we dock."

Zac considered her.

They'd been friends as well as lovers, for four good years. She'd wanted him more than anyone else in the world, trusted him more than anyone except her sisters. If he turned on her now...

"What do you need?" Zac asked.

Xena could have cried.

She gulped hard instead. "We need to tie him up and stow him somewhere," she said. "Here would be fine if we could guarantee no one would come in."

Zac nodded. "On it," he said, and stepped out of the room.

"When will Mommy be here?" Lucian asked.

"As soon as she can, buddy. She's just been delayed." She looked at his face. "It'll be okay," she added, with no idea of whether she was lying to him.

She checked the mostly-unconscious man again, checking his head. There was a gash, bleeding a lot in the way that head wounds did, and a swelling bump that would probably be tender, but there wasn't anything spongy or broken when she probed the skull with her fingertips.

The man groaned, and Xena eyed him narrowly. She didn't think he had much fight left in him. He'd be lucky to escape without a nasty concussion. But she still didn't want him free to move around or call for help, especially when she wasn't doing too well herself. Her ribs ached, and the various bruises and contusions of the last few days were making themselves known, now that the adrenaline had ebbed.

"Xena," Lucian said. "I want Mommy now, okay?"

"Soon, buddy."

"No, now," Lucian said, and when she stared at him, stymied by how to explain that she couldn't deliver the impossible, he burst into noisy tears.

"Uck," Xena said, or something like it. Her exposure to upset children was even more limited than her experience with guns, and this felt potentially more dangerous. Lucian had absolutely no restraint. He was howling, mouth wide open, snot and tears descending freely down his face. What if someone came in?

Someone did. Zac slipped through the door and triumphantly held up an "Out of Order" sign and a stick of Blu Tack.

"Oh, good. Where'd you find that?"

"Janitor's closet. Wasn't even locked." He affixed the signto the out-side of the door and produced a screwdriver, presumably from the same source. He screwed the door latch back in place and spun the lock. It was wobbly, but something.

Lucian's meltdown hadn't died down, but Zac didn't seem worried. He had twin nieces, Xena remembered. They'd been babies when they'd broken up.

She gestured frantically at Lucian. "Help," she mouthed.

Zac folded to sit cross-legged on the floor. "You're doing great," he assured her. "Sometimes they just do this."

Xena felt this was unfair to Lucian, who definitely had good reason to cry. She kind of felt like howling herself. "Shh, honey," she said, and hugged him closer. "I'm sorry. I know it's really scary. But I'm here. I'll help."

He hiccuped and sobbed something mostly incoherent. She caught the words "Anna" and "Elena".

"No one's going to care," Zac assured her. "There's probably like three crying kids out there."

"We just put an out-of-order sign on the door," Xena reminded him. Lucian seemed to be tiring himself out.

The man on the floor groaned again, shifting his limbs uncertainly, and Xena looked at him sharply.

"Any rope in that janitor's closet?" she asked.

"Nope," Zac said, and then pulled a boxcutter from his shorts. "But I had another idea."

Xena looked at the man's bespoke suit jacket and white business shirt. Quality cotton, tight weave. "I might be having the same idea," she said thoughtfully.

Forming bonds out of her assailant's cut-up clothes was easier than she'd thought. She and Zac dragged him into the toilet cubicle, with another makeshift rope securing him to the pipe. They had to spend the rest of the journey in the family bathroom, listening to occasional bursts of noise come down the bathroom corridor from the lounge as the doors opened and closed.

About halfway through, the man woke up, and tried yelling through his improvised gag for help, thumping his bound legs against the wall.

Zac and Lucian were playing Go Fish with a ferry-themed pack of playing cards, and they both looked up.

Xena went inside. "Stop," she said quietly.

The man glared at her, and thumped again.

Xena considered the gun parts weighing down her pockets, and sighed. "Seriously," she said wearily. "You know I don't want to kill you, right?"

He looked at her with contempt.

Xena leaned in close and grabbed his jaw. "But I will," she said quietly, and showed him the boxcutter in her other hand, the blade pushed out to its full extent, the edge gleaming in the harsh florescent light.

The man stilled.

"If I think you're going to take that boy away, if I think you're going to hurt him or me or my friend, I'll kill you." She squeezed his jaw tightly, letting her fingers crawl over bone and bruises. "I'll probably feel bad about it afterwards. If I get caught, I'll go to jail. But that won't matter to you, because you'll be dead. So don't fucking push me. I've thought about it carefully, and I'll do it. You know, I'm curious. Is that more or less scary than someone who'll kill on instinct? Or for pay?"

"Go fish!" Lucian said gleefully, on the other side of the cubicle wall.

"Do we understand each other?" Xena asked, holding the man's gaze.

He nodded. The movement was minute, his eyes still boring hatred into her skull, but it was an agreement.

Xena stood up and slid the blade back into the housing. "I'm glad," she said, and went back out to the main room.

It took a while for her hands to stop shaking.

***

The SUV took another route around the back of the estate, rather than trying to move through the crowds. Cressida had been hoping she could talk them into dropping her off partway, but the mansion loomed before them, and the SUV pulled up on a back terrace, just inside the security fence.

"Thanks for the ride," Cressida said brightly. "See you Monday?"

Dammond smiled. "You don't want to come in? Have a drink with me?"

"You must be so busy. Besides, I promised I'd go watch the Archers."

"The lesbian band? They're not on until much later."

Cressida resisted the urge to roll her eyes—of course Dammond would refer to an all-female queer folk-indie group as "the lesbian band"—and tried to look confused instead. "Oh, I must have mixed up the schedule."

"Then come for that drink," Dammond said.

"It's like, ten-thirty in the morning."

"That never stopped you before."

"On my old schedule, that was pretty much a nightcap," she pointed out. "Moms have to take it easy with the day drinking."

Dammond's eyes darkened. "Mine didn't," he said, and Cressida winced. She wasn't the biggest fan of Dei Argive, and the woman certainly didn't like her, but she hadn't meant to jab at Dammond's mother.

The big bodyguard was touching his ear piece, frowning. "Mr. Argive?" he said.

"Just a second," Dammond told her, and the two of them walked a few steps away, voices lowered.

Cressida hesitated. She needed to get back into the crowd and find her own way off the island. But if she left now, it might look more suspicious.

"Then find him!" Dammond snapped at the bodyguard. The sound scraped across her nerves. Even worse was the horror on Dammond's face as he hurried towards her.

"Lucian is not with Elena," he said urgently.

Cressida made a split second decision. "What?" she asked. "Dammond, what do you mean?"

"Elena isn't at the daycare center. Neither is Lucian."

"*What?* Where are they?"

"We don't—" Dammond looked at the big man, then back at her. "Elena didn't show up for work at all. Was she there when you dropped Lucian off? Did you meet her along the way and hand him over?"

"I don't remember! I—where is he, Dammond? Did somebody *take* them?" She hoped she wasn't dropping Elena deep in shit creek, but concealing Lucian's escape was more important for now. She was acutely aware the ferry couldn't have made it to shore yet.

The big guy said something into his wristcuff, and then came to join them. "The nanny's baggage is still in her room, sir," he said. It was the first time Cressida had heard his voice clearly, a rough British burr. "There might be a few things missing, but she didn't pack up." He paused a second and added, "No signs of a struggle."

"Did Elena seem off?" Dammond said. "Did she act weird around Lucian, or behave—"

"She seemed completely normal!" Cressida was worried that she was overselling the shock, but Dammond made a soothing noise and rubbed her shoulder. Crap. She couldn't get away now—Dammond might accept some strange behavior from her, but he'd never buy that she could happily head out to the festival with their son missing. She twisted her hands together, her anxiety entirely real.

"I'm going to check our rooms," she said. "He might have gone back there."

"We've checked," Dammond said.

Any minute now, they were going to check with the gate guards, who would say they'd seen her leave with Lucian and Xena, and then she was fucked.

Cressida considered her options and burst into tears. "Call the police!" she said. "Dammond, you have to call the police right now!"

Dammond and his bodyguard exchanged looks they probably thought she couldn't interpret.

"Hey, it's okay, we'll find him," Dammond said. "He's probably just hiding somewhere."

Cressida nodded, eyes wide open, the better for tears to pour out. She stumbled up the steps—Dammond made as if to comfort her, but she waved him off—and found herself in a wide foyer she'd never seen before. She turned to Dammond. "Where's my suite?" she said. "I'll go find his blankie. Lucian would never sleep without his blankie. He'll want it when you find him."

"Through that door, up the stairs, then you're in—let me come with you, Cressida."

"No! No, you find him!"

She dashed through the door and up the stairs, sobbing noisily, and through luck and good guesswork, found herself back in her suite. Thank goodness she hadn't returned the keys.

First step, get out of sight. Check.

Second step, get out of this house. She scanned the space and considered her options, regretting that she hadn't just left once she'd lost Dammond. She'd been too into the role, that was the problem. The character she was playing would have rushed to her suite, so she'd rushed to her suite. Now she was on the second floor.

She looked out the window of the sitting room. There was a trellis there, with winding ivy climbing up the wall. It looked sturdy, and she was athletic, so maybe, if she was careful...

"Cressida," Dammond said behind her, pushing the door to the suite open. The big man was behind him. The big man was the problem. If she had to, and she could take him by surprise, Cressida thought she might have a shot at besting Dammond, but she'd never beat the big guy in a physical contest.

"I can't believe this has happened," Cressida said. It wasn't hard to let some of her real worry and distress into her voice. "How could he just disappear?"

Dammond was frowning. "Did you personally drop him off at the daycare center," he said, "or did you let *her* do it?"

"I did," she said.

"Because no one at daycare remembers you doing it," Dammond said, his voice too gentle.

"Well, that's ridiculous," Cressida said, and tossed her hair. Wait, no, the denial was too fast. She should have gone for not being able to understand what he was talking about. Well, she was in it now. "They've lost my son, and they want to blame me!" She glared at him. "You promised he would be safe!"

Dammond didn't respond with anger or guilt, and Cressida felt fear wind along her limbs.

"Mmm," he said thoughtfully. "They could have forgotten you, and be trying to blame you. That's one way of looking at it. Another might be that you never dropped him off at all. Another way of looking at it might be that you wanted to keep my son away from me, Cressida and you lied to me."

"I don't know what you're talking about. What are you talking about?" Were tears an option? If she could fake hysteria...

Dammond strode forward, and she put all of her energy into not flinching.

"My guys talked to the taxi driver, Cressida," he said. "I know that you and Lucian and fucking Xena Troiades went to the docks together. Did she leave with him? Did you give our son to a stranger?"

Cressida burst into tears, pleased to see a flicker of discomfort dash across Dammond's face. "You're *horrible*," she sobbed. "I just want to know Lucian's safe! I can't believe you'd—" And she broke for the bedroom door in the middle of the sentence

He was on her at once, his hand on her wrist like a vice, his other scooping around her waist and pulling her tightly against him. He'd never once touched her in violence. Never once touched her when she didn't want to be touched.

She shrieked and tried to claw at his face.

"Stop it," Dammond said sharply and shook her. Her head snapped back and forth, the whiplash enough to shock her free of the terror.

The big man moved in, but Dammond jerked his head, and he stepped back again, waiting by the door to the suite.

"You gave our son away, Cressida! Do you have any idea what you've done?"

"He's *my* son," Cressida snarled. "He's under *my* custody. And now you're threatening me, hurting me? I have every right to ask a friend to look after him or take him away."

"So you lied to me?"

Cressida let her scorn show in her face. "I had every right to do that too. You have *no* rights to him, Dammond. You gave them all up when you backed your grandfather instead of me. I'm *glad* he's never met you. Now he never will."

Dammond went white. He shoved her backwards. It was a reflexive gesture, as if he was trying to get away from something that had hurt him, and it gave her a few steps distance.

It wasn't much of an opening, but it was all she had. She pushed off, dancer's legs propelling her through the bedroom door, and slammed it shut on Dammond's face. The deadbolt snapped into place under her fumbling fingers, and she backed away.

"Don't be stupid, Cressida," Dammond growled through the door.

Cressida darted for the window, then swore. The trellis didn't continue on this side of the house. If she jumped for it, even if she dangled from the window, she risked serious injury. Her eye snagged on the bed, on the sheets that had been rumpled by herself and Xena barely hours before.

There was a mumble of voices in the suite. Cressida picked up a pewter figurine and hurled it through the window. The festival music surged in, and her spirits lifted. There were people out there, thousands of them. If she could just get their attention... "Help!" she screamed out the window. "Help me!"

She didn't wait for a response, but snatched the sheets, knotting them hurriedly together. It had been years since she'd done aerials, but the muscle memory was probably still there, right? She tied one end of the sheet around the leg of the massive bed, tugged hard to test it, and was heading for the window when Dammond's security chief kicked through the door.

He was on her in a second, way too strong and completely implacable, trapping her even as she tried to fight and claw. This man wasn't going to be distracted by tears or insults. He got a hand over her mouth and squeezed, giant fingers pressing tightly into her jawbone.

Cressida panicked. She flung her weight back, which did nothing, and tried to bite him, which earned her a tap to the side of the head which made the room spin around. By the time she regained her wits, she was on her knees, arms trapped behind her back, and her mouth still covered.

Dammond swaggered into the room and crouched in front of her.

"Stop being stupid, Cressida," he said. "I can give Lucian everything." He swept his arm around the room. "And you want it too. Don't pretend you don't like the luxury. Don't pretend you haven't thought about what you could do with my money." He reached out, and smoothed her rumpled curls. "I know you're angry now. But you'll see it my way."

She would have spat at him, but a glare was all she could manage.

Dammond's lips curved. "Lucian can have the best of everything," he said. "The best schools, the best colleges, the best job. He'll know all the best people." He patted her hair again. "And he'll have you. The best mother."

Oh, shit.

"We need a more secure location," the security chief said. His voice was a low hum, unexpectedly soft, with what Cressida thought was a British accent of some kind. Not Scottish or Irish was about the best she could guess.

"My study," Dammond said. "But how are we going to get her there?"

"She's going to walk," the big man said, and hoisted Cressida to her feet. "You won't be any trouble, will you, darling?"

Cressida shook her head. As soon as she saw someone, she'd call for help or scream—

The big man put his mouth next to her ear. "Because if you're any trouble, I'll kill you," he said, sounding very reasonable. "If you call for help, or try to signal anyone, I'll kill them too."

"Nigel," Dammond said. "There's no need for that."

"No. Because she's not going to do anything. That right, darling? Because Dammond, he wants you around, and that's nice. But I don't care." There was an easy sincerity to the words that was so much scarier than if he'd shouted or sneered.

"You'll be fine," Dammond told her, his tone reassuring. Who was he trying to convince, Cressida or himself? For the first time, Cressida wondered if she'd read the power dynamic wrong here. She'd thought Dammond was the boss, and Nigel the silent goon at his shoulder. Now that Nigel was talking, he seemed to have a lot more authority than she'd assumed.

And Dammond didn't like it. His eyes went to Nigel, then back to her.

"Let her go," he said, the words an order, and Nigel immediately removed his hands from Cressida's mouth and wrists.

"No screaming, love," he said, and moved in front of her, pushing his jacket flap open so she could see the hidden gun harness under the exquisite tailoring.

Cressida closed her eyes and nodded sharply.

Dammond tucked his arm around her and hustled her to the door.

When he opened it, there was one pissed off woman in the hallway, staring daggers at them as they emerged. Cressida's screaming and the sounds of the struggle had bought that much attention at least.

"Why is there so much shouting?" Kithara demanded. "I must have my pre-show nap! It is *essential*!"

"She took something that disagreed with her," Dammond said. "Sorry to disturb you." His arm tightened around her waist. "We're just going somewhere quieter to sleep it off."

To Cressida's surprise, Kithara looked at her more closely. "Are you not well?" she asked, her voice actually softening.

Cressida nodded, trying to look shamefaced. "I took a couple pills," she said, her voice raspy. Would Nigel really shoot a famous pop star, right in the hallway? She could feel his bulk at her back. A trained fighter would know what to do in this situation. They'd know how to get the gun off him, shoot him, stop Dammond, and end this nightmare.

Xena would know.

But Cressida only had herself, and the killer at her back wasn't someone she could stop. She stared at Kithara, then let her eyes go unfocused. "You know how it goes," she said. "One pill, two pill, red pill, blue pill."

She laughed, and then leaned on Dammond, letting him take more of her weight. "I'm tired," she whined. "Make the colors stop. It's a whole marching band."

"You must buy from reputable suppliers," Kithara said, shaking her head. "Quality, it is key." She shot Dammond another virulent glare, and stalked back to her suite.

"Nice one," Nigel rumbled in Cressida's ear. He sounded amused. "You're a good little actress."

Too good, Cressida thought. She'd hoped that Kithara would see through the lie and figure out that she needed help.

"This way," Dammond said, and led them down the hallway to the elevator. His voice was tense, and the arm Cressida was leaning on was tight with stress.

It was impossible to summon any sympathy for him. Every bit of hope left in Cressida was focused on Lucian's escape.

Chapter Sixteen

Zac seemed to be enjoying an opportunity to play the role of hero. He booked them into a hotel under his own name, and insisted that Lucian and Xena wait outside.

"Just in case anyone's watching," he said. His voice was serious, but there was a gleam in his eye that said part of him was finding this exciting.

They waited until the concierge was busy with a group of new arrivals, and then slipped through the lobby. The unexpected early retreat from Lotophagi was making a difference here too, but in this resort hotel, there were still rooms available.

Xena's first priority was her phone. She borrowed Zac's charger and checked her notifications. A lot, but nothing from Cressida. Her texts went unanswered, and two calls went straight to voicemail. Either the island network was up to its tricks again, or Cressida couldn't answer.

How the hell was she going to get in touch with Anna? She didn't know the woman's last name, and even if she worked under her real first name, combing through online escort ads for "Anna" seemed like it might be a fruitless waste of time.

Lucian was bent over Zac's phone, watching *Bluey* clips. She sat on the couch beside him. "Lucian, buddy," she said. "Do you know Anna's last name?"

"She's Anna Zabala," Lucian said instantly.

Well, that was a lot easier to look for than "Smith".

"Are we going to talk to her on the phone?" Lucian said hopefully.

"I want to, but I need to find her number first. "

"I know her number!" Lucian said. "We made a song!"

Zac gave him a doubtful look, but Lucian jumped off the couch and sang through the ten-digit cell number with gusto. Also, with gestures. "That's Anna, that's Anna Zabala, that's Anna's number," he concluded, his little-boy voice loud and not particularly tuneful.

Xena laughed and gave him a high five, breathless with relief. "Let me get a pen and we'll do that again," she told him, and Lucian repeated himself, this time with some delightfully awkward hip swivels.

"I know Mommy's number too," he told her, and sang that as an encore while she dialled, hoping that Anna wouldn't automatically reject the unknown caller.

"Hello?" a woman's voice said.

Xena exhaled. "Hello," she said. "I'm Xena Troiades, a friend of Cressida's. We met at Lotophagi. I have Lucian here with me."

"Anna!" Lucian yelled, and grabbed for the phone. "Where are you?"

The woman's voice tightened. "I'm at home, Goose. What's wrong?" A brief pause. "Xena, may I speak to Lucian, please?"

Xena handed over the phone.

The resulting explanation couldn't have been easy to unwind. Xena couldn't hear most of what Anna was saying, but she could see Lucian getting visibly calmer as he started responding to queries.

"Yes," he said. "Um, yes? Xena is my friend."

Xena swallowed hard at the unexpected tightness in her throat.

"Okay," Lucian said, and turned to Xena, holding out the phone.

"Hi," Xena said.

"Hey," Anna said. "I assume you can't tell me everything in front of certain listeners. Can you go somewhere with some privacy?"

Zac had booked them two adjoining rooms. Xena caught his eye, nodded towards Lucian, and walked to the connecting door, shutting herself in. "He can't hear me now," she said quietly.

"Is Cressida alive?" Anna asked, her voice flat, and Xena sucked in air.

"As far as I know," she managed. "Hopefully she's caught another ferry. Or maybe a plane."

"But you don't think she did."

"She was talking to Dammond. She was going to distract him. I don't know if he caught on."

"Dammond," Anna said, her voice rich with disgust. "What an absolute waste of oxygen. Okay, tell me what's going on."

Xena paused. "I can try," she said, and outlined as much as she could about Dammond's activities. It felt good to tell someone else. She skimmed over how she knew—Anna didn't need to know about Laodice's experience at Halcyon, nor Cassie's column—but that he was a money launderer under active investigation definitely seemed worth sharing.

"Wow," Anna said when she was done. "I'd say that I didn't think he could be this kind of human garbage, but actually, it totally fits. And you think Cressida's still with him?" She paused. "This isn't what I'd normally suggest, but have you considered calling the police?"

"The federal agent I spoke to said the local law was probably in Dammond's pocket."

"That tracks," Anna conceded. "But it's also possible the fed told you that because he knows local law might mess up his investigation."

"I didn't think of that." It sounded horribly plausible. Xena didn't think Gus would directly harm Cressida, but she'd definitely gotten the impression that his most serious goal was putting Dammond away. "But what would I tell them? I've got a shaky story from a contact who will definitely deny it, and no direct evidence of any crimes. I don't have Gus's number, to put them in touch with him, even if he'd speak to them. And Cressida stayed behind of her own free will."

"But she hasn't contacted you since."

"No."

Anna made a thoughtful noise. "There's the guy who jumped you in a ferry bathroom. You have two witnesses to that."

"The one I concussed and tied to a toilet, with the help of my ex?" Xena asked. "Not that I think he's going to go to the cops, either, but if he did, it wouldn't look good for me. I don't actually care about that, but they're going to be less likely to listen if they're trying to arrest me."

"So what next?"

"Would you be able to come and get Lucian? Getting him safe was Cressida's first priority. I'm worried that the ferry guy might come after him, and I want to get him away. I can buy you a ticket or—"

"Honey, I started canceling my clients for the next few days the second that Lucian told me his mom wasn't there," Anna said, sounding amused. "The car service is on its way to take me to the airport. I'm packing now."

Xena exhaled. "Thank you."

"You could bring him to me, you know," Anna said. "It's not safe for you, either."

"I know," Xena said.

"But?"

Xena squared her shoulders. "But if Cressida hasn't arrived by the time you do, I'm going back for her."

There was a pause on the other end of the line. "Yes," Anna said quietly. "I believe that you will."

***

Dammond's study was on the third floor, toward the back of the house, in the part that Dammond hadn't opened to his VIP guests. It was a small, windowless room, full of bookshelves holding the American and British canon of old white dudes, bound in identical brown leather covers. There was a heavy desk, also brown, with a neat stack of brown manila folders, and a landscape of a hunting lodge in fall. The artist's palette had trended heavily towards brown.

Cressida had had ample time to inspect every shade and detail while she waited, gagged and handcuffed to the radiator, and under the guardianship of one of Nigel's men, a man named Max.

Max hadn't been cruel. He'd treated Cressida the same way that she might treat a friend's pet that she didn't like very much, but had an obligation to look after. He'd given her water and a couple of protein bars, and kept his gun trained on her while she chewed and swallowed, in case she was tempted to shout for help.

She'd been allowed one potty break in the half-bath next door, also under guard, but her gag had stayed firmly in place for that, presumably because she didn't need to open her mouth to pee. Fumbling open her shorts with her hands bound in front of her had been awkward and embarrassing. Peeing in front of someone else was hardly the most intimate thing she'd done with a stranger, but on those occasions she'd been getting paid, and making her own choices accordingly.

And not in terror for her life.

Cressida had briefly flirted with the idea of trying to seduce Max into dropping his guard, and just as swiftly dropped it. His behavior towards her was purely professional. Besides, he scared the crap out of her.

So instead of trying longing looks and sly glances, she'd calculated her chances of surviving through the night. They didn't look good. Even if Dammond was currently entertaining a fantasy of retrieving Lucian and making her play the good mother, his buddy Nigel was definitely more practical. Her guess was that he was just humoring Dammond for now.

When Cressida craned her neck and strained to the limit of her bonds, she could see a wooden (brown) clock on one of the shelves. The ticking was driving her insane, but she was grateful for it anyway. Without her phone or natural light, she had no other way to judge how long she'd been here, but the clock said it was late afternoon, heading into evening. She thought—she hoped, with every part of her—that Dammond's lack of reappearance meant Xena and Lucian had gotten away clean.

She went over the litany of reassurance in her own head, her only comfort right now. Xena would get Lucian to Anna. Anna was named as Lucian's guardian in Cressida's will, and even more importantly, she had clients in law enforcement, business and government. It would be a fundamental betrayal of her own ethics, but Cressida knew that she wouldn't hesitate to pressure them into acting on Lucian's behalf.

It was much quieter back here, away from the festival, but she occasionally heard snatches of music. It seemed insane, totally unreal, that thousands of people were dancing and singing out there, using up whatever they'd managed to slip past security, stumbling around in the mud, and making millions for murderers. While she was trapped, wrists and jaw aching. Once, she heard something wild with violins that might even have been the Archers. Playing without Paris, playing without Xena there to film them.

That was a question no one had answered yet. Who had been sabotaging the Spiegeltent? And why? Nigel wouldn't have done it; if he wanted someone dead, he wouldn't fuck around with electrical shocks and falling spotlights.

She let her brain worry around the problem for a while, her forehead pressed against the smooth, cool metal of the radiator, and without even realizing it was happening, drifted into sleep.

Cressida woke sometime later, disoriented and sore. Dammond was shaking her shoulder, which didn't help with the disorientation, and her throat was unbearably dry.

He looked furious, and her heart sank, even as she lifted her chin. She didn't like the look of his pupils, huge and black. Max was standing in a kind of parade ground stance, while Nigel lurked by the door.

Dammond untied the gag, not gently, and Cressida coughed, and coughed again, unable to stop. Dammond put an open bottle of water in her bound hands, and she got most of it down her throat, swallowing gratefully.

Dammond's eyes lingered on her throat, on the droplets that had scattered over her top.

Seducing Max was out, but seducing Dammond had some possibilities.

Her gut roiled at the thought of touching him. But it might be her best chance to get away. So she croaked, "Thank you," and attempted a smile Dammond didn't return.

"So your butch *friend* isn't just a gal pal," he said tightly.

Cressida frowned. "You must have figured that out already."

"Yeah," Dammond said. "And then I had to *listen* to it. Listen to you two fucking, in my house."

Oh shit. They *had* been recorded. And by now, Dammond had thought to listen to the tapes from last night. Which meant he knew that they knew about the money laundering. And about the federal agent embedded in festival security. And—

"Where's Lucian, Cressida?" he demanded.

Not Chrissy. *Fuck.*

"I genuinely don't know," she told him wearily.

Dammond rubbed the end of his nose, looking equally tired. "He's my son. I want him back."

"You never had him," Cressida snapped.

"And whose fault is that?"

"Yours, you asshole!"

Max was looking impassive, but behind Dammond, Nigel met Cressida's eyes and smirked. Well, at least someone was enjoying the show.

"Look," Dammond said, visibly trying to relax his jaw. "I want us to be a family, okay? I acknowledge that I've made some mistakes in the past, but we were both much younger then. You never had a real family, and mine was a little unusual. I'd like a second chance."

The worst thing was, Cressida thought he meant it. His eyes were a little glazed, and he was definitely on something, but despite the swaying and the dilated pupils, there was a plaintive note in his voice.

"Family's important, Chrissy," he said, his voice dropping to a whisper.

Cressida bit her lip, and watched his eyes track the motion. Was it better to go along with the delusion, or resist it? Nigel was frowning now, and that decided her. Nigel wanted a clean solution. Well, Cressida was good at messy.

"I thought you didn't want me in your family," she said, letting her voice tremble.

"I did," Dammond said softly. "I do. It was Grandfather. He couldn't see what you were really like, what you could be if you didn't have to do that job."

"Your mother wouldn't welcome me," Cressida said. It was a shot in the dark, but it landed.

Dammond flinched. "She would," he said, his voice raw. "She wants to see her grandson, before she—"

"Before what, Dammond?"

Dammond looked straight at her, his eyes haunted. The redness around his eyes probably wasn't just the drugs. "Before she dies," he said quietly. "Cancer. We've tried everything, but she doesn't have long."

Cressida let her own eyes soften, her voice go gentle. She was drawing Dammond in, and watching Nigel and Max with her peripheral vision. "I'm sorry," she said.

"Do you even care?" Dammond asked.

The real answer was, not much. Dammond's mother had been horrified by her only son's stripper fiancee. She had no respect for Cressida or her work. But the woman had never done or said anything to her, at least to her face. She'd been a pale, wispy slip of a person, her tyrannical father's presence shadowing every thought. She didn't deserve an agonizing death.

"I do," Cressida said. "If you'd just told me that from the beginning, Dammond, I would have been happy to set up a meeting between your mom and Lucian." She took a deep breath, deliberately inflating her chest, and let her bottom lip tremble. "I wish you'd told me. Maybe it's not too late."

Dammond went still. "Really?"

"I think so. If you let me go, we can work something out."

Nigel coughed. Cressida ignored him and leaned in so that her forehead almost touched Dammond's, making a small, private space between them. "I'm not saying it will be easy," she said softly. "We've both made a lot of mistakes. But letting me go could start a new beginning."

Dammond eyes were wet. For a moment, she thought she had him.

And then he pulled back from her, mouth curling up in a sneer.

"Sure," he said. "And then you turn me over to the feds and skip off with your new girlfriend."

"It doesn't have to be like that," Cressida said, but she could see she'd lost him. Nigel relaxed against the doorframe.

"I can't believe you fucked her," Dammond said. "In the bed my parents used to sleep in, while our son was asleep in the room that used to be mine.

Oh, ugh. Had he given her that suite out of some weird fantasy of reliving family holidays? Had he thought he'd be joining her in that bed?

"Well, I'm sure your parents fucked in it too," she said.

Dammond made a face like an eight-year-old who'd just realized that his parents must have had sex at least once.

"And I'm not sure what's so hard to believe," Cressida continued. "Xena's hot, determined, protective, funny…"

"A failure," Dammond said. "An ex-D-lister."

"And not a felon," Cressida said. "Which, you know, I kind of thought was a low bar to meet, but you crawled right under it."

Dammond rolled his eyes. "Everybody tries to avoid the government take."

"Uh-huh," Cressida said. "People like drug cartels. Terrorists. Whatever the fuck this guy is." She jerked her chin at Nigel, who was looking amused again. Like his buddy's pet had learned a mildly entertaining trick. "And that's why you're never seeing Lucian again."

Dammond reached out and grabbed a handful of her curls. He shook her head lightly from side to side, his eyes narrowing. "Never say never, Chrissy. When Lucian gets here, you're not going to tell him any of this shit, you understand? You're going to look after him, and you're going to treat me with the respect I deserve. I'm the head of this household."

Cressida laughed in his face. "The respect you deserve? I've got a good grip on that."

Dammond's fist tightened in her hair. "I've been patient up till now, Cressida. But I'm not going to take this defiant crap anymore. You're going to act like a proper woman."

Cressida rolled her eyes. "Oh, please. What fucking braindead podcasts have you been listening to? The ones for lonely assholes who just can't work out why they can't get a girlfriend?"

Dammond's face went purple with rage, and he tossed her backwards. Her head thumped into the radiator, the sharp pain shooting across her skull and pulling tears from her eyes. By the time she blinked them free, Dammond was storming out the door, spine rigid.

Nigel lingered, grinning at her. "Feisty, aren't you?" he said, again with that weird note of approval. He bent down and reattached her gag, flicking her nose when she tried to bite him. It was even tighter than before, and her throat heaved in reflex. "Watch it, darling. I think you know this only ends one way, right? You're a smart girl. But whether it ends fast or slow, that can be up to you." He sat back on his haunches and regarded her. "Strange, what a man will do for love. Do you remember that couple who got handsy with you in the tent?"

Mr. and Ms. Grabby Hands? Cressida blinked at him, confused.

"My boy Dammond was really unhappy about that. Doesn't like people touching his things. He asked me to take care of the problem." He shrugged nonchalantly, and watched as she began to understand.

"It was fast for them," he said pleasantly. "No need to linger. What do you think he's going to have me do to your lady love?"

Cressida screamed through the gag. She tried to lash out with her feet. But her legs were stiff from being curled up under her so long, and Nigel only grinned and moved away, shaking his head.

"Nigel!" Dammond snapped from the hallway.

"Coming, boss," Nigel said, and winked at Cressida. "Max, you're with me. We're clearing the basement, and this little lady isn't going anywhere."

Cressida wouldn't give him the satisfaction of tears. She sat there, frozen, until they were all gone, the door locking firmly behind them.

Dammond had had two people killed for touching her. He had some crazy vision about making himself a family to present to his dying mother. And he wanted her son.

Well, fuck that noise. It was time for her to escape.

***

[Xena] I'm back on the mainland

[Laodice] WHEW

[Laodice] I'm so relieved

[Laodice] And I'm so sorry

[Cassie] Group video chat?

She couldn't do that, no matter how desperately she wanted to see their faces and hear them speak. Xena had no intention of telling her sisters she was going *back* to the island. Laodice would instantly intuit what she meant to do, and Cassie would give kind but firm advice, laying out all the reasons why Xena should leave retrieving Cressida to the authorities already in place. And if they thought she was going to ignore that advice, they were both fully capable of notifying the authorities themselves to make sure Xena didn't run back into danger.

[Xena] Can't chat. Low battery

[Laodice] Are you coming back soon?

[Xena] hope so

She almost left it there, but she was all too aware that this might be the final time she ever spoke to her sisters. There was so much she wanted to say to them, about how much she wanted them to have long, happy lives, about how grateful she was for their support and unstinting love, about how proud she was of everything they were. But any kind of speech along those lines would ring alarm bells at once.

[Xena] love you nerds

[Laodice] Love you too!!

[Cassie] Ditto. See you soon.

"All good?" Zac asked, as he did another circuit of the room.

Lucian was napping on the couch, his mouth slack with sleep. Xena had been worried that he'd take being confined to yet another room badly, but apparently he was too tired to care. It was Zac who was restless, unhappy that he couldn't take advantage of the resort pool or gym, and disgruntled about not being able to film any content. He definitely preferred the glory of a heroic role to the sacrifices it might demand.

But Xena had held firm. They didn't know what their ferry friend was up to, or if Dammond had sent more goons from the island. Getting Lucian to the airport in a few hours was going to be a big enough risk.

"Just talking to my sisters," Xena said.

"Say hi from me."

"Um, no," Xena said. "That would definitely let them know something was wrong."

"How do you mean?"

Xena stared at him. "Zac, my sisters hate your guts."

He looked startled. "What? Why?"

Okay. They were doing this. "Because you broke my heart!" Lucian stirred on the couch, and she lowered her voice. "And yes, I fucked up big time. I should never have pressured you to marry me in front of thousands of people. But I proposed because I loved you, and thought you loved me too. I thought you wanted to be with me forever. And I thought that because you *told me so.*"

"Oh," he said.

"Yeah, *oh.* It wasn't your *fault.* My sisters know that. But they also know I spent a year being a total mess. It took me a while to climb out of the hole. And no, it's not fair, but they're never going to like you. And if I send a message that implies we're voluntarily hanging out, they're going to know that something's up."

Zac was frowning at his knees, restless hands picking at the fabric. She'd seen him do that so many times, in so many hotel rooms. Restless, reckless, ready to get to the next big thing. It had used to make her smile.

Now, she was just tired.

"I'm sorry," he said abruptly, and then he looked up to meet her eyes. "You're not going to do that reconciliation video, are you?"

"No. I'm happy that we *are* reconciled. But I don't want to live my life in public anymore. I'm not saying I didn't like my job. I loved it. I was so sad to lose it. But even if I could take it back with no drama, that's not the life I want to live anymore." She sighed. "I need to figure out what that is."

"Well, you could definitely work behind the scenes," Zac said. "The Archers stuff is really taking off."

"Is it? I haven't even looked."

Zac gaped at her, as if this was an even bigger shock than Laodice and Cassie not liking him. "Uh, *yeah*," he said. "Look now!"

She did, and it was her mouth that fell open now. The numbers had gone viral.

Not *huge* viral, not global viral, but they'd moved from the feminist folk audience that usually liked the Archers to a wider audience. And wow, the engagement ratio was amazing. The Archers social channels had nearly doubled their follower count overnight.

Paris had added a couple more sad hospital videos, and Prax had managed to upload a get-ready-with-me video from the tent, where she talked followers through changing her hair routine and estradiol patch before the show. The numbers on that were a little flat; the hashtags needed some work. Xena's fingers moved to edit them, and then she hesitated. She was probably fired, right? Even if she still had account permissions, she shouldn't use them. At least not until she had a chance to talk to Paris.

"You really hit something," Zac said earnestly. "Are you looking for work? Madison is taking maternity leave soon, and I need to hire a short-term replacement."

"Zac," Xena said, shaking her head. "I can't be your socials manager."

Zac gave her sad puppy eyes. "I thought we were reconciled?"

"Sure. But that doesn't mean I want to work for you. And even if I did, shouldn't that be something you discuss with your fiancée first? Pretty sure she gets first refusal on you hiring your ex."

"Shit. Yeah. I didn't even think about that."

"Well, think about it," Xena said, more snappishly than she wanted to. "It's your job as a partner."

Zac scrunched up his face, and Xena stood up. "Anna's not here for a few hours yet," she said. "I'm going to follow Lucian's lead and take a nap. Will you wake me if I don't get up?"

"Yeah."

"Okay, then." She turned back to him at the door. "Zac? You really helped us out today. Thank you for being a good ex."

"Where's that coming from?"

Xena shrugged. "I guess... Lately, I've seen too much of the other kind."

Chapter Seventeen

Cressida took stock of her immediate resources. The list was depressingly meager.

Cute outfit, looking worse for wear. Handcuffs around both wrists, hooked around the radiator pipe, which meant her arm reach was severely restricted. With some strain, she could twist around to touch the gag with her fingertips, but she didn't have the positioning or the slack to yank the awful thing down. Even if she got it off, she'd only be able to scream for help, and she was betting the wrong people would hear. And worst of all, she had no bobby pins in her hair today, and therefore no chance of using her mouth to try and pick the handcuffs lock.

Okay. Her legs were unrestrained. She could try beating her feet against the floor. The rug would muffle the sound, but if there was someone on the floor below, and they weren't on Dammond's side, maybe they'd be confused enough to investigate, or at least complain about the noise.

But they'd probably complain to Dammond.

Cressida was going to have to hope that they wouldn't shoot her here. If they transferred her to another location, she might get a shot at escape, or at least a chance to go down fighting. And that meant her body had to be ready for it. A fight for your life probably shouldn't involve less preparation than a dance routine, right?

She started with simple, gentle stretches, rolling her neck and rounding and hollowing her spine. Stiff muscles protested, but she kept going, pointing and flexing her feet until the prickling sensation faded and she felt the warm fluidity of muscles ready to use. She tried some flexibility stretches next, and accidentally bumped her left foot against the desk leg.

Hm.

She sat back, knees drawn up, and regarded the desk with narrowed eyes. It was an old-fashioned, carved monster of a thing, with ornate curved legs, fussy drawers with brass handles and a bunch of little cubby-holes on top.

And it was within reach of her legs.

And desk drawers held *stationery.*

Cressida stretched out, fingers digging into the radiator as best she could for leverage and hooked her ankles around the closest desk leg. She tugged.

Nothing moved. The desk legs were sunk deep into the pile of the rug, and it was absurdly heavy. She took as deep a breath as she could through the gag, and toed off her sandals, for any extra grip that might give her. Core engaged and thighs tensed, she put everything she had into one mighty heave.

The desk jerked perhaps a half-inch closer.

Before it could sink back into the divot, she tugged again, drawing it closer to her with the flexibility and strength she'd trained over years. By the time she'd yanked it close enough, her abs were aching and she was starting to shake, but she was grinning around the gag, hope rising inexorably in her heart.

The stack of manila folders hadn't survived the journey. They'd slid all over the desk and onto the floor, paperwork spilling out of them. Cressida ignored them and wrapped her legs around the desk leg closest to her. If Dammond was smart, he'd have locked everything away. She might be betting her life on him not being smart.

She tilted the desk forward, and watched the drawers. There was a nerve-wracking moment when she was terrified she'd lose control and smash the stupid thing into the floor, but she caught it in time and set it back. Okay, adjust the grip, turn a little more to the right, get her knee a bit higher...

The top two desk drawers slid gently forward. And when she let the desk go back to upright, they stayed there, jutting out of the front.

Cressida flexed her foot against the exposed underside of the closest drawer and pulled it forward until it slid free of the desk and thumped onto the rug with a reassuring clatter. She hooked her foot inside and pulled it closer. There were things rattling in there. There were *paper-clips*. There were *scissors*.

Cressida could have cried with relief, but she absolutely didn't have time. With feet and knees and elbows, she fumbled the scissors up her body and into her bound hands. She cut off the gag, and a few curls with it, and took what felt like the first real breath she'd had all day. The paperclips were harder, and she dropped more than a few, but having her mouth free helped a lot. She opened one out, clutched it with tongue and lips and teeth, and fed it into the handcuff keyhole. Every atom in her body was focused on pressing down and turning the makeshift pick with a firm and steady pressure.

Her neck was aching, her jaw so tense that she was distantly worried that she might crack a tooth.

The click of the handcuff pin releasing reverberated through her skull like a trumpet fanfare.

Cressida let the handcuffs slither free, stretched her hands and fingers—ow, ow, ow—then stood up. Freedom was like a drug, shooting frantic energy into her limbs and down her spine. She crossed the room and grabbed a heavy brass candlestick from a bookshelf. It had a reassuring heft in her hand, and she shoved it into her waistband.

Armed and potentially dangerous, check.

The door, as she'd expected, was locked. A paperclip wasn't going to cut it, and her lockpicking skills probably weren't up to the job either, so she rifled through the desk, hoping for a spare key.

She had no luck there, but two small leather-bound notebooks, one red, and one black, caught her eye, mostly because they weren't brown. She flipped through them, eyebrows raising when she realized they were handwritten in some sort of code. There were initials and numbers, abbreviations she didn't understand, strings of 16 digits, and some stuff she thought might be latitude and longitude coordinates. About two-thirds of the way through, the handwriting changed from slanted cursive to Dammond's decisive capital letters.

Okay. Interesting, but clearly a puzzle to worry about later. Cressida slid the notebooks into her pockets. The manila folders scattered all over the floor seemed to be paperwork for the festival. Waivers, insurance policies, health and safety sign-offs. Weird, but another puzzle for later. She caught sight of the folder with her own name on it, and slipped the sheaf of paperwork out, shoving it down the front of her blouse. It wasn't a great silhouette, but she was kind of beyond wondering if her tits looked good.

Next step. Try and pick the door lock with a paperclip, or smash the hinges off with the candlestick? Xena would have made short work of the hinges, but Cressida wasn't sure she could summon the same force.

What are your other options? she thought grimly. *Do it now, before you lose your nerve.*

Something clicked in the lock.

Cressida didn't think about it. She'd spent hours in this shitty room, simultaneously terrified and bored out of her skull, and now the time for thinking was over. She stepped to the right, out of sight of the man opening the door, and as he came in she swung the candlestick down. At the last moment, warned by some change in air or shadow, or even just an animal instinct that let him know something was wrong, he jerked, and instead of crashing into the back of his skull, most of the candlestick's force came down where his neck and shoulder met.

It was still a stunning blow. Max staggered forward and fell, sprawling full-length on the study floor.

Cressida's own animal instincts wanted her to flee, but she had enough presence of mind to grab the phone that had fallen from his slack hand before she skittered out the door, closing it behind her. The key was still in the lock. She turned it, and pocketed the key.

Then, still clutching the candlestick, she raced down the hall, searching for the stairs and a way out of this nightmare.

*****

Anna didn't look like Xena had expected. She hadn't been consciously thinking about it, but from the throaty alto voice and Cressida's disclosure of her profession, she'd been expecting someone tall and thin and blonde, the kind of woman who played high class prostitutes in the movie.

But that just showed you couldn't trust the movies.

Anna was short, maybe just over five feet, and round, with luscious breasts and thighs and hips. She had ruddy cheeks and gorgeous brown curly hair that bounced as she moved. She reminded Xena of a juicy, shiny apple, just waiting for that first delicious bite.

Xena might have been head over heels for Cressida, but she wasn't *blind*.

But identifying the hot stranger as Anna wasn't a problem, because the second Lucian saw her, he let out a high yip and ran, his chubby legs pumping. They were both in tears by the time Xena and Zac reached them, but Anna stripped the water from her face and looked keenly at Xena.

"Ah," she said. "You *are* the XO Xena."

"I was."

"Cressida used to send me your videos. Don't let her pretend she didn't."

Xena's face warmed. "Thank you?"

Anna nodded, a glint in her eye, and then turned to the boy in her arms. "Okay, Lucy Goose, we have to rush," she said. "We need to get back on a plane and go home so Mommy can come find us."

Lucian, predictably, had some questions and concerns, but Anna caught Xena's eye and titled her head meaningfully towards the exit. Right, quick exit, no lengthy goodbyes.

"Bye, Lucian," Xena said, and hugged him. He squeezed her back, his little arms tightening.

"Can we play again soon?" he asked.

"I sure hope so, buddy." She kissed him on the cheek, his soft baby skin tender under her lips.

Anna used the moment to get Lucian moving, and Xena watched until they disappeared back through security. Safe. As safe as she could make them, at least, and Anna didn't seem to be any kind of fool.

Zac was still lingering. "Are you really going back?" he asked.

"Yes."

"Um. Do you want me to come with you?"

"I appreciate the offer," Xena said. "But no. It's stupid that *I'm* doing it."

"Yeah. But you're going to do it anyway." He flashed her a grin, bright and confident, and she could see the echo of the man she'd loved.

"Not going to try to talk me out of it?"

Zac shook his head. "No one can talk you out of anything, and I'm not dumb enough to try," he said. And then, in a rush: "I really did love you. I really did think I wanted to be with you forever. But when you asked me, in that moment, I knew I was wrong, and I knew it all at once." He looked thoughtful. "You know how, if you're trying to decide between two things, you flip a coin? Not necessarily because you're going to do what the coin says, but because you know that if you get heads and you're disappointed, then you need to go with what the tails choice was."

Xena's eyebrows lifted. "My proposal was a coin flip?"

"I guess? I just meant that, yeah, you definitely did it the wrong way. But even if you'd done it the right way, my answer would have been the same. I would still have broken your heart. So *I'm* sorry about that, and I understand why your sisters hate me. But I hope you don't."

"No," Xena said. "Never, Zac. Be well, okay? And for the love of whatever you hold holy, *don't* go online to talk about anything that happened in the last twelve hours. *Ever.*"

He looked just a little offended. "I'm not *that* much of a glory hound."

Xena had her doubts, but she thought it would probably be too mean to express them. A moment later, she was glad she hadn't, when Zac gave her his remaining cash reserves before heading off to catch his own plane.

Zac's idea of walking around money was nearly three grand. Xena stuffed the wad into her bag and took a cab to the docks. There were still ferries running, but she definitely wanted something more discreet. The flat, pointy-nosed speedboats down at the end seemed the most promising. Xena found one being hosed down by a morose teenager, who got a lot less morose when she handed him a hundred-dollar bill. He ran to fetch his uncle, the actual owner, and came back with a twinkly-eyed man with weathered skin, whose portrait Xena would have put under the dictionary definition of "scoundrel."

"I need to get to Aea by boat," she said. "Then I need you to wait there, for me and one other person."

The man stroked his luxuriant mustache. "Well, why don't we talk about what that might involve?"

"It involves two grand, cash."

The man's teeth gleamed. "Welcome on board, madame. Matt, did you refuel her?"

"Yes, Uncle Cy."

"Good. You can go home now."

"But—"

"Nope," Cy said firmly. "I'm not explaining this to your mother. Get."

Matt went back to being morose and sulked away, while Xena climbed on board. She gave Cy half the cash, showed him the rest, and put it back in her bag. From his half-impressed look, she knew he'd seen the handgun in there. She'd reassembled and reloaded it, but the safety was on and there was no bullet in the chamber. Having a gun didn't make her a shooter. But perhaps it would be useful as a threat.

Xena was ignoring a lot of alarm bells, because none of this was safe. Not just entrusting herself to a stranger on the ocean, but going back at all, for a woman who might be imprisoned, or dead. Or Cressida could be perfectly fine and coming on the first ferry in the morning, but Xena didn't believe that. Cressida had meant to distract Dammond, and she would have wanted to give them time to make their escape. So she'd probably kept distracting him, until he'd discovered what had happened, or maybe some of the stuff she and Xena had talked about, and then...

Well. Xena was really hoping for imprisoned, but alive. If Cressida was dead, she wasn't sure what she'd do, but it would probably be both bloody and ineffectual.

The sensible thing would be to tell Cy to take her back. She wasn't feeling very sensible.

"You're traveling light," Cy said, his tone as conversational as it could be on a boat with the engine running.

"Yeah." What was she likely to encounter? She should have been thinking of that, instead of endlessly cycling thoughts about Cressida being injured or dead. She should have gotten more prepared. "Do you have a toolbox?"

"Under the bench you're sitting on." Cy glanced back at her, then focused on the water again. "It's getting dark," he said, his voice neutral. "You want me to turn on the lights?"

"Um. How unsafe is it if you don't?"

"Running dark it is," he said cheerfully. "And I'm guessing you don't want to tie up at the docks either?"

"No. Can you get me somewhere close to the festival?"

"The one at the Argive place? I can take you right up to their family beach."

Of *course* Dammond had a private beach on an island resort. Xena felt a moment's disloyalty for her mean thought, because Cassie and Manny had a private dock at Lake Lydia, but that was different. Docks and beaches weren't the same.

Stop it, she told her brain, and focused on the toolbox. She found wirecutters and a flashlight, both of which seemed like they might be helpful. "Another two hundred for these?"

"Hm, no. I don't need you leaving tools somewhere they can be traced back to me."

"I'm not doing anything illegal," Xena said, and then reconsidered. She was probably aiming for trespassing, breaking and entering, and maybe assault and battery. "Eight hundred."

Cy sighed. "Done. But only because you seem like a nice girl."

Xena snorted.

"A determined woman, anyway." Cy did something with a lever, and the boat shuddered, then jumped forward, perceptibly faster. "There should be a rag and some rubbing alcohol in there. Do me a favor and wipe my fingerprints off my stuff, would you?"

Xena obeyed. Her thoughts were still circling, but the motion was helpful, steadying her hands as she wiped down the tools and stowed them in her bag.

They slowed down as they approached the island, Cy making adjustments that Xena didn't understand as they pulled closer to the shore. The light was fading from the sky, but the island was all lit up, music and light shimmering up like heat. She sensed more than saw the quiet beach, the lush growth surrounding it on all sides.

"There are steps cut into the hill there," Cy said. Xena squinted, but she couldn't make them out. The flashlight would have to do the work for her, when she got closer. The boat's engine dropped several notches, until it was more of a restless grumble than a roar. Then the motor cut out completely, and Cy lowered the anchor.

"You're going to have to swim for it," he warned her. "I'm not running aground for you."

"I figured," Xena said, and stripped off her shoes, shirt and cargo pants. In a moment, she was crouching in the boat in her underwear, hair in a tight bun on the very top of her head. She bundled her clothes and bag into the two plastic trash bags she'd lifted from the fancy hotel, and strapped the package tightly onto her back.

"Have you done this before?" Cy asked.

"Night swimming?"

"Covert ops."

He didn't sound as if he was joking.

"Sure," Xena said, glad he couldn't see her face clearly. She was a terrible liar. But if he thought she'd come after him if he took off, he might be more inclined to stick around, instead of taking the thousand she'd already given him and getting the hell out of dodge. "When we get back to the beach, I'll flash you SOS. You put a light on, and we'll swim out."

Could Cressida swim? Well, Xena could tow her if she couldn't. She could tow her unconscious, if she had to.

"How long is this going to take?" Cy asked.

"You got somewhere to be?" Xena didn't wait for the answer. She slipped over the side of the boat, grateful for the warmth of the water, and headed for shore.

It was almost relaxing. She'd always been a strong swimmer, and for a while she didn't have to think about anything but the pull of the water under her hands and the kicks propelling her to shore. In less time than she would have guessed, she felt sand beneath her feet. She swam in a little closer, then stood and waded in the rest of the way. The tide had been with her. It felt like a blessing on a day of curses.

She stripped the water from her limbs, dabbed at her underwear, and dressed again. The damp underwear was uncomfortable, but this wasn't a situation she intended to go into half-naked. She brushed her feet off carefully, but of course there were still a few grains of sand she could only feel once she'd gotten her shoes on. It seemed unfair that this totally ordinary annoyance should still apply while she was staging a rescue, but that was life for you—frustratingly mundane even in extraordinary circumstances.

Xena flashed the light around until she saw the steps, and crept up, using her hands more than her eyes to guide her. There was a little winding path through the rich foliage up here. A heavy fragrance drifted from the trees. Something flapped overhead—a night bird or giant bat. She followed another turn, and the mansion was abruptly looming over her, a little further up the slope. She was looking at what she'd thought was the back, but as she stared at the lit up building, the curving driveway, and the family camping ground that didn't even fill the lush lawn, she realized that the building didn't really *have* a back. Every room had a view. Every aspect was designed to impress or intimidate. She walked forward, eyes straining, and managed to spot the wire link security fence before she crashed into it. It made sense. Dammond would not have opened his private beach to his festival-attending marks.

Xena used the wirecutters then, keeping her ears perked for security or curious wanderers. She was congratulating herself on her stealth and preparing to peel the cut wire open, when the voice behind her said, "Stop. Hands up."

The voice was quiet and calm, but Xena still might have reacted badly if part of her hadn't recognized it.

"Gus?" she said.

"Don't—" he said, and then sighed in exasperation as she turned to face him, her hands falling to her sides.

"Hands *up*," said another voice, from the bushes off the side. The voice was accompanied by an ominous clicking sound, and Xena froze. *That* voice, she didn't recognize.

"Lower your weapon," Gus said, quiet but sharp, and the silence was somehow sulky. Then there was a rustling noise, and Xena let herself exhale.

"This way," Gus said, but if he was gesturing, Xena couldn't make it out.

"Uh," she said, squinting. "I can't really see."

A square, gloved hand closed firmly about her wrist, and drew her a few steps further down the path, then off it, into the bushes. Xena stumbled in his wake, trying not to hurt herself or make too much noise. Her eyes were readjusting to the dim light, now that she wasn't staring at the lit-up house. Gus stopped, and Xena realized they were standing in a small, natural clearing.

"What the hell are you doing here?" Gus asked. He kept his voice low, but there was no doubting the frustration.

"I could ask you the same thing," Xena said. The other person was just a shadow, lurking. From the voice she was predicting they were a woman, but she had no idea who. "Aren't you supposed to be pretending to be a security guard?"

"I was," Gus said. "But I'm guessing someone gave me away, because a few of my fellow guards wanted to take me somewhere for a quiet talk about my loyalties."

Xena winced. "Sorry."

"You told Cressida O'Brien, didn't you?"

"In my defense, you didn't tell me we'd be under surveillance."

"I told you," the woman said, obviously to Gus, and he grunted.

"I'm sorry," Xena repeated. "I'm glad you're okay."

"Uh-huh. And why are you here?"

"We were leaving. But Dammond came down to the ferry terminal, and Cressida stayed behind to distract him. She was supposed to come as soon as she could, but she hasn't."

"Where's Lucian?" the woman said, her voice sharp.

"He's safe," Xena said. "He's off the island." Should she be giving all of this away? She stamped on the impulse to tell them more, and looked in the general direction of the woman's face. "Who are you, anyway?"

"What, don't you recognize me, Xena?" the woman said, in an accent that did seem kind of familiar.

"Elena! Lucian's nanny?"

"More or less," Elena said, dropping the New Zealand accent again. "I was there to get him and Cressida out if it all went to shit. But you seem to have managed that between the two of you."

"Hey," Xena said, her temper rousing. "Don't blame me for catching Gus in the middle of his creeping around."

"I don't blame *you*," Elena returned, her voice silky smooth, and Gus grunted again.

"Enough," he said wearily. "Elena, you don't have to agree with all of my actions, but I'm the senior officer on site, all right?"

"Yes, sir."

"And as for you, Xena... What were you going to do? Break into a heavily guarded mansion full of Dammond's friends and lackeys, rescue his ex, and shoot your way out again? *Without* getting killed?"

"So she is in there?" Xena said sharply.

Gus hesitated. "We observed her entering with Dammond some hours ago," he said reluctantly.

"And our comms unit intercepted an anonymous call to the local police," Elena added. "Some woman saw Cressida walking away with two men after a yelling match in her room. The men said she was high, but the caller said there was a weird vibe, and she wasn't sure Cressida was safe."

"Then why haven't you gone after Dammond?" Xena asked. "You know he has a hostage. Aren't you supposed to serve and protect?"

"Cressida's not the only civilian in that building," Gus said firmly. "Even if we had backup, we couldn't risk a frontal assault."

"*Our* job is to secure evidence," Elena said. "Except they'll have destroyed all of that by now. They're going to slip away from us, *again*."

"Maybe," Gus conceded.

"Definitely," Elena said. "Ernest, you and I both know we need to get this guy now. He's slipped away too many times, and taken up too many agency resources. The bean counters are going to add up all that time and money and conclude Operation Boar Hunt needs to be wound down. If we don't pin him to the mat, now, he's never going down."

"Nigel Stafford is a practical man," Gus said. "If he spooks, he'll destroy all the evidence and if we arrest him he won't say a word. But Dammond's more erratic. And he talks."

"He won't talk to us," Elena said. "I don't care how erratic he is, that's the kind of guy who lawyers up the second you take him into custody." Her head snapped towards Xena, like a cat spotting prey. "Ahhh."

"He'll talk to me," Xena said. She hoped she sounded more confident than she felt.

"I can't ask you to do that," Gus said, which notably wasn't, "I can't let you do that."

"I wasn't planning on shooting my way out." *Unless it went really bad.* "This may shock you, but I actually have a plan." The plan depended on her doing some boldfaced lying, which she was worried about, but she could see a way that Gus could help her with that too.

A pause, longer this time. Xena could feel Elena willing Gus to make the same decision she wanted. Not for the first time, she wondered about this mysterious agency they worked for.

"Okay," Gus said at last. "Tell me this plan."

Chapter Eighteen

Cressida really hated this enormous, horrible house.

The guest areas had lulled her into a false sense of normality. It had been luxurious, and a little old-fashioned, in a money-is-class kind of way, but the layout had been comprehensible. This part of the house was much more difficult to navigate. There were weird steps going up and down, and a lot of short, closed off passages that might open into another short passage, but just as easily might open into a bedroom or a toilet.

She opened another door onto a storage room, heard the shuffle further down the passage that announced someone was coming, and hid inside, pressed up against a mop that smelled like a sickly combination of barf and bleach.

Her first thought had been to get to the public areas. True, most of the VIPs would be at the festival, but there might be entourage members she could appeal to. Nigel had threatened to kill anyone she asked for help, but released from the immediate threat, she could see that as the bluff it was.

Surely.

Unfortunately, when she'd followed her hazy, terror-ridden memories to the door that led to the guest space, she'd found a security door, locked by a keycard she didn't have. And when she'd crept closer, pressing her ear against it, she'd heard the murmuring of voices. Guards. No exit there.

Now her aim was to find her way downstairs, to a room with a patio door, or a window she could wriggle through. The house was most certainly not her ally.

The person in the hallway went past, and she waited until she heard the click of the closing door before she escaped from the mop's nauseating stench and cracked the storeroom door, peering out. Okay, she wasn't going to follow the person who'd just left, but there was a door across the hall, up one of those weird half-steps.

She darted across and tried the door.

It opened onto a bedroom, where a shaven-headed man with his back to her was pulling a white shirt over his head.

Cressida forced herself to close the door with quiet control, and went for the only remaining exit from the hallway, which the unseen walker had used a moment before.

No one was lurking behind the door. Instead, it opened on a narrow flight of stairs, heading straight down.

Oh, thank goodness, the ground floor at last. Down the steps, she found another narrow hallway, a utility closet, and finally, an empty sitting room, illuminated only by the light coming through the wide windows.

Yes. She slipped inside. The key she'd used to lock Max in worked on this door, too, and she locked it behind her, feeling some of the tension go out of her shoulders, even at this minor barrier. The window ledge had a handy overstuffed couch in front of it, and Cressida sat on the back of the couch, dangling her legs into the gap, while she used the ambient light to inspect the window latch. It was annoyingly modern, one of those things that only let you get the window open ten inches or so. She could smash the catch off with her candlestick (and risk noise) or try to squeeze through the gap as it was (and risk getting stuck).

She hesitated just long enough to hear the voices from outside, then the horrifying sound of another key in the lock.

Fuck. She dropped behind the couch, stifling the grunt as she hit the carpet. The couch had a solid back, so she couldn't be seen, which was good, or see anything herself, which was bad.

"—don't know why you think I have Cressida," Dammond said as he entered. Cressida felt her jaw lock in rage and anger at the sound of the voice. The lights in the room flickered on.

"She was observed entering the house."

If Cressida hadn't already been holding herself very still, she would have frozen in surprise at that. The second voice was *Xena.* Was it just the two of them? From the footsteps, she thought there was at least one more person.

"Observed? By who?" Dammond said sharply.

Whom, Cressida thought.

"By the authorities," Xena said steadily. "You know they're watching this place, right?"

Someone—*not* Dammond—swore. A British accent; probably Nigel.

"And they told *you* their observations," Dammond said, his voice contemptuous.

"Yes," Xena told him. "While they were wiring me up to come in and get you to talk." There was a muffled sound, and an intake of breath.

"Stand *down,*" Dammond said sharply.

"I'm disconnecting it now," Xena said, and there was a crackling sound, plastic and metal being yanked apart. "See? I don't care about the law. I just want Cressida safe."

It sounded heartbreakingly sincere, but oh fuck, what had Xena just done?

"They don't have enough evidence to lay a case," Xena continued. "That's why they tried to do it through me."

"Then why should I—"

"Because *I* have evidence," Xena said sharply. "I've been filming all over the festival, remember? You tried to stop me, but I didn't delete shit. That footage is in secure data storage with a timelock on it. If I don't walk out of here—with Cressida—and send the right code, the footage gets sent to every major media outlet. And maybe the feds won't be able to build a case on that, but what's that going to do to the reputation of Argive Holdings?"

It all sounded very plausible. Xena *had* been filming, and if she had caught something dubious on film, that would be a smart thing to do with it.

But Xena's voice was strained, as if she was trying to be convincing, rather than just letting the facts stand for themselves. Cressida had the sinking sensation that she was bluffing on a pair of twos.

"Where's your proof of this footage?" Nigel said, and from *his* tone, suddenly too bland, Cressida knew that he hadn't bought it either. "You must have made a copy of it, yes? To blackmail Dammond."

"No copies," Xena said, after a pause that was way too long. "Data security."

"I see. Well, I suppose we'd better take you to Cressida."

"Bring her here." Xena was trying to sound firm, but there was an uncertain note in her voice.

Dammond heard it too. "No, I don't think so. Nigel here will pat you down, and then we'll go somewhere more private."

He was going to move her to another location, where Nigel could quietly murder her. And Xena, brave, reckless Xena, would walk to her own death if she thought she was saving Cressida.

Cressida stood up. The gap between the couch and the window wasn't wide enough for her to do it smoothly, which had an impact on the drama of her entrance, but Dammond and Xena seemed appropriately shocked to see her anyway. Nigel didn't look shocked, but his eyes narrowed in a way she really didn't like.

"He can't trade me," she told Xena. "Because he doesn't have me."

Xena had stripped down to her cargo pants and sports bra. There was a wire taped to the outside, that presumably had been connected to the box riding on her hip until she'd torn it free. Her smile was blinding, a burst of joy and relief so intense that Cressida felt her own eyes well up.

"What the fuck?" Dammond said, his eyes darting between the two of them, and then scanning over Cressida's disheveled state. "Cressida, what happ—"

"I broke out, of course. Didn't you always tell me I was *inventive*?" She edged out from behind the couch, circling towards Xena's position. The big, black window at her back was making her shoulder blades itch. The part about the cops sending Xena in had sounded true, and if they were out there, they'd be watching. Possibly down a target scope. They could probably see the candlestick she was holding in a clenched fist behind her back.

"Where's Max?" Nigel demanded.

"Napping," Cressida said, which was better than "lying downstairs with a probable traumatic brain injury."

"It was a *bad* idea to lock me in your study, with all your sketchy little plans," she said, just to give Dammond something else to worry about.

Dammond had reacted to *study* and *plans*, but there'd been a microscopic eye-flicker towards Nigel. That was interesting. On a hunch, Cressida pulled out the thick sheaf of paper stuffed down her front and waved it at Dammond.

"I found the performer contracts," she announced, and Dammond's expression was too tightly controlled to be sure, but she thought she'd scored another hit. See, this was why she should be doing the talking, not Xena. Xena could do the scooping her up and kissing her part, as soon as they were in the clear. That sounded like something she'd be good at.

The mystery was why Dammond was worried about performer paperwork, or why it had even been in the study in the first place. Nothing else from the festival had been there. The contracts were mostly just standard festival stuff. The liability statement for her act, the part about having your act certified safe which everyone lied about, the—oh no. The weird insurance claim contract. Money you could claim in the event of an injury, but that Lotophagi would claim *for* you...

... and then, *not* pay to the performers who'd lied about getting their health and safety certification.

"You asshole," she said. "*You* killed Troy."

Xena jerked, staring at her in amazement.

"No, I didn't," Dammond said, way too fast for an honest denial. Like he'd been anticipating the accusation.

"Oh, not personally," she said, scornfully. "What did you do, pay off one of the stagehands? Or one of Nigel's guys?" Klara's wobbling

stepladder, the stripped wire in a puddle, the light falling from the rig…
"You sabotaged the Spiegeltent for the performers insurance money. But
it backfired, didn't it? It drew a lot of attention your way."

Nigel was watching Dammond thoughtfully and even through her
rage, Cressida felt a rush of triumph. There it was, the wedge she could
widen between Dammond and his terrifying ally. She took another
few steps towards Xena. She wanted very badly to beat the shit out of
Dammond with her candlestick, but he was too far away, and even if he
wasn't armed, Nigel definitely was.

But they were still listening to her, and that, she could use. "You're
greedy," she said flatly. "Even while you were cleaning all that cash, you
couldn't help running a scam on top of a scam. Did your European
buddies know about that? Did they know you were going to get the
Spiegeltent shut down, cut off that revenue stream for them?"

"Hey," Dammond said, but not to her. He was looking at Nigel, who
had drawn his gun. The muzzle was pointing down, for now. "Put that
away."

"You've got it, Dammond," Nigel said easily. "As soon as you tell me
what she's talking about."

"Nothing! She's crazy. She'll lie just for kicks."

Nigel raised his eyebrows. "She seems pretty sharp to me."

"Xena and I talked about it in my room," Cressida said helpfully. "Did
Dammond let you listen to those tapes?"

Nigel's eyes flickered towards Dammond again. "That's not a bad
idea."

Dammond went purple. "I'm not letting you listen to Cressida fucking this bitch," he snarled.

Xena had been standing still. Now, with Nigel's attention diverted, she stepped sideways, until she was pressed against Cressida's side. Cressida nearly melted at the warm, solid reassurance. She shifted her arm down and around, tapping the candlestick in the middle of the broad back. After a moment, she felt Xena's hand curl around it, under her own fingers, and let go. If only one of them could be armed, Cressida knew who she wanted it to be.

"We can stop before we get to the sex," Nigel said.

Dammond was visibly uncomfortable, sweat sheening on his forehead. "I'm not running another scam," he told Nigel. He was probably trying to sound confident and reassuring, but it came off whiny.

"Really? This insurance thing sounds like a goer. How much extra did it bring in? You've been warned about your ideas, Dammond, but if you've been skimming off the top while you make choices that restrict profits... Well. That would make you a very naughty boy."

"This idea's working out pretty well for you," Dammond said, waving in the direction of the festival grounds. "Come on, Nigel. I've made a few missteps in the past, but you know Argive Holdings is solid."

"Adrestus Argive was solid," Nigel corrected. "Your grandfather was a real gent. And a hard bastard, of course, but the kind of hard bastard I like doing business with."

"I can show you exactly what he was doing," Cressida said, and moved towards Nigel, holding the sheaf of paper out in front of her. She was planning to throw it in his face when she got close enough. He might have tagged Xena as a threat, but he'd already shown he wasn't scared of Cressida. So she could jump for the gun, and Xena could take care of Dammond with the candlestick, and then come and help her take Nigel down—

The shot echoed through the room. Cressida jerked to stare at Xena, but she looked unhurt, if equally shocked. She turned back to Nigel, who was folding gently onto his knees, a look of startled annoyance on his big face. There was a bright red spot on his white shirt, the stain spreading.

"Fuck," he said, his tone level. Then he pitched forward onto his face and went still.

"Dammond," Cressida said. He was holding a small, slim gun in one hand. Cressida couldn't stop looking at it. "Dammond, no."

It was a dumb thing to say, because he'd already done it, and she couldn't negate it. His eyes were wide, his breath coming fast and shocky. Cressida was willing to bet it was the first time he'd ever shot someone. Xena made a motion and he turned towards her, the gun moving with him.

"*No*," Cressida said, and leaped in front of Xena. She probably wasn't much of a barrier, if it came to that, but Dammond had hesitated, and that was good enough for now. "Dammond, *please*. Please just let us go. It's all gone too far."

"Why did you tell, Chrissy?" Dammond asked. He sounded lost and sad, as if *he* were the wronged party.

"Because you killed Troy and hurt Paris," Cressida said through clenched teeth. "And I'm sure there were a ton of near-misses. You got the Spiegeltent shut *down*."

"That's no place for you," Dammond said. "Not for the mother of my child."

Cressida gaped at him. His concern about the timing that night suddenly made sense. "You ordered the spotlight accident for before midnight, didn't you? You tried to stop the show *before my act*. I can't believe this! You were ready to murder someone just so that I couldn't perform!"

Something flashed in Dammond's eyes. "Stop being hysterical, Chrissy," he said, and Cressida was seized with a deja vu so powerful that red flared in her vision. He'd said something similar when she'd told him she needed his support at the rehearsal dinner. *Don't be so dramatic, Chrissy. Sit your ass down.*

She drew in her breath with a sharp hiss.

And Xena cleared her throat. "He's right, Cressida," she said. *"Calm down."*

Cressida flinched in reflexive outrage, then stilled, remembering their earlier conversation. *"I would never tell someone to calm down,"* Xena had said.

Xena had a plan. It was Cressida's job to make sure she was able to pull it off.

***

"Sorry," Cressida said, her voice only a little flat. "Lots of heightened emotion here."

Xena had never been more impressed with anyone in her entire life. While she'd been grimly focused on rescuing Cressida, Cressida had not only rescued *herself*, she'd been able to solve the mystery of Troy's death.

Unfortunately, it didn't look as if either of them would live to enjoy it for long. Dammond's face was a sickly greenish hue, but his hands were steady on the gun. Cressida was between her and the weapon, which made most of Xena's unarmed gun defense training useless. And while Dammond was close enough to rush, he was also close enough that he wouldn't miss.

She tightened her grip on the candlestick behind her back. She could always try to throw it. She'd get shot immediately afterwards, maybe fatally, but it might give Cressida a second to run.

Except that Xena wanted to live, maybe more now than she had in the last two years. She wanted to take Cressida out dancing, and buy Lucian ice-cream in Ida park, and show them both her large and too-empty apartment. She wanted to teach Cressida self-defense, and have Cressida teach her pole-dancing. She wanted to spend Saturday nights in bed with her, and Sunday mornings sipping coffee and talking about their plans for the day.

And if Cressida lost her temper, they were both going to miss out on all of that.

"Cressida, getting angry won't help," she said, staring at Dammond over the blonde head. "Remember my irresponsible videos?"

It was a risk to remind Dammond of her presence. He clearly hated her guts, and his eyes focused on her for a moment, chilly and clear.

But Cressida had gotten the message. Her shoulders went down, with what must have been a real effort of will, and she stepped forward, drawing his attention. "I'm trying to be calm, Dammond," she said. Xena couldn't see her face, but her voice had gone sweet, and even a little bit wheedling. "But the gun is kind of scary. You did shoot Nigel."

"I shot him to protect you," Dammond said, his eyes focusing back on her. Xena did not like the possessive glint there. "I'll never let anyone hurt you, Chrissy."

"I know," Cressida said, somehow managing to sound sincere, and even grateful. "I appreciate it, Dammond, I really do. Nigel told me that you had him take care of those nasty people who grabbed me in the tent."

What? Xena clearly had some news to catch up on.

But Dammond was puffing up under Cressida's approving tone. "I did that for you too," he told her. "I've been protecting you for a long time, Cressida. Even when you hurt me so badly, I wouldn't let Grandfather go after you. I told him that if anything happened to you, I'd walk away, from him, from the business, everything. He told me that with you gone, I'd have Lucian. But I wanted you too."

Cressida's back went rigid. "Thank you," she said, after a chilling moment. She might even have meant it. "I'm so grateful you did that."

Dammond beamed at her, and then his eyes slid over her shoulder to Xena. "So I just need to take care of *her*," he told Cressida. "Then we can get out of here. We can get Lucian, and be together, the way we should be."

"*No*," Cressida said, too sharp, and then as Dammond frowned at her, she laughed, a light, carefree little tingle, and made a big gesture with her arms that covered for her gentle sidestep. "We can be together, of course. But you don't need to hurt her, Dammond. She's not worth your time. She's nothing."

And *ow*, that would have hit Xena right in the heart, but Cressida had pulled Dammond's eyes with her to the side. His gun hand swung around to follow, but then he realized he wasn't covering *Xena*, and he tried to correct. There was that crucial moment where the muzzle wasn't pointing at either woman and Xena was already stepping in and swinging. The candlestick effectively gave her half an arm's length of extra reach. She brought it down on Dammond's forearm with a sharp crack.

He yelled, more at the impact than the pain—that would come later—and the gun went off, too loud and too close, but definitely pointing at the floor. He pulled his arm back, and she followed the motion, catching his hand and forcing it in inwards, twisting the gun free with a sharp yank. His grip strength had loosened, so she'd definitely done some damage to his arm.

But he was still dangerous. Adrenaline would drive him on until he was incapacitated. She stepped in, lifted her knee, and delivered a beautiful sidekick to his left kneecap. It made a wet popping sound, and Dammond collapsed, his mouth falling open.

There. He could keep going with a broken arm, but he couldn't chase them on a dislocated knee.

It had all taken maybe a second. Xena shoved the gun in the biggest pocket on her pants, scooped up the candlestick from the floor, grabbed Cressida by the wrist, and bolted into the hallway.

There were guards on all the doors to the outside. Xena felt as if she could smash through all of them, but that was just the adrenaline talking. "We need a window," she said.

"Fire alarm first," Cressida gasped, and darted for a red box on the wall.

The shrill ringing was immediate and deafening. Dammond's lackeys might have ignored the sound of shots, and the other guests had probably told themselves it was just a weird bang, but *everyone* was going to hear this.

So now the guards were distracted, the civilians would self-evacuate, and once they got outside, she and Cressida could mingle with the crowd.

"You're so smart," Xena said.

She'd knocked the air out of Dammond, probably broken his arm, and done serious damage to his knee. Plus, she had his gun. Any sensible person would be giving up around now. But she didn't think Dammond was at all sensible, and she had no idea what he'd do next. She wanted to get both Cressida and herself away before he decided.

"Here!" Cressida said, and opened a door to the left.

It was a toilet, with a window over the cistern. "Cover your eyes," Xena said, and smashed the glass out with the candlestick. She swept it up and around in a big square, clearing most of the jagged shards. "You first."

"You first," Cressida countered. "I don't have shoes. I need you to catch me."

That made too much sense to argue with. Xena handed her the candlestick and grabbed two rolls of toilet paper, using them as makeshift pads to protect her hands from the glass as she clambered out. Cressida followed her, with much more grace, and Xena caught her in her arms, keeping Cressida's feet clear of the glass.

Cressida was staring down at her. "You came back for me," she said, her voice shaking. "I thought I was on my own."

"Of course I did," Xena said fiercely. She was striding away as she spoke, taking them around the building to the front door, where confused people in various states of undress were flooding out. Emergency crews from the festival were converging on the house in their golf-carts. The guards were clearly overwhelmed. They were talking urgently to each other and staring up at the windows as if they were waiting for orders. One of them had opened the security gates to accommodate the evacuation, and that was where they headed.

Cressida buried her face in Xena's shoulder, and Xena hunched and let her hair fall forward to give her some concealment. No one even looked as they went right through the gate.

Cressida breathed a shaky sigh into Xena's neck, and Xena's arms tightened around her. "We're nearly there," she said quietly.

"Right," Cressida said, her voice only trembling a little. "Are we on grass? I can walk from here."

"Okay," Xena said, and set her down, not without some reluctance. She pulled up the loose material of her cargo pants, to where her phone had been taped to the inside of her knee. The sidekick and rush of escape hadn't even jostled it. She peeled the tape loose, at the cost of some hair and skin cells, and put it to her ear. "Did you get all of that, Gus?"

Cressida made a startled noise.

"I got it," Gus said. "You two clear?"

"Nearly."

"Good. Rendezvous at the meeting point. And stay on the line."

"But you were wearing a wire!" Cressida said.

"Misdirection," Xena said. She was feeling pretty smug about that, even if her "I have evidence" bluff had failed. Gus had told her they'd search her for bugs, so she'd shown them a bug to worry about and had her phone running the whole time, with backup voice recording in case the network failed.

It took them a while, keeping to the shadows and working around the edges, and halfway there Xena remembered that she had a probably-loaded gun in her pocket and had to stop to do a safety check. But they got to her hole in the fence and stepped through, and Elena and Gus were waiting for them.

"I'm glad you're all right," Cressida told Elena. "Uh, but since you're here...were you really qualified to look after my son?"

"I do have a psychology degree," Elena said. "I don't usually put it to use for child-minding. And yet, here I am." She was setting a fast pace down the path to the beachside steps. The second time Cressida winced from standing on a twig, Xena picked her up again, going for a piggyback this time.

"Is she mad at us?" Cressida whispered in her ear.

"I might be in some trouble," Xena admitted.

"Yes, you are," Elena said. The woman had ears like a bat. "For interfering in an active investigation."

"But Xena got your evidence," Cressida protested. "She got Dammond on tape shooting Nigel!"

"That should get him a medal," Elena muttered.

"What my colleague is trying to say is that would be great if we wanted one man for second-degree murder," Gus said. "We had larger ambitions. Plus, we really do try to discourage civilians from interfering in this kind of thing. It nearly always turns out badly."

Xena wasn't paying much attention. In her mind, they'd either charge her or they wouldn't, and she considered it a small cost to pay for Cressida's safety. But mostly, she was distracted. They'd reached the top of the hillside path, and instead of the dark ocean, with Cy's single light flashing from his speedboat, the beach was a hive of activity. Quiet activity, only lit sparingly by blue flashlights, but there were boats discharging people. She caught glimpses of heavy body armor and gleaming weapons.

"What the hell is that?" she asked, setting Cressida down again.

"That's our backup," Elena said, sounding very satisfied. "Finally! Right. You two stay here and *don't* interfere. You've done enough to fuck this up."

"Then I guess you don't want these?" Cressida said sweetly, and pulled two notebooks out of her pockets.

"What are those?" Gus said sharply.

"Oh, nothing," Cressida said, and made a motion in the dim light that Xena instantly recognized as tossing her hair. "Just some little notebooks, with a lot of 16-digit numbers, and some initials and notes, a few dollar amounts, that kind of thing."

"Where did you get them?"

"Dammond's study," Cressida said. She handed them over to Gus, who opened them instantly. "And wouldn't you know it, I noticed that the last third or so was in his handwriting. The first two-thirds is probably Adrestus's work. Is that the kind of evidence you need?"

"Oh, yes," Gus said, sounding stunned. He was playing his flashlight over the pages, his eyes widening as he went further back. The notes obviously meant something to him. "This will do nicely."

"Then you can go after the real criminals and leave Xena alone," Cressida said, her voice turning from playful to icy. "Or I'll get on the stand and swear up and down that I wrote those notebooks myself and planted them in Dammond's study to frame him."

"Fine," Gus said.

"Sir!"

"Let it rest, Corporal." Gus was holding the notebooks in a distinctly covetous grip. "This is the missing piece. We're going to nail a lot of people to the wall." He pointed sternly at Xena. "This is your official warning. Don't do it again."

"Definitely not," Xena said, and reached for Cressida's hand. The small fingers curled around hers, squeezing. "From now on, I'm living the quiet life."

Chapter Nineteen

Cressida wasn't able to see Xena until nearly a week after they both got back to the city. Lucian was understandably reluctant to let her go anywhere without him.

And Cressida, she had to admit, had been similarly clingy. It had been difficult to let Lucian out of her sight for long enough to go to debriefing interviews with a lot of people who carefully weren't wearing name badges and worked in suspiciously bland office buildings. She'd compensated by spending the rest of her time with him.

Anna, as always, had been a rock. But she kept giving Cressida speculative glances when she thought she wasn't looking.

"Okay, what is it?" Cressida asked. Lucian had finally fallen asleep in their bed, after another extended crying jag.

"Nothing," Anna said hurriedly. She'd taken the week off, to watch Lucian while Cressida went to her debriefings, and she was wearing what she called her "goblin mode" outfit—pajama pants with a sloth print, a faded Maenad College T-shirt and her glasses instead of contacts. Her hair was clustered on top of her head in an octopus clip. It still looked perfect. Anna's hair always did. "How's he doing?"

"Not great," Cressida admitted. "I think he needs to see someone. Professionally, I mean."

"So do you," Anna said bluntly. "You were abducted at gunpoint, assaulted by your ex, forced to witness a murder—"

"I know, Anna. I was there." Cressida stretched, letting her neck pop. "I have to talk about it all day. Can we not do it here?"

"Sorry."

"It's okay."

Anna nodded. "So. How's Xena?"

"We're texting," Cressida admitted.

"No, really? Every time I look at you, you're grinning at your phone. You're like a human heart-eyes emoji."

"It's just..." Cressida slid onto the couch and hugged a throw cushion, aware that this didn't make her look any *less* like a lovestruck teenager. "She's just so great, you know? She's got this dry sense of humor, and she can be mean in a way that's really funny, and she's been so many places and done so many things. I felt like a fangirl at first, asking about her old job, but now it's just comfortable. I love talking to her."

"Plus she's really buff."

"Oh boy. *So* buff. Did I tell you she literally *carried* me out of that place?"

"We like a girl with biceps," Anna said, her eyes gleaming.

"And she came back for me," Cressida said. "No one else would have done that." She waved off Anna's half-formed protest. "Oh, I know you *would* have, but you couldn't. Getting Lucian safe had to come first." She smiled. "And Xena knew that too. But *then* she came back for me."

Anna pointed at her. "Human heart-eyes emoji."

"And Lucian likes her too," Cressida said.

"Then stop texting and start dating," Anna said. "Tomorrow's my last evening off. Lucian and I will have Anna-time, and you'll get laid."

"I can't—" Cressida began, looking guiltily back at the room where Lucian was sleeping.

"Cressida," Anna said, with unusual firmness. She had a few clients who enjoyed being dominated, but she didn't usually use that voice at home. "The whole reason you went to that festival was so you could be Lucian's mom *and* yourself, right?"

Cressida hugged the cushion tighter. "And look how well that turned out."

"Honey, I know. But you weren't wrong to want that. You *should* be yourself. You *should* perform, and teach, and go out with this hot Amazon who's clearly gagging for you." Anna looked sympathetic, but absolutely sure of what she was saying, and Cressida took heart from it.

"I should," she agreed. "But it's hard."

"When has hard ever stopped you?" Anna asked. "Don't let fucking Dammond ruin this for you too."

That struck home. "Fine," Cressida said, and picked up her phone. She texted Xena a suggestion for dinner and dancing the next evening, and glared half-heartedly at Anna. "But if Lucian gets upset, call me."

"I will not," Anna said. "I will love him and care for him and cater to all his emotional and practical needs, but I won't let his needs sabotage your own. And if you come home before the morning, I'm going to kick you back out. You just watch me." She made a stern face, only half-teasing. "I'll even wear my kicking boots."

***

[Xena] Okay, how about this?

[Laodice] Looks great!

[Cassie] How do you get your pony tail that sleek?

[Xena] so much gel

[Laodice] Well, have a great time and look after yourself and when do I get to meet her?

[Xena] um maybe AFTER our first date??

Xena's lobby doorbell buzzed, and she checked the video. The pinhole video made Cressida's face look weird, but it was definitely her. She hit the entry button to send the elevator down for her, and checked herself in the full-length mirror one more time. She didn't wear a lot of dresses, but Cressida had never seen her dressed up. At least, not in person.

She'd bought the black mini months ago, and never worn it—not on camera, not out, not anywhere. It seemed appropriate for what she was hoping was the first date of many. The hemline did incredible things for her long legs, and the built in bustier top lifted and molded her cleavage, exposing the tanned skin of her upper chest, shoulders, and arms. She'd spotted Cressida looking at her arms.

Plus, she'd paired the dress with gold sneakers she could run in, and the skirt was short and stretchy enough that kicking would be easy. She wasn't going to feel comfortable going anywhere in anything she couldn't fight in for a long time.

Her doorbell rang. She swallowed hard, resisted the urge to touch her hair (really, so much gel) and opened the door.

Cressida stared at her.

Xena stared back. Cressida was wearing a mini dress too, a silky, tight thing, printed with swirls of rich green and reddish-brown. Her golden hair was topped with a sparkling headpiece, her eyes had been made up to look even more enormous, and her mouth was bright red.

"You look..." Xena said, and then her brain tried to supply too many adjectives at once. "Great. So great."

Cressida didn't say anything for a moment long enough that Xena was briefly afraid she'd offended her somehow. Then she stepped inside and closed the door behind her. "We can't go out," she said, her voice husky.

"Um? Why?"

"Are you kidding me? With you looking like that? I'd be fucking you in the restaurant bathroom before we even got past the appetizers."

Xena felt her pussy clench and swell at the words. "That doesn't sound like a *bad* idea."

Cressida tossed her bag on the entryway table. "It is. Because you'll be loud, won't you?"

Xena's breath caught in her throat. "I could be quiet," she said.

"I want you loud," Cressida said. She stepped in and smiled up at Xena, her eyes glinting with intent. "I want you screaming for me. Are you wearing panties?"

"Yes."

"Will you take them off for me?"

Xena's pussy clenched again. She could already feel the moisture gathering between her thighs, making her slick and ready. "Sure," she said, and her hands dropped to the hem of her dress.

Cressida shook her head. "Not here," she said. "Go in the bedroom and take them off. I'll be out here." She strolled past Xena into the open-plan living room, her hips working behind the thin silk of the dress. If she was wearing panties herself, they weren't visible under the fabric.

Xena went to her bedroom and did a quick check while she was there. She'd had a few fantasies about the evening ending like this, so she'd already made her bed and tidied away the laundry piles that usually sat on the designated chair. She stripped the panties off—oh, yeah, she was really getting juicy down there—and walked back into the living room.

Cressida was sprawled on the couch, looking out the wide glass windows. Xena wasn't wealthy enough to go penthouse, but her apartment was high enough up to catch some city lights, and she owned it free and clear.

"I love this view," Cressida said.

"Me too," Xena said, winking at her, and Cressida laughed.

"That's so corny."

"You make me feel corny," Xena said.

"That's only one letter off what I was aiming for," Cressida said, and while Xena was working that one out, she beckoned her closer, her face imperious.

Xena went to her knees at Cressida's feet, and Cressida leaned over and kissed her.

It was the first time they'd touched in days. The contact sent sparks cascading down Xena's nerve endings, and she gasped into Cressida's mouth, and surged up against her. Her hands slid up Cressida's bare thighs. "Can I—" she began, lowering her face, but Cressida caught her ponytail at the root and held her still.

Xena blinked, startled at how effective the gesture was. From Cressida's startled grin, she hadn't expected it either.

"This okay?" she asked, tugging lightly. The roots tightened, and Xena felt the prickling sensation wash over her scalp, and then down her entire body.

"Apparently," Xena said, still startled. "Um, take it slow?"

"You got it," Cressida said, and without increasing the pressure, she used her grip to guide Xena up her body, twisting to the side as she went, until Cressida was flat on her back and Xena was braced over her. "You're gorgeous," Cressida told her.

"That's my line," Xena said, and kissed her again. She slid her hands up Cressida's body, marveling at the smoothness of the silk, and Cressida laughed and wriggled underneath, letting go of Xena's hair so she could pull her dress up and off. She *was* wearing underwear - a thong and bra in gold and white.

"I love the way you glitter," Xena said, and licked a jutting nipple through the thin fabric.

Cressida moaned and thrust her breasts up, and Xena took the hint, nuzzling and mouthing at the sweet flesh. Cressida had used some kind of scented body lotion, and she was fragrant and sweet, with the salty tang of her skin underneath.

"Wait," Cressida gasped. "I was going to make you scream for me."

"In a minute," Xena promised, and worked her way down Cressida's body, peeling her thong down the tanned legs. She kissed her way back up to Cressida's pussy, and spread her apart, admiring. The pretty pink lips, shining with Cressida's desire, the thatch of golden curls. "I could feast on you all day."

Cressida sat up on her elbows, and reached for Xena's head. No, her *ponytail*, and Xena made an involuntary noise as Cressida increased the pressure, bringing her face down. "Please do," she said, eyes glittering, and Xena gratefully obeyed.

***

Cressida's mouth was dry, her thighs quivering, as Xena delved between her legs. She hadn't bothered with the tease this time—a fast learner, her Xena. She'd gone straight for strong pressure, tongue flat and hungry against her clit. Cressida pulled on the ponytail, and felt Xena's moan reverberate against her pussy.

"Fingers," she ordered, a little too breathless to be really commanding, but Xena obeyed instantly, slipping two inside her. Cressida clenched down, wanting more pressure, more filling, and Xena's hand shifted, until there were three fingers sunk deep, stretching her out. Oh, yes, she needed this. Did Xena have toys? If not, Cressida had a nice collection she'd be happy to show her, locked in her nightstand drawer.

The thought was fleeting, disappearing when Xena crooked her fingers and pressed *up*, unerringly finding that spot in Cressida she could never reach herself. "Fuck!" she said, and her fist tightened involuntarily in Xena's hair.

"Mmgh!" Xena agreed, and the pressure on Cressida's clit increased, going faster and harder, winding her up and up and until she was soaring. She managed to release her grip on Xena's hair before the crash came, and just as well—her toes curled and her entire body jerked and shuddered, the release overwhelmingly fierce.

Xena had backed off immediately, apparently remembering that too.

"You okay?" she asked, touching her now-disheveled hair. Oh, Cressida had nearly yanked her hair tie right out. Okay, they needed some more ground rules about that.

"I am fantastic," Cressida said, and let her body fall limp into the couch. She felt as if she'd gone through an exhilarating sky-dive and a relaxing three-hour massage, all at once. Her pussy was sending little shocks through her nervous system. "Don't touch me just yet."

"Do you need a blanket? Some water?"

"Anyone would think you were the one bossing me around," Cressida said, amused. "No. Come here. Lift your skirt. Aren't you clever, wearing a skirt for me tonight?"

Xena was slowly going beet red, the color washing down her face and throat. Cressida sat up and wriggled to the edge of the couch, then went to her knees, her face hovering at crotch height.

Xena made a stifled noise in the back of her throat.

Cressida inhaled, relishing that rich, salty scent of a woman ripe with desire.

"Now, you're going to have to be very strong," she told Xena. "You can't fall down, however good you feel. But you can make as much noise as you like."

And she dove in, lips and tongue and teeth working, until Xena screamed her name.

***

Later, while they were cuddled up together in Xena's enormous bed, kissing and touching without any immediate urge for more, Cressida wiped some of her own eyeshadow off Xena's lips and showed it to her, grinning. "Are you sure you like the way I glitter?" she teased.

Xena laughed. "Yes. You belong in the spotlight."

Oh. Cressida pressed her hand against her heart, and smiled through the tears that prickled at her eyes. "I love it," she said. "I love it so much. But I think the festival circuit is well and truly closed to me now. Lotophagi was my last shot, and you know how that went."

"I had some ideas about that," Xena said cautiously. "If you wanted to hear them."

"Sure."

"It turns out I can be pretty good at making content for other people," Xena said. She was picking her words carefully. "Paris and the Archers are getting some good offers now. Enough that Paris might even forgive me for abandoning them."

Cressida laughed. "The part where you were saving a damsel in distress and her son wasn't explanation enough?"

"It's a mitigating factor," Xena conceded. "Although Paris would have been happier if I'd somehow found a way to do both things at once, and is miffed that I didn't. Anyway, I have a lot of time, and not much to do with it, and I figured...maybe I could help you out for a bit? I can film content, talk to some old contacts. Your charisma would do the rest."

Cressida sat up. "I can't possibly afford you."

"I'm not asking to be paid," Xena said steadily. "And I'm not proposing this for the long-term. Once you take off, you should hire someone else. I think I've learned my lesson about working with people I lo—uh, mixing business and romance. But I can give you that boost. I mean. I think I can? I'm not sure. I understand if you'd want to wait and maybe try with—"

Cressida pressed her fingers over her lover's mouth. "No," she said firmly. "You can do it. I can do it. Let's—"

"Do it?" Xena offered, grinning.

"Go ahead," Cressida said. Her brain was buzzing, the possibilities blooming and expanding as she thought it through. She'd never done much social media herself, there hadn't seemed any point with her career on hold, but with Xena's expertise and her own contacts, she could see the sense in it right away. And Xena wanted to help her, let her be her best self in front of the widest audience possible. Not like Dammond, who'd wanted to lock her away in his delusion of a happy family. "Xena! Tell me the lesson you learned?"

"About mixing business with pleasure?"

"About working with people you love," Cressida said, and grinned at Xena's face, gone wide and wondering. "Screw it. Lucian likes you, I'm completely crazy about you, and I don't have time to fuck around. Let's be the lesbian cliche who get together after the first date. Do you want to be my girlfriend?"

"Technically, we didn't even get to the date part," Xena pointed out, but she was sitting up too, reaching out to hug Cressida to her. "Yes," she said, her face pressed into Cressida's hair. "I want to be your girlfriend." Despite the words, her voice was still uncertain.

"But?" Cressida said, gently probing.

Xena pulled back. Her eyes were wet. "But I'm worried it's too fast," she said. "And not because of the cliche, but because... Well, we met in a weird situation, and it was all really awful and we were hopped up on adrenaline. I like you. I really, really like you. But I don't know if I can trust myself to care this much again. What if it goes wrong?"

Cressida put her hand on Xena's heart, feeling it thump strong and fast under her palm. "Then it goes wrong. And we'll both be really sad. And then we'll heal, and go back into the world and try again. That's what we do, you and I. We're survivors."

Xena nodded, her mouth still mournful at the corners.

"But, Xena...what if it goes right? What if we're amazing together?" She cupped Xena's wet cheek in her other hand. "You risked your life to save mine," she said quietly. "And true, this is a different kind of risk and a different kind of courage. But I believe you can do it. If you can't trust yourself, can you trust me?"

"Oh," Xena gasped, and the tears spilled unheeded down her cheeks, but she was smiling through them, smiling at Cressida as if she'd just given her an enormous gift. "I can. I can do that."

"Fuck, yes," Cressida said, and kissed her hard. "Stick with me, babe. We're going places."

SIX MONTHS LATER

"Are you having regrets?" Xena asked Cassie.

"Every second minute of the last three days," Cassie said. They were in the well-appointed kitchen of Cassie and Manny's home, scrubbing the last of the dinner plates. Cassie and Manny had decided to host a mid-winter gathering for their expansive (and expanding) family, and Xena had never seen her calm, collected, sensible sister so frantic. "Manny's the hospitable one. He's *built* for this kind of thing. I'm the one who volunteers for the dishes so that I can get away from our mothers trading sex tips."

"I'm going to be just like them when I grow up," Laodice said, drying a crystal wine glass. "Xena, can you put these away?"

"Sure," Xena said, wiping the last of the suds off her hands. "As long as it doesn't come with any sex tips."

Laodice laughed. "You and Cressida don't need my advice. I'm a little too dick-oriented."

"We use dicks," Xena protested, opening the cupboard over the microwave. "They're not attached to a man, which some might see as a bonus, *and* we can choose from a wide array, but they're definitely still—"

"What part of escaping the sex tips did you two not understand?" Cassie demanded. Her cheeks were flushed and her curls were flying around her face with the force of her scrubbing. Xena took a good look at her and decided not to tease.

"So," she said casually. "Cressida and Lucian are moving in with me."

"Oh, yay!" Laodice said, and hugged her enthusiastically. "That's great news. And a big change. How's Lucian handling it?"

"We're doing it in stages," Xena said. "Cressida and Anna have worked out a visiting schedule, and Lucian is looking forward to Anna-time sleepovers." She smiled, knowing she looked a little goofy, and not really caring. "But it's finally happening. I think this is for real."

"Of course it is," Cassie said. She let a plate splash into the sink. "You know what? Let's leave this until tomorrow and sneak up to my office. Tantalus's organic pinot noir needs more taste testing."

"That is an *excellent* idea," Laodice said. "I'll just let Telfer know." She darted out of the kitchen, her velvety long-sleeved gown flowing behind her, and Xena followed.

It was a good thing the ancestral Pelopson home was big, because this weekend, it was full of people. In the dining room, Hecuba and Manny's mother were talking to each other and giggling a suspicious amount. The kids were mostly in the games room, where Manny's oldest niece was keeping an eye on them. Lucian was happily playing some complicated game of pretend with the youngest Pelopson, Chrys, that involved a lot of pointing sternly at a cushion while they chanted "spells." In the corner, Priam and Telfer's Uncle Burak were playing a game of chess they were treating like a life-or-death occasion.

Manny was circulating, making sure everyone had snacks and drinks at hand, and Telfer was sitting in the den with Cressida, talking about her burgeoning business. Her natural charm and obvious expertise had hit the online burlesque scene with a vengeance. A month after the first sponsorship offers had come in, Cressida had taken Xena to dinner and fired her, and Xena couldn't be happier about it. Her own social media management business was picking up, though she was still steadfastly refusing to work with Zac.

"Iulus and Leia are *kissing*," Laodice hissed in her ear.

Xena followed her gaze, expecting something scandalous, but in fact their younger brother had just kissed his girlfriend on the cheek while he got up to fetch her cardigan. "You can't be a prude about that," she said, amused. "I know for a fact that Cassie walked in on you and Telfer in the attic yesterday."

"I cannot express to you how much this disturbs me," Laodice said plaintively. "Our younger brother is dating my *boss's daughter*. If he breaks her heart, Hera will fire me. If she breaks his heart, I'll have to kick her ass, and *then* Hera will fire me."

"Uh-huh," Xena said. "Hera's Telfer's boss, too. What does he think?"

"Oh, he thinks they're a cute couple," Laodice said. She was rolling her eyes, but her voice was fond. "But then, he's a hopeless romantic."

As they walked over to interrupt their partners, Telfer didn't sound like a hopeless romantic. He sounded like he was pitching Cressida a cross-media deal for one of the titles he oversaw the marketing budget for.

"Are you two discussing business at the holidays?" Xena asked, taking Cressida's hand.

Cressida squeezed it, and looked innocent. "Of course not," she said, sounding completely sincere, and she was a perfect liar, and so adorable that Xena just had to kiss the tip of her nose. Telfer had turned to Laodice as soon as he realized she was there, clearly barely aware that anyone else was in the room.

"I'm going upstairs to get some sister gossip in," Xena said quietly. "Are you okay down here?"

"I'm having a wonderful time," Cressida assured her. "Although if Manny's brother tries to give me "boy-raising" tips again, I may commit some mild atrocities."

"Oh? Where is Augie?"

"Ness dragged him away. I think they're talking to Gus in the library."

"Poor Gus," Xena said involuntarily.

"He chose to come," Cressida said heartlessly. She still held a grudge against Gus for his threat to charge Xena with interference.

Xena didn't. She'd seen quite a bit of him through the on-going Argive Holdings case, and had, gradually, and with Manny's anxious permission, broached the subject of a family reunion. Gus had been suspicious and reluctant, but he'd warmed to the idea after meeting Manny for a drink, because Manny was a lovely teddy bear who made everyone around him feel welcome. This might not have been the best preparation for the full Pelopson Experience.

"He's fine," Cressida said, easily reading her expression. "He's faced live fire and survived the trauma of his dad being murdered. I don't think an awkward conversation with a blowhard is going to hurt him, especially when he's getting a tidy inheritance."

"You're probably right," Xena decided.

"I'm *always* right," Cressida said. "And don't you forget it."

"I love you," Xena said.

"I love you too," Cressida said. Despite her flippant tone, her eyes were steady. "So much. Now go upstairs and gossip, and don't forget to report back later."

"Yes, ma'am," Xena said. Despite the words, she stood there a moment longer, gazing into her girlfriend's face.

"Something wrong?" Cressida asked.

"No," Xena said. "Everything is just right. Everything is *perfect*." And in that house full of noise and warmth, laughter and love, she kissed the woman she loved with all her heart, and knew that finally, it was the truth.

The Love Labyrinth

I hope you enjoyed *XO, Xena*, the last (for now) novel in the Olympus Inc. series. But don't despair: read on for a sneak peek of a novella set in the same world!

Also, if you want to know what's coming up, do sign up for my newsletter at http://thathealeygirl.com . It is less of an author update newsletter, and more of a weeklyish column about weird research rabbit holes, my latest hobbies, things I've been reading or writing, and what it's like to be a part-time teacher, full-time writer in New Zealand, occasionally interspersed with "Oh, yeah, this is coming out, maybe you'll like it!". People seem to enjoy it.

***

THE LOVE LABYRINTH

Ariadne Spinner had often dreamed of her homecoming. Realistically, she'd known most of it wouldn't come true, but she'd really been hoping *someone* from her old life would see her arrive and be appropriately impressed.

Unfortunately, as she pulled up outside her brother's side hustle, the Weeping Rock streets remained tragically empty.

Labyrinth Escapes wasn't in what could be charitably called the central business district of Weeping Rock. It was a refurbished office complex in a strip mall on the less fashionable side of town, squeezed in between a used bookshop and a pet store, neither of which appeared to be open at 9:32 a.m. on a summery Saturday morning.

In her homecoming fantasies, Ariadne had imagined returning to her hometown in a convertible. She'd imagined herself gleaming in a ballgown, like Audrey Hepburn's Sabrina stepping into the courtyard, shining in Givenchy.

She'd pictured thoughtful nods from the elderly Mora sisters as they acknowledged that the Spinner girl was back.

She'd envisioned Phaedra Klack, still somehow wearing her cheerleading uniform, reacting with drop-jawed outrage to her victim's triumphant revival. She'd even dreamed of Theo Banks staring at her, stupefied, as he dropped to one knee and produced a sparkling diamond ring.

In real life, the convertible was a used Toyota Rav4, a little dusty, but still perfectly acceptable. Ariadne wasn't wearing Givenchy, but a bubblegum pink double gauze dress of her own design that she'd confidently show at any spring runway show. Her shoes were pistachio strappy heels with a pretty bow at the ankle. Her hair was perfect. Her lipstick was pristine.

And no one was there to see her.

She waited another minute, just in case Theo Banks urgently needed some fish food or something.

Then she sighed and slid out of the car. No one responded to her tentative knock, but the door proved to be open.

Her brother Andy had started Labyrinth Escapes two years ago, with a friend he'd met online in one of his puzzle enthusiast forums. His real income came from his work as an accountant, but with even the little he'd told her about the place, he was clearly much more enthusiastic about the escape room business.

That enthusiasm had not translated into a plush location for his side hustle.

The reception area was dingy and generic: a big box store couch piled with sad cushions and a few plastic chairs, opposite a high reception desk that had probably come with the lease. The door behind the desk had a Staff-Only sign on it, so she'd likely find Andy there. A corridor to the left of the reception area had three doors, each labeled with a sign - probably the actual escape rooms.

One off-white wall had a carved wooden sign declaring it the Champion's Circle, and seemed to be the place where the escapees took their photos after completing the challenge. The sign was rather nice, actually, but the walls needed a good scrub, the carpet had obviously been there a long time, and the curtains were limp, beige polyester things that conveyed "sad office" rather more effectively than "fun experience".

There was the bang of a door opening behind her, and Ariadne turned away from her inspection of the curtains, smiling widely.

But the man walking out of Andy's office wasn't her brother. He was an enormous stranger with a craggy face and a limp human form casually slung over his huge shoulders.

"Oh good, you're here early," he said. "Come and help me hide the body."

Weirdly, this was not a sentence that had featured in any of Ariadne's homecoming fantasies.

***

Ariadne Spinner, newly graduated fashion designer, has returned to her hometown. She's ready to prove herself a woman transformed—to her old crush, to her high school nemesis, and to everyone else in Weeping Rock that ever doubted her. But when she gets involved with her brother's escape room business—and his big, grumpy business partner—the path to triumph gets a lot more tangled.

Can Ariadne find her way to revenge, validation *and* the guy?

Read *The Love Labyrinth*, a sparkling Ariadne-and-the-Minotaur take on the myth of Theseus!

Afterword

In the tales of Troy, neither Polyxena nor Cressida have happy fates.

Polyxena, the youngest daughter of Hecuba and Priam, doesn't appear in the Iliad, but does appear in the works of later poets, and her fate is recounted in Euripides' plays *Hecuba* and *The Trojan Women*. There, she is sacrificed at the tomb of Achilles. (Some accounts say she was engaged to him; some that she betrayed him.) The accounts usually emphasize how dignified and modest Polyxena is about it, practically begging her murderer to strike the killing blow, while she exposes her breasts to make it easier for him. But! She also modestly makes sure that her legs are covered while she falls, so no one gets an upskirt look.

This all sounds super realistic and normal, like a thing that a woman would definitely do in the middle of being uselessly slaughtered to appease male pride, and not at all like a story someone might tell later to make himself feel better about it.

Cressida, on the other hand, isn't part of the Trojan War stories until centuries after the Iliad and the Greek dramatists. She was invented by a 12th-century French poet, retold by a 14th-century Italian, picked up by Chaucer, and then dramatized by Shakespeare in *The Tragedy of Troilus and Cressida*. The story goes that she was beloved of Troilus, a prince of Troy, but when her father switches sides, she must go to the Greek camp, where she is courted by and ultimately succumbs to the Greek hero Diomedes. She's a brazen hussy! A faithless harlot! She's broken Troilus's heart! Most stories end there, but Robert Henryson shows her being cast off by Diomedes, and becoming a beggar, full of repentance and grief for her faithlessness, before she succumbs to leprosy and dies. One of your classic happy endings.

The Olympus Inc. series has been my attempt to wrestle self-determination and romantic success for women from these mythological (and medieval) archetypes. What if Xena, so calm in her moment of crisis, was a warrior, not a victim? What if Cressida, excoriated for acting like a whore, was actually a sex worker, and unashamed of it? What if they met and liked each other in one of those moments of life transition and transformation where liking can so quickly crystallize into love?

Hanging over this cross-millennia textual collision is the aura of a much more modern story: *Xena: Warrior Princess*, a seminal text of my not-yet-aware-I-was-a-baby-bi teenage years. It might be difficult for today's audiences to understand just how rare same-sex attraction (even hinted) between women was in the bad old days of the 90s mainstream. Xena and Gabrielle's devotion to each other, however subtly coded, was genuinely ground-breaking.

I haven't used any plot elements from *Xena* in creating this story, and this novel is not a *Xena* fic or AU retelling (sorry!) But in a political climate where the backlash against queer stories is getting ever nastier, it seems only right to acknowledge the impact of that series on its audience and on the greater media landscape. My brunette warrior and bubbly blonde entertainer owe *Xena* something. Thank you, Lucy and Renee.

Acknowledgements

Robyn Fleming pulled triple duty on this one, as editor, martial artist and maternal advisor. I'm honored to have you in my life, bb. Alison Cooley's lovely illustrated cover art has been a real treat, and I've learned so much from the process of working directly with this wonderful artist and friend. I'm extremely thankful for Lizzie Tollemache and Kim Dalton, who provided answers to many of my questions about burlesque performance—any errors or exaggerations are my fault, and I'm sorry.

I'm grateful to Erin Harrington and Chloe Sutherland for providing emotional and literal sustenance during various crunch points. I appreciate my lovely dayjob co-workers for putting up with all my deadline moaning and the Critshow crew for giving me advice on handguns.

Finally, I want to thank everyone in my group chats, especially the ones where we're safe to start with, "Can I be really petty for a second?" Bitch chat is best chat.

About the Author

Karen Healey lives in New Zealand and writes cozy fantasy romance, science fiction, and young adult fiction. Kate Healey, who looks suspiciously similar, lives in New Zealand and writes spicy contemporary romance and urban fantasy.

Karen is an Aurealis and Sir Julius Vogel Award winner and has been a finalist for the ALA Morris Award, the New Zealand Book Award for Children and Young Adults, and the Andre Norton Award. Kate hasn't won anything yet, but give her time.

They both drink far too much coffee.

Sign up for my newsletter at http://thathealeygirl.com . You'll get the first news on new books, weird research rabbitholes, frequent rambling on living a creative life, and occasional freebies!

Also by the Author

As Kate Healey

Olympus Inc. Series:

Penelope Pops the Question (a series prequel and newsletter freebie, available when you sign up at http://thathealeygirl.com!)
The Love Labyrinth (standalone novella)

Arc One: The Olympians (now available on Kindle Unlimited!)
#1 *Persephone in Bloom*
#2 *Aphrodite Unbound*
#3 *Hera Takes Charge*

Arc Two: The Trojan Women
#4 *Ask Cassandra*
#5 *Love, Laodice*
#6 *XO, Xena*

As Karen Healey

The Movie Magic Series:

"Jingle Spells" (a newsletter freebie, available when you sign up at http:
//thathealeygirl.com)
Bespoke & Bespelled
Savory & Supernatural

The Hidden Histories Series (with Robyn Fleming):

The Empress of Timbra
The Spymaster's Apprentice

Young Adult Works:

What We Reach For: Three Stories of Love and Magic
Guardian of the Dead
The Shattering
When We Wake
While We Run